DETECTIVES 3

DETECTIVES 3

An Aristocratic Detective
Richard Marsh

Jane Sprood, Detective
Ellis Parker Butler

The Deliberate Detective
E. Phillips Oppenheim

Coachwhip Publications
Greenville, Ohio

3 Detectives: An Aristocratic Detective / Jane Sprood, Detective / The Deliberate Detective (Edited by Chad Arment)
© 2014 Coachwhip Publications
No claim made on public domain material.
Front cover: Blimp (cc) Peter DeWit

The Hon. Augustus Champnell stories by Richard Marsh
The Jane Sprood stories by Ellis Parker Butler
The Stanley Brooke stories by E. Phillips Oppenheim

Richard Marsh (1857-1915)
Ellis Parker Butler (1869-1937)
E. Phillips Oppenheim (1866-1946)

ISBN 1-61646-229-9
ISBN-13 978-1-61646-229-1

CoachwhipBooks.com

CONTENTS

AN ARISTOCRATIC DETECTIVE

RICHARD MARSH

I

THE LOST LETTER

Chapter 1

The Letter is Lost

When the Hon. Augustus Champnell observed that he had travelled to the family seat in the Northern Highlands for the sole purpose of asking his father if he had any insuperable objection to his adopting the profession of a detective, the Earl of Glenlean stared. He looked as if he could scarcely believe his eyes—and ears.

"A what?"

"A detective."

"Do you mean a policeman?"

"My dear father!"

The Hon. Augustus smiled. He was a tall, well-built, good-looking young fellow, with fair hair, a slight moustache, a manner which was apt to be all things to all men—and women, and a pair of light-blue eyes which were curiously keen. As the Earl continued to stare, he explained,—

"That sort of thing is all the rage just now. There's a heap of money to be made at it—that is if you are up to the mark. And I flatter myself I am. Of course, I should only take up cases of a certain kind, to which, also, there was attached a certain fee. Whatever else have I to do? I have, practically, no money of my own; you have none to give me. I have no taste for heiress-hunting. The thing is at least as decent as the tea-trade, or the Stock Exchange. As you are aware, I have always had a sleuth-hound sort of instinct ever since I was a child."

9

"I am aware of nothing of the kind. I don't know if you are in earnest, but, in any case, I take leave to tell you, sir, that I never heard such nonsense in my life. Heaven knows I have been worried enough in my time, but that a son of mine, a Champnell, should ever ask me if I had any objection to his becoming a common policeman—the thing is nothing else, sir, nothing else!—is a situation I never expected to encounter." The Hon. Augustus evinced an inclination to speak, but the earl waved him down with both his hands.

"Not another word, sir; not another word."

So the Hon Augustus, who knew his father, allowed the subject to drop—at least for the time.

But the next morning, as he was wondering if he should go for a stroll over the hills, or try a cast with a fly, there came a hurried tapping at the door of his sanctum, and Philpotts, the butler, entered.

"The earl wishes to know, sir, if you will go to him in his study at once."

The Hon. Augustus put down his pipe.

"Very good, Philpotts. Anything the matter?"

"Well, sir, I think there must be something the matter. The earl's in such a—such a—"

The servitor hesitating, the Hon. Augustus finished his sentence.

"Yes, I know—a devil of a temper. All right. I'll be with him in a moment."

As the Hon. Augustus was passing the countess's own sitting-room—everybody knows that the Earl of Glenlean has been married twice, and that the present countess is about the age of his youngest daughter—young Ronald, the countess's first-born, came rushing out.

"Hullo! 'Gustus, the earl and the countess *have* been going it." That is how the Hon. Ronald Champnell spoke of his father and mother. "And ma's gone crying to her bedroom, and she said she'd help me with my kite, and nurse is not a bit of good, and I wish you'd come and help me."

The young gentleman was holding a large kite in his hands, which required, apparently, some finishing touches.

"Sorry, Ronald, I cannot stop just now. Possibly I may be able to place my valuable services at your disposal a little later on."

As the Hon. Augustus entered the study, a moment's glance at his father showed him that it was something out of the common. The Earl of Glenlean was in a state of quite unusual excitement—unusual, even for him. He kept getting in and out of his chair as if he was unable to either sit or stand comfortably.

"Philpotts tells me, sir, that you wish to speak to me."

"I do, Augustus, I do. A most extraordinary thing has happened—a most extraordinary thing."

"I hope that it is nothing unpleasant?"

"It is unpleasant—it's dashed unpleasant. A paper—to be plain with you, a letter of an extremely confidential character—has been taken from my table here."

"Indeed, sir, when?"

"Just now!"

"I do not quite understand you, sir."

"You'll understand me if you'll allow me to explain. You were talking yesterday about what you called your sleuth-hound instinct, so I thought I'd give you an opportunity to put it to some practical use." The earl was, plainly, snappish. His son contented himself with bowing. "I went upstairs to speak to the countess, leaving this letter on the table, and when I came down the letter was gone."

The Hon. Augustus scrutinised his father with his keen, blue eyes. He perceived not only that the old gentleman's agitation was genuine, but also that he was endeavouring to conceal rather than to display it.

"What was in the letter?"

"Never mind! I tell you that it was of an extremely confidential character, and that I would not have it meet anybody else's eyes but my own, and the person's for whom it was intended, for—for a good deal."

His son understood. He was aware that the earl's record was of a curious sort, and could easily believe that he might have had a finger in a good many letters which he would rather keep from publication.

"Was it a letter you had received?"

"No, it was one I was writing. In fact, I had nearly finished it when the countess sent down to say that she wished to speak to me."

"Who brought the message?"

"Her maid—but she could have had nothing to do with the matter, because she went upstairs in front of me, and I saw her go into the countess's bedroom."

"How long were you gone?"

"Certainly not more than ten minutes, probably less. It was the consciousness of having left the letter lying on the table which made me hasten back."

"Did you shut the door when you went?"

"Yes, and it was shut when I came back."

"Was anything taken except the letter?"

"Nothing—not a thing had been touched. To all appearances the table was exactly as it was when I left it."

"Tell me precisely where the letter was."

"It was on my blotting case. When Mills—that is the maid's name—came in, I was writing it. When I went out I turned the leaf of the blotter, so as to cover it."

"You are sure you did cover it?"

"I am not prepared to swear to it. I am under the impression that I did—I intended to, but the fact is, I was anxious to hear what the countess had to say."

"Did the maid see that you were writing?"

"I take it that she did—she could scarcely have helped it. But I am sure that she did not know what I was writing, and, as I have told you, I am convinced that she could have had no hand in the abstraction of the letter."

"I am not suggesting that she had. Was there anybody about the house who knew that you might be writing such a letter?"

"Not a creature! Not a soul! I swear it!" The earl's agitation became almost painful. "I will be frank with you, Augustus. Rather than that anybody about the house should become acquainted with the contents of that letter I would give ten years of my life. I am relying both on your honour and on your discretion."

"In so doing you are perfectly safe. Have you inquired if anybody entered the room during your absence?"

"That is not the least extraordinary part of the affair. I have asked Philpotts. He says he was busy in the morning-room, and he is sure that nobody did."

"Is that what Philpotts says?"

"Yes." The father glanced sharply at his son. "You are not suggesting that Philpotts might have had a hand in it?"

"Not I. Philpotts dangled me in his arms when I was a baby. I have not known him all these years without taking his measure. I was only wondering if he had any particular cause for noticing."

"If, as he says, he was busy at the sideboard, and the morning-room door was open, as it was, he could not have helped but notice. Aren't the rooms right opposite each other?"

"Precisely. That is so. Then, if no one came through the door, someone must have come through the window."

"The window has been wide open all the time, just as you see it now. But no one could very well have got through the window without damaging either the roses or the flowers, and nothing of the kind has happened, because I have looked to see."

The Hon. Augustus leaned through the open window. It was raised, perhaps, five feet off the ground. Not only did a wide bed of flowers run along the wall at the foot, but the wall itself was covered with climbing roses, which, just then, were a mass of blossoms. As the earl observed, it seemed that anybody climbing through the window would have been forced to leave marks of his presence either on the flower-bed or among the roses. But, so far from anything of the kind being visible, everything was in spotless order. Not a petal lay upon the ground.

The Hon. Augustus returned into the room. He went to the writing-table. Something on it caught his eye.

"What are these?" he asked.

The writing-table, like the rest of the furniture, was of black oak. It had a leather top. On this leather top were spots of what looked like oil or grease. At these the Hon. Augustus pointed.

"That's what I can't make out," replied the earl. "They weren't there when I left the room. They seem to be some sticky stuff."

Kneeling down, the Hon. Augustus examined the spots by means of a reading-glass which was lying on the table.

"As you say, sir, it is some sticky stuff, and something with a strong capacity for sticking, too. Something that is meant to stick. Anybody standing outside the window, with, say a fishing-rod in his hand, and a float at the end of his line, smeared with this stuff, if he was to swing that float into the room, might cause it to adhere to a letter lying on a table, and he might make of the letter a prize."

The earl stared.

"Good heavens—who do you suppose would be likely to go through a performance of that kind? How could anyone know that such a letter was lying on the table?—or, indeed, that any letter was lying there? How could he time his appearance on the scene to fit in with the few minutes I was out of the room? How could he know that I was likely to be out of the room at all?"

"Precisely. Your questions are shrewd ones. They will have to be determined. I suppose, sir, you are sure that you did leave the letter lying on the table?"

"Sure! Of course I'm sure! What the dickens do you mean?"

And the earl stamped his foot on the ground in a fashion that suggested that his irritation had very far from decreased. His son stood up. He regarded his father with a close attention which the earl showed signs of resenting.

"If I find this letter for you, sir, what reward will you give me?"

"If you find the letter—what do you mean?"

"If I find the letter, and return it to you, with its contents unread, and no one in the world, except yourself, with an inkling of what those contents are—what reward will you give me?"

The earl glowered at his son, not only in unmistakable surprise, but with also something like a glimmering of suspicion.

"Do you know where the letter is?"

"I do not. I know no more about it than you do yourself. But I am prepared to take your view of the matter, and to accept this case as a test as to whether I do or do not possess something of the instinct of a sleuth-hound. If I prove, by my success, that I do, I shall expect you to give your consent to my adopting, as my own, the profession of detective."

"You shall have it—gad, you shall! Find out what scoundrel has laid felonious hands on that letter and return it to me unread—unread, mind!—and I'll not only give you my consent—I'll also give you your first professional fee of a hundred guineas."

"Very good, sir. I will do my best to earn it." The young man turned to go. His father stopped him.

"Where the deuce are you off to? What are you going to do?"

"You must forgive my saying that that is my affair. Afterwards, if I succeed, I will explain to you, in detail, if you wish it, my method of procedure. Until then you must allow me to go my way unquestioned."

The Hon. Augustus left the room.

With an exclamation the earl threw himself into a chair. "If," said he, "there is an art in which the rising generation is proficient, it is, without any doubt whatever, the art of being cocksure."

The Earl of Glenlean went upstairs to have a few words with the countess. And the countess had a few words with him. Which exchange of conversational sweetmeats did him so much good, that, encountering Philpotts as he was leaving the lady's room, he shouted at that fortunately well-seasoned domestic, as if he supposed that the man had suddenly gone stone-deaf.

"Where's Augustus?"

"Mr. Augustus has gone out, my lord."

"Gone out,"—the earl glared. "Where to?"

"I do not know, my lord. I saw Mr. Augustus a few minutes ago strolling across the lawn."

The earl returned to his study.

"I should like to be told what idiotic nonsense he is up to now! I decline to allow myself to be trifled with by such a puppy. The scoundrel who has stolen the letter is miles away, by now, or, worse still, the letter itself is on its way to town! Good heavens—To think of it!" The earl threw his hands above his head, as if the mere idea of such a catastrophe was more than he could bear. "I'll wire at once to half a dozen decent detectives to come down from town to help me search for it. Who's there?"

"Am I interrupting you, sir?"

CHAPTER II
AND FOUND

THE SPEAKER, who was holding the handle of the open door in his hand, was the Hon. Augustus. The sight of him did not appear to calm his father.

"By the way, Augustus, I have decided that it is altogether out of the question that I should place a matter of this paramount importance in such inexperienced hands as yours. I don't want to hurt your feelings by suggesting that you have a higher opinion of your own powers than I have, but I have resolved to telegraph for half a dozen properly qualified men from town!"

"Very good, sir. Will you telegraph before I have returned you the letter or afterwards?"

"What the dickens do you mean?"

"I mean, sir, that the letter is already found."

"Found—good gracious!" The earl dropped into an arm chair bounded out of it again. "Who was the thief?"

"I fancy, sir, that you yourself were the thief."

"I was the thief!" For a moment it almost seemed as if the earl was about to have an apoplectic fit. "Allow me to remind you, Augustus Champnell, that I am the unhappy individual who has the misfortune to be your father!"

"I was merely stating facts, sir."

"Facts—and this is a son of mine!" The earl dropped back into his armchair. "Go on, sir, go on! Insult me further. Pray where is the letter which I have stolen?"

"Here, sir." The Hon. Augustus opened the door wider. "Come in, Ronald."

There entered—looking as if he would much rather have stayed outside—the Hon. Ronald Champnell—who had nearly struck seven—and who was holding, with both his hands, a very large kite, which had a very long tail. Taking it from the youngster, the Hon. Augustus held the kite up in front of the earl.

"Here is the letter, sir."

Placing his glasses on his nose, the earl looked at the kite with a mystified air.

"Where?"

"Here, sir, here!"

As he spoke, the Hon. Augustus shook the kite. Just for a second, he more than half suspected that the earl was about to throw a ruler at his head—the august nobleman had thrown such things at people's heads more than once in his time. But on this occasion he refrained. He contented himself with addressing his son in a tone which resembled, in some respects, the highly rectified extract of vitriolic acid.

"I have to assure you, Augustus Champnell, that there is a limit even to your father's power of endurance."

"I have no desire whatever to try your power of endurance. You will find, sir, that the letter is here. You will observe that the kite has a very long tail—it balances it exactly, doesn't it, Ronald? The tail is constructed of pieces of paper. Will you kindly cut off the third piece of paper from the end?"

"I shall do nothing of the kind. I have had enough of your tomfoolery."

"Then, sir, I will do it for you. I thought that if you cut it off yourself you would be certain that the letter had remained unread. But perhaps it will be equally satisfactory if I cut it off in your presence."

The tail of the kite was formed of pieces of paper tied to a string—as tails of kites are apt to be. With a penknife, the Hon. Augustus removed the piece of paper which was third from the bottom of the string—and having freed it from its bonds, handed it, still screwed up anyhow, to his father.

"There is the letter, sir."

The earl unfolded the piece of paper, which he had taken—gingerly enough—between his fingers, staring at it as if he had quite decided that, at last, his eyes must be deceiving him.

"It is—good—good—" The earl floundered in his speech to such an extent that he was actually unable to find a word which was sufficiently strong to enable him to give adequate expression to his feelings. Then he sprang from his seat, and roared at Ronald,—

"So you stole it, did you, sir?"

The Hon. Augustus interposed.

"You are under a misapprehension. If you will permit me, I will explain." He turned to the youngster. "Here's your kite, Ronald. I'll make a better tail for you in a minute or two, in exchange for the one I have spoilt. Off you go, old chap."

Off the "old chap" went—evincing no symptom of unwillingness to get out of the paternal study. After he was gone the earl continued to examine the restored letter in silence, as if he did not know exactly what to say. So his son spoke instead,—

"I believe, sir, that I have earned the stipulated reward."

"I'll be hanged if you haven't, and you shall have it!" Taking a cheque-book from a drawer, the earl scribbled off a cheque for one hundred guineas then and there. As he was about to hand it to his son, he hesitated. "But how am I to know that the letter has remained unread?"

"You will have sufficient proof of that when I tell you how I tracked it down, or rather up, for, when I first caught sight of it, it was careering through the air. It was in this way. When you told me how it was impossible that anyone could know that such a letter was being written, and it seemed pretty certain that during your absence from the room no one had entered either through the door or through the window, it became obvious to me that you yourself must have been responsible for its disappearance."

"The devil it did!"

"When," continued Augustus, "I saw the spots on the table—which I see are still there—I had at once a glimpse of how the disappearance had been effected."

"How do you make that out?"

"Very simply. These things, like conjurors tricks, always are simple when they are explained. I had previously noticed that some of the contents of a bottle of mucilage had been spilled on one of the book-shelves—here, sir, they still are."

"Jove, now you've mentioned it, I remember spilling the bottle as I was getting down the Red Book."

"Exactly. Anyhow, there were some of the contents. I saw that the spots on the table resembled those contents, and what was more, I noticed that, as I had expected, you had got some of the contents on to the sleeve of your coat. You see, sir?"

The Hon. Augustus turned his father's right coat sleeve upwards. Sure enough on it, near the cuff, was a greasy smear.

"In covering the letter, as you supposed, with the blotter, nothing was easier in your haste—you told me, sir, you were in a hurry—than for you, with that strong mucilage there, actually, though unconsciously, to attach it to the sleeve of your coat. That, I take it, is what you did do. The question to be determined was—where had you dropped it? You had not dropped it in the room; you must have dropped it before you saw the countess, otherwise she would have seen it sticking to your sleeve, and have pointed it out to you. It seemed to me probable that you had brushed it off your sleeve against the door, as you were entering the countess's room. That again is what I believe you did do. The room was empty when I reached it, but a number of scraps of paper were littered about on the floor. I knew Ronald had been making a tail to his kite, and as your letter was not among the torn paper, I jumped to the conclusion that Ronald had used it as an addition to his kite's tail. I started off in chase of him, I brought his kite to the ground, perceived that a sheet of your letter-paper was attached to the tail, and straightway brought him and his kite back to you. I submit, sir, that the evidence goes to show that no one has seen the letter but Ronald—he says himself he picked it up from the floor and tied it to the tail! and what is Ronald's capacity, or rather incapacity, to read your hand-writing you are well aware. You perceive, sir, that the whole affair is very simple."

"Simple," growled the earl. "Simple beyond the verge of peurility! Here is your cheque, sir. I hope you may earn other cheques as easily. If this sort of thing is the art of detection it is an art which any simpleton may master. As, therefore, the profession of a detective should be within the range even of your capacities, you have my permission to adopt it as your own."

So the Hon. Augustus did.

II
LADY MAJENDIE'S DISAPPEARANCE

CHAPTER I
THE VANISHING WIFE

THE HON. AUGUSTUS CHAMPNELL'S first professional case of any importance was the rather curious one of Lady Majendie.

It began with the arrival, as he was finishing breakfast, of a letter which not only appeared to have been written with the wrong end of a broom stick, the lines zig-zagging up and down the page so as to form a sort of delirious pattern, but which was also couched in language of an extravagant kind—language which showed scant regard to spelling and none to grammar.

> "South Molton Street.
> "Dear Champnell,—If you have the feelings of a human being in your nature I entreat you to come to me at once this instant minute!!!
>
> "Never was a man plunged into a more deplorable situation or dashed nearer to the brink of suicide—for all I know, unknown to myself or to anyone else, I may already have been guilty of murder!!!
>
> "I implore you, if you have a drop of the milk of human kindness rushing through your veins, to hasten instantly to your almost, if not quite mad,
>> Cyril Majendie."

As the Hon. Augustus was starting, with a view of promptly responding to this poignant appeal, he encountered, on the doorstep, Mr. Frederic Parker—widely known as "Perky Parker," owing not only to the peculiarity of his manner, but also to the way in which the little moustache he had pointed upwards. It was Mr. Frederic Parker who electrified society last season by marrying Miss Scraggs, the American millionairess—though why she married him nobody knows. Mr. Frederic Parker looked pallid—for him.

"Mr. Champnell, I wish to see you, at once, on particular business."

"I am sorry that, at the moment, I have a pressing engagement. With your permission I will call on you directly I am free."

"Very good. I will wait." Mr. Frederic Parker was about to take his departure when he turned again towards Mr. Champnell. "By-the-by, Champnell, I may as well tell you that I have hesitated a good deal before coming to you, but there comes a time when even a man must assert his manhood. Our fellows all think I married my wife for money, but I didn't—I yielded to the promptings of affection." The little man hammered his gloved hand against the side of his chest where his heart was not. "But when it comes to seeing her leave the house in broad daylight, in the garb of a common flower-girl, with blotches on her face and I don't know what besides, and accost a common vagabond, in a raffish ulster, and slip her arm through his, and walk away with him, I tell you that even the most deeply-rooted affection totters on its foundation. You will find me waiting for you when you come."

When the Hon. Augustus arrived at Sir Cyril Majendie's that gentleman bore every appearance of having just got out of bed—and not out of a bed of roses either. To have seen him then no one would have supposed him to be, in general, one of the best-dressed men in town. Possibly a collection of bottles and of glasses, which were on the table, might have had something to do with the singularity of his costume and of his demeanour.

He came rushing towards Mr. Champnell with outstretched hands.

"My dear Champnell, I can't tell you how glad I am to see you; I declare you are the best fellow in the world! I do believe if you had been ten minutes longer I should have gone stark mad! What will you have to drink?"

"Nothing, thank you." As Sir Cyril was about to fill a tumbler, presumably for himself, the Hon. Augustus checked him. "And if you take my advice, you won't take anything either till you have told me what is the trouble."

"You're quite right, Champnell—I won't! I only have it to drown thought, upon my honour—you've no idea what a lot of drowning it takes. Have you heard anything about Nora and me?"

Sir Cyril looked at Mr. Champnell with anxious eyes.

"Absolutely nothing."

Everyone always is hearing something about that most extraordinary pair—the Hon. Augustus meant that he had heard nothing out of the common. Sir Cyril broke into a torrent of speech which, if it was remarkable for neither coherence nor eloquence, was at least remarkable for fluency.

"My wife's gone, Champnell—clean gone. I give you my word! This day week we had a row, we always are having rows, but this was a regular flare up. It was all that confounded wife of Perky Parker's—and so I'm always telling Nora. Mrs. Parker's got no end of money of her own, and Nora's got none, and she is always landing Nora in a heap of expenses, and how on earth am I to pay for them when, as everybody knows, I myself spend more money than I've got! I was five thousand to the bad at Epsom, so I told Nora she had ruined me, and that if I couldn't find the five thousand nothing remained for me but suicide—or something of the kind; I don't know quite what I did say. Anyhow, she said she couldn't think of living if she'd ruined me, and she walked straight out of the room—I didn't know what she meant—I never do know what she means. The next morning she never showed—of course, that was nothing; but when I came back at night—lateish, you know— the servants came and said that they had seen and heard nothing of Nora, but her door was locked, and they couldn't make her hear. I had the door broken open but she wasn't there—and that's the last I've seen of her; I haven't even had either a wire or a post-card. And this morning I found this inside a pair of my trousers—what it was doing there I don't know, it's given me quite the creeps."

Sir Cyril drew Mr. Champnell's attention to a white silk hand-kerchief, which lay among the bottles and the glasses on the table, and which contained rings, brooches, and a miscellaneous collection of women's *bijouterie*, a lace handkerchief which was stained with what looked like blood, a very large silver bodkin which was also stained with blood—indeed, the whole contents of the hand-kerchief were disfigured with ugly dark red blotches. Sir Cyril's voice dropped to a tremulous whisper.

"Champnell, do you think that it is a case of murder or of suicide? Just think what my feelings are when I reflect that all that remains of Nora may be down the sink, or buried somewhere in the basement."

The husband's hand stole in the direction of a bottle and a glass. The Hon. Augustus caught his wrist in a grip of steel.

"You will be so good as not to drink anything more. I think it only too possible, Sir Cyril Majendie, that rather than continue to live with a tippling and a spendthrift husband, Lady Majendie may have been urged to fatal courses."

Sir Cyril seemed surprised. "I say, Champnell,—don't!"

"And I take the liberty to tell you that the law looks with reasonable suspicion upon the man who, having concealed the disappearance of his wife for a whole week, resorts to alcohol to ease the pinchings of a remorseful conscience."

Sir Cyril seemed still more surprised.

"Upon my word, Champnell, if I'd have thought you were going to go on at me I'll be hanged if I'd have sent for you."

"In that case I will go at once. I will place the matter in the hands of the first policeman I meet." Sir Cyril caught him by the arm.

"My word, Champnell, how you do go on! I give you my word, dear boy, you are under an entire misapprehension. If it's the presence of the bottles you object to, I'll have them removed."

"Be so good as to have them removed."

Sir Cyril had them removed—watching their removal with very much the air of a man who is assisting at his own execution.

It was some time before Mr. Champnell had done with him—Sir Cyril's story required a good deal of sifting. When he had done with him and was going downstairs, Neave, the butler, meeting him at the foot of the staircase, drew Mr. Champnell, with an air of mystery, into a little room on one side.

"Excuse my taking the liberty, Mr. Champnell, but I have heard that you have become a detective."

"I have become something of the kind."

"Then I make so bold, sir, as to inform you that some very strange things have been taking place in this house—as, perhaps, Sir Cyril may have told you."

"To what do you particularly refer?"

Neave pursed his lips and rubbed his hands—a little viciously.

"I refer, sir, to the behaviour of this new footman, which his name is Perkins—might Sir Cyril have mentioned his name?"

The Hon. Augustus shook his head.

"I thought as much, begging Sir Cyril's pardon, though heaven knows I have mentioned it to him often enough. He came to us from Lady Sarah Mason's, which is a most religious household—twice to church each Sunday every servant in the house has got to go, I know of my own knowledge!—and he came with the very best of characters, though how he got it is more than I can understand. I never saw his match for impudence. He hadn't been in the house four-and-twenty hours before he told me to my face he'd punch my head. Anything like his goings-on I never heard of; poking and prying in every hole and corner of the house, by night and by day, and never minding in the least a word I say to him. Only yesterday I caught him at the drawers in which Sir Cyril keeps his trousers. 'What are you doing there?' I asked him. 'Running the rule over the governor's kicksies,' he said, as bold as brass. So I said to him, 'I would have you know, young man, that when Sir Cyril has finished with his trousers they come to me.' And what do you think he answered, sir? I will be candid with you, begging your pardon! 'Seems to me that everything about the house comes to you, old coxy bird. Sort of place where they shoot rubbish, ain't you, Jimmy?' Now, sir, I am not accustomed to being called 'old coxy bird' by the under-servants, nor is my name Jimmy; and I ask you, sir—"

The aggrieved butler asked Mr. Champnell a good deal. Indeed, the Hon. Augustus found a difficulty in shaking him off—as Sir Cyril had declined to listen—Sir Cyril always declined to listen to any-one, on any subject whatever, upon principle—it seemed that the injured Neave had made up his mind that someone should listen. When, at last, Mr. Champnell had got into the street, having strolled perhaps fifty yards from the house, chancing to look over his shoulder, he saw, issuing from Sir Cyril's area gate, a man. A young man, evidently of the servant class, who wore a remarkably hang-dog air. Without pausing to look either to right or left of him he began to move quickly in the opposite direction to that in which Mr. Champnell was going. Quick as thought Mr. Champnell turned on his heel and followed. Fast as the young man moved his pur-suer moved still faster. As he was going round the corner, the Hon. Augustus laid his hand upon his arm. With a movement of startled surprise the young man turned and faced his captor—terror writ large on every muscle of his face.

"Now, my man, I have you. What is the meaning of this game of yours which you have been playing?"

Mr. Champnell's tone was curt and hard. He kept his steely blue eyes fixed upon the other's countenance. The young man quailed before his glance. He stammered out an answer,—

"If you please, sir, it is not I who am to blame, I have been driven into it by others."

"We will soon see about that. You come with me."

So the young man went with him—looking not unlike a cur who expects a whipping.

Chapter II
The New Footman

SOMETHING LIKE an hour afterwards a handsome cab bore the Hon. Augustus Champnell to Sir Cyril Majendie's door. Neave opened to him.

"Sir Cyril in?"

"Sir Cyril has gone to bed, sir."

"Gone to bed!—at this hour of the day?"

Mr. Champnell might be surprised—but the thing was a fact, as he proved by a personal inspection. He found Sir Cyril in bed, with the blankets drawn up to his chin, and in an extremely lachrymose frame of mind. Mr. Champnell routed him from between the sheets, hurried him into his clothes, and got him downstairs into the cab before he had succeeded in gaining a clear idea of what was happening. The cab drove off with the two men sitting in it, side by side—Sir Cyril still in a graveyard sort of mood.

"Give you my word, Champnell, I feel as if all the people in the street were pointing their fingers at me. Suppose they were to find my wife's remains in the dust-bin, or some horrid place like that, I should never be able to hold up my head again."

"You should have been a more kindly husband, Majendie."

"You wrong me, old man. I give you my word, I've threatened to commit suicide quite as often as she has. As a rule, we are a united couple, as people go. You wouldn't feel married if you weren't always having rows. Hullo, Champnell, where are you taking me to? The Johnny's pulling up at Perky's!"

Just then the cabman was pulling up at Mr. Frederic Parker's. Mr. Champnell sprang on to the pavement.

"All right, Sir Cyril, stop where you are. I want to speak to Mr. Parker."

Mr. Champnell already had his hand raised to salute the hall door, when it opened, to disclose Mr. Frederic Parker himself, equipped for out of doors. Mr. Parker seemed indignant. "Really Mr. Champnell, I think it's about time you did come. I don't know if you suppose that my business is of such slight importance that you can put it off till you have finished with everybody else's."

"I beg ten thousand pardons, Mr. Parker, but, with your permission, I will place myself at your service now."

Slipping his arm through Mr. Frederic Parker's, the Hon. Augustus led him down the steps, and in a trice, Mr. Frederic Parker found himself seated by Sir Cyril Majendie's side in the cab. Mr. Champnell followed him.

"There is plenty of room for me, gentlemen, upon your knees. All right, driver, you know where to go."

And the cab was off. Which of the two gentlemen was the more surprised at finding himself with such a neighbour, it would be impossible to say. Mr. Frederic Parker was the first to speak.

"Hang it, Mr. Champnell, sir, what do you mean by this? How dare you thrust me into a cab, and expect me to sit side by side with this individual?"

Sir Cyril explained.

"You see, Champnell, it's this way—we're not on speaking terms, Parker and me."

"No, sir, we are not on speaking terms, nor are we ever likely to be."

Mr. Frederic Parker essayed to rise. Mr. Champnell, who was partially dependent on him for a seat, kept him in his place by exercising a judicious pressure on his knees.

"Now, Mr. Parker, sit still if you please. Pray don't make an exhibition of yourself in the street and in a common cab."

Sir Cyril cast oil upon the troubled waters.

"I don't know, Parker, why you need keep up your quarrel with me, now that my wife's been murdered."

"Murdered!—Good God—Majendie!—You don't mean it?"

"I expect that she has been something of the kind; for all I know, her body may be turning up at any moment. It's a week ago since she disappeared."

"I am not so sure, Majendie, that you're not to be envied. My wife hasn't disappeared; I almost wish she had. She has been misconducting herself with an individual whom I take to be an Italian organ-grinder out of work."

"Ah, Parker, I was always telling you that your wife would do something like that—it was she who drove my wife to her ruin."

"On the contrary, Majendie, it was your wife who was continually instilling evil principles into my wife's mind."

"Hang me, Parker, if I don't chuck you out of the cab."

"If you touch me with one of your fingers, sir, I'll knock you down."

Mr. Champnell interposed—it seemed to be almost time.

"Now, gentlemen! Gentlemen! I can easily understand how it is your matrimonial speculations have gone so utterly astray when I perceive how incapable you are of exercising self-restraint, even in, your present unfortunate situation."

The cab had entered a distinctly unfashionable neighbourhood. It stopped in front of a dirty house, which was in a dirty street. Mr. Champnell got out. The others followed him. Mr. Champnell paid the cabman his fare. The man drove off.

"Have the kindness, gentlemen, to follow me."

They had the kindness—each first looking askance at the other. It is possible that, if they had been on speaking terms, they would have inquired whither they were being led. As it was, each seemed unwilling to allow the other to hear the sound of his voice.

The dirty door of the dirty house stood open. The Hon. Augustus led the way up three flights of dirty stairs to a room at the back. The room was not only dirty, like the rest of the premises—it was unfurnished. The Hon. Augustus shut the door behind them as they entered. Then Mr. Frederic Parker spoke.

"Might I inquire, Mr. Champnell, what is the meaning of the wild-goose chase which you appear to have brought me on?"

"Your question, Mr. Parker, shall shortly receive a satisfactory answer. Hush!" He stood in an attitude of listening. "Sooner, even, I think, than I fancied. Is that not someone coming upstairs?"

Someone was ascending—they could hear the sound of footsteps clattering up the uncarpeted stairs. Mr. Frederic Parker, opening the door about an inch—unchecked by the Hon. Augustus—peeped out to see who the newcomer was. Suddenly, starting back into the room, he gasped,—

"I'll be hanged!—my wife—gone into the next room!—in the garb of a common flower-girl!"

Sir Cyril seemed interested—he occupied the position which Mr. Frederic Parker had vacated.

"I give you my word—my new footman!—the beggar who's been giving old Neave such a time of it—gone into the next room, too!" Sir Cyril came away from the door. "On my honour, Parker, I don't admire your wife's taste—the man's almost as black as a nigger."

Every hair on Mr. Frederic Parker's moustache was bristling. He favoured Sir Cyril Majendie with a frenzied glare. He burst into a roar of rage.

"Stand away from the door!"

He dashed through the door into the adjoining room, Sir Cyril treading hard upon his heels, the Hon. Augustus bringing up the rear. He struck an attitude, which was a mingling of fury with despair, and addressing himself to a lady, the most prominent articles of whose attire were a vivid check shawl and a large hat, which were adorned with a gorgeous feather, exclaimed, "So, Mrs. Frederic Parker, I have discovered you at last!"

Sir Cyril advanced to the new footman.

"I give you my word, Perkins, I admire your modesty. I suppose that nothing would do for a man in your position but a young married woman who was in the possession of. millions."

Mr. Champnell came to the front—doffing his hat as he did so.

"Permit me, Mr. Parker, to have the honour of introducing you to Lady Majendie." The Hon. Augustus motioned towards the new footman. "Sir Cyril, I have much pleasure in making known to you your wife."

There was a momentary pause. Then a sound, which was half laugh, half sob. The new footman, snatching off a wig, revealed a head of curly golden hair. An unmistakably feminine voice rang out,—

"Oh, Cyril, this is too much—that I should have been suspected of an intrigue with Maria and by Mr. Parker, too! What an actress I must be. It's the walnut juice has done it—I shan't get it off my face for months!"

Sir Cyril looked what he felt, not a little bewildered. "I give you my word, Nora, that this is a pretty trick to play your husband."

"My dear Cyril, I did it all for you!"

"For me?" Sir Cyril seemed doubtful.

"Yes, for you! When you told me that you'd be ruined if you couldn't lay your hands upon five thousand pounds, I made up my mind that you shouldn't be ruined for want of that. So I just stepped across the road to Maria—Maria's a trump, aren't you, dear?"

The lady in the check shawl dropped a curtsey. "I are that, my ducky."

"And I said, 'Maria, I want to have a bet with you.' And she said, 'I'm on.' So I said, 'I bet you that I'll go as footman in my own home for a week, and that Cyril won't recognise me all the time.' So she said, 'It's done. How much?' So I said, 'It must be for something worth having, Maria. This is a regular sporting bet, this is. Will you make it five thousand pounds?'"

The lady in the check shawl struck in,—

"When she said that I knew she was a trump—bless you, don't I know the girl? I knew that she had a special use for that five thousand!" Placing her hands on her hips, in the orthodox way, the lady confronted Sir Cyril,

"Yes, Sir Cyril Majendie, I knew that, at any price to herself, she was going to do a good turn to you—don't I tell you I knew the girl?" She turned to Mr. Champnell, "And pray, sir, how did you find out what your betters failed to do?"

"For that, Mrs. Parker, I am indebted, in no slight degree, to the real Perkins, whose substitute Lady Majendie has been. I made a prize of him directly he had come up the area steps."

"I was afraid," cried Lady Majendie, "that the fellow would spoil me—and that, although it cost us a stiffish sum to square him. He was always hanging about the place—he made out that his conscience wouldn't allow him to keep away; the man is too good to live! But how did you find out this address—that you didn't get from him?"

"That I found on a slip of paper which was under the odds and ends which were contained in the white silk handkerchief, Lady Majendie, which yesterday you put inside a pair of your husband's trousers—that time the scandalized Mr. Neave came and almost caught you in the act. The slip of paper had escaped Sir Cyril's notice, and I imagine, yours also."

"It had—although you must have had sharp wits, Mr. Champnell, to have guessed at what the address might mean. We intended to keep our little frolic to ourselves, didn't we, Maria?"

"We did that, my Lady Majendie—you shall have that five thou— there never was a fairer won bet—when we get home. And now, if you married men will get into the next room, we married women will get into our own clothes." She turned to Mr. Champnell. "We married people will have to fight this out between ourselves—I don't think, sir, we need detain you."

He acquiesced. "I don't think you need."

So the Hon. Augustus Champnell went downstairs.

III
THE BURGLARY AT AZALEA VILLA

Chapter I
The Burglar

It was when the Hon. Augustus Champnell was recovering from a slight touch of influenza that the servant came to announce that Lord George Carman particularly wished to see him.

"Haw!" began Lord George—it struck Mr. Champnell that he seemed more transcendental even than usual—"sorry to hear you're seedy. Awkward affair last night. Burglary, and I don't know what. Devil of a nuisance."

Stretching out his long thin legs in front of him, Lord George surveyed the pointed toes of his polished shoes through his eye-glass. He appeared to be under the impression that he had made himself quite plain.

"Is that all you have come to say, Carman?"

Lord George glanced up. He seemed surprised.

"Haw! Fact is, I've come to see you."

"So I perceive."

"Yes." A pause. Another attempt at speech. "Fact is, don't you know, there's been a rumpus at Azalea Villa, the residence of a friend of mine—Miss Tottie Darling."

Mr. Champnell knew all about Azalea Villa, and also about Miss Tottie Darling, as Lord George was probably aware. After a pause of considerable magnitude, Lord George went on,—

"Fact is, fellow broke in last night. Collared no end of things. Yes."

"Indeed."

"Lots of jewellery. Things I've given Miss Darling, don't you know. They will have cost me no end of money by the time they're paid for. Not that I mind. Though the lady don't seem to like it. But that's not the worst."

"What is the worst?"

It may sound incredible to those who are acquainted with Lord George Carman, he actually betrayed symptoms of uneasiness. He looked up at the ceiling, as if seeking for inspiration there, then looked back again at Mr. Champnell.

"Fact is, I couldn't go to the beastly police, don't you know, really. So I've come to you. You're one of us. So it's different."

"If you're asking me, Carman, if you may rely upon my regarding anything which you may say to me as strictly private and confidential, I answer that you unhesitatingly may."

"That's a comfort."

Lord George sighed. He became conversational—for him.

"Fact is, I gave Miss Darling a written promise of marriage. She kept it at the bottom of her jewel-box. And that's gone along with the rest of the things. I wouldn't have it hawked about for any amount of money. The Lord knows what would happen if it came to my father's ears. Especially just now—when they're all at me to marry somebody else, you know."

Mr. Champnell did know. He pictured the Marquis of Hammersmith's face—that most evangelical of noblemen—finding himself confronted by such a document in his son's calligraphy. What would the Carmans exclaim at the notion of having Miss Tottie Darling as the future queen of their beer-vats!

"The loss of such a document may turn out to be rather an awkward thing."

"Rather. You've no notion!" Lord George edged his chair a little closer. "Between you and me, Champnell—I don't say it is so, mind—but we've had a word or two lately, and I shouldn't be surprised if she's stolen the thing herself. Pretended there's been a burglary, don't you know, and then gone and given my promise of marriage to a friend, for him to put the screw on."

"Have you evidence which points to something of the kind?"

"Not a shred! not a tittle! It's only my idea. I tell you I don't half like it."

"Who lives in the house besides Miss Darling?"

"Only a girl. It's only a doll's-house sort of a place. There's only Tottie and a maid."

"What has been taken besides the letter?"

"No idea. Know nothing about it. Only what she's just told me. Come straight from there. She seems to be in a deuce of a way. May be genuine. Thought I'd come to you and see what you could make of it. I tell you, I don't half like the idea of that promise of marriage of mine being handed round the town—especially situated as I am just now."

"A little fresh air will do me good. I'll come round to Azalea Villa as soon as I'm dressed. Perhaps you will meet me there."

"Yes." A pause. "I might." Another pause. "In fact, I will. Yes. Good-bye."

The servant could hardly have seen Lord George Carman off the premises when the man returned to announce that a person desired to see the Hon. Augustus, who refused to give his name. The Hon. Augustus, who was about to prepare for his journey to Azalea Villa, evinced no desire to see the person.

"Go and ask him to tell you what it is he wishes to see me about."

A husky voice supplied an unexpected answer.

"All right, guv'nor. That's what I've come for to tell you."

The answer came from an individual who was standing behind the servant, and who evidently had surreptitiously followed him up the stairs. Now, without waiting for any more ceremonious invitation, pushing past the scandalized lackey, he entered the room. He looked at Mr. Champnell and Mr. Champnell looked at him. The Hon. Augustus spoke to the servant.

"You can go." The servant went. "Be so good, my man, as to be as brief as possible in telling me what it is you want with me."

The visitor was an under-sized young fellow, apparently not more than twenty-four or twenty-five, whose endeavour to pass himself off as a respectable artisan was rather handicapped by the suspicious closeness with which his hair was cropped. He carried a seedy billycock in one hand and an ordinary black handbag in the other. For some cause he did not appear to be in the most amiable of tempers. When Mr. Champnell had ceased speaking he crooked his elbow towards the window which looked out into the street.

"Yes! I see him! Don't let him make no error—oh, no! Lord George Carman he calls himself—a nice bloke he is."

Mr. Champnell began to be amused, both by his visitor's tone and manner.

"You know Lord George Carman?"

"Know him?—rather! What do you think? His father's worth millions, his father is, yet it's the likes of him as goes and takes the bread out of the mouths of honest men."

"Indeed. I was not aware that he had any inclination in that direction. What has he done to you?"

"Done to me? Why, he's served me a dirty trick, the like of which I wouldn't do to a blind tomcat. I know what he's come to you about. He's come to tell you that his crib's been cracked—what he calls Azalea Villa. He wants to know who done it. I tell you, though I wouldn't tell him. Me!"

Mr. Champnell's amusement increased.

"Frankness would seem to be a marked trait in your character. Am I to understand that it was you who, last night, burglariously entered Azalea Villa?"

"That's what you are to understand. I'm told as how you calls yourself a detective—and you're the son of a hearl. My sakes! I don't know what things are a-coming to! We shall soon have the Prince of Wales a-sweeping of a crossing! You look like a common slop, you do."

"It strikes me that it's a common slop you want, my man. Am I to send for one?"

"Go on! I don't mind! There's only my own words again' me, and they're not evidence. Besides—you put me in the dock and I'll say all I've got to say, and that'll make someone look a little funny."

The man hesitated. He was evidently divided between two desires, a desire to relieve his mind—it was plain that something of a most unusual sort was on his mind—and a desire for his own safety. Finally he threw discretion to the winds—he relieved his mind.

"I've been readying the place a month and more, and no end of trouble I've had to do it. But when I do a thing I like to do it well; I'm as good a tradesman as there is in the profesh, though I say it myself, so don't you go and forget it. It ain't all skittles, crib-cracking ain't, it's fair hard work. Well, last night I put it up. I got in all right and I did my little business, what I'd got to do, all right, and I never so much as upset a rat. I was going away through the window of a little room what had got white walls, what I'd come through, when I sees upon the table a bottle and a glass. So I douses my glim, and I puts down my bag and I has a sup. If you'll believe me, guv'nor, as I was standing there in the darkness, just as I was raising the glass to my lips, a bright light shone into the room, like a halo like, on the wall, and there was Lord George Carman his own self, a-staring at me. It was all gone in a moment, him and the light and all, but it had been there quite long enough for me. I didn't want to stop to do no telling, so I catches up my bag and I cuts my lucky."

Drawing the back of his hand across his lips, the fellow looked at Mr. Champnell as if defying contradiction.

"Do you expect me to believe, my man, that Lord George Carman actually detected you in the act of committing burglary on his own premises, yet made no attempt to stop you?"

"I wouldn't have minded his doing that so much—I take some stopping, I do—but that would have been fair and above board, and all in the way of business, like; but he done worse than that, by chalks. When I gets back to my own little place, I opens my bag to have a look at my earnings, and so help you might have knocked me down with a feather! I'd filled the bag with my own hands, pretty nigh chock of diamond jewels and such-like, and when I came to reckon it up, well, there! you take and have a squint at it yourself, guv'nor, and tell me what you think of it! Here is the blooming bag."

Placing the bag which he had been carrying on the table, the man opened it for Mr. Champnell's inspection. It certainly contained rather a curious collection, hardly of the kind which the average burglar might be expected to covet.

"There you are! Did you ever see anything like it? Crusts of bread, lumps of dripping, bits of scrap meat, old noggins of cheese—like as if I was some blooming tramp and had been cadging for a meal! Ain't that a nice sort of thing to fetch away from a crib what I had been readying for a month and more?"

"Am I to understand you to say that someone in Azalea Villa took out what you had placed in the bag and put these things in it instead?"

"You ain't to understand nothing of the sort; you're to understand that the blessed bags was swapped. This ain't unlike my bag, but it ain't my bag; as I see only too well when it was too late. That there sneaking old rooster, and so I'd call him to his face—Lord George Carman, he calls himself—had nicked my bag and put this here, with this musty-fusty muck inside, instead of it. I thought that little job would set me up for a year and more—there was such lovely things I put inside my bag! I know what they corst! And when I did see what I had brought home I could have died. Gar on! If I was a nob, s'help me, James, I wouldn't play a poor, struggling, hard-working bloke a trick like that."

The fellow's disgust had a tragic as well as a comic side, but the Hon. Augustus Champnell only laughed.

CHAPTER II

AND THE LADY

AZALEA VILLA was one of those retiring bandbox villas in the wood, chastely shut in by high brick walls which even the tallest Life Guardsman could not peep over. Miss Tottie Darling was a beautiful lady, whose taste in costume was undeniable and expensive, and whose bearing could be, on occasion, infinitely more glacial than that of the historic Lady Clara Vere de Vere. The lady was in one of her frosty moods when the Hon. Augustus arrived. She was reclining on a couch in her pretty little drawing-room, and as the maidservant ushered him in she glanced at his visiting card, which she was holding in her hand, then up at him with a languid air.

"Mr. Champnell?" Mr. Champnell bowed. "Pleased to meet you."

The Hon. Augustus explained.

"My visit, Miss Darling, on this occasion is one rather of business than of pleasure. I am here with reference to the burglary which, I understand, took place last night."

"Oh!" The lady, visibly, was not interested. "I suppose George Carman has sent you. He need not have troubled. I know all about it."

"Indeed. Nothing had been discovered when I saw him. What has been discovered since?"

"Nothing." The lady pillowed her head in a still softer place among the cushions. "There was nothing to discover. You don't suppose that George Carman can hoodwink me? Burglary! George Carman was himself the burglar."

"Is it possible?"

"It is not only possible, it's sure. If he was in want of money I might have forgiven his pawning my jewels without first going through the form of asking my leave. It is, however, a different thing when it comes to his stealing his own written promise to marry me."

Mr. Champnell went to the window, which looked on to the garden. He changed the subject.

"I suppose your house is called after the azaleas which I see you have in your garden. What fine ones they are."

"Seen better."

Mr. Champnell was silent for a moment. When he spoke again he still retained his position before the window.

"May I ask, Miss Darling, if you have a list of the jewels which are missing?"

"Oh, dear, yes. As, when he tries to pawn them, George Carman will discover."

"Were you yourself disturbed in the night in anyway?"

"Not I. George Carman was too clever. He wouldn't have dared to face me. I'll own, if he likes, that he managed his part of the business very well, though it's just possible that he got someone to do his dirty work for him."

There was a ring at the garden door.

"There is Lord George; I asked him to meet me here." Mr. Champnell turned towards the lady. "Before he enters the room, you may take it from me, Miss Darling, that, whoever had a hand in this business, Lord George Carman hadn't. Of that I am sure."

The lady ceased to recline. She sat up on the couch. Her languor seemed suddenly to disappear. "What do you mean by that?"

"Exactly what I say."

The lady stood up. She exchanged glances with the gentleman. Some communication seemed to pass from one to the other. Her manner became, in an instant, quite the opposite of languid.

"Oh, you men! You stand shoulder to shoulder, and stick to each other through thick and thin, and think you can rob and cheat us women, and play any hanky-panky tricks with us you please, but sometimes you're mistaken! Don't fancy you can come the old soldier over me, Mr. Champnell. I tell you that George Carman planned the whole affair, from first to last—and I know it! And you can tell him from me that if he doesn't give me back that promise of marriage, or another one in its place before to-night, I'll go right straight away to his father—and then we'll see."

The lady moved majestically towards the door. As she reached it Lord George came in. He stared at her, blocking the way.

"Haw! Anything wrong?"

"Yes, George Carman, everything's wrong; so don't make any mistake about it!"

And the lady, sweeping past him, disappeared. Lord George stared after her, dropped his eyeglass, picked it up again, and having refixed it in his eye, stared at Mr. Champnell askance.

"What's up?"

"It would seem, if you will excuse my saying so, that Miss Darling's temper is up."

Lord George moved across the room towards Mr. Champnell. He lowered his voice to a confidential whisper.

"Do you think she did it?"

"She says you did it."

"Me! Lor'!" Lord George paused. "That's good. Why, I wasn't near the place all night."

"Are you sure of that?"

Lord George seemed to flinch before the other's scrutinizing gaze.

"Sure? Of course I'm sure! I suppose I ought to know."

"As you say, you certainly ought to know." Mr. Champnell turned aside. "Perhaps, Carman, you wouldn't mind showing me over the premises."

"Pleasure! Not that there's anything to show."

There did not seem to be anything to show. The tour of inspection only occupied a short time; they only made one pause.

"Believe this is where the fellow broke in. Am told so."

Mr. Champnell looked round him. He recognized the room which his visitor had described—the little room with the white walls. It was a small room with a table in the centre, on which had probably stood the bottle and the glass whose presence had induced the gentleman to put down his bag. On going to the window, Mr. Champnell perceived that it opened directly into the garden; it was an ideal place for a burglar to effect an entry. The walls were painted a vivid white.

"Did the man leave behind him any token of his presence?"

"Don't know. Think not. Heard of nothing."

Lord George was taciturn. He looked depressed. Possibly he was thinking of Miss Darling's temper.

"Rather curious to have the walls of a room painted such a very vivid white."

"She would have it. Said it was cool. I don't know." He seemed more depressed than ever—as if he were tired.

"Ain't you finished?"

"Nearly. Now, I want to see the room from which the jewels were taken, and the case itself from which the jewels were abstracted, and in which also, as I understand, your promise to marry Miss Darling was kept."

Lord George looked doubtful.

"That's Tottie's bedroom. I expect she's in it. She generally bolts to it when she's upset."

Mr. Champnell was suave but firm.

"I should be sorry in any way to inconvenience Miss Darling, but I have no doubt that when she hears what we want she will be delighted to allow us to examine the actual scene of the robbery. She herself will see so clearly the absolute necessity of such an examination taking place."

Lord George continued to look doubtful, and the event proved that his doubt was justified. They had to knock at the lady's bedroom door two or three times before its occupant condescended to answer, and after she had answered they had to parley for some time longer before admission was gained. Finally, with a flourish, Miss Darling threw the door wide open.

"Oh, by all means, force an entrance into a lady's bedroom. Of course, where George Carman is no woman can expect to enjoy the privacy of her own apartment. I don't know, George Carman, how you suppose that you're going to find your promise to marry me in here, when all the time you know it's in your pocket."

Lord George seemed to be positively terrified.

"Tottie, I'll take my oath—"

Miss Darling cut him short.

"You needn't! I've heard you take your oath before."

It is to be feared that she possibly had.

Regardless of this little war of words, Mr. Champnell advanced into the room. It was luxuriously furnished, conspicuously regardless of cost. The prevailing colour was pink, pink silk. The dressing-table, for instance, was charmingly decorated with voluminous folds of silk, which were of so light a pink that they might almost have been called flesh-colour. On the table stood a beautiful leather box—pink Russia! Mr. Champnell admired it—externally.

"Is this the dressing-case, Miss Darling?"

"What's left of it." There seemed to be a good deal left of it, so far as one could see. "Oh, you can open it. Anyone can open it now. The burglar—with a glance at Lord George—"smashed the lock."

Mr. Champnell did open it. As the lady suggested, it opened quite easily.

"That burglar seems to have left a good many of your jewels behind, Miss Darling; more of them, indeed, than the average burglar is apt to do."

The lady gave a little exclamation.

"Left some of them behind!" She rushed to the dressing-table. She stamped her foot. She gave a decided scream. She turned upon Lord George.

"You—you brute! So you've thought better of it after all. I suppose you knew I had a list, and you've put them back again."

Lord George stared at the jewel-case in what seemed to be genuine surprise. It did seem, just then, to be about as full of jewels as it very well could be—beauties some of then were. In face of the lady's attack the gentleman managed to pluck up some semblance of spirit. He retorted with a sort of sulky ferocity.

"I don't believe they were ever taken."

"Oh, no; of course you wouldn't now. I wonder if you've put the promise of marriage back as well." Miss Darling took out tray after tray full of jewels. At the bottom of the box she pressed a spring, which being pressed revealed a little secret hiding-place. This was empty. "So you have kept the promise of marriage. Just as I expected. Now, we do know where we are!"

"Do you think I'm an idiot?" inquired Lord George Carman. "Do you think I don't know that you've taken it yourself?

Just then the maid came in.

"Did you ring, ma'am?"

It was Mr. Champnell who answered, he had moved to the fireplace.

"It was I who rang." He addressed Miss Darling. "I ventured to take advantage of my being near it to touch the bell, Miss Darling." He turned again to the maid: "That was a mistake of yours to replace the jewels; a gross one. You would have done better to have allowed Mr. Miles to take them with him. Though I do homage to the desire to make partial restitution."

"I beg your pardon, sir."

The girl looked, or tried to look, as if she did not understand—though a slight tell-tale flush showed in her cheeks.

"Not at all." Mr. Champnell turned to Miss Darling. "This is the person, Miss Darling, who has put back your jewels in the case. The little document of the nature of a promise to marry, she retains."

The girl—she was a pretty one—went as red as fire, then all white. She made a quick backward movement towards the door—she had come some distance into the room—in an instant Mr. Champnell was between her and it. She turned and confronted him, grasping for breath.

"Let me go!" she said.

"One moment, if you please," Mr. Champnell motioned towards her with his hand. "Your cousin, Miss Darling, I believe?"

"How do you know she's my cousin?" demanded Miss Darling, who seemed to be herself slightly disconcerted.

Mr. Champnell shrugged his shoulders.

"How? Especially as, I am afraid, she has used you in rather uncousinly fashion. She has had, for some time, her eye on that promise of marriage, touching which, I fear, you have been slightly indiscreet. She imagined that if she could only get it into her possession, it would be worth a fortune to her, and also, that she would have you at her mercy. The scheme she formed to get hold of it, and yet prevent suspicion falling on to her, was ingenious. Her fault has been that she has been too clever."

Miss Darling's eyes had been fixed upon the maid, whose demeanour betrayed her.

"I never thought it of you, Pollie!" exclaimed the lady.

But the girl was still. Mr. Champnell went on.

"A gentleman, whose name is Miles, and whose profession is burglary, formed some time ago the intention of burglariously entering Azalea Villa. Experience had taught him that the best aid to a burglar was a maid whom he could pump. But, in endeavouring to pump the maid at Azalea Villa, Mr. Miles, unconsciously, had met more than his match. While he thought he was pumping her, she in reality was pumping him. She perceived that here was the opportunity offered which she had so long been seeking. She decided to allow Mr. Miles to commit his burglary, and then, under cover of his burglary, to steal that little document. The idea, one must own, was in its way, a neat one."

"It's a lie!" gasped the girl. "It's a lie!"

"Really, it is unkind of you to say so—and uncivil too. Last night Mr. Miles did commit his burglary. Although he did not know it, the maid was expecting him. She permitted him to abstract the jewels from the case. But, as he was about to take his departure through the window in the little room with the white walls he saw a bottle and a glass on the table, which the maid had placed there, knowing that Mr. Miles was of a thirsty nature. Mr. Miles rose to the bait. He put down his bag with its precious contents, he filled the tumbler from the bottle and he darkened his lantern. That same second the maid, who all the time was concealed behind a curtain, exchanged his bag for one of her own, which she had already prepared, and, simultaneously, removed the cap from a magic lantern, which I noticed is still in the little room with the white walls, and which she lighted and focused and fitted with a slide which took the shape of a capital coloured portrait of Lord George Carman. The startled Mr. Miles, expecting nothing of the kind, and taken unawares, not unnaturally imagined that the picture which he saw on the wall—the white wall served as an excellent screen— was the man himself. He snatched up the substituted bag, without perceiving in his haste the substitution which had been effected, and ran for his life. The maid, therefore, was left in possession of the spoils. I fancy that, when it came to the point, she did not dare to retain them in her possession. But to return them was a tactical blunder. The document which she removed before Mr. Miles' arrival on the scene, as I have said, she retains."

As she listened, the girl's face had been a picture of varying emotions. She shrank from him as if he had been some uncanny thing.

"It's a lie!" she gasped again, mechanically rather than of her own volition.

"So far from its being a lie, you have that document upon your person at this moment. Give it to me—take my advice—before it is too late!"

Mr. Champnell's tone became stern, his manner commanding. The girl quailed before his searching glance. His force dominated hers. With trembling fingers, unfastening the buttons of her bodice, she drew from her breast a paper. In an instant the Hon. Augustus had snatched it from her. As he did so, with a cry as of fear, she sank on to the floor and burst into a flood of hysterical tears.

Mr. Champnell handed the paper which he had taken from her to Miss Darling.

"That, I believe you will find, is the promise of marriage."

It was.

IV
THE STOLEN TREATY

Chapter I
At the Foreign Office

THE POSITION of confidential agent, which the Hon. Augustus Champnell came to occupy in high political circles was owing, in the first place, in no slight degree to his handling of the case of the Stolen Treaty.

When he reached the Foreign Office—within five minutes of his receiving the note requesting his attendance—he was at once ushered into the presence of the then Foreign Secretary, Viscount Horsham. The viscount thanked the Hon. Augustus for his prompt attendance, reminded him that his father, the Earl of Glenlean, was an old schoolfellow of his own, then at once proceeded to the business in hand.

"The fact is, Mr. Champnell, the copy of a treaty—indeed, the treaty itself—which, for the present at least, is of a confidential character, and which we have negotiated with the Government of Mexico, has been stolen from this office, from underneath my very nose."

Mr. Champnell looked what possibly he might not have felt—surprised.

"Have you no suspicion, my lord, of who the thief is?"

"That, Mr. Champnell, is the delicate part of the position. We have not only a suspicion, we have something which approaches to a certainty."

The Hon. Augustus bowed. As yet he did not clearly understand.

Leaning towards Mr. Champnell across the table, the viscount lowered his voice.

"We have only too much reason to believe that the thief is the Plenipotentiary from Panama."

The Hon. Augustus began to see the viscount's drift.

"In that case, I presume, you desire not so much the detection of the thief as the recovery of the treaty?"

"Exactly—you have hit it on the head. As you are, of course, aware, we could not arrest the man even if we wished; he is protected by his office. But, apart from our disability, we desire to avoid a scandal. He is accredited to us as Don Joaquim de Coronads—which, by the way, we have again reason to believe has not always been his name."

Pausing, the viscount exchanged with Mr. Champnell a glance which was full of meaning.

"We have cause to suspect that he has not stolen the treaty for his own use, but with a view of selling or otherwise disposing of it, to the Plenipotentiary from Caracas. You have no notion, Mr. Champnell, what curious representatives are sometimes sent to us by South American states."

"So I should imagine."

The viscount raised his hands.

"Indeed! The name of the Plenipotentiary from Caracas is Don Martinez Sutierrez. I will merely observe that while he speaks Spanish, and indeed, for the matter of that, English also, with a marked German-American accent, his colleague, de Coronads, speaks practically no language but English—and that with a strong Irish-American accent. The stolen treaty contains a clause having a particular personal reference to Sutierrez, and to affairs in which he is personally interested. He, no doubt suspecting the existence of this clause, and being conscious of the vital necessity of his obtaining early and exact knowledge of its purport, has instigated de Coronads, who is a personal friend of his own, to get it into his possession."

The viscount stopped. The Hon. Augustus considered.

"I suppose that there is no doubt that de Coronads did steal the treaty?"

"Unfortunately, none whatever. The impudence of the act was not the least amazing part of it. I assure you, between ourselves, Mr. Champnell, that neither gentleman is an individual who is at all likely to stick at trifles. The treaty had been returned by the Queen. The Panama and Caracas Plenipotentiaries suddenly arriving together, requested, in a somewhat blustering fashion, an immediate interview. They were shown in to me. The interview was of a not altogether pleasant kind. Towards the close of it, Sutierrez drew me aside into the bow-window there, under the pretext of saying something to me in confidence. While I was standing with him I actually saw de Coronads fingering the papers on my table. But it was not till after he had gone that I discovered that it was the treaty with Mexico that the scoundrel had stolen. It was as impudent and as barefaced a robbery as I ever heard of."

"When did this take place?"

"Not an hour ago."

"So recently. Then, in that case, there is a possibility of the contents of the treaty not having yet been communicated to Sutierrez."

"There is, as you say, a possibility, but it is a slight one. He is only too well aware of the necessity of receiving early information."

"What sort of a man is de Coronads personally?"

"A man of about forty-five, with black hair and whiskers, an impudent-looking fellow. Very big and very broad; possessed, I should think, of the strength of a Hercules. As Irish-looking a Spaniard as I ever saw—or heard."

"And Sutierrez?"

"He is about the same age, tall and thin, with fair hair and moustache, a shifty, disagreeable manner, and a dry, sarcastic fashion of speech; as German a Spaniard as his friend is Irish. To be frank with you, Mr. Champnell, I take it that both men are natives of Europe who have resided for many years in the United States, who have obtained the positions which they now hold during the recent political convulsions in Panama and Caracas, and who, for men in such positions, have about as bad a record as men very well could have."

"Where does de Coronads live?"

"In very modest fashion in Chepstow Villas, Notting Hill. Sutierrez lives in better style in Westbourne Terrace. I take it that neither man is well-to-do. They are adventurers who have come to England in the hope of being able to recruit their own finances at the expense of the finances of their adopted countries. A good many diplomatists come from South America on precisely the same errand. Fortunately, not all of them adopt the same means to attain their ends which de Coronads has done. If the Government of Mexico learns that Sutierrez has gained access to the contents of the treaty, we may have serious trouble."

The Hon. Augustus rose as if to go.

"Well, Mr. Champnell, what do you propose to do?"

"To recover for you the stolen treaty."

"You understand that, to be of any service, it must be recovered at once. I may mention that the treaty is drawn up in Spanish, and that, as de Coronads' knowledge of that language, like Sam Weller's knowledge of London, is peculiar; we, for our part, shall be content if it is returned to us before it reaches Sutierrez."

"I understand." The Hon. Augustus went to the door. He stood for a moment looking inside the crown of his hat. "May I take it, my lord, that, in the judgment of the Foreign Office, there are occasions on which the end justifies the means?"

Viscount Horsham looked sharply up, then down again.

"That is a point on which I, personally, am unable to express an opinion. Don Joaquim de Coronads seems to think so." He began to play with a paper-knife. "You understand that we must decline to accept any responsibility in matters which I would call extraneous."

"Precisely. I quite understand."

The Hon. Augustus left the room. When he was gone the Viscount murmured to himself and smiled.

"I should not be surprised if Mr. Champnell meditates a piece of dare-devilry to match de Coronads' own."

The Foreign Secretary was right—the Hon. Augustus did.

CHAPTER II

AT THE PANAMA PLENIPOTENTIARY

As VISCOUNT HORSHAM had said, the Plenipotentiary from Panama lived in modest fashion at Notting Hill—for a Plenipotentiary, in very modest fashion indeed. To be plain, the Panama Embassy took the shape of lodgings; a sitting and dining-room on the ground floor, and a bedroom overhead; and the rent of the Panama Embassy was a little in arrear.

Don Joaquim de Coronads had just finished dinner—and not a very sumptuous dinner either. Nothing could have been simpler than the usual conduct of the establishment of the Panama Embassy, except the manners of the Plenipotentiary. Panama was the very newest thing in South American republics, and it seemed doubtful if it would survive its novelty. The Plenipotentiary himself was beginning to incline to the opinion that it would not. As he put his feet on the table and lit his cigar, and examined the whisky which was left in the bottle, his mood was gloomy.

"If some dollars don't come along pretty soon I'll have to skip. This Embassy business is a failure—it is that! Here's my salary four months overdue; and it's no use me telegraphing because I don't get no answer. I'd have done better to have run for president, though they wouldn't have had me if I had."

Don Joaquim de Coronads poured some whisky into a glass.

"I ought to have done what Gustav's done—taken a block in Westbourne Terrace, and made things hum. I wouldn't have had so much difficulty in getting into debt. No one's going to trust an Embassy what's located in these rooms. Gustav owes thousands. Fifty would see me through; and it's likely to. A sorrowful man I am to have to say it."

Don Joaquim de Coronads thrust his thumbs into the armholes of his waistcoat. He puffed at his cigar as he pondered.

"It's a comfort I laid my hand on that there darned treaty. It was a bold stroke, so it was! Gustav'll sit up when he knows, though he suspicioned me directly we got outside the room. He'll have to pay before he has a peep at it, the mean-sowled German thief. I thought I'd have a peep at it first of all myself, I did. But the blamed thing's writ in Spanish, and it's tarnation little I know of my natural tongue. That's the worst of not being a native of your own country. I'll have another try at it now, I will. I may find out a trifle of what it means by guessing."

Don Joaquim de Coronads removed his thumbs from his waistcoat arm-holes, his feet from the table, and was about to rise leisurely to a perpendicular position, when a cord was thrown over him from behind, twisted with very considerable dexterity and rapidity two or three times round him, and before he had woke to a reality of the situation, he found himself tied to his chair. In front of him stood a tall man, who was attired in a long dark ulster—which he kept well turned up about his ears—and a long soft felt hat. This gentleman was pointing the barrel of a revolver directly at Don Joaquim's face.

When he had recovered from his not unnatural astonishment, Don Joaquim addressed the new Collier as if he knew him.

"This is friendly, Gustav, to drop in on me, through the window, in this unexpected kind of way—upon my conscience, so it is."

The newcomer replied with that curious twang in his speech which is characteristic of a certain type of German-American.

"You think so, Mr. Timothy O'Rourke, eh?"

Don Joaquim looked about him with a startled air.

"Ssh! You've left the window open. Maybe someone will be hearing. Haven't I asked you to forget to remember the O'Rourke?"

"And have I not asked you to remember that I am Martinez Sutierrez, Mr. Timothy O'Rourke? Blathering Tim, Soapy-mouthed Pat, or whatever you call yourself, you dirty Irishman—eh?"

Don Joaquim regarded his visitor with what seemed to be increasing astonishment.

"You've a friendly way of speaking, Gustav, so you have. And might I trouble you to tell me what's the meaning of your coming through the window? Wasn't there a door? And have you taken off your feet that I never heard you tread on them? Is it a trifle of a game you're having with the best friend you ever had—to tie him to his chair?"

"You behaved to me like a true friend this afternoon—eh?"

"Is it about the treaty you're meaning?"

"What about the treaty—eh?"

"I'll be honest with you, Gustav, as I always am. I lied to you this afternoon when I said I hadn't taken it, so I did. I slipped it into a pocket in my coat which has come in handy more than once or twice before. I don't know how I came to lie to you, I done it before I thought; but I meant to let you have it in the morning, and that's the truth!"

"Then you won't mind my having it now—eh?"

"Not the least bit in the world. Why should I? It was for you I stole it. You're welcome."

Don Joaquim stopped. He looked at the other as if he expected— and hoped—that he would give him some kind of a cue. But his visitor was silent. Don Joaquim's tone became unctuously wheedling.

"It's you who won't forget to give his friend a trifle to recompense him for the trouble which he took."

"Is there—is there any reference to that—affair of mine?"

"You mean in the treaty? And that's what I myself would like to know. I'll be frank with you. I've been spelling of it through; but it's a tricky lingo is the one which I'm supposed to be speaking, and they've hashed it up in a fashion which makes it worse than ever; so that devil a word can I understand at all, at all."

"Where is it?"

"Now, Gustav, there's a word of business I'd like to have with you before we reach the pleasure."

"Where is it?"

"You're handy with the barker, Gustav, and there's a friendly something in your tone which is new; but what I'm after knowing is what you're going to give me."

"If you don't tell me where that treaty is inside of sixty seconds I'll give you the contents of six barrels."

"Oh, no, you won't. I'm not afraid. This isn't a country in which shooting's free, and you know it. This isn't Caracas, or one of them happy hunting-grounds; but a mean-spirited, low-down place where you have to pay for every drop of whisky you put your lips to. Steady, Gustav! Keep yourself to yourself. Don't you start to overhaul the Panama secret archives—and keep your hands off my tobacco-box. That desk's where I keep my cigars; if you're smoking, blaze away at weeds of your own. Steady, I say! Don't you think that because you've tied your friend to his chair that you're going to rob him to suit yourself. If you lay a finger on what isn't yours—and there's nothing here that is—I'll holler. And if I holler I'll raise glory; and there'll be trouble for the Plenipotentiary from Caracas. D'ye hear me? Hi—hi!"

Regardless of Don Joaquim's remonstrances the other was proceeding to treat the contents of the room as if they were his own. The Plenipotentiary from Panama opened his mouth with intent to carry out his threat of "hollering." On which the stranger behaved in a really surprising manner. Taking the helpless de Coronads by the throat with one hand, with the other he slipped something over his nose and mouth, which he held there in spite of his victim's struggles. Don Joaquim writhed and twisted. His body stiffened on his chair as if seized with a sudden convulsion, then went limp, and then was still. If it had not been for the cords which held him in place, he would have fallen to the floor. His arms dangled loosely at his sides, his head hung forward on his chest, his breath came in sterterous, unnatural gasps, then seemed to cease. For the representative of a great nation, the Plenipotentiary from Panama presented as undignified a spectacle as could be very well conceived. He had been chloroformed.

CHAPTER III
DIPLOMATISTS

IT WAS A LITTLE later in the evening. The Plenipotentiary from Caracas called to see his colleague from Panama. He showed himself upstairs in the informal fashion which obtained in the diplomatic circles in which he had been wont to move. He even turned the handle of his colleague's door without troubling to announce his arrival.

"Dim, are you busy—eh?" He paused for an appreciable instant to remove the cigar from between his lips. There was no answer. "No? Right! I gome in."

He went in—to stare in amazement at what he saw.

"What—what in dunder! Drunk? Already? What a man!"

A further examination caused doubts to cross his mind.

"He does not look as if he was drunk. I did not dink dere was enough drink in de world to make Dim O'Rourke so drunk as dis; dere is not enough money in Banama to bay for it. Died? Died to his chair? What in dunder! Dere is—dere is a little game here. Ah! He wakes! Dat is better."

A slight convulsive movement passed over Don Joaquim's body. His limbs twitched. There seemed to be a slight attempt at respiration. His colleague observed these signs with interest; he treated him to a gentle shaking.

"Dim, you are awake? No? All right; you will be soon. Berhaps if I were to dake away dis cord it would be as well. Dere is someding here a liddle funny. We shall see. My dear life, it is so dight dis cord, it is a wonder it has not cut him half in two. Do cut it is de best."

The Plenipotentiary from Caracas took a penknife from his pocket—a really serviceable article, with a blade some seven or eight inches long. He cut the cord at Don Joaquim's back with but a touch from its razor-like edge. So sudden, indeed, was the parting of the strands, and the captive's consequent release, that before Don Martinez was prepared for such an eventuality, the Plenipotentiary from Panama tumbled face forward on to the floor. The tall, collected-looking gentleman, with the cigar between his teeth and the gleaming steel in his hand, showed no sign of being distressed by this untoward little incident.

"Dat do him good; shake him up; rouse his sluggish liver."

Something seemed to have done him good. Either the release from galling bondage or the shock of the tumble. Or, perhaps, the effects of the drug were wearing off: At any rate, so soon as he reached the floor he began to show signs of objecting to the position in which he lay. Presently he rolled over on to his back, and finally raised himself to a sitting posture. Looking about him with not unnatural bewilderment, he pressed both palms to his throbbing temples.

"The holy saints! And if there's another head like mine I'd like to see the man as carries it upon his shoulders."

"A liddle ill—eh, Dim?"

Don Joaquim twisted round his head with a degree of celerity which suggested that he had already proceeded some distance on the road to recovery.

"You're still there? You're still there?"

"To be sure. Where would I be if not near my friend when he's in a liddle drouble—eh?"

"By the—by the living jingo, you're a—you're a curiosity. Standing there as cool and calm as if it wasn't straight from hell you've come."

"Dat so? Still feeling a liddle so-so—eh, Dim?"

"I'm feeling a good deal more than a little so-so, and I'm likely to keep on feeling till I've had a few words with you. It's about my turn to talk. Blessed St Patrick, the head I've on me!"

The Plenipotentiary from Panama scrambled to his feet. It was a process not altogether unattended with difficulty. When he attained to a perpendicular position he swayed to and fro in a manner which suggested a fresh descent. Don Martinez advanced with the apparent intention of helping him to stand. But the other would have none of him. His friendly design had a restorative effect which was, possibly, unintended. Don Joaquim swung round on his heels with unexpected agility. With fists clenched he stood and glared at him.

"Keep off! Keep away with you! If you so much as touch me with one of your dirty fingers I'll prove to you that I am still a man."

"You're more than a man, my Dim."

"Snigger! Let the sneers slip off the tongue of you! I'm laughing! Maybe you'll be before this meeting rises. Stand where you are."

"I'm standing."

"Then keep standing."

The Plenipotentiary from Panama, with a step which was still a little uncertain, moved towards the door. He turned the key; took it from the lock; placed it in his pocket. His colleague observed him with cigar held between his fingers.

"For what do you lock the door, Dim?"

"To keep you from going through it. Maybe this time it was through the door you came, for a change."

"It is generally through the door that I do gome."

"Except when you come through the window."

"Just so. Except. But that is not often. It is some time since I game through a window."

"About an hour ago—or it may be two. You sausage-faced Dutchman, why it's still gaping!"

One of the windows was wide open. He closed it with an amount of bang and clatter which was perhaps a little more than was needed.

"It is a liddle joking you are—eh, Dim? A kind of game you have wid me?"

"You've your own notions of a game; by the saints in Paradise, you have!" He clapped both hands to his head. "It may turn out, before we're through, that I have mine. Now, you long-legged black-guard, I'll give you one fair chance. Have you took it?"

"Dook what? De whisky?"

"The whisky to blazes! You know very well what I'm after. None of your fooling."

"It's you who have done all de fooling up do now."

"I'm coming to business soon. Answer me: Have you took the treaty?"

At the mention of the word treaty, a slight alteration took place in the other's demeanour. He became more alert; a little eager—a change which was not concealed by the ostentatious air of indif-ference with which he replaced the cigar between his lips.

"It is you who dook the dready. Yet you dold me you did not. I know, posidively, dat is a lie."

"Quit it! You've been through that already!"

"Already? When already? It is about dat I have come now."

"And a pretty way you have of corning, by the life of me. I knew you weren't white, but it's learning I am how black you are. You've had your chance. But since a straight answer's not to be got from a crooked mouth, it's seeing for myself I'll be."

He went to an old-fashioned bureau which stood in a corner of the room. Throwing open the two doors he began to throw out on to the floor the very miscellaneous contents of one of the shelves. Having reached the end without lighting on that which he was looking for, he again turned towards his colleague.

"As I'm a live man, you have took it. So it's a thief you are." He continued his researches on another shelf. When he once more faced the other he had a revolver in his hand. "Now, it's me that's got the drop on you. Is it a little target practice I'm to have, or will you be returning of the treaty?"

"You're very drunk—eh, Dim?"

"I'm sober enough to send a splinter of lead through the wooden head of you."

"Dim!"

Don Martinez made a movement towards the table. The other stopped him.

"Keep where you are. I wouldn't trust you to move half the breadth of one of the hairs off your own head unless I'd been shooting of you first. I know you for the blackguard that your mother sorrowed for."

"It seems do me dat we're a liddle off de level you and me. I said, 'Dere is a dready I would like to see.' You replied, 'Very good; I will come wid you. I will dalk to Milord Horsham; you will your dready sdeal.' It durn out de oder way round. I dalk to Milord Horsham, you sdeal de dready—my dready."

"You've stole it from me since. It's you, that's the thief; it's no gentleman you are."

"Dim, what are you blaying?"

"I'm playing on the square; it's you that's crooked. You come through that window—"

"I gome drough dat window?"

"You tie me with your dirty cords—"

"I die you? We march."

"Is it denying it you are?"

"I deny noding—noding at all. Only I beg you do understand dat I see your liddle game. You wish me to suppose de dready is lost dat you may ask for its broduction a larger brice; not so? Very well, den, whad is de figure?"

"You talk to me like that when it's in your pocket all the time?"

"In my pocket? So! Now do get it in my pocket; how much?"

"Listen to me, my bonny boy. You came through the window; you tied me to my chair; you monkeyed with your popgun; you took away my senses with the filth you had. Of all these things I'm not now talking; we'll reach them later. But, before we come to them, you'll hand me back that treaty. Business first, and after that we'll enjoy ourselves as, under the circumstances, two gentlemen should. I'm always ready for a bit of fun."

"You don't sound as if you were drunk, and somehow you don't look as if you were drunk. But if you're sober, den you're away beyond me. Again I ask you, Dim, what is it you are blaying?"

"I'll talk no more to you! You're in the right line from Judas. Hand me back that treaty before I put a bullet in you."

"You can but a bullet in me if you like, but if you do you will be a fool for your pains. Let me explain. If, as you seem to infer, some-one did come drough de window—"

"If! By St. Peter and the Holy Keys, he stands there just saying 'if'!"

"What extraordinary accident can cause you do subbose it was I—"

"Extraordinary accident is what he calls it! I'll tell you what it was; it was my own two eyes. It was them was the extraordinary accident."

"If you'll let me know at what dime you say de oggurrence dook blace—"

"As if he didn't know! The innocence of him! The amazing face!"

"I do not know. What it is you're blaying at I don't understand; but I will give you broof, more dan enough, dat I was not out of my house donight dill I game in here just now."

"I've all the proof I want—my own eyesight. Do you call my two eyes liars? Don't I say I saw you?"

"Drough a glass of whisky—eh, Dim?"

"Hark to me, Mr. Gustav Schneider, or whatever it is you've not pluck enough to call your dirty old Dutch name. I'm not drunk, I'm sober; worse luck for you! I not only saw you, I heard you; I felt you; I smelt you. And that you should stand there pretending that it wasn't you mishandled me, it's beyond believing so it is, entirely.

"But that wasn't the worst. I might have forgiven you if you hadn't rammed your filthy muck into my mouth to draw my senses out. Bah! I taste it now; and the stink of it! And then, when I was like a babe unborn for ignorance, to steal from me that which—at the peril of my good name, which is, as you know very well, to me a jewel, and of my liberty, for which in the cause of a friend I care not that—I stole first of all for you, it bangs Banagher—so it does. It's beyond black ingratitude by all the way from here to nowhere—it is that!

"But I've done with you! I've finished! Hand me back that treaty before I fill you up with lead, and I'll return it to the Saxon hound I had it from—the curse of Cromwell on him! Do you hear me? Hand it back or, when I've counted three, I'll fire, and away'll fly the sowl of you. One! I'm pointing at the very middle of your heart. Two! The bullet's marking of the road it's going to cut right through you."

The Plenipotentiary from Panama would doubtless have said "three"—apparently the word was trembling on his lips—only, in the exuberance of his own verbosity he had not allowed for the alertness of his friend. Before the syllable was actually uttered the Plenipotentiary from Caracas, ducking, dashed across the room with the swiftness of some wild creature. Gripping his colleague by the wrist and jerking up his arm before he had a chance to fire, he repeated his former inquiry,—

"What is it you're blaying at?"

"Playing, am I? Then, if you will have a game, and it's for diversion you are, it's that I'm playing at."

With his disengaged hand he struck at his friend, who did his best to counter, but without meeting with complete success. Don Martinez received the finish of the blow upon his ear. It did not seem to improve his temper.

"You Irish pig! I'll have your life for dat!"

"Pig, is it? Pig, am I? I'll show you the kind of pig I am! You German swine, I'll tear the heart right out of you!"

The Plenipotentiary from Panama took his colleague by the throat, and his colleague gripped him round the waist for all he was worth, each putting forth an amount of energy which was hardly suggestive of that perfect amity between the representatives of two great nations which might have been desired by the lovers of international concord.

CHAPTER IV

THE FOREIGN OFFICE AGAIN

VISCOUNT HORSHAM turned the card over in his hand, as if wondering if there could be anything on the back which might throw light upon the situation,

"Who is it you say wishes to see me?"

"The Plenipotentiary from Caracas."

The viscount was silent for an instant.

"I hope I may be excused for remarking that, things being as they are, his visit's rather—surprising. However, I don't know what harm will be done by seeing him. He can hardly propose, already, to display an interest in other of our papers. Tell them to show him in; and, Mr. Daintrey, seat yourself at your own table. This time I'll have a witness who'll keep an eye upon the Plenipotentiary's proceedings."

Presently there entered a tall, thin individual, who spoke with a very curious accent.

"You see, I gome again already. It is about a madder which is a liddle odd. It is about a dready."

The viscount pricked up his ears.

"Indeed."

"Yes, indeed. About de dready with Mexico." His lordship pricked up his ears still more; his visitor spoke with such a very matter-of-fact kind of air. "By a gurious goincidence, yesterday afdernoon, when I go away from here, I find it in my pocket."

"That is singular."

"Dat is right; it was singular. So I gome to redurn it do you now."

He handed the Foreign Secretary a document which he took from an inner pocket of his coat. His lordship regarded it askance, as if somewhat taken aback by his visitor's truly remarkable presence of mind.

"Do I understand you to say that you discovered its presence in your pocket directly you went away from here?"

"Dat is so."

"And that you have retained it in your possession ever since?"

"Only since last night, my lord."

The change in the speaker's tone and manner was as sudden as it was striking. The viscount looked up with a start. His visitor had removed something from his head and face. The minister stared.

"Mr. Champnell!"

"At your lordship's service."

"What on earth is the meaning of this?"

"It means that I have returned the treaty as your lordship desired. I can give you my personal assurance that it has been seen by no one who can comprehend a word of it."

"But—how did it come into your possession?"

"That is one of the matters on which, as your lordship gave me to understand, your office accepts no responsibility."

"I see." The minister looked down. "I hear there has been friction between the Plenipotentiaries from Panama and Caracas."

"So I am told."

"Actual violence."

"Very considerable violence."

"Nearly killed each other."

"I believe they would have quite, if the police had not appeared upon the scene in the nick of time."

"That's—odd."

"Very odd."

"I wonder what was the cause of the trouble?"

The minister looked up.

"I associate myself with your lordship's wonder."

The two men exchanged glances. A smile gleamed in the viscount's eyes and wrinkled the corners of his lips. Mr. Champnell never moved a muscle.

When the visitor had gone, the viscount observed to his private secretary, "Daintrey, that's rather a remarkable young man."

"Rather," agreed Mr. Daintrey.

The minister smiled.

Perhaps he was thinking of the "friction" between the Plenipotentiaries from Panama and Caracas.

V

THE ROBBERY ON THE "STORMY PETREL"

I

THE CASE OF THE robbery on board the *Stormy Petrel* was notable for one thing if for no other—in it the Hon. Augustus Champnell received fees from three separate and, indeed, antagonistic individuals.

The Hon. Augustus had finished reading the morning papers, and was wondering—for business was slack—what the day might bring forth, when there came a tapping at the door, and there immediately entered two servants in livery, bearing between them an iron box, which they placed on a chair. One of them spoke—as if he had been an automaton.

"The Marquis of Bewlay's compliments to Mr. Champnell, and will Mr. Champnell drown the box in a cistern full of water, till the Marquis arrives."

Mr. Champnell stared.

"And when will the Marquis arrive?"

The Marquis arrived almost as soon as the servants had gone. That ancient peer came hobbling into the room, leaning on two sticks, and as soon as he saw the box on the chair he seemed more than half disposed to back out again.

"Didn't the rascals tell you to drown the box in a cistern of water?"

"The rascals did. But the Marquis of Bewlay will permit me to observe that I always require a sufficient explanation before I act on instructions which I receive from strangers."

64

With Mr. Champnell's assistance the Marquis took refuge in a chair.

"What's your fee?"

"My lowest fee is one hundred guineas."

"Too much."

"In the case of the Marquis of Bewlay my lowest fee will be one hundred and fifty guineas."

The Marquis glanced up at him—and leered.

"You shall have it for your impudence—the Champnells always were an impudent lot. Find out who sent what is in that box, and you shall have your hundred and fifty. Here's the key, look inside—only mind, gently does it."

Unlocking the iron box with the key the Marquis gave him, Mr. Champnell found that it contained other smaller wooden boxes, which were divided from each other by layers of cotton wool. Removing the covers of these wooden boxes he perceived that each contained what seemed to be some sort of oil can.

"Thirteen of them, aren't they?" On counting them Mr. Champnell discovered that the number was correct. "Lucky number, and pretty playthings, every one of them. All infernal machines, or I'm a hatter. They've come raining in on me by every post—if you look at them you'll see that there is a different postmark on every one of them."

"Are you certain that they are infernal machines?"

"I'll lay you ten to one in anything you like to name that they are, and leave you to prove the contrary—that's the extent of my certainty, Mr. Champnell. Only if you take my advice you'll keep them immersed in water until the thing has been shown to demonstration, either one way or the other. I have no desire to be blown to pieces, if you have."

"Have you no sort of idea where they come from?"

"Once upon a time I was fool enough to enroll myself as a member of a certain secret society. I have broken since then pretty nearly every one of its rules, which I swore to observe, and I think it quite on the cards that these things may have come from some of the society's agents. I'll tell you what I'll do; instead of a hundred and fifty guineas, I'll give you two hundred, if you prove, beyond a shadow of doubt, that they don't. I've come to you instead of going to the police, because I want the thing kept private, but at the same time I am particularly anxious to know if at last the beggars are beginning to try to do what they have threatened to do, times without number."

The Marquis's story was a long one, and not a little involved; some of Mr. Champnell's questions he declined, point blank, to answer. When he had gone, Mr. Champnell still found himself in possession of very slight data to enable him to prosecute his researches. He summed the data up in his mind telling himself, finally, that they really amounted to nothing at all, and had almost resolved to write to the Marquis and decline the conduct of the case unless he furnished him with fuller information on certain points on which he had refused to give any information at all, when the servant came to announce that Mr. Golden, of the firm of Messrs. Ruby and Golden, was at the door and desirous of an interview.

A minute later Mr. Champnell found himself face to face with the junior partner of the famous firm of jewellers—a shrewd, sharp-looking man, who wasted no time in coming to the point.

"I have been made the victim, Mr. Champnell, of an atrocious outrage, and I come to you first, because the matter is one which requires delicate handling, and second, because the author of the outrage is a member of your own order. I may add that if you succeed in this matter we may be able to place a good deal of business in your hands—business of a kind which requires the intervention of a diplomatist rather than of a policeman."

The Hon. Augustus bowed.

"You are acquainted with Lord Hardaway?" Another bow from Mr. Champnell. "His lordship has been a customer of ours for some time, and is so largely in our debt that some months ago we felt bound to intimate that we could not allow him to add to the already large figure of his account.

"We have recently received information, through side channels, that his lordship was paying his addresses to Miss Bonnyer-Lees, the sole child and heiress of the eminent soap-boiler. And, ten days ago, we received a letter from his lordship himself, which was to the effect that he was about to start for a cruise in his yacht, the *Stormy Petrel*; that Miss Bonnyer-Lees was to accompany him, with other friends; that he had hopes of making Miss Bonnyer-Lees his wife; and he desired us to send him, at once, for his inspection and the lady's, a selection of the finest things we had in stock; in fact, he gave us to understand that matters had reached a stage in which he was anxious to make the lady a handsome present. His lordship went on to add that if he married Miss Bonnyer-Lees our account should receive an immediate settlement; while, on the other hand, if he did not marry her, it was quite possible that we should have to whistle—the word was his lordship's own."

"Where was Lord Hardaway when he wrote this letter?"

"Staying at Miss Bonnyer-Lees' own residence in Kent. But the day after we received a telegram from him stating that they had decided to commence the cruise sooner than they had originally intended; that the day following they would be off Deal, on board the yacht, and that the goods were to be sent on board to be examined. The telegram also contained what seemed to me, under the circumstances, to be a somewhat brutal intimation to the effect that if we did not telegraph a reply to say that the goods would be sent off at once the order would be placed elsewhere."

"Did you send the goods?"

"My impulse was to telegraph a refusal. In several little matters Lord Hardaway had not used us altogether well, and it seemed to me that in this matter he was not using us altogether well either; there was no necessity, for instance, for him to threaten us with the loss of his custom. My partner, however, Mr. Ruby, would not hear of a refusal. He was naturally unwilling to lose the business which would be associated with what would, probably, be one of the weddings of the season. On one point I did stand firm. As I feared that, if he was the bearer of the goods, Mr. Ruby would quite probably allow himself to be wheedled out of them, without receiving any satisfactory promise of payment, I resolved to take the goods myself. Which I did do."

Mr. Golden paused. At this point of his narrative, which he had reached, a certain uneasiness seemed to possess him.

"It was about midday when I reached Deal. It was both blowing and raining, and what I should have called a regular gale was on. A sailor with the words 'Stormy Petrel' on his cap came to me at the station, and, when I told him who I was, informed me that we must go off to the yacht at once, because his lordship had resolved to weigh anchor if I did not arrive by that train. I had never been to Deal in my life before, and I had some idea that the yacht might be anchored to the pier. But when I got down to the beach I found that there was no pier, and the sailor, pointing to what was merely a speck on the horizon, said, "There's the *Stormy Petrel*." When he said that, and I saw that the yacht was heaven knows how far from land, if I had not felt that the fellow was covertly grinning at me, and that I should never have heard the last of it from Ruby, I should have come straight back to town, which would have been a wiser thing than what I actually did do. I entrusted myself in a cranky boat to the mercy of the, literally, foaming billows."

Again Mr. Golden paused. It might have been imagination, but it seemed to the Hon. Augustus that, at the mere recollection of that experience of the horrors of the ocean, Mr. Golden became a little yellow.

"I am not ashamed, Mr. Champnell, to own that I am no sailor. I have felt qualms upon the Thames. What I suffered in that cockleshell of a boat, tossed hither and thither amidst that seething mass of waters—I don't know if it was blowing or raining hardest—I will not now attempt to describe. When I reached the *Stormy Petrel* I was more dead than alive. Lord Hardaway received me on deck; he was, evidently, suffering no inconvenience from the weather. 'Hollo, Golden,' he said, 'you're looking queer.' 'If, my lord,' I answered, 'I am looking as queer as I feel I must be looking very queer indeed. I had no idea before I left town that such a storm was raging.' 'Storm!' he said, 'you don't call this a storm. It's only a capful of wind! Come below and have a peg?' I went downstairs and I had some brandy; then I must have had another attack of illness, because the next thing I can remember is Lord Hardaway clapping me on the shoulder and exclaiming, 'I say, Golden, where are those jewels of yours?'"

Once more there was a break in Mr. Golden's narrative—he seemed to be oppressed by the weight of his recollections.

"It will give you, Mr. Champnell, an adequate idea of my physical condition when I tell you that, until that moment, I had forgotten that I had the jewels on me, and when I add that I had taken with me from town jewels to the gross value of nearly £20,000 you will understand what that statement means. They were contained in a locked leather case, which was attached to a steel belt which was locked about my waist. The keys both of the belt and of the case were in a secret pocket of my waistcoat—see here."

Unbuttoning his waistcoat, Mr. Golden disclosed a tiny pocket, which was ingeniously contrived in the lining.

"When his lordship spoke I put my hand to my waist and found that the belt and case had gone, and not only so, my waistcoat was unbuttoned and the keys had vanished.

"'My lord,' I cried, as I staggered to my feet, 'I've been robbed.'

"'By Jove,' he exclaimed, 'if I didn't think so. Come along, Golden, the thief has just gone overboard with the spoil—if you don't look alive he'll get clear away.' You will understand, Mr. Champnell, that I was disorganised both in mind and body—really incapable, in fact, of collecting my thoughts. I allowed his lordship to drag me up above. It seemed to me when I got into the open air that the storm was raging worse than ever; and taking me to the side of the deck, he pointed out a solitary individual who was rowing away from the ship in a little boat. 'There's the thief! I thought there was something suspicious about the way in which he came sneaking up from below. Before we knew what he was up to he had dropped into his boat and was off. If you look alive, Golden, you'll catch him yet, red-handed.' The boat in which I had come from shore was still alongside, and, before I had a chance to collect my scattered senses, his lordship had not only bundled me into it, but the boat itself was pushed off from the yacht.

"We chased that boat which contained the solitary rower, as it appeared to me, for hours. I will not dilate on what I still continued to suffer, but through all my agony I urged the rowers in pursuit. As soon as we were within hailing distance I shouted to the fellow, 'Stop!' Directly I did so, standing up in his boat, he dropped something into the sea. I distinctly saw that he dropped something, but what he was too far off for me to see. When we reached him he declared that he had merely thrown overboard some rubbish, but why he had chosen that singularly inopportune moment he did not condescend to explain. We took him in tow, he seeming not at all unwilling, and at last we reached the land. How thankful I was to do so no one but myself can have the faintest conception.

"Hardly had I set foot on *terra firma* than I became convinced that I had been duped from first to last. The fellow we had chased turned out to be an honest, simple fisherman, who had been employed to take a telegram from the post office to the yacht, and who protested that he had never left his boat, and that he knew nothing of my belt or case. I believed, and I believe him. I have no doubt whatever that Lord Hardaway was himself the thief. I would have instituted a prosecution directly I returned to town only Ruby would not hear of it. Mr. Ruby is always fearful of anything in the shape of a scandal. A week has passed. We have heard nothing of his lordship or of the jewels. That, at present, is how the matter stands."

"What is it you wish me to do?"

"To see that the jewels are returned to us."

"And in default?"

"We must either have the jewels or a guarantee of payment—a sufficient guarantee!—or we prosecute. Here is a list of the jewels that are missing, with the several values attached." Mr. Golden handed the Hon. Augustus a sheet of paper. "You perceive that it is a matter which requires delicate handling."

"Quite so. Where is Lord Hardaway now?"

"No one seems to have the least idea. As you are aware, the weather has been very boisterous during the last few days, and, for all anyone seems to know, he and the *Stormy Petrel* may be at the bottom of the sea together. Altogether, for us, it is a pleasant state of things!"

"Was Miss Bonnyer-Lees on board?"

"She was not. It appears only too probable that the whole business was a deliberately planned conspiracy. As I told you at the beginning, Mr. Champnell, I have been made the victim of an atrocious outrage."

II

WHEN, MR. GOLDEN having departed, the Hon. Augustus was left alone he laughed. The story of the jeweller's sufferings appealed to his sense of humour. He studied the list of the missing jewels.

"There appears to be some pretty baubles among them, and they appear to be marked at pretty prices. If Hardaway has got clean away with the spoil they ought to provide him with a pleasant little nest egg with which to start afresh."

He turned to the mantelpiece to get a light for his pipe. Just as he struck a match his ears were saluted by a curious sound which proceeded from behind his back.

"What's that?"

With the lighted match in his hand he turned to listen. The sound continued—it seemed to increase in volume. It was as if some rusty clockwork mechanism had suddenly been set in motion.

"It seems to come from the interior of the Marquis of Bewlay's precious iron case." The case in question still remained where it had originally been placed, upon a chair. Mr. Champnell went to it and raised the lid. "By George! it does! It strikes me that it comes from inside one of these pretty wooden boxes—from inside this one, unless I am mistaken."

He removed the cover from the box in question—the noise did seem to come from inside it. No sooner had he done so than there was a sound as if a damp squib had been exploded, a quantity of what seemed like water was dashed into his face, and there drifted through the room a most unpleasant smoke. The Hon. Augustus was amazed.

"It occurs to me that the Marquis was right, and that these ingenious contrivances are infernal machines. Unless I err, one of them has justified its existence by exploding. Considering that there are twelve more of them, I seem to be in a truly comfortable situation. It is a pity Bewlay did not keep them in his possession a little longer, and allow them to explode on his own premises instead of on mine. What is this stuff on my face?" His head and face were covered with moisture. He allowed a drop to trickle into his mouth. "It tastes like seawater. What is the meaning of this thing? I'll have a look at myself in the glass."

As he was moving towards a mirror something caught his eye which was lying on the floor.

"What the something's that?"

He might well ask—what seemed to be a circlet of scintillating light was lying almost at his feet. He picked it up, staring at it, when he had it in his hand, with growing bewilderment.

"A bracelet!—of diamonds!—As I am a sinner!—How on earth did it get here?" An idea flashed into his brain. "Can it be—it can't be—I do believe it is one of Golden's."

He examined with eager eyes the list of the missing jewels.

"It is!—Here's the thing itself!—'A bracelet of twenty-four diamonds, in a plain gold setting, with pearl fastenings. When closed the fastening is heart-shaped. Five pearls in fastening.' It is Golden's. Hollo, another of the Marquis's infernal machines seems to be evincing an inclination to go off."

The words were hardly out of his mouth when it did go off; indeed, the whole thirteen had gone off within ten minutes. They had evidently been ingeniously contrived to go off, as rapidly as possible, one after the other, so, as the schoolboys have it, to "keep the pot a-boiling." The room was full of suffocating smoke, Mr. Champnell was drenched with what seemed like sea-water, and he was in the possession of the whole of the missing jewels—they had been vomited forth by the infernal machines.

"Although this looks as if it were a fairy tale," he told himself, "I fancy it has a very simple explanation."

As, some half-hour after, he was driving down Bond Street in a cab, his attention was attracted to an individual who was advancing along the Piccadilly pavement.

"The man himself! So whatever may have become of the *Stormy Petrel*, milord himself is above water."

Stopping the cab, springing out of it, hastening towards the individual in question, Mr. Champnell accosted him—a tall, willowy man, with a dark, oval face, and big, wild, black eyes.

"I am glad to see, Hardaway, that you're not drowned, in spite of the boisterous weather which has recently prevailed in the Channel. You have probably been kept alive in order to be arrested on a warrant emanating from Scotland Yard."

"Champnell, you don't mean it?"

"Don't I? When a man steals jewels to the value of twenty thousand pounds, puts them, with about two gallons of sea-water, into thirteen infernal machines; sends those infernal machines to the address of the Marquis of Bewlay; and they are brought to me, and explode, and nearly blow me up, and the whole place besides, it is generally supposed that that man has done something which necessitates the issue of a warrant."

"My dear fellow!—it was only a joke."

"For less pointed jokes men have been sent to penal servitude."

Lord Hardaway slipped his arm through Mr. Champnell's.

"I was so devilish wild, and Golden was so devilish sick, that I couldn't help but spoof him. As for Bewlay, I owe him one for a dozen different things; I was bound to be even with him some time. There was nothing in the tins but water and Golden's jewels."

"Then it doesn't occur to you that you have been guilty of felony, and also of what a hanging judge might construe as an attempt to murder?"

"I say, Champnell, spare my blushes! I hear, dear boy, you've turned detective; you might do me a good turn, and all in the way of business. The fact is, I'm engaged to be married—the Bonnyer-Lees." Lord Hardaway winked. "It will set me on my legs."

"I thought that Miss Bonnyer-Lees was not on board the *Stormy Petrel*."

"She wasn't. That's what made me so devilish wild. She was to have gone, but when it began to blow she hoisted the white feather. I felt that I must have it out of somebody, so I had it out of Golden. But I saw her yesterday, and I made it all right, we're going to be married at once. I'm going to run straight—I swear I am! But if this tale got wind, it might spoil everything. I tell you what, old man, if, in the way of business, you'll make things square with Ruby and Golden, and with old Bewlay, I'll give you any sum in reason you like to name, say a couple of hundred guineas, cash down."

"A couple of hundred guineas, you say?" Mr. Champnell smiled; what at at the moment was not quite plain. "You don't seem conscious that it is a rather curious proposition which you are making me, especially as I happen to be already retained upon the other side, but I'll do the best for you I can."

When the Hon. Augustus reached Messrs. Ruby and Golden's establishment in Bond Street he was received by both the partners in a private room.

"Do I understand, gentlemen, if I return to you the missing jewels, exactly as they left Mr. Golden's hands, that, as they say in the advertisements, no questions will be asked?" Both partners were profuse in their protestations that he might so understand. "Then, in that case, gentlemen, here they are." He placed a leather case before them on the table. The partners stared. "If you will be so good as to examine them, at once, in my presence, you will perceive that they are intact. You quite understand, that no questions are to be asked of anyone, and, in particular, nothing is to be said to Lord Hardaway. I may mention, by the way, that Lord Hardaway is to be married, almost immediately, to Miss Bonnyer-Lees."

Mr. Ruby rubbed his hands and smiled.

"We are delighted to hear it, Mr. Champnell—delighted! You may rely on us not to breathe a word to Lord Hardaway; we quite understand that it was only a little joke of his. His lordship is so full of humour."

Mr. Golden's tone—he was examining the jewels as he spoke—was not quite so effusive.

"If you had been in my place, and had suffered what I suffered, you might not have seen the joke quite so clearly, Ruby. There is such a thing as being almost too full of humour."

Mr. Champnell went straight from Bond Street to the Marquis of Bewlay's. He found the Marquis in his smoking-room.

"You may make your mind easy on the subject of those infernal machines. Here they are." Mr. Champnell took thirteen empty tins from a bag which he was carrying. "They have all gone off, but as they were all filled with water it would seem as if somebody had been planning a practical joke at your expense. That sort of infernal machine hardly savours of a secret society."

"It certainly does not, and though you mayn't think it, Mr. Champnell, it's worth all of two hundred guineas to me to know it."

"I am very glad indeed to hear it."

And so the Hon. Augustus told himself again, when, having returned to his own quarters, he had propped up his feet against the mantel-shelf and was lighting a cigar.

"I don't think that's a bad morning's stroke of business—five hundred guineas for doing nothing at all."

JANE SPROOD, DETECTIVE

ELLIS PARKER BUTLER

I
A CAREER OF CRIME

SHORTLY AFTER MIDNIGHT, one January night Henry Sprood cautiously raised one of the dining-room windows in the home of Enderbury Wick and climbed inside. He knew the exact location of the sideboard and in just which drawer the Wick spoons and forks lay; he walked to it silently, removed the silver and placed it in the thickly padded bag he carried. For a moment, then, he stood motionless, surprised that burglary was such a safe and simple occupation. He was almost disappointed that nothing more thrilling had occurred. It was at the end of this moment that his eyes turned toward the dining-room window and saw a head silhouetted there.

To understand why a respected, elderly man like Henry Sprood was stealing Enderbury Wicks silver is not difficult; ages ago some one discovered that pendulums swing. Henry Sprood had swung— that is the answer.

For many years Henry Sprood had been a modest, honest and upright citizen of the village of Westcote, which is on Long Island, near New York. His wife, while she lived, had rather ruled Henry, as did his six sons and daughters. His wife had now been dead many years, and five of the sons and daughters were married. It seemed, however, as if the ruling proclivities of his wife and all his sons and daughters had unified in Jane Sprood, the daughter who did not marry and who remained at home.

"I hope I know my duty when I see it," Jane Sprood had said, eying her father rather sternly. "While you live, I shall preserve your home." So she did. It would not be quite fair to Jane Sprood

to say she preserved it in vinegar. You will know what I mean, perhaps, when I say she wore square-toed boots, perfectly awful hats
and considered cigarette-smoking a weak, feminine trait.

"The day may come when I shall smoke a pipe," she once told
me, "but I consider cigarette-smoking a childish fad."

Quite frequently I have known Jane Sprood to sit on the platform at important female-suffrage meetings with her hat wrong
side in front, but no one ever so much as smiled. Jane Sprood was
above hats. She was an earnest person. It was an education to see
her striding along the street when she was in haste. She was capable of stepping on a Newfoundland dog without noticing she had
stepped on it.

Henry Sprood, her father, was on the other hand the most inconspicuous of men. He was a small man and gave the impression
that if he did not wear side-whiskers he could not be seen at all.
He had a habit of pulling at the side-whiskers, which were short
and neat, as if he were attempting to pull them off and thus disappear from view entirely.

It was the belated realization that he was a nobody in a world
of famous (or notorious) men that led Henry Sprood, in his old
age, to decide, with deliberate forethought, to lead a life of crime—
that and the fact that Jane Sprood was Jane Sprood. He knew that
Jane, who watched his every waking action and who believed that
it was part of her life-work to keep her father's latter days placid
and calm, would set her square-toed foot down firmly if, for example, he decided to surpass Stefansson as an Arctic explorer. And
yet the world teemed with men who were, like Stefansson, each
the greatest in his particular line of endeavor. To Henry Sprood
the thought that he would never be the "greatest" in anything became abhorrent. It was then that he thought of a life of crime.

For a man who is, so to speak, henpecked by a daughter who
will not let him undertake even such a simple thing as learning a
new game of solitaire, the life of crime is ideal. I wonder that more
henpecked men do not take it up. It can be lived at night and secretly—indeed, it *must* be lived secretly to reach the greatest
heights of success.

Henry Sprood did not jump into a life of crime prematurely. He gave it deep thought and made his preparations carefully. For many nights, as he sat at his side of the parlor table, seeming to read the newspaper, while Jane Sprood sat opposite reading a book, and his granddaughter Elsie—a charming girl, just out of high school—read or sewed or knit at their side, he was, in fact, planning and studying, laying out the steps of his career.

No one seeing the little family around the parlor table would have imagined that one of the group was planning burglary, arson, robbery, abduction and murder; but such was the case. Henry Sprood, intent on being known forever in the annals of wickedness as the King of Crime, was deep in such thoughts even when Jane Sprood thought he was dozing over his newspaper.

Several things aided Henry Sprood and simplified his plans. He was a light sleeper and troubled with indigestion. He had for many years worried about the furnace going out at night. At any time of the night he might be heard going to the bathroom medicine-closet for a dose of pepsin, going down cellar to see how the furnace was behaving, or moving restlessly about his room. Often he sat for hours in the cellar, nursing his indigestion and watching the furnace.

As the time neared when he meant to begin his criminal career, he intentionally increased his night wanderings, so that when the time came he might sally forth by way of the cellar for hours at a time without arousing Jane's suspicion. He did other things. He gradually and cautiously acquired a set of burglar's tools, revolvers, et cetera. He pottered around the cellar and dug an "ash pit" under the furnace. In reality it was a hiding place for the loot he meant to bring home.

This January night had found his preparations complete. At the minute he had set for his first step into actual crime, he got out of bed, reached out of his window and cut the telephone wire. This was because he wished to sever Enderbury Wick from communication with the outside world. The telephone wire was a "party" wire that served both houses. Mr. Sprood had decided to commit his first burglary upon the premises of Enderbury Wick, his nearest neighbor to the east.

WHEN HENRY SPROOD saw the head silhouetted in the dining-room window, he drew a revolver from his pocket and leveled it.

"Hands up, or I'll shoot!" he whispered.

"No, don't you dare shoot, Grandpa," came a sweet answering whisper. "It's Elsie. I'm coming in."

As she said this, the high-school graduate put her foot over the windowsill, drew herself up and landed lightly in the room.

"What larks!" she whispered gleefully. "Have you got the spoons already? Are you going upstairs to get the jewelry? Look, I've got on my gym-costume. It's dandy for burgling, isn't it? Well, what are we going to do next? We can't stand here all night, can we?"

Mr. Sprood was greatly distressed.

"You must go home, my dear," he said earnestly. "I cannot imagine how you could ever guess—"

"Oh, you dear, stupid thing!" the girl exclaimed. "Do you think you can hide anything from me, Grandpa? Not from little bright-eyes! Why, I believe even Aunt Jane would have suspected something—and she's dense, very dense, you know—if she made your bed every morning and saw just heaps and heaps of crime books—'Raffles' and everything. Why, Grandpa, I *knew* the very minute I found all the lovely jimmies and things. They're simply adorable!"

"Jimmies?" said Mr. Sprood uneasily. "How did you find jimmies?"

"Snooping, of course," said Elsie lightly. "In the cellar! And the perfectly sweet place you made under the furnace to hide our swag in! That's the right word, isn't it? And nitroglycerin! The very minute I saw the nitroglycerin I changed my mind."

"You changed your mind?" said Mr. Sprood weakly.

"About being a detective," said Elsie. "I always meant to be a detective, of course. Such larks, catching criminals! I had to be a detective instead of a criminal, you understand, Grandpa, because a nice girl can't take up a career of crime ordinarily—not a really nice girl. It is not proper—going around everywhere at night without a chaperon, I mean. But of course, with you along, it is all right. Nobody can object to a girl's being a criminal if her grandfather chaperons her. Come on—let's go up and get the jewelry. Mrs. Wick has a perfectly lovely wristwatch."

"No, my dear," said Henry Sprood firmly, "nothing of that sort to-night. You, with the impetuosity of youth, might be tempted to venture, but I chose this house for the reason that felt it safer to begin simply and work toward bigger things. I chose this house because I know that Mr. Wick and his wife are afraid of burglars and lock themselves in their room."

"I know," said Elsie lightly. "They say that if they hear a burglar they will push the dresser against their door and keep quiet until the burglars go away. But I do think you might let me go up and boo at them or something."

"No," said Mr. Sprood firmly, "no foolhardiness!"

"Well, anyway," said Elsie, "let's go to the kitchen and have a burglar feast. You've got to let me have some fun. You got the silver."

"Very well," said Mr. Sprood after brief consideration of the suggestion. "It will undoubtedly cause more comment if we steal a meal before we depart."

The next moment Elsie threw her arms around her grandfather's neck and kissed him ecstatically.

"Grandpa," she exclaimed, "you are a perfect old peach of a dear! You're the nicest burglar I ever heard of."

The Wick kitchen was spotlessly clean, and so Elsie Sprood immediately proceeded to render it less so.

"Because that's the way burglars do," she explained. "Folks are never satisfied with their burglars unless they muss things up."

For her part of the stolen feast, Elsie lunched simply but amply on cake on which she spread marshmallow-whip generously. Mr. Sprood ate cheese, sliced thin and sprinkled with powdered sugar, a combination of which he was very fond, and which he was seldom allowed at home, Jane Sprood declaring that cheese gave him indigestion and that putting sugar on cheese was unheard of and unholy, if not worse.

"But I'll eat what I please here," he told Elsie. "If a burglar can't eat what he pleases, what is the use of being a criminal?"

"Of course, there is some logic in that," Elsie admitted, "but I wouldn't eat too much. It is all right to be brazenly unafraid of Aunt Jane, but that's no reason why you should tie yourself up in knots for the next year. If I am to lead this gang—"

"You, my dear child!" exclaimed Mr. Sprood. "*I* am to be the leader."

Elsie let a slice of cake and marshmallow-whip pause halfway to her mouth.

"Grandpa," she said seriously, "I can't think of any such thing. Why, don't you see it can't be? How could I ever be Queen of Rogues if I let you be leader? No, you can be my chaperon, and go with me everywhere when I have a job on hand—"

"But my child," said Mr. Sprood, "this is my career of crime, not yours. How can I become known as the King of Criminals if I am to let you lead?"

He was quite stubborn about it, and so was Elsie.

"I dare you to let me ask Aunt Jane, or Miss Perk, or anybody, which of us would make the best crime-leader," Elsie said. "You know very well they would say I would."

"But I *won't* be under a woman's thumb, not even under yours, Elsie," said Mr. Sprood. "By day—yes. In crime—no! It was to escape—"

"Well, you're eating too much of that cheese, I know that," said Elsie, tossing the empty cardboard marshmallow-whip container on the floor.

"Anyway, I'm not going to quarrel with my dear old pal. We'll wait and see. Maybe we'll be the King and Queen of Crime."

"To that," said Mr. Sprood, returning the cheese to the ice-box, "I might consent. Shall I carry the swag?"

"No, we'll both carry it," said Elsie; and so, each carrying one corner of the padded bag, they returned to the Sprood home, which had now become a veritable den of thieves.

The next morning Mr. Sprood did not get out of bed. He was indeed suffering great agony, and only the tremendous success of his burglary kept him from shedding tears of remorse. Ordinarily Jane Sprood would have spent every moment at the bedside of her suffering father on such a morning of pain, but although she came up now and then, this morning she spent for the most part in Mrs. Enderbury Wick's home, hearing the story of the burglary, which had naturally caused the utmost commotion in the immediate neighborhood.

It must be said that Jane Sprood was not much interested in the burglary itself. Small things like earthquakes, deluges and burglaries did not interest her. Had she been on the ark with Noah, she might have remarked, if the other passengers had pestered her with details of the flood too long, "Yes, I dare say it is quite a heavy shower," but she would have spent her time trying to convince Shem that Mrs. Shem deserved the privilege of voting, or in attempts to convert Noah from his well-known anti-prohibition slant. Jane Sprood's interest in the burglary was mainly in wondering how any woman could be as excited over an ordinary matter as Mrs. Enderbury Wick was over a simple, uncomplicated burglary that had occurred hours before and was now completely a thing of the past

"If they had killed you and your husband," she told Mrs. Wick, "you might have reason to be excited."

"But a burglary—right here in my own house!" twittered little Mrs. Wick.

"Fiddlesticks!" said Jane Sprood. "One gets nowhere fussing over a petty thievery like this. Crime is recognized as a fact. There always have been burglaries; there always will be. They run true to type. One is like another. We know all that is to be known of their psychology. There is nothing new to learn. Now, if my father or my niece suddenly took up a life of crime, we would have something to twitter about."

"Mr. Sprood and Elsie!" giggled Mrs. Wick hysterically. "What an idea!"

Even Jane Sprood smiled then. She had, she felt, gone a little too far in choosing an example to illustrate her meaning.

The detectives—for, of course, Mr. Wick had telephoned for them as soon as he discovered the burglary—seemed to bear out Jane Sprood's contention. There were three of the detectives, and the leader seemed to be Sergeant Gulpin, who was an uninterested, red-faced, thick-necked man. The three examined the premises in a bored way, and Sergeant Gulpin jotted down a memorandum of the stolen forks and spoons, with a detailed description.

"This here burglary," be told Mrs. Wick, "probably looks like a mighty big business to you, but to us detectives it's just part of the day's work, as you might say. Get me? We get so many of 'em, mostly worse than this one, that we don't think much of 'em. Most women think their burglary is the most important that ever was pulled off, if you know what I mean."

"I'm trying not to be too puffed up about it," said Mrs. Wick.

"What I mean, if you get me," said Sergeant Gulpin, "is that most folks that's been burgled thinks we ought to go right out on the front porch or somewheres and fetch in the burglar in about two minutes with irons on him. That ain't the way we go to work."

"I'm sure it is not," said Jane Sprood, and Sergeant Gulpin glanced at her doubtfully.

"What I mean," said Sergeant Gulpin, "is that in a case like this it's a hundred to one we don't never catch the burglar unless he goes and pawns the stuff, and then it is fifty to one we don't get him, anyway. What I always say to folks when they send for us on a case like this is: 'Don't expect nothing; it's a hundred to one shot.'"

"I can easily see," said Jane Sprood, with what seemed to Sergeant Gulpin a touch of sarcasm, "that that is the wisest advice under the circumstances."

Sergeant Gulpin looked at her as if he could say something about women with big chins if he chose, but he turned away. "Come on, men," he said. "We got all we want here."

ELSIE, REPORTING to her partner in crime the progress of the investigation, was able to bring the best of news. "That coarse-looking policeman don't know a thing," she told her grandfather. "He says it is a hopeless case. I stopped him on the porch as he was coming out of Mrs. Wick's, and I gave him a smile, Grandpa—like this."

It was a smile that would have made a brass statue pause and give up its innermost secrets.

"Well, my dear?" asked Mr. Sprood.

"He told me it was undoubtedly the work of old and expert professional burglars," Elsie said, "and that there was hardly a chance of ever catching them. Isn't it jolly? I think we ought to rob a bank next, don't you, Grandpa? I think we ought to consider ourselves above stealing spoons, don't you? Anyway, we might rob a shop of some kind—a grocery-store or a delicatessen-shop."

Mr. Sprood smiled, but he groaned too.

"Not a delicatessen, my dear. Nothing with cheese in it," he declared. "A hardware-store, or a car-barn."

"I knew you were eating too much of that cheese," said Elsie. "You mustn't do it, Grandpa. Just see what it leads to! We might go out to-night and hold up a street-car, or do something to keep in practice, and here you are fast in bed. I expect you'll be here for days and days, with hot-water bottles and pepsin, when we ought to be making the names of the King and Queen of Crime famous."

"I'm going to get up in a few hours," said Mr. Sprood feebly. "I'll be on my pins again soon. I'm not wasting time here. I'm thinking of crimes to commit."

"Well, perhaps it may be just as well," said Elsie. "It does give you time to think, doesn't it? The main thing is that we're safe. We've shown ourselves we can be trusted. We can baffle the detectives."

"I fear no minion of the law," said Mr. Sprood.

"We needn't fear anyone," agreed Elsie, and she went down to learn the latest reports from the Wick home.

Not until the next evening was Henry Sprood able to dress and go downstairs. He was still very pale and wobbly in the legs. He looked so ill that Jane Sprood was quite worried. She put a stool for his feet and tucked a pillow at his back.

"There, now!" she said. "You ought to be in bed, but I suppose you must be up, or you wont be satisfied. My advice to you is to go to bed in half an hour and get a good night's rest. Susan Perk is coming over, and I know well enough you don't fancy her, but it will be all the better for you if she drives you to bed. You ought to be in bed, anyway."

Elsie sat as close to her grandfather as she dared, giving him now and then a little squeeze of the hand. In a few minutes all were reading.

The arrival of Susan Perk was announced by a gentle, apologetic cough even before she reached the front door.

"Land sakes!" she exclaimed, when she saw Mr. Sprood. "You look like a corpse! You do look and appear like my poor brother Thomas the very day and date his indigestion carried him to a better land. Have you got a kind of puffy feeling in the chest?"

"I'm all right, Susan," said Mr. Sprood. "I'll be all right tomorrow."

"The very words my brother said not an hour before he passed beyond!" said Susan Perk, shaking her head. "The very words! Well, hope for the best, I say. That's my motto—'Hope for the best.' If the worst comes, Jane, I'll be right at home across the street. Some hate to touch a corpse, but I do my duty as I see it."

"Sit down, Susan," said Jane Sprood. "Don't be a fool. You've been having Father dead every week for the last twenty years, and you know it."

"I make my mistakes, being mortal like all," said Miss Perk, seating herself and sighing, "but time will tell. What did you send for me for, Jane Sprood? 'Her father's dead,' I said to myself the moment I heard your voice over the telephone. If it ain't that, what is it?"

She looked at Mr. Sprood a little resentfully, he thought, as if he had somehow cheated her by not being dead.

"Susan," said Jane Sprood, "women are brighter than men; their minds are keener."

"Well, I hope so, at least," said Susan Perk sadly, "but it has been said: 'The mind of man passeth understanding.'"

"Fiddlesticks!" said Jane Sprood. "Nothing of the sort! Susan, did we or did we not secure female suffrage in this State?"

"For myself I say nothing, Jane. I was but an humble gleaner in the fields, but you did more than most."

"And did we get national Prohibition, or didn't we?"

"It's got. I'll say that," said Miss Perk.

Jane Sprood tapped the floor with her broad shoe-toe.

"What man can half do, woman can do well, Susan Perk," she said. "I have brains, have I not? Susan—"

"Yes, Jane?"

"Of all the incompetent, hopeless, helpless human beings I have ever seen, the detectives in this town are the worst! Susan Perk, do you know any reason why a woman should not be a detective?"

Miss Perk smoothed her dress across her knees.

"No, Jane," she said, but it was evident she was agitated. For his part Mr. Sprood gazed at Jane with actual alarm. Even his granddaughter Elsie caught her breath nervously.

"I'm glad to hear you say so," Jane Sprood said dryly, "because it wouldn't make any difference if you said otherwise. Susan, I am going to be a detective."

"Land sakes!" exclaimed Susan.

"A real detective," said Jane Sprood, implying that some she had met recently were but poor imitations. "And you are going to be my assistant, Susan Perk."

Susan Perk shook her head sadly.

"Well, what must be, must be, Jane," she said with an enormous lack of enthusiasm. "I dare say you know best, but I expect we'll both be murdered in our beds. I look for nothing less. Murdered in bed with our throats cut from ear to ear, and a warning pinned on our breasts!"

"Nonsense!" said Jane Sprood. "Nothing of the sort. I generally know what I'm doing, Susan Perk, and I've given this my best thought. I'll not have a lot of hirelings loafing about barrooms while I pay for their time, for one thing. *Jane Sprood, Detective*, means business, Elsie!" she said sharply.

"Yes, Aunt Jane!" said Elsie nervously.

"You have a good head, for a chit. You'll be one of my men."

"Yes, Aunt Jane."

"Father!"

"Yes, Jane, dear?" said Mr. Sprood.

"You'll do the best you can for me. Men can still go where women cannot. I can depend on you?"

"Yes, Jane," said Mr. Sprood in an almost inaudible voice.

"Very well," said Jane Sprood briskly. "We understand each other. While I shall not scorn such monetary rewards as may come as the result of our work, our first aim shall be to ferret out the criminal and see that he is punished to the limit of the law—to the utmost limit, Susan."

"I'm sure he ought to be satisfied with that, Jane," said Miss Perk.

"Humph!" said Jane Sprood. "Now for our first case: who burglarized the Enderbury Wick home? I give myself two days to settle *that* question."

Mr. Sprood, who had been growing paler and paler, now uttered a gurgling sound and slid down in his chair until his gray side-whiskers were on a level with his knees. He pawed feebly at the air with his left foot, and then became quite inert. He had fainted.

THE NEXT DAY was a very unhappy one for the King and Queen of Crime. The facts that Mr. Sprood felt unable to leave his bed, and that Elsie was consequently excused from detective-duty to minister to his needs, did not comfort them. They had had too many examples of Jane Sprood's tireless efficiency in the past. Early this morning she had put her nondescript hat on her head and had gone forth in company with Susan Perk to study the scene of the crime, and she had come to the house but once, when she went to the cellar.

"How long," asked Henry Sprood gloomily, about four in the afternoon, "is the penitentiary-term for burglary?"

"Don't, please, Grandpa," said Elsie.

"If it is twenty years," said Mr. Sprood, "I won't last that long."

"We may only get five," said Elsie consolingly. "It was our first crime."

By six o'clock Mr. Sprood felt much better. The period of pain which followed any indulgence in cheese had passed then, and he felt the rebound to optimism and hope common in dyspeptics. Jane Sprood was still out.

"She hasn't found a clue; that's what's the matter," said Mr. Sprood gleefully. "And she won't find one. We didn't leave any. She'll fuss around and potter around, but she won't find one. I think we are safe—absolutely safe."

Even Elsie thought so now.

"Of course Susan Perk will do a great deal to keep Aunt Jane's attention scattered," she said. "That's something. There's nobody like Susan Perk to get off the subject and stay off of it, and to keep everyone else off of it. Grandfather, I *don't* believe we left a clue. I've been thinking all day, and I can't remember one."

"And no one would suspect *us*," said Mr. Sprood. "We are the last anyone would suspect. I think that I'll get up now."

JANE SPROOD CAME home to dinner. She seemed her usual self and ate heartily, spearing a baked potato across the table when she wished one. She mentioned Susan Perk once, saying Susan would never, she feared, make an ideal detective, being pessimistic by nature and too talkative. After supper Elsie, doing her best to seem calm and nonchalant, asked a question:

"Did you have any luck, Aunt Jane?"

"Luck? No—no luck. I do not depend on luck."

"I mean," said Elsie, "did you find any clues or anything?"

"We discovered the burglar, if that is what you mean," said Jane Sprood dryly. "My opinion is that a blind cow could have discovered the burglar. Susan, did we find any clues?"

Susan Perk raised her hands and turned her eyes to the ceiling to indicate that they had found millions.

"Why, I ask," said Jane Sprood, "should a burglar wishing to rob Enderbury Wick house cut the telephone-wire outside a second-story window in this house when he could have cut it from the ground, just outside Enderbury Wick's?"

No one answered, least of all Henry Sprood.

"I mention no names," said Jane Sprood, "but why did Sergeant Gulpin say there were no clues when remnants of cheese sprinkled with powdered sugar were found in the Wicks' kitchen? Who has a depraved taste for cheese and sugar?"

There was no answer. Mr. Sprood's tongue was too dry for speech.

"I say nothing about the wire's being cut just outside your window, Father. I say nothing about the nicks in the blades of your shears. Susan, how many finger-prints did we find?"

"Eight hundred and seven," answered Susan.

"Seven hundred and eight, Susan; learn to be exact!" said Jane Sprood. "Seven hundred and eight! But I say nothing about them—about their being identical with yours, Father. I say nothing about finding Mrs. Wick's spoons and forks in the ash-pit under our furnace—absolutely nothing. These are but subsidiary clues. The burglar might have cut the wire outside Father's window, using Father's shears, to give a false scent. He might have used rubber gloves with the finger tips molded to reproduce Father's fingerprints. He might have hidden the silver under our furnace to inculpate Father. I say nothing of these things, Father, because you might still have known nothing of the burglary."

Henry Sprood was now sitting on the edge of his chair. His mouth was opening and closing in a vain effort to confess, but not a word would issue from his dry throat. A thought flashed through his brain that he had never really known his daughter Jane before, for as she tortured him she smiled. There was no anger in her eyes or in her voice. She spoke as a keen-scented crime-hound would speak, without malice, without triumph.

"All these things, Father, might still have happened to be without your guilty knowledge, but—"

"Aunt Jane," said Elsie here, "do you mean to sit there and say Grandpa is a burglar? Do you mean to say my grandfather stole those spoons? I'm surprised, Aunt Jane, that you should call your own father a thief."

Mr. Sprood was making vain, unintelligible gestures with his hands. Now Jane Sprood turned to him.

"I don't wonder, Father, that you are surprised, because you are the last man in the world to suspect yourself of burglary, as I well know. This is a great surprise to you, I'm sure. But it is the truth. You, Father, stole the Enderbury Wick spoons and forks."

"Glug—glug-glug," said Henry Sprood thickly.

"It was cheese," said Susan Perk. "Goodness knows—"

"You had been eating cheese and walking in your sleep, Father," said Jane Sprood gently. "You had been reading crime-stories. Of course, dear, you remember nothing of it, but you went to the Wicks' and stole their silver and hid it in the hole under our furnace."

"And goodness knows it's a wonder Enderbury Wick didn't come down and kill you with a pistol," said Susan Perk, "as he would have done if he hadn't been such a peeving specimen of man. It's a blessing you didn't fall down the cellar stairs and break your neck, gallivanting around in your night-shirt."

"Father wears pajamas, Susan," said Jane sharply. "And now, Father, do you wonder how I know you stole the silver when you were walking in your sleep?"

"Yes," said Elsie eagerly, "he wonders."

"Because," said Jane Sprood, "last night you got up in your sleep, Father, went to the cellar, got the silver and took it back to the Enderbury Wicks'."

Henry Sprood raised himself feebly from his chair, his career of crime at an end.

"Thank you, Jane," he said tremulously. "I think I'll go up to bed. Now I know how I got that splinter in the palm of my foot."

"Splinter, hey?" said Susan Perk briskly. "You want to look out for blood-poison. My Cousin Hiram Pork had to have his leg cut off above the knee from the very same reason and cause. 'It's nothing,' he says; and the next thing he knew, his toes swelled up—"

"Susan!" said Jane Sprood sharply. "If you can't talk more cheerful, you'd better go home. You talk too much."

For that was Jane Sprood's frank, outspoken way.

II
THE AVALANCHE

JANE SPROOD, FORTY, unmarried, strong-jawed and square of toe, stood in her parlor, pinning one of her awful hats onto her head. As she stood, her feet well apart, her arms raised, jabbing a rebellious hatpin into the hat, she looked more mannish than her weak and gentle father, who sat watching her, pulling at his inconspicuous side-whiskers as he watched. Susan Perk, her dearest friend, sat watching her too.

"I don't know that what I say ever makes any difference to you, Jane Sprood," she said, "but that hat's on wrong-side before. Not that it looks worse—it couldn't."

"Mind your own business, Susan," said Jane Sprood. "This hat feels perfectly comfortable."

"But Auntie," said Elsie, the redoubtable Jane's pretty niece, "you might just as well wear it the right way if you are going to wear it at all."

"Fiddlesticks!" said Jane Sprood. "Now, then, for the last time, shall it be Jane Sprood & Father, or Jane Sprood & Partners?"

Jane Sprood, having, as she felt, won female suffrage and national prohibition for the town of Westcote, had recently made up her mind to be a detective. As usual, she had made up her mind with all the strength and vim of a steel bear-trap snapping shut. It made no difference to Jane Sprood that she had never detected before. That was an unimportant detail. Shocked by the inefficiency of the detective police of Westcote, with Sergeant Gulpin at its head, she had decided to take a hand. Her aides were Elsie Sprood—

her pretty niece, just out of high school; Henry Sprood, Jane's gentle father; and Susan Perk, from across the street, the leanest, gossipiest spinster in Westcote.

"If you ask *me*," said Susan Perk, "I'd put your poor dear father's name first and foremost, him being male and having, by all signs, but a short time to be among us. He don't look well right now. Far be it from me, Jane Sprood, to urge daughterly ways upon you, such not being your habit, but my motto is 'Father first,' and always was. If I had my say, it would be 'Henry Sprood & Co.'"

"Well, you haven't," said Jane Sprood. "Jane Sprood this company is, and Jane Sprood it is going to be named. And you want to make up your mind now, Susan, or it will be plain 'Jane Sprood' and nothing else. If you want to be in it, say so and don't sit there like a silent clam. You don't, usually."

"I want to help you, Auntie," said Elsie Sprood. "You know I do. I only said that people might think it odd to see a sign on the house."

"Susan?" said Jane Sprood.

"Well, goodness knows I don't want to go sneaking and snooping around in gum shoes, although I do admit I wear rubbers, and have ever since Mother caught cold and died in less than a fortnight, as I told her she would. But that's the way she was. Good advice rolled off her like water off a duck's back. I says to her: 'Mother, if you will go out to-day, with my corns telling me rain is in the air, as plain as the nose on my face—'"

"Do you or don't you want to be a detective, Susan Perk?" asked Jane Sprood.

"You snap a person up so, Jane! Have it your own way, then. But I dare say no good will come of it. To my mind—"

"Your mind never bothered you much, and it never will," said Jane Sprood, for she was accustomed to speaking plainly, especially to Susan Perk. "Jane Sprood & Associates is what I will have painted on the sign. And don't wait lunch for me. I'm going to the sign-painter's, and then to the printer's, and I dare say I'll go over to New York and put advertisements in the newspapers. There is not enough crime in this town to suit me. To my mind the work of a detective is to detect and not to sit waiting forever for something to detect. If I'm not home in time for dinner—"

She was interrupted by a gentle ringing of the doorbell, followed by the entrance of little Mrs. Enderbury Wick, the neighbor next on the east. Mrs. Wick entered without waiting for the door to be opened, and it was easy to see that she was agitated.

"Well, Caroline, what now?" asked Jane Sprood, who could not bear the flutterings of feminine women. "Has the teakettle boiled dry?"

"A robbery!" exclaimed Mrs. Wick. "The bank has been robbed. Enderbury just telephoned—"

"Good!" cried Jane Sprood, her manner changing entirely. "It is time something happened. What was stolen?"

"The safe," said little Mrs. Wick. "They stole the whole safe. Enderbury says—"

"Now, be calm," said Jane Sprood severely. "Be quite calm."

"I am calm," said Mrs. Wick resentfully, although it was evident she was not in the least so.

"Remember you are speaking to a detective," said Jane Sprood. "Every word you speak is important. Now, proceed."

"Enderbury telephoned," said Mrs. Wick. "He said he thought he had better, because I might hear a rumor and think he was shot or something."

"It makes no difference to us whether he was shot or not," said Jane Sprood severely. "We want the facts."

"Well, I'm trying to tell you, Jane, dear," said Mrs. Wick.

"Be concise," said Jane Sprood. "Everybody talks too much. Don't you know time may be the important factor, Carrie Wick? Proceed, please."

"And goodness knows," said Susan Perk, "I hope your husband manages to keep his shirts clean, but I have my doubts."

"My husband told me it was all an absolute surprise to him," said Mrs. Wick, as if that was quite sufficient, and she proceeded to tell what he had telephoned her regarding one of the most remarkable of bank-robberies.

The Westcote State Bank was a comparatively young institution, having been in existence only some six years, and it did not yet own a banking building. It occupied the street floor, on the corner of Main and Verity streets, of what was known as the Rockminster Building, an aged structure owned until recently by Dr. Abel Rockminster, the elderly dentist who was also president of the bank. The Doctor's son, Jim Rockminster, was cashier of the bank, and Enderbury Wick was teller.

While Dr. Rockminster was reputed to have been, at one time, a very prosperous citizen, it was generally admitted that he was so no longer. His investments had been unfortunate, particularly one he had made in the Blackstone & Gray Point Ferry Company, and his dental practice had fallen off greatly, so much so that it was known he intended leaving Westcote and that he had rented an office in the small village of Blackstone, on Long Island Sound, some two miles from Westcote. Blackstone promised to become something of a manufacturing center, and as Dr. Rockminster was no longer in demand among those wishing expensive dentistry, he meant to go where there was more plain work wanted.

Mrs. Wick did not say all this, because it was known to her hearers. Neither did she say that Dr. Rockminster was executor of the estate inherited by Arabella and Ardelia Fliegelmeister, two very elderly maiden ladies whose father had much admired the Doctor. What Mrs. Wick did say was this:

"Well, Enderbury got to the bank at five minutes before nine. He never varies a minute; I see to that. So he got there and opened the door—unlocked it, of course—and the first thing he noticed was the ceiling. There was a big, rough-edged, square hole in the ceiling. He knew immediately that the bank had been robbed."

"Naturally," said Jane Sprood.

"And it had been," said Mrs. Wick. "As soon as Enderbury looked inside the railing, he saw that the small safe was gone—absolutely gone! It had gone up through the hole in the ceiling."

"Wait," said Jane Sprood. "You say 'small' safe—"

"Because there had been two—the big one and the small one. The bank has no vault. And the little sale was gone."

"How big was the small safe?" Jane Sprood asked.

"Taller than I am," said Mrs. Wick, "and—four feet wide, I guess."

"And heavy?"

"Of course—solid iron, or steel, or whatever they are. Two men couldn't move it—not ordinarily."

"And it went up through the ceiling?" asked Jane Sprood.

"It went up," said Mrs. Wick. "And what is more, Jane, it went up between a quarter of eight and five minutes of nine this morning, because when Rocco, the janitor, got through sweeping and dusting and fixing the furnace-fire at seven-forty-five, the safe was still there."

"Humph!" said Jane Sprood dryly. "Remember Rocco, Susan!"

"But that is not what Enderbury says is the strangest," continued Mrs. Wick. "Four men stole the safe, and at least forty saw them steal it; and a policeman—that same Sergeant Gulpin you don't like, Jane—was there and made the crowd stand safely back when the safe came down."

"Down? What do you mean by 'down'?"

"Why, down—out of Dr. Rockminster's office," explained Mrs. Wick. "You see, Jane, these four men—the robbers—came with a big gray auto-truck and backed up to the curb under Dr. Rockminster's window and threw all their planks and ropes and block-and-tackles onto the sidewalk, and one stayed there while the three others went up the side stairs and broke into Dr. Rockminster's office and made the hole in the floor and raised the bank safe up to Dr. Rockminster's office. And then, of course, they lowered it out of Dr. Rockminster's window and put it on the truck, and drove away. Enderbury says they wrapped the safe in burlap, but everyone thought that was to keep it from getting scratched. Enderbury says no one thought anything of the safe coming out of the Doctor's office, because everyone knows he is going to move to Blackstone."

"And where did the truck go then?" asked Jane Sprood.

"Well, Enderbury says that is the funniest thing," said Mrs. Wick. "It didn't turn the corner into Main Street. It went up Verity Street. That was not strange, but nobody remembers seeing it after it reached the corner of Verity and Ash. Of course, Jane, it was several minutes after Enderbury entered the bank that he telephoned to the police, because he telephoned Jim Rockminster first.

And the truck had been gone fifteen or twenty minutes when Enderbury reached the bank. And of course Sergeant Gulpin and the policemen took half an hour or so to look things over before they began telephoning, but when they did begin, they couldn't find a person that had seen the truck. It just disappeared."

"It is a habit big auto-trucks have, of course!" said Jane Sprood scornfully. "Father, go out and crank up my flivver and bring it to the front, please, and then go down to that bank and snoop out all the news you can, and come back here. Carrie Wick, what was the name of that truck?"

"Name? Oh, I know what you mean—the kind of truck, and the name of the owner, and all that. I don't know. Enderbury did speak of that, but nobody noticed. Everyone was watching the safe come down."

"I can believe it!" said Jane Sprood. "Human beings don't observe details. They will gawp at a safe. —Elsie!"

"Yes, Aunt Jane?"

"Get on your hat and go down to Verity Street," said Jane Sprood briskly. "You like children, and they like you. Do you know Dettomarino?"

"The Italian shoemaker, back of the bank?"

"With ten or twenty children—yes. You can depend on it that fifteen or sixteen of them were climbing all over that truck. They'll know. Pick out a boy. A boy will know the names on that truck. Get the boy that knows most and bring him here. I'll be back in an hour."

She turned to the telephone and asked Enderbury Wick if he had heard anything new. He had not. Dr. Rockminster, he said, could not be found, and Jim Rockminster was tremendously distressed by the robbery.

"But it really doesn't amount to much," said Enderbury Wick. "We did not use the small safe much. All our securities and collateral were in the big safe. There was only about twenty thousand dollars—all in cash—the money we keep on hand for my use, as teller, in case Jim does not get down early."

"Heard anything of the truck with the safe on it?"

"Not a thing," said Enderbury. "But the police say the robbers can't get off the island. They have telephoned and have closed every avenue of escape."

Jane Sprood drew on her gloves briskly.

"You get your hat and climb into my flivver, Susan Perk," she ordered. "You're going with me. I don't know what is at the bottom of all this, but if anybody knows all the mean gossip about the Rockminsters and Enderburys and the rest, it's you! For once in my life I'm going to let you talk your limit. Those fool detectives may have their card-files and rogues' galleries, but I've got you!"

When Jane Sprood returned, her hat considerably on one side of her head and her hair more or less in disorder, she wore a grim but satisfied look, as if her part of the investigation had proceeded well. Susan Perk was still talking, but her voice was rather hoarse, an indication that she had been talking continuously.

"Now, hold your tongue, if you can," Jane Sprood told her as she saw Elsie and a somewhat soiled boy in the parlor. "Well?"

"It was a Murray-Coe, and the name on it was Bryce & Briggs, Safes and Pianos Moved, Orotown, L. I., and the number began with an 8, gimme a quarter, you said you would," said the young Dettomarino all in one breath.

Jane Sprood gave him half a dollar.

"How many of the men were Italians?" she asked.

"One was," said the boy.

"Did you ever see him before," Jane asked.

"No."

"Would you know him if you saw him again?"

"Sure!"

"Well, go home. There's no use telling you not to make yourself sick eating candy—"

"I'm going to buy Thrif' Stamps," said the boy, grinning, and he took his cap and went.

Jane Sprood threw herself into a chair and covered her eyes with her hands. She let her head rest upon the back of the chair. She was thinking—trying to piece together all she had learned or find some way that satisfied her. She had just put one foot on the seat of a chair in front of her, for greater comfort, when the bell of the telephone rang. She jumped up, brisk again in an instant.

"Enderbury Wick speaking," she heard. "I thought you would like to know, Miss Sprood, that the police have found out about the truck and the tackle. It was stolen out of the yard of Bryce & Briggs, at Orotown, this morning. It hasn't been returned yet."

"Humph!" said Jane Sprood. "I knew that before. Do you think anybody would bring back that truck and say, 'Here's your truck; we had a very successful robbery; thank you'? Don't be a fool, Enderbury Wick." She turned to Elsie. "Where's Father?"

"He's not back yet," the girl said.

But he came in a minute later, and with him was Dr. Abel Rockminster.

"I brought the Doctor to you, Jane," said Mr. Sprood. "I told him you had gone into the detective line, and he thought—"

"I thought, perhaps," said the old dentist, "you might help me, Jane. I know you haven't been coming to me lately; I'm out of style and out of date, I dare say. But I have always admired your efficiency. Yes! I don't know—I thought perhaps—"

The old man seemed greatly broken since Jane Sprood had last seen him. His hands trembled, and his face was drawn, and his eyes showed fear and indecision. He was a striking contrast to Jane Sprood's natty little father, for Dr. Rockminster was a large, heavy man, and now his shoulders slouched, and he was loose and spineless.

"May I see you alone, Jane?" he asked nervously. Jane Sprood led him into the dining-room and closed the doors. "As soon as I can get at it, Doctor," she said briskly, "I'm going to have an office—a room I can call an office. I'm going into this detective work heart and soul. That's my way. Efficiency, effectiveness, effort! Well?"

The Doctor hesitated, and Jane Sprood put her hand on his arm to reassure him.

"Speak out, to the bottom of your heart," she said. "Tell me everything. Whatever it is, it will not be as bad as I have heard. Susan Perk has been talking to me for an hour."

"Poor Susan!" said Dr. Rockminster. "Well, Jane, I'm afraid I'm in a nasty hole—a bad hole, Jane. I'm afraid it is all up with me, I suppose," he said, sighing. "I should be beyond caring—everything has gone so wrong with me, and I'm so old now; but it's Jim I'm thinking of too—Jim and myself. Yes!"

"Tell me about it," urged Jane Sprood. "They suspect you? Or Jim?"

"Jane," said the dentist, "you know how I have been running downhill financially, with that Blackstone & Gray Point Ferry stock as a final stab. You knew of that—you owned a share or two. Daggett robbed us when he sold us that stock."

"He did not rob me of much," said Jane Sprood dryly. "He was here last night, trying to get me to join a pool to keep the ferry running until he could sell it to some noodle. I gave him a slice of my mind. Well?"

"That stock about finished me, Jane," said the dentist. "I have a few irons in the fire—affairs that may pull through and set me on my feet again if I have a little more time—a year or so. But they are matters that offer hope only if I can keep the confidence of the men who are with me in them. That is the tragedy. I have the chance, but it is going! In a day the avalanche will fall. It will be ruin for me—for me and for Jim."

"Now, Doctor," said Jane briskly, "we will never get anywhere this way. Speak out. Be plain."

The old man took a fresh grasp on himself. "Jane," he said, "I do not care whether the men who stole that safe are ever found or not, but the safe must be found. It must be found, and intact, or the Rockminster name will be blackened forever. I am executor of the estate left to those poor Fliegelmeister girls. You may have heard that. I thank God I did not put their money into ferry-stock as I once meant to do, although it would have been better for me had I done so. Yesterday, Jane, I bought forty thousand dollars' worth of bonds for them with their money. I bought Liberty Bonds— coupon bonds."

"That was wise enough, wasn't it?"

"Wait! I went to New York to buy them, and brought them back myself. I reached Westcote about four o'clock. Jim was in the bank, alone, and I rapped on the door, and he let me in. I did not want to trust the bonds in my rickety old safe, and we opened the security drawer of the small safe—"

"You say 'we'?"

"We, because one of us alone could not open it," said the Doctor. "You know how security-drawer locks are made? Two keys are needed to open them. The 'master-key' must first set the lock, then the drawer key can throw the bolt. Since the bank began business, I have held the master-key, Jane."

"And Jim has the other key?"

"Yes. Neither of us, alone, could open the drawer. We must work together to open it. You see what it means?"

"I know what Susan Perk would say it meant," said Jane Sprood. "Susan would say you and Jim were in league to rob the bank—to rob the Fliegelmeister girls."

"To cover up the peculations I could no longer hide," said the Doctor. "Because, Jane, last night I saw the two old maiden ladies and told them their bonds were locked in that security drawer."

"But—"

"I know what you mean to say," said the Doctor. "'How could you prevent the robbery?' Jane, I hired those men!"

"Doctor!"

"I hired them to move a safe," repeated the dentist. "One of them came to my office—months ago, I think—and asked to have some work done, dental work. A rough fellow! I have been at work on his teeth ever since. It came out that I meant to move, and he wondered if he could pay my bill, or part of it, by moving my safe. I agreed to that. He was coming this afternoon. Instead he came this morning."

The Doctor laughed ironically.

"Who would believe that story?" he went on. "'He hired them, true enough,' they will say. 'But there were no bonds in that safe. They never were put there. The old rascal is trying to cover his thefts, and the young rascal, his son, was willing enough to help him.' That is what they will be saying in an hour, or to-morrow. And then the avalanche!"

Jane Sprood nodded her understanding.

"I see you need that safe, Doctor," she said. "Have the police no news?"

"The safe, the truck, the men, all have disappeared utterly!"

JANE SPROOD WALKED to the window and looked out upon the street where her flivver stood. Her forehead was creased, and she clasped her hands behind her back. Suddenly she turned.

"This man, Doctor," she demanded, "the man who had his teeth fixed, the one you hired to move the safe—describe him."

The Doctor closed his eyes, the better to see a mental photograph of the man.

"He was an Italian—short, rather heavy, black hair—curly hair, oily-looking; you might call it short ringlets. Hard, large, rough hands, hairy on the backs, a short clipped mustache, brown eyes, wide, low forehead—"

"One gold tooth, about here or here, in front?"

"Yes," said the dentist with surprise. "It was one I put in. How did you know?"

"A young Dettomarino may have told me," said Jane. "I am not entirely a fool, Doctor—not entirely, but almost, because—"

She paused.

"Because," she said slowly, "I hoped to catch the four robbers myself. A detective needs a reputation for success more than all else, Doctor. In a week, in four days, perhaps, I might have had those men. In a week, in four days, in two hours, Doctor, your avalanche may have fallen. So I choose to think, now, that it is more important to stay your avalanche than to set my fame going by catching those men."

"You are a good woman, Jane."

She did not pay attention to this. "You will go downtown," she said like an adult giving directions to a child. "Go to the bank. Go to Enderbury Wick first, then to your son. You will be eager, happy, positive. You will say 'Jane Sprood has found the safe and the truck, and the safe has not been opened.' Do you understand?"

"But—"

"No matter! You'll say that. A five-ton truck and a bank safe six feet tall and four feet wide cannot disappear utterly. That is common sense, isn't it? To-day or to-morrow or the next day the police, if left alone, will find the truck and the safe. In the meantime what is most needed is to prevent the first gossip from starting the rumor that you have peculated or that you and Jim are in collusion. That is what we must prevent, Doctor. I will look out for myself."

"But if they come to you—as they will?"

"I've always been able to take care of myself," said Jane Sprood, "and I hope I can do it still."

"Jane, I'll never forget this," said the Doctor, taking his hat.

"I hope you don't," said Jane Sprood.

WITHIN FIFTEEN MINUTES of the departure of Dr. Rockminster the telephone-bell jangled; and Jane Sprood, who had been yawning while Susan Perk talked uninterruptedly, jumped for the telephone. As she suspected, it was the bank. It was Enderbury Wick's voice that accosted her.

"That you, Miss Sprood? This is Wick—Enderbury Wick. Dr. Rockminster is here. He says you found the safe—"

"Well," snapped Jane Sprood, "what of it? Can't you believe him? I never knew him to lie. If he says I said I found it, I did say so."

"But *did* you?" asked Enderbury.

It was evident that Jim Rockminster took the receiver from Enderbury Wick.

"Is that you, Miss Sprood?" Jim's voice came over the wire. "Father is here, saying you found our safe. Where was it?"

"Now, look here, Jim Rockminster!" said Jane Sprood. "Don't you know me well enough to know that if I had wanted to tell where that safe is I would have told your father?"

"Yes, but Miss Sprood—"

"Good-by!"

Jane hung up.

"When a man is that Jim Rockminster's age," she complained, "he is as inquisitive as a woman. I expect I'll have all the newspaper reporters in the world here next! A nice howdy-do!"

"But what is it all about, Aunt Jane?" asked Elsie. "Did you tell Dr. Rockminster something you have not told us?"

"Dr. Rockminster is a gibble-gabble," said Jane Sprood. "What were you saying about Mrs. Brilling's first husband, Susan?"

"Like a fish!" said Susan willingly. "Although, come to think of it, I don't know that I ever heard of a fish that drank rum by the barrel, like that man did. Never a sober minute until he was in his coffin; that's my idea of him."

Before she had quite completed her reminiscences of Mrs. Brilling's first husband, a touring-car dashed to the curb outside and stopped, and eight men, among whom was Sergeant Gulpin, jumped out and ran for the front door.

"Let them in, Elsie," said Jane Sprood. "If you don't, they'll break the door down, I dare say!"

Of the men two, including Sergeant Gulpin, were of the detective police, and the remainder were reporters. It was evident that it was more from policy than from desire that they gave Sergeant Gulpin the right to speak first. The Sergeant seemed impressed with his importance.

"What's this about finding that safe?" he asked violently. "Who found it? Which of you?"

Jane Sprood looked Mr. Gulpin squarely in the eye.

"What safe?" she asked. "The safe the police can't find?"

"Never mind that now," said Sergeant Gulpin, getting red in the face as the youngest reporter laughed. "Are you Jane Sprood?"

"Jane Sprood, detective, yes!" said Jane. "Jane Sprood, of Jane Sprood & Associates, detectives. Yes, I'm Jane Sprood, and these are my associates. Is there anything Jane Sprood & Associates can do to assist the remarkably polite and efficient police force of Westcote?"

"So that's it, hey?" said Sergeant Gulpin, growing still redder in the face. "Advertising dodge, is it, getting all these reporters up here to hear you guy me? Well, I ain't got no time to waste at that sort of business, if you know what I mean. Did you find that safe, or didn't you?"

Jane Sprood walked to the window and stood with her broad back showing her contempt.

"Safe?" she said. "You mean the Westcote State Bank's safe? I think perhaps we did some work on that case recently, but it was so simple I've forgotten. I leave all such very simple matters to our secretary. Susan Perk, do you remember whether Jane Sprood & Associates found a safe anywhere this day?"

"My lands of goodness!" exclaimed Susan Perk, bouncing straight up in her chair in her surprise. "I declare this is the first I ever knew I was secretary of the thing, Jane Sprood, and a pretty way you have of slinging it in my face when least expected. Secretary, she says! Secretary, and not a book, or a sheet of paper, or even a pencil, to secretary with!"

"Cut that!" said Sergeant Gulpin. "If you are the mouthpiece of this bunch, talk it out. Did anybody find that safe?"

"Hear the man!" said Susan Perk. "What do you suppose Jane Sprood went out in that joltsome car of hers for if it wasn't to find the safe?"

"And the man, Susan," suggested Jane. "Don't forget the man with the gold tooth."

"Land sakes!" cried Susan Perk. "Was he a robber? If I'd known that, I'd have passed away where I sat! A robber I did *not* expect to see, as Jane Sprood well knows, nor safe or truck, for that matter, if you want the truth, although Jane Sprood says to me the moment we got into that Satan's-imp of a car of hers: 'Susan, prepare to see that safe.'"

"Then you did find it? Where?" asked the youngest reporter.

"'Jane,' I says," continued Susan Perk, not heeding the interruption, "'a safe I don't expect to see, when all the police in the world can't find it.' 'Fiddlesticks!' she says. 'I use my brains, Susan Perk. Those men had time to get off this island by ferry or bridge, and if they had done so, some memory of them would exist. And hide here in town they couldn't,' she says; 'so what would anyone with brains think?' I told her I never pretended to have 'em—brains, I mean. 'I didn't invest several hundred of my good dollars in a fool scheme for nothing,' Jane Sprood said to me. 'I know, and old Doc Rockminster knows, and some few others may know, that the Blackstone-Gray-Point-Ferry stopped running last night, but I'll warrant those safe-stealers didn't know it. What they did,' said Jane, 'was to make for the nearest ferry.'"

Sergeant Gulpin, who had forgotten to remove his hat, now did so, to wipe his forehead.

"I knew it wasn't running," he blustered.

"So Jane said. 'The fool police will know it is not running,' she said, 'likely being notified, and won't think it worth their while to look there. We'll look, Susan.' So we did, and sure enough, there was the truck, and the safe on the ferry."

"And it is there?"

"Or was," said Susan Perk.

Sergeant Gulpin made his way toward the door.

"And what about the man with the gold tooth?" asked a reporter.

"Oh, him!" said Susan. "Jane hired him to watch the truck and the safe."

"Because he was one of the robbers," said Jane Sprood over her shoulder.

"Come on!" said Sergeant Gulpin. "I've got the straight dope now. We'll have the safe and the truck in ten minutes. And that gold-toothed Italian, too."

They left hurriedly, all of them, without another word to Jane Sprood, but at the curb one of the reporters drew back after he had put his foot on the running-board of the car.

"That's all right," he said; "you fellows go ahead; I can get the dope from you when you come back. I think my big story is right here."

He watched the car disappear and then turned toward the house. He was a wise reporter.

"Twenty lines is the limit for a suburban bank-robbery," he said, "but Jane Sprood, the female detective, is good for two columns and a double-column photograph. Jane, here comes Fame."

Jane Sprood, at the window, saw the reporter returning. She turned.

"Open the door, Elsie," she said. "Here comes Free Advertising."

III

TOLUARDOROL

ONE FEBRUARY AFTERNOON two remarkable-looking middle-aged women stood on the front porch of a house in the village of Westcote, Long Island, a few miles from New York, watching Sam Denning attach a neat sign to the front of the house at one side of the front door. One of the women who lived in the house was quite stout, with large feet clad in strong square-toed shoes that matched the general mannishness of her attire. Her face was severe, with a strong chin, but her eyes were keen and cool. She wore a remarkably unhandsome hat that seemed to have been treated in a most cruel and degrading manner. It looked as if it had been quite frequently sat on.

The other woman was different. Her most striking feature was her nose, which was extremely prominent. She appeared to be somewhat washed-out and faded, her eyes being rather watery, but withal she had a certain sprightliness which showed in her garments. These may be briefly described by saying that she was quite fluffy.

The sign Sam Denning was attaching to the house bore the names of these two women. It read thus: *Jane Sprood And Miss Susan Perk, Detectives*; and Susan Perk had hurried across the street from her modest cottage to see the sign put in place.

"Well, I dare say business is business, Jane Sprood," said Susan Perk, "but seeing my name blazoned to one and all like this makes me feel like poor dear Mother looked when she started to church under her blue-silk parasol, but without her dress-skirt, and her striped tick petticoat coming no lower than her knees, if that. Never did I expect to see my name made a sight for the common gaze, although I must say the '*Miss*' removes the sting to that extent. I trust and hope that those who read may think I have some womanly qualities left."

"If it worries you," said Jane Sprood, "Sam Denning can take the sign back and put '*Spinster*' after your name. Sometimes, Susan, I think you're a fool."

"If it comes to that," said Susan Perk, "I dare say I am. Often, when I think I let you talk me into being a detective, Jane Sprood, I am of the same opinion myself."

Never, perhaps, had a human being entered into a partnership more reluctantly than Susan Perk when she joined with Jane Sprood to embark in the detective profession. Only her lifelong friendship for Jane Sprood had finally induced her to agree.

"Susan Perk," Jane Sprood had told her, "I have put up with your gabble and gossip ever since we were girls, and now that you can be of some use to me, I'll not let you back out. Card systems and rogues' galleries I haven't got, nor will I need while I have you; for if there is any scandal you don't know, it's not worth knowing. You are a poor, brainless creature when it comes to common sense, but for information—true and false—I don't know your beat, and you can't go back on me now."

Such was Jane Sprood's influence over Susan Perk that Susan found herself a member of the detective farm in spite of her reluctance. She had objected the less because the concern was to be, as first planned, "Jane Sprood and Associates," Miss Sprood's father and niece Elsie being included; but Elsie Sprood had decided to enter Vassar, and Henry Sprood had recently gone to a better land (as Susan Perk phrased it). Being one of a group of associates had not seemed brazenly daring, but to be a member of the firm of Sprood & Perk, Detectives, set poor Miss Perk quivering and fluttering, for she realized only too well that she did not know even the first simple rudiments of detecting. It might be well enough when the efficient, self-reliant Jane Sprood was at hand, but Miss

Perk trembled when she thought that sometime Jane Sprood might be absent, and a distracted client, accused of murder perhaps, might come to her demanding the solution of his mystery within a few hours.

"What I would do then, Heaven only knows," said Susan Perk, "although I dare say I might talk to him until Jane came back if my breath held out, for goodness knows that's all I could do."

ON THE DAY following the placing of the sign, Jane Sprood got into her light and ill-used motorcar and went to New York. She had important business there, and thought she might remain all night. She stopped to tell Susan Perk.

"I'm sent for," she told her. "To my mind I'm not sent for because I'm a detective, but because I'm a female one, and the party wants to get newspaper advertising out of it—'Famous Female Detective Takes Case in Hand.' But that is nothing to me, Susan Perk. Business is business, whatever the way it comes."

"I'm sure you'll do your best," said Miss Perk. "What is it? I hope it is not a murder, where you will have to paw over a bloody remains. Laying out a decently dead person is no disgrace, Jane Sprood, but oft have I laid awake since you got me into this business, dreading I'd be called upon to turn the victim over and find where the dagger was stuck into him. I hope it was no murder."

"What it is, you'll know in good time, Susan," said Jane Sprood, "but not now. Better you should not know. If you got an ear to talk into, you'd keep the secret about as secret as Dr. Cook kept his voyage to the North Pole. What you don't know, you won't tell—which is more than can be said for him."

Hardly had Jane Sprood disappeared down the street in her dusty car than a young woman paused before the Sprood house, looked at the sign at the side of the door, and climbing the porch steps, rang the bell. Miss Sprood's maid came to the door.

"Miss Sprood? No'm, she ain't in," the maid said. "She's gone and maybe won't be back until to-morrow. Was it something to do with detective business?"

"Well—yes."

"Then I guess you'd better go across the street and see Miss Perk. She's Miss Sprood's partner—like. Maybe," said the maid, "she might help you."

The young woman hesitated. She looked across the street.

"I don't know," she said doubtfully. "You see, I didn't know Miss Sprood was a detective. I came to her for advice, more than anything else, but if she is a detective, now, it might be even better. Is her partner a detective too?"

"Well, as for that," said the maid, "her name's on the sign the same as Miss Sprood's is. It's not for me to judge."

"I think I'll see her, anyway," said the girl doubtfully.

It was evident that the young woman was in no little distress. She was a pretty, rather slight person, of the sort the slangy New Yorker would have described as "Some chicken!" with considerable enthusiasm. She tried, anyone could see, to make the most of her attractions and was not innocent of cosmetics. Her lips were not entirely free from artificial red, and her eyebrows were not exactly as Nature had planned them, and her hair had been given great attention, to say the least. Her neat shoes, silk-clad ankles, slithery silken dress, her furs and hat were all meant to catch the eye, and presumably the male eye. In spite of all this, she had a certain air of self-respecting frankness that indicated she was able to be straight and stay straight. She might have been a manicurist from some high-grade parlor patronized largely by men. One thing was clear; some problem confronted her that was too big for her none too deep mind to cope with unaided.

The girl was Mayette (once plain *Mary*) Spurling, who had been born and reared in Westcote. In her trouble she had remembered Jane Sprood and had come to ask advice of that woman's sound common sense. She crossed the street to visit Susan Perk, but with far less hopefulness than she had pushed the bell-button beside Jane Sprood's door. She had made a bluff at bravery when approaching Jane Sprood's door, but she was frightened, now that she was to face an unknown detective. She was not, however, half as frightened as Susan Perk was when she opened the door and guessed that a "case" had actually come to consult her.

"My goodness gracious sakes alive!" she exclaimed, fluttering like an aspen-leaf. "Why, yes'm, I'm the Susan Perk you're looking for, and I do hope you've not come to ask me to turn over bloody corpses, looking for dagger-holes, because I'll tell you plain and straight I don't hanker for it. No ma'am!"

"This is about money," said Mayette Spurling.

Miss Perk looked at her visitor keenly.

"Stolen money?" asked Miss Perk, thrilling in spite of herself. "My lands, I do wish Jane Sprood was here! Well, I dare say I've got to do the best I can for you, poor child! Who stole it? Well, of course you don't know that, or you wouldn't be here, would you?"

"It—it was not stolen," said Mayette with hesitancy. She had taken off her gloves, and now she began twisting and untwisting them nervously. "I—I shouldn't have come to you. I think I'll go. I—"

She bent her head.

"Miss Perk," she said, looking up suddenly, as if she had made a resolution, "I wanted to ask Miss Sprood's advice and—borrow some money from her if she would lend it to me! I—it was foolish of me, but when I found she was not home, I thought perhaps I dared ask her partner. But I see now I have no right—"

"How much is it?" asked Susan Perk. "I don't say I'm rich, like some folks, but I'm not a pauper."

"It is one hundred dollars," said Mayette.

"Land of mercy!" cried Miss Perk. "One hundred dollars! Did you lose it?"

"No," said Mayette. "No, not just that. I spoiled it, Miss Perk."

For a moment or two she twisted her gloves. It was evident she was greatly agitated.

"I spoiled it, and I am afraid to tell," she said with a rush of words. "It was money I had to account for—had to give back; and now I can't do it. They'll think I'm lying if I tell the truth; they'll think I stole it."

She fumbled in her handbag and brought out a soggy wad of manila wrapping-paper as large as a walnut. Nervously she removed the wet wrapper and disclosed a smaller wet wad of a greenish-gray pulp. Miss Perk took this in her hand and examined it closely. Here and there through the mass were short, colored silk threads.

"And that," said Mayette tragically, "is all that is left of one hundred dollars."

"'Tain't much," agreed Miss Perk. "How come it this way?"

"Have you any money—paper money—in the house?" asked Mayette.

"Not what you would call much," said Susan Perk suspiciously, "and what I've got I aim to keep."

The young woman made a hopeless gesture.

"I'm not asking for it," she said. "I only want you to look at it. Will you do that for me, please? Just look at it?"

"Well, I might do that," said Miss Perk, "if I knew what good it would do any living soul."

"It will help prove that I am telling the truth," said the girl earnestly.

"I'll look at it," said Susan, and she disappeared. When she returned, she had her purse; from it she took a number of bills.

"Do you see anything peculiar about the money, Miss Perk?" asked Mayette, and Susan examined the bills closely. She handled them daintily, with the tips of her fingers,

"I ain't a money-expert," she said, "and unless the picture of G. Washington was printed upside down, or something like that, I wouldn't know if they was counterfeit or not. About all I can notice is that dirtier money I never handled in my born days, and it's a wonder folks don't get diseases from such filthy stuff. Filthy lucre this money is, if ever there was filthy lucre."

"You see!" exclaimed Miss Spurling eagerly. "Even you noticed that the very first thing!"

"Well, I'm a detective," said Miss Perk. "Maybe that accounts for it."

"Oh, no! I'm sure it doesn't," said Miss Spurling. "You just noticed it. And now, Miss Perk, won't you please wash one of those bills—wash it carefully, and let it dry?"

"Good lands!" exclaimed Susan Perk, but she let herself be persuaded. Miss Spurling went with her.

It does not take long to wash and dry a dollar bill. Miss Perk, in a few minutes, having dried the bill in a towel and then let it wave above the hot-air register, had a neatly washed and dried bill in her hand.

"And now," said Miss Spurling, "your bill is nice and clean, but if you look at it closely, you'll see that the creases still show, and that the black engraving on it is grayed. Just compare it with this bill, Miss Perk."

She took a crisp, sharp dollar-bill from her hand-bag. The difference was very apparent. The one was plainly a washed-out bill; the other appeared to be a crisp new bill just from the mint.

"Miss Perk," said the girl, "before the war I had a nice little business of my own, and I was getting along very nicely. I bought and sold old hand-made lace in a small way, but that was the least of my business. Cleaning rare and delicate old laces was my money-maker. The best people—the Vandergoulds, the Osterbilts, everyone—intrusted their old lace to me, priceless lace so old and delicate that it seemed a breath might destroy it, and I cleaned it. Then the war came."

"So I've heard," said Miss Perk.

"Yes, and in a day my business ended. No one thought of old lace or of having it cleaned. My little shop was ruined, and I lost all I had saved. It was pretty hard, Miss Perk. I thought I was done for. Then I thought of my new business."

"What's it?" asked Susan Perk.

"I am a money-laundress," said Miss Spurling. "You thought this bill I showed you was new money. It is old money. It was dirtier than the bill you washed. It is because I had learned the highest form of laundry art while cleaning lace that I am able to launder money and render it absolutely equal to new."

"Well, if you ask me," said Susan. "I'd say it was a mighty poor business to be in. So far as has come to my notice, folks is just as willing to take money dirty as money clean."

"But that is where my city knowledge came in," said Miss Spurling. "Do you know that many of the big hotels never give any bills in change except mint-new bills? Especially in their restaurants and dining-rooms? Imagine, Miss Perk, a refined lady like Mrs. Vandergould, eating dinner at the Orocourt Hotel and receiving on a golden plate her change in filthy bills such as you have in your purse! It would nauseate her. She would never go there again. It is estimated, Miss Perk that when the shortage of new money began this winter, and new bills were not to be had, the patronage of the really swell hotels fell off eighteen per cent. Nice people simply would not dine out; they dined at home. Hotels like the Orocourt were especially hard hit. I knew this, Miss Perk. And I knew I could launder the worst money so it would look and feel like new."

"Saints alive, and did you, now!" exclaimed Miss Perk.

"So I went to the manager of the Orocourt Hotel, and made an arrangement with him to launder all his money," continued Miss Spurling. "I have laundered thousands and hundreds of thousands of dollars for him. He gave me a room in the hotel, fitted it with a small porcelain washtub; with electric irons. I chose an inside room without a window and without a door. Some days I had eighty thousand dollars in that room at one time."

"Goodness!" exclaimed Miss Perk.

"The Orocourt had crisp 'new' money when no other hotel had it. The restaurant receipts ran thirty-seven per cent above normal. Nice people went there and dined just to get the clean, 'new' money in change. And the secret of my success, Miss Perk, was toluardorol. I suppose you never heard of it."

"Never in my born days," said Miss Perk.

"It is the new chemical used for etching glass," explained Miss Spurling. "It is so powerful that one drop spilled on a glass plate set on a mahogany table will eat a hole through the plate, through the table and halfway through the floor underneath. No one has ever dared to think of it for laundry work, but I dared. My secret was to dilute it. I used one drop of toluardorol to three quarts of water. Two drops is too much. One drop in three quarts of water will clean delicate old lace without damaging it; one drop in three quarts of water makes a solution of such strength that a filthy piece of paper money that is allowed to remain in it three minutes comes out spotlessly clean, but without injury. It removes the dirt, kills the germs and restores mint-crispness. It makes the old bill look like a new one. Even bankers cannot detect the difference."

Miss Spurling paused and looked at Susan Perk's face.

"Well, I don't see what that has to do with losing one hundred dollars and folks' thinking you stole it," said Susan Perk; and Miss Spurling, who had reached for her handbag, drew back her hand.

"I was coming to that," she said.

"Being a detective," said Miss Perk, "I hoped you would."

As a matter of fact, Miss Perk, now that her first fright was over, was enjoying the visit of her first client exceedingly. She felt a sharpening of all her senses. Like a true detective she had sorted and arranged all Miss Spurling had told her, and she was keen to hear the further details so that she might sort and arrange them, too, and thus construct a perfect whole.

"I am glad you are interested," said Mayette. "It makes it easier. So first I must tell you, Miss Perk, that because of the immense amount of money-laundering I have to do at the Orocourt I had to hire an assistant—a colored girl named Rosaline. I had the utmost faith in her honesty."

"Humph " said Miss Perk, as if she doubted the honesty.

"Rosaline irons the money for me," explained Mayette, "and I have never missed so much as one dollar-bill since I have had her, until to-day. In fact, I do not believe she could have had anything to do with my trouble. And neither could Augustus."

"Who is Augustus?" asked Miss Perk. "I never did like the name."

"He is my fiancé," said Miss Spurling. "At least, I think we are engaged. He has never spoken. But oh, Miss Perk, he is such a lovely man!"

"Well, for my part," said Miss Perk, "for lovely men I never had any use. What does he do for a living?"

"He—he helps at a dance-palace," said Miss Spurling, but with some reluctance. "He dances with ladies when there are not enough other men."

"Do you mean to tell me this Augustus man is what folks call a lounge-lizard?" asked Miss Perk.

"They have no right—" began Mayette, but Miss Perk would not let her finish.

"Well, I have my opinion of your Augustus!" she said. "Go on."

"You have no right to suspect him of anything whatever," said Mayette with considerable spirit. "I would trust him with all the money in the world. And anyway, he let the house-detective search him before he left the room."

"What room?" asked Miss Perk excitedly.

"My laundry-room," said Mayette. "He just dropped in from his room next door to ask me if I would take supper with him at a cabaret to-night. Rosaline was there, and she will tell you the same. He was almost broken-hearted when he saw what he had done, and he was the very first one to think I might be suspected of something wrong. It was Augustus, Miss Perk, who asked—asked, you understand—to have the house-detective search all of us."

"Well, I dare say it was noble and grand of him," said Miss Perk, "but I'd know more about it if you told me what it was all about. Jane Sprood says a good detective don't make up her mind at once and in the beginning, but if there's any crooked work been done, I will say here and now I don't take any stock in a lounge-lizard that a girl don't know whether she is engaged to or not and comes snooping into a money-laundry to ask her if she will go to one of them miserable cabaret shows that, from all I hear of them, ain't no better than they should be. Go on!"

Miss Spurling seemed abashed by this.

"Do you really think Augustus could— But I can't believe it! Only—"

"Only what?"

"You are a detective and know human nature," said Miss Spurling.

"It's my business to, now that Jane Sprood has got me hitched up to her, anyway," said Miss Perk. "And human nature I do know, if I do say it myself, for if there's anything mean in mortal life, it's human nature. Go on."

"Well, Miss Perk," said Mayette, "this morning I stopped at the cashier's desk at the Orocourt, and he gave me the soiled-money wash for the day. It is always done up in thousand-dollar bundles, and before I give him a receipt for it, I count the money. It was just the amount he said it was, this morning. I took the money to my laundry-room, where Rosaline was waiting for me, and we began work."

"Washing the money?"

"Washing and ironing it. And first I locked the door, because I can't take a chance of anyone's coming in. It is too dangerous. So I locked the door and opened the first bundle of money. I wash only a little at a time. I let three quarts of hot water run into the small porcelain washtub, and then take my bottle of toluardorol from the glass shelf above the washtub and drop just one drop into the water. Then I put eight or ten bills into the water and let them soak for a few minutes. They are then clean, and I take them out and give them to Rosaline to iron. Her ironing-board is at the opposite side of the room. While she is ironing one batch, I wash the next, and so on."

"Yes. Go on!"

"I had washed about nine thousand dollars this morning," said Mayette, "when Augustus knocked at the door. I let him in, and he talked a few minutes and asked me to go to the cabaret. I had the tag end of a bundle of ten-dollar bills on the table by the ironing board, and the next bundle was thousand-dollar bills. It was the first time Augustus had seen me at work, and I said: 'Gussie, I'll show you how I wash ten thousand dollars in one batch, the most valuable tub of wash you ever saw.'"

Miss Perk was sitting on the edge of her chair now, keen with excitement.

"Ten thousand dollars!" she breathed.

"Yes, I meant to put ten of the big bills in the tub," said Mayette. "I crossed the room and let three quarts of hot water run into the tub, and dropped one drop of toluardorol in it. I put the stopper into the bottle and set the bottle on the glass shelf above the tub. Then I went to the table for the bills. Rosaline was ironing the last batch. Augustus was standing by the tub. When I got to the table, some trick of routine made me decide to finish the ten-dollar bills before I opened the thousand-dollar bundle, and I took the ten bills and carried them to the tub and plunged them into the toluardorol water. Then I walked over to Rosaline. The next moment I heard an exclamation of horror from Augustus."

"My sakes!" exclaimed Miss Perk. "What was it?"

"He had dropped the bottle of toluardorol, and its entire contents had spilled in the tub! I knew better than to put my hand in the water. I rushed to the other side of the room for a small ladle I sometimes used, but when I reached the tub again, I was too late. The ten ten-dollar bills were pulp—the pulp you see there!"

"Goodness gracious mercy sakes!" exclaimed Miss Perk.

"I scraped up the pulp with the ladle," said Miss Spurling, "but—you can see it no longer resembles money. 'Augustus! Augustus!' I cried. 'What have you done!'

"'Ten thousand dollars destroyed!' he cried.

"I was too excited to think of the amount or to correct him. To me one hundred dollars was as impossible to replace as ten thousand would have been. I was distracted. It was Augustus who then thought of the house-detective.

"'You must call the house-detective,' he said, 'and have us all searched.'

"'Why?' I asked him.

"'Why?' he replied. 'Because no one as suspicious as these hotel people will ever believe this was an accident. Look at it as they will: they gave you money, and you say a bottle broke, and the money turned to pulp. Will they believe that? Not unless they are sure you have not taken the money and substituted a lot of old paper pulp in its place.'

"I saw he was right. I might have done that very thing."

"Aha!" said Miss Perk. "Pretty slick, that lounge-lizard!"

"What do you mean?"

"He took that money out and put the pulp in," said Miss Perk.

"No," said Miss Spurling, "because the house-detective did come, and he did search all and every one of us, and every nook and cranny of the room. There was no money hidden. That is positive. 'Just the same, May,' he said to me, 'the house won't believe it. The house will think you got away with it.' So that is why I came to Jane Sprood. It is why I came to you. Oh, Miss Perk, if you will lend me one hundred dollars, so my loss need never be known to the hotel, I will revere you forever. I will pay you back ten dollars a week. Otherwise I will be branded a thief, and my money-laundry work is killed forever."

"Humph!" she said. "The way some folks is taken in by a nice-spoken man beats all! They dazzle and deceive. Thank my stars, I never had use for any man, young or old. Miss Spurling, it's plain to see you've been made a fool of, but Susan Perk don't mean to sit by and see a Gussie lounge-lizard do and deceive a member of her sex. Many a time I've said to Jane Sprood: 'Sorry the day I took upon myself to be a detective!' But I'll say different now. That Augustus lounge-lizard got that money!"

"Miss Perk!"

"I do say and I so mean," said Susan. "Ten thousand dollars he thought it was, and ten thousand dollars he meant to see in that tub before ever he left that room. Ten thousand dollars he thought he was getting, and little he cares if you go to jail for it! Never did I expect to take a case of detecting on my own hook, Miss Spurling, but rout that Augustus lounge-lizard out I mean to do! I hate and despise the very breed!"

"But that will do me no good," said Miss Spurling. "Unless I have the hundred dollars to-night when I return the rest of the money, I will be branded as a thief."

"That's not my affair," said Susan.

Mayette Spurling looked up and then looked down.

"Miss Perk," she said, "I'll be glad to have you take this case as a detective, whatever the outcome may be, but what good will it do to have Augustus put in jail if my business is ruined? Here!"

She took from the hand-bag a small bottle of colorless liquid.

"What's that?" asked Miss Perk.

"It is toluardorol," said Miss Spurling. "It is the last bottle of it in America, and no more can be imported until the enemy-trading laws are repealed. It is worth five hundred dollars, Miss Perk, and it is by the use of it, alone, that I can continue my money-laundry. Miss Perk, let me have one hundred dollars, only until tomorrow, and I will be saved."

Miss Perk took the bottle in a gingerly grasp and considered it.

"To my notion," she said, "that Augustus lounge-lizard got your money. I'm no such detective as Jane Sprood is, but I've got some brains, I do hope and believe. Was there a plug in the bottom of that tub to let the money run out?"

"Of course, Miss Perk."

"Very well," said Susan Perk triumphantly. "That's where your money went, to my notion. Augustus lounge-lizard lifted the plug and let the bills go down the pipe, and put the plug back and put a handful of pulp in the tub. That's what happened—mark my word!"

Miss Spurling stared at Susan Perk in amazement.

"It might be!" she breathed. "I don't know where the waste-pipe goes. It might go through Augustus' room."

"It does, I'll warrant that," said Susan Perk. "Well, I'll show Jane Sprood she's not the only brain in this detective firm. I'll let you have one hundred dollars until to-morrow, young lady, but when I come to that Orocourt Hotel to-morrow, to finish up this case, I want the money back. And I'll just keep this toluardorol until I do get it back."

"But be careful with it," urged Mayette Spurling. "My business depends on it."

"Careful I will be," said Susan Perk, and careful she was.

AN HOUR AFTER the departure of Mayette Spurling, Jane Sprood, after stopping at her own home, drove her noisy little car to the door of Susan Perk's cottage and leaped out. She slammed the car door and strode up the walk, knocking on the door with her gloved knuckles. Miss Perk, all aflutter with excitement, admitted her.

"Who came?" demanded Jane Sprood. "I hope, if it was somebody wanting detective work, you told them to come back."

"I did better than that, Jane," said Susan. "I fixed it. I took the case."

"Well, I hope you didn't make a fool of us," said Jane Sprood, "although that is almost too much to hope. What and who was it?"

Excitedly Susan Perk told Jane Sprood the whole story of the money-laundress and the disintegrated bills.

"Humph!" said Jane Sprood when Miss Perk had ended her recital. "You needn't expect me to give you back half of that hundred dollars, Susan Perk, even if we are partners. Maybe it will teach you to have some sense."

"What do you mean, Jane?" asked Susan, growing pale.

"I mean this folderol about toluardorol and all," said Jane Sprood. "You've been took in; that's what I mean."

"I made her leave the toluardorol with me, Jane," said Suzan. "Here it is."

"Yes," said Jane Sprood. "Toluardorol! It is so powerful that one drop would eat a hole in a glass plate, is it? How do you keep it in that glass bottle then, I'd like to know?"

"Land sakes!" exclaimed Susan Perk. Miss Sprood took the bottle, drew the cork and sniffed the liquid.

"Plain water!" she said. "Before you gave that money to that woman, why didn't you telephone to the hotel and find out whether there was such a person as a money-laundress? If you had a mite of sense, Susan Perk, you would have telephoned to the hotel detective to find out if there was any truth in the whole story. To my notion you've been stung!"

Susan Perk took the toluardorol bottle.

"It does smell like plain water," she admitted, "but that's no proof the poor creature ain't a money-laundress and in sad trouble. You think yourself mighty wise, Jane Sprood, but you would be surprised if I went to the Orocourt Hotel to-morrow and found all as Mayette Spurling said it was."

"I would indeed, Susan Perk," said Jane Sprood, "and the reason is that I ate my lunch with the money-laundress of the Orocourt

Hotel not two hours ago, and her name is Sarah Pettingill, and she is sixty-four years old and has a husband in Brazil. Now I suppose I'll have to catch the lady that buncoed you!"

For a full minute Susan Perk said nothing. Then she thrust the bottle of toluardorol at Jane Sprood.

"Here's your clue!" she said spitefully. "Take it! I don't want it!"

IV

ON SUSPICION

Detective Jane Sprood opened her front door herself in order to save time, for she knew that Susan Perk, who had just hurried across the street, would take more than enough when she began talking, and Miss Sprood was about to go out. Her paintless flivver—known in Westcote as Jane Sprood's Jazz Band—stood at the curb, waiting to be cranked, its sides camouflaged with splotches of reddish rust, and a long tongue of loose rubber hanging from one wheel where the tread of the shoe had peeled from its under-fabric. This injury to the tire had occurred only this morning, adding a rapid, melodious *flap-flap-flap-flap* to the other noises of Jane Sprood's Jazz Band when it was in motion.

As a vehicle for a detective Jane Sprood's Jazz Band had one good quality and one bad one: it never failed to carry Jane Sprood where she wanted to go, but it made so much noise that people in Westcote said, "If Jane Sprood wanted to sneak up on a criminal, she'd have to pick up that automobile of hers and carry it." This was not exaggeration. I myself have said, more than once: "If Jane Sprood wants to sneak up on a criminal, she'll have to carry that tin Liz of hers under her arm, wrapped in an old shawl." My meaning was that if she did not wrap it in something soundproof it would rattle like a fistful of glass marbles in a baking-powder can.

The fact that the so-called automobile stood at the curb was evidence that Miss Sprood meant to go forth on some detective mission, for she never used the car when on ordinary journeys

to and fro, because it was such a jolty car. As poor, stiff-backed
Susan Perk put it, "It jounces a body."

By "stiff-backed" I do not mean that Susan Perk suffered from
curvature of the spine, hardening of the joints of the spinal column, or anything to excite your pity. She was stiff-backed in the
meaning of perpendicularity and thinness, her general architec-
tural scheme being that of a lead pencil, but with a larger nose.
When seated in Jane Sprood's car, Miss Perk was, from the base of
her spine to the base of her brain, a straight line, and every whack
of the wheels of the car on the stones of the road ran up her spine
and thumped her brain. After a short ride in Jane Sprood's Jazz
Band Miss Perk's brain felt as if it had been spanked from below
by a rapidly repeating brain-spanker.

Jane Sprood, grim-jawed, efficient and relentless, was therefore surprised to see Miss Perk appear at her door since, by ap-
pearing at such a moment, Miss Perk opened herself to the danger
of being asked to accompany Miss Sprood. Although Jane Sprood
was a rather large and cruel-looking woman, with mannish clothes
and a hat that might have been taken for a discarded bird-nest,
Susan Perk (who was thin and unmarried) was no less a detective.
The sign on Jane Sprood's door—"Jane Sprood and Miss Susan
Perk, Detectives"—was proof of this. By coming across the street
just as Jane Sprood was drawing on her driving gloves, Susan Perk
seemed to invite a jouncy ride in the flivver. It was quite as much
Susan Perk's duty to hunt criminals as it was the duty and pleasure of Jane Sprood.

Since Jane Sprood and Susan Perk had embarked upon the
detective profession, they had become nationally famous and, indeed, had deserved to become so, for they had made some remarkable captures and had solved some almost unsolvable mysteries.
In all of these Miss Perk had taken quite as much part as was taken
by Jane Sprood herself, but for a week or more now Susan Perk
had asked to be excused temporarily from such labors.

"Goodness knows, Jane Sprood, I'm not one to shirk," she said
to her partner, "nor have, although unladylike this detective work
I do, and must, call, as I have many times told you, and will again
so tell, if the Lord preserves my health so to do."

"Well, what is it? What do you want this time, Susan Perk?" Jane Sprood asked. "Can't you ever learn to ask for what you want without telling me the history of the world from Eve to everlasting?"

"Unladylike I call it, whether it is biting a burglar or strapping a revolver on the calf of my limb, which to you seems less than nothing, if not an actual pleasure, you being so constituted and having, as I will say for you, Jane Sprood, an ankle that you need not be ashamed of, mine being otherwise."

"Fiddlesticks!" said Jane Sprood.

"If you so wish to call them," said Susan Perk rather resentfully, "I have no way to prevent your so doing, although I have always found them perfectly serviceable, not needing them to support a grand piano. Ankles are not all, Jane Sprood!" she added tartly.

"My stars!" exclaimed Jane Sprood. "Did anyone ever see such a woman! Susan Perk, you are enough to drive me crazy! I have not said ten words to you, and here you are all riled up and fighting like cats and dogs over a pair of legs that nobody has mentioned but you! What do you want of me? If you came over to get me to say you are a Venus Adonis, or whatever the name is, I won't!"

Miss Perk was somewhat surprised by this return attack. She often talked herself so far from the idea originally in her mind that even she was amazed when she discovered how far she had traveled.

"Why, Jane!" she said. "Jane, I only asked you—"

"You asked me nothing, Susan Perk," Jane Sprood said. "If you wish to ask, ask! Don't go chasing yourself to Beersheba and back like a—like a centipede!"

It appeared, when Miss Perk was thus nailed down to a simple statement, that she desired to be omitted from any detective plans Miss Sprood might have on hand for immediate attention.

"For you know as well as I do, or should, that when a person's mother's second cousin's only son, even if from a place no better than Billtown, Iowa, as I dare say it may be, although I have no means of knowing," said Susan Perk to Jane Sprood, "still, even if it is, her duty remains the same."

"Whose duty remains what same?" asked Jane.

"My duty to my relation," said Susan. "To Orlando M. Biddlebury and his sister."

"Never heard of them," said Jane Sprood.

Neither, it seemed, had Susan Perk directly. She had known there were Biddleburys and Kipps and Dolsens in Bill County, Iowa, all more or less related to the Perks, and with all of whom Susan's mother had corresponded rather irregularly. As soon as Susan Perk received the letter from Desdemona Biddlebury, however, she had looked up the family connections in the book her mother had used for such things, and found there were indeed an Orlando and a Desdemona Biddlebury, and that they dwelt on Rural Free Delivery, Route 6, Billtown, Iowa.

With this in mind, it was natural enough to expect that when Orlando and Desdemona felt called to visit New York they should propose a short visit with their somewhat, if not very, distant connection, Susan Perk.

It was for this reason Susan Perk had asked to be excused temporarily from taking part in any mystery solutions, crime detecting or criminal capturing that Jane Sprood might have on hand while the visitors remained, and Jane had granted Miss Perk this favor. For that reason, too, it seemed quite safe for Susan Perk to cross the street, even if Jane Sprood's Jazz Band stood at the curb ready for departure. She was, we may say, temporarily immune from danger of spine shocks. She was on vacation from detective duties. She was not on vacation from her inbred and insatiable curiosity.

"Well, Jane," she said, "I see you're at it again. Land knows it's none of my affair, being at present free from a business I don't like and never did like, but am still a partner of, for which reason I dare say I have a right to know what is going on, if anything, although I have little enough hope you will tell me unless you choose to do so, being so tight-mouthed."

"If you mean you want to know what case I am working on," said Jane Sprood, "there is an easy way to find out. Send that coffin-faced cousin and his goo-goo sister packing, and get back to work."

Miss Perk looked at Jane Sprood resentfully.

"Goo-goo the sister may be, Jane Sprood, although what it means I do not know, unless eyes, but coffin-faced you have no right to say, although Orlando's chin may be too long and flat for beauty, which is no test of manly merit, when you come to that."

"If his face is not shaped like a coffin, what is it shaped like?" asked Jane Sprood with a bitterness that was not usual with her. Miss Perk, thus questioned, defended Mr. Biddlebury's face with the first words that came.

"Handsome is as handsome does," she said.

"Indeed!" said Jane Sprood. "And what, may I ask, Susan Perk, does his face do? All I have seen it do is grin like a monkey."

Susan Perk had seated herself in a leather chair. She sat on the extreme edge, for sinking back comfortably into the depths of a chair had, to her mind, something immoral in it. Now she folded her arms across her stomach and looked Jane Sprood in the eye.

"Jealous!" she said.

Jane Sprood put up her hand and gave her hat a whack. It sent the hat over one eye, giving her a dangerous, piratical look.

"Fiddlesticks, Susan Perk!" she said.

"If not, what?" asked Susan.

Jane Sprood looked at her partner steadily for a few moments.

"Susan Perk," she said finally, "there are times when I wonder whether you have a single gill of brains in your head, and there are times when I know you have not. This is one of them."

And with that she went out of the room and out of the house. She strode to her car, gave the crank a mighty whirl, climbed into the car and drove angrily down the street. When the rattle of the car had faded in the far distance, Miss Perk tossed her head.

"Well!" she exclaimed angrily, and she went across the street again.

Orlando Biddlebury was resting comfortably in a hammock in the shade created on the front porch by the climbing vines. He had a magazine in his hand, and as Susan appeared, he yawned and tossed it to the foot of the hammock. He let his vast feet come slowly to the porch floor and straightened his long body to a sitting posture.

"Well, Susan?" he queried.

He had long since begun to call her Susan.

Miss Perk seated herself in a porch chair. She was agitated. Mr. Biddlebury reached out one of his huge, hairy paws and took one of her hands.

"Did that old she-bear claw ye?" he asked soothingly.

"Outrageous!" said Susan. "Outrageous is the only name for the treatment I have received, Orlando, and, as you well know, I am not one to speak harshly of man, woman or beast, being otherwise brought up. But outrageous I was treated and outrageous I will say!"

"She spoke to you like that, did she? Drat her!" Orlando said angrily. "You wait till I get face to face with that fine lady, Susan. I'll outrageous her. I'll give her a piece of my mind she won't forget! Now, don't you go and cry—"

Miss Perk had had no thought of crying, but since he mentioned it, she dabbed her eyes with a handkerchief, using her free hand.

"There! There!" he said, patting the hand he held. "It ain't right you should be hitched up with no such she-bear. If you say the word, Susan, drat me if I don't get right out of this hammick and go over and scratch your name off that sign. Drat me if I don't! If you say the word!"

"Friends from childhood," said Susan Perk woefully, for being comforted intensified her feeling of injustice. "Friends Jane Sprood and me have been from childhood, Orlando, and could be yet but for her manner of brutality, than which a more so I have never seen, hard as the world is in general to a person alone and unmarried—"

"But you won't be long," said Orlando. "Not if I have my say-so."

"Alone and unmarried," continued Susan Perk dolefully, "although I may say, and those who say different do not tell the truth, I've had chances in plenty."

"I'll bet you have," said Orlando. "All that I can't understand is how it comes some of them even didn't just up and force you to marry them. That's all I can't understand. No spunk; that's what ailed them."

"There wasn't any of them as—as spunky as you are, Orlando."

"I bet you!" said Orlando, rising. "Spunk's my motto, Susan. I wonder if you've got a hunk of that gingerbread nobody wants. I get so blamed hungry when you ain't right here where I can look at you, Susan."

"You flatterer!" Susan simpered, and went into the house to get a plate of her famous gingerbread.

It was wonderful gingerbread, thick, lightly porous, stickily glistening on top and fragrant with an appetizing fragrance. Orlando Biddlebury was passionately fond of it, so fond of it that every day the enticing odor of freshly baked gingerbread permeated the house. He liked it best when fresh, and that may have been why he ate all there was every day. He was sure, then, to have it fresh the next day.

As he stood beside the hammock, looking through the vines at the street, Orlando Biddlebury was no common stature of a man. He was very close to seven feet tall and something like eighteen inches more had been turned under to make his feet. His feet were enormous. They were not only long but wide, and, judged by his shoes, they were thick.

His hands were huge, too. If one looked at his hands or feet one would reckon him a powerful man, but looking him up and down, one lost this impression. A full view of him suggested, for some reason, a tall, fatigued sheep. He was, probably, the laziest-looking man in the world. When he moved, he seemed too lazy to lift his big hands and great feet, and all his actions suggested a sufferer from the worst form of permanent ague. A glance at his face was disillusioning, too. It was a flabby, coffin-shaped face, with a long, flat, weak chin and pale, watery eyes.

Orlando had been thin from top to toe when he reached the home of Susan Perk but the good feeding he was receiving there was beginning to show, especially under his vest, for he was expanded in the manner of a serpent that has swallowed a rabbit.

Desdemona Biddlebury, of the goo-goo eyes, was far livelier.

"While I'm near New York, I'm going to see New York," she had said, and she wasted little time at Susan's.

"New York ain't nothing to me," Orlando had said. "I'm all tired out, and I'm going to rest up while I have the chance."

In this, which might have been truthful enough, for rest he certainly did, he was not entirely free from guile. Desdemona seemed to know, instinctively, and with a sister's keenness, that Susan Perk had "intentions" toward Orlando.

"She's that way," Orlando told Susan. "She's jealous-like. The first sign of anything, she'll snatch me back to Iowa quick as a wink."

For this reason the courtship of

Orlando Biddlebury and Susan Perk was conducted sub rosa. There was no holding of hands or passing of fond glances when Desdemona was about. Then one might have taken Orlando and Susan for strangers or, at the worst, newly met distant cousins. For Susan this added to the piquancy of the courtship. It cannot be said it added piquancy of any sort to Orlando. He was about as piquant as a piece of wet leather. He was as snappy as a cold buckwheat cake. Orlando had, at the best, just about as much fervor as a dead clam.

"That Miss Sprood," he drawled, when Susan returned with a plate of gingerbread, "ain't no fit companion for a person that's going to be Mrs. Orlando Biddlebury."

Susan put down the plate hastily. Her heart actually stood still. Although Orlando's back was still toward her and he still looked out at the street, this was the supreme moment of her life. Not before this had Orlando spoken so plainly. Although he had shown his affection in many ways, he had not before said in plain words that he intended marriage. Having stopped for one or two beats, Miss Perk's heart beat with tremendous rapidity.

Susan liked his masterful way of speaking of her as if she had already consented to be his wife. It was not namby-pamby trifling such as might be indulged in by boys and girls. Both she and Orlando were old enough to know their own minds; that was certain.

"You know best, Orlando," she said weakly.

"You keep away from her," he said, turning and picking up a thick chunk of gingerbread. "I won't have the wife I'm going to be married to insulted right and left. It ain't fitting."

Susan Perk was proud at that moment.

"Orlando," she said softly—for a woman ever loves to make tests of love—"are you sure you want to marry me?"

"I'm sure of one thing," he said in a tone that sent a thrill of joy through Susan's being; "I'm sure I'm going to. And if that don't prove it, I don't know what does. And I ain't going to shilly-shally like a moon-calf, either. Matter of fact," he said, biting into the gingerbread, "it won't do to."

"No, Orlando?" queried Susan weakly.

"It won't," he mumbled, for his mouth was as full as Miss Susan's heart. "Jealous, that's what Desdemona is. Naggin' me to go away from here."

"The spite-cat!" said Susan.

"I guess so," said Orlando. "Anyway, that's how it is. What I'd like," he continued, "would be a swell wedding—all the neighbors in, and everything; but there wouldn't be any wedding. You don't know Desdemona like I do. She's a terror when she gets up on her hind legs. Claws and bites, yells and raves. There's only one thing to do. We got to elope."

Another delicious thrill passed through Susan. Elope!

"Do—do you think so, Orlando?" she asked.

"Know so," he said. "And to-morrow's the time. We'll take the noon train to New York, get married in Jersey and sort of disappear until Desdemona quiets down a mite or two. Twelve-fourteen."

"Don't you want to kiss me, Orlando?" asked Susan.

"Well, I don't mind," he answered, and he did.

When Susan was released from his arms, she went into the house to get together the few things she would be able to take on the hurried wedding trip, for it was also necessary for her to go to the bank to draw some money. Orlando had advised this.

"If you've got it to spare," he told her, "you'd better get a thousand—or maybe two thousand dollars, if you've got it, Susan. Not but what I've got plenty myself, being what you might call well-off My farm out of Billtown ain't worth a cent less than forty thousand. And I've got cash right here."

He slapped his pocket   He did more than that. He drew front his pocket a great roll of greenbacks and yellowbacks. There seemed to be hundreds, if not thousands, of dollars in the roll.

"I got plenty, you see," he drawled, "but I got to throw Desdemona off the scent, as you may say. I got to get her entirely unsuspicious for to-morrow. I'm going to give her all this money to keep for me. Going to give it to her to-night and say: 'Desdemona, you keep this cash awhile. I ain't going to need it soon.' Then she won't think suspicious."

"Will she give it back?" asked Susan.

Orlando laughed.

"When she gets over being huffed, she's got to give it back," he said, and that seemed reasonable.

At five o'clock that afternoon, when Susan Perk was in her kitchen preparing a dinner for herself and her guests, she heard—far and faint—the rattle of Jane Sprood's approaching automobile. Orlando and Desdemona were on the front porch.

"Jane Sprood won't have much more chance to talk to me like a bear," Susan thought with satisfaction.

She heard Jane Sprood's Jazz Band come to a noisy stop, and instantly, it seemed, there was a scream, a shout, loud voices and a chaos of rough stamping on the Perk porch. Miss Susan ran toward the porch. Midway, she met Jane Sprood coming toward the kitchen,

"It's all over, Susan," said Jane Sprood. "They've got the handcuffs on Orlando."

"On Orlando!" cried Susan Perk.

"And about two hundred and eighty years in the penitentiary is what he'll get," said Jane Sprood grimly, "—that being twenty years per wife for fourteen wives."

"Fourteen wives!"

"Thirteen, is what I should say," said Jane Sprood, always exact; "for the first, I dare say, was legitimate and not a crime in the eyes of the law."

"Thirteen? Thirteen wives? Orlando has—"

"Fourteen he has," said Jane Sprood, "and you can thank me and your stars, Susan Perk, that you are not the fifteenth."

It was not until several days later that Susan Perk was able to hear the whole story of Orlando's perfidy or to learn that Desdemona was in fact his fourteenth and, probably last victim, although he had intended, for purely financial reasons, to make of Susan a fifteenth.

"Land sakes!" said Susan weakly. "And that's the case you were working on all the time, Jane Sprood! However did you find out about him?"

"I went to New York and asked if there was any kind of bigamist or other sort of marrying crook loose in the land," said Jane Sprood. "If so, I had sense enough to know Orlando Biddlebury was the man."

Susan Perk sat straight.

"And him such a nice, innocent-appearing gentleman!" she said. "What in the land ever set you to thinking he was a marrying crook, I'd like to know, Jane Sprood."

"Well, Susan," said Jane Sprood, "I'm not quite a fool. He was making love to you, wasn't he?"

V
THE PSYCHIC HUNCH

SHORTLY AFTER MIDDAY, on June 18, the same being a bright and cheerful day, Jane Sprood's telephone bell rang and Miss Sprood answered it. The famous female detective had been on the point of going down into the village to transact a bit of small business at her bank, and her renowned automobile, known as Jane Sprood's Jazz Band because of its noisiness, stood at the curb. Jane Sprood herself was attired in her usual mannish costume, and her hard-worn hat was jammed on her head.

"Well, what is it?" she called into the receiver with some annoyance. There was no reply, and she jiggled the receiver hook up and down angrily. "Central! Operator! Did anyone call me?" she demanded impatiently. "Do you think I have nothing to do all day but stand here and—"

"Hello! Is that Miss Sprood?" a voice came faintly. "Am I speaking to Miss Jane Sprood, the detective?"

"I'm Jane Sprood. What do you want?"

"Is it the detective speaking?"

"Now listen!" called Jane Sprood. "This is Jane Sprood. I said so once and I don't mean to say it again. This is Jane Sprood, detective, of the firm of Jane Sprood & Miss Susan Perk, detectives, and if you want anything, say so. If you don't, get off the wire. I'm a busy woman and—"

The voice that replied was gentle and mollifying in tone. "I'm sorry to disturb you, Miss Sprood," it said, "but something dreadful has happened. I need your services immediately." Instantly Jane Sprood's manner changed.

"What is it, a murder?" she asked eagerly, for she had not yet had a murder case.

"It may be worse—than that," said the gentle yoke. "Can you come at once? This is Mr. Bradley-Orr speaking—Mr. Augustus Bradley-Orr, 876 Willow Avenue. Will you come at once, please?"

"I'll be there," said Jane Sprood, and she had jammed the receiver on its hook before she had finished the sentence. In another minute she was saying, over the phone:

"Is that you, Susan Perk? Get your hat on; we've got a case. Start immediately. Hurry up."

As a precaution Jane Sprood slipped a dangerous-looking revolver into her skirt pocket. By the time she had turned her car and was at Susan Perk's curb Miss Perk was waiting, in a flutter of excitement. She was as unlike the mannish Miss Sprood as might be, although of the same age. Miss Perk was the sort of well-along-in-years maiden-lady one would more naturally associate with tabby cats and knitting than with detective adventures.

"Have you got your pistol?" asked Jane Sprood abruptly.

"My goodness, no!" exclaimed Susan Perk. "I hope, Jane Sprood, I'm not so foolish, at my time of life, as to meddle with that awful-looking instrument. It is safe where it is, Jane Sprood, and there it shall stay."

"Where is that pistol, Susan Perk?" Jane Sprood demanded.

"Well, if you must know," said Susan Perk, "it is down cellar in a tea-canister, in a garbage pail, in the stone washtub."

"Get it!" said Jane Sprood grimly.

"Now, Jane—"

"Get it!"

Reluctantly Susan Perk entered the house, and when she returned, she had the pistol. It was in the tea canister, which she carried with great care and placed timorously in the automobile.

"Humph!" said Jane Sprood dryly. "A lot of good that will do you if you have to use it suddenly! Where are the bullets?"

She meant, of course, the cartridges.

"In the canister," said Susan Perk.

Miss Sprood picked up the canister and shook it. The rattle of the cartridges and the thumping of the revolver against the sides of the canister assured her that Susan Perk was telling the truth. Although a revolver in a tin canister was not as quickly available as it might be, she felt that no more closely personal association with a dangerous firearm could be expected of Susan Perk in her present stage of development. She would have been less pleased if she had known that Miss Perk had bribed the butcher boy to entwine the revolver in about eight yards of wire to make sure the hammer would not, in some inexplicable way, begin flopping up and down. The wiring had been done so well that even an expert would have required several hours in which to unwrap the wire. But Jane Sprood did not know this. She sent the automobile forward with a jump that made Susan Perk's head jerk backward. Miss Sprood was a self-taught and what may be called a hit-or-miss driver. Sometimes she hit all the rough spots in the road, and sometimes she missed all the smooth ones.

The home of Mr. Bradley-Orr, who was a middle-aged bachelor, stood on the outskirts of the village of Westcote in the general direction of Blackstone, and was a large, old-fashioned house in good repair. It stood in an immense tract of ground, much of which was cut up into flower gardens, in which Mr. Bradley-Orr spent most of his time. When Jane Sprood and Susan Perk walked up the long, neat gravel walk to the front door, the door opened to greet them, and an aged negro manservant received them.

"Misto O'," he said in a tone hardly louder than a whisper, "is a-waitin' fo' you. Kin'ly step dis way."

They entered the parlor, which was huge and high-ceiled, gloomy in its ancient dark paper and chill even on this bright June day, for the blinds were closed. Out of this gloom—for the detectives were still blinded by their entrance from the glaring sunlight— a soft, gentle voice greeted them.

"Ah, Miss Sprood and Miss—"

"Perk—Susan Perk," said Jane Sprood. "She is my partner."

"Much pleased," said Mr. Bradley-Orr, as if he were conducting an afternoon tea rather than merely receiving crime-chasers.

Out of the dusk he now emerged and placed a cool, soft hand in Jane Sprood's. It was so dark in the room that it was only with the greatest difficulty that anything could be seen, but Jane Sprood was sure she was in close proximity to Mr. Bradley-Orr, for there was no doubting the friendly clasp of his hand, and she was quite certain that the white she saw must be his face and his snowy white hair. She had sometimes seen him at work in his garden.

Mr. Bradley-Orr, having taken Miss Sprood's hand, took Miss Perk's hand. Although Miss Sprood did not know it, he took their hands at one and the same time, one in each of his. He held Miss Sprood's hand until she jerked it away.

"Well," she said, making her voice even more rough than it normally was, "you phoned for me, didn't you? What do you want?"

"Ah!" said Mr. Bradley-Orr. "That is it. What do I want!"

"You ought to know; you sent for us," said Jane Sprood in a matter-of-fact tone. "If you don't know, I'll tell you one thing—I'm a busy person."

"Wait!" said Mr. Bradley-Orr.

He drew a small table from the wall to the center of the floor and placed three small chairs around it.

"Be seated, please, ladies," he urged. "You will pardon me if I close my eyes. May I take your hand?"

"No," said Jane Sprood flatly, "you may not."

For a moment Mr. Bradley-Orr was silent.

"I hoped," he said gently, "you might bear with me to that extent, considering the very remarkable mystery that I hope to ask you to solve. I hoped—I more than hoped—I should not have to tell you. I hoped you would, with me, feel it. Are you, either of you, psychic?"

"Great stars!" exclaimed Susan Perk, nearly jumping out of her chair. "What do you want us to do? See ghosts?"

"Be still, Susan," said Jane Sprood. "Don't be a fool. There are no ghosts."

"If you will not clasp hands with me," said Mr. Bradley-Orr in his gentle voice, "let us sit still. Perhaps you may feel it."

Susan Perk moved uneasily.

"Sit still, Susan," said Jane Sprood. "Who knows what this will lead to? Remember, you are a detective. This may seem strange to you, Susan, but we may have far stranger experiences before our careers are ended. —If you told us what you expected us to feel," she added, to Mr. Bradley-Orr, "we might come closer to feeling it."

"Mystery," said Mr. Bradley-Orr in an awed voice, "a sense of mystery and crime; a feeling of undiscovered crime close at hand. It comes to me again and again. I do not know what it is or where it is, but it seems close at hand. There!"

He uttered the last word so suddenly and unexpectedly that Susan Perk gave forth a little squeal of fright.

"Did you feel it? Did you sense it?" asked Mr. Bradley-Orr eagerly. "It came to me then, again. Ah! Now! Now!"

He drew a deep, quivering breath and lay back in his chair. Jane Sprood could see, now that her eyes were somewhat accustomed to the darkness, that his eyes were closed. His chest rose and fell with the gasping for breath. A look of horror spread over his face.

"See it! See it!" he cried. "It *is* a murder. It *is* a corpse!"

There was something startlingly convincing in his voice. When he spoke, it seemed that he did indeed see a corpse. Jane Sprood leaned forward and kept her eyes on his face. Susan Perk was frozen with fear.

"It comes like that," said Mr. Bradley-Orr, opening his eyes. "It grows stronger each time. Never before did I see the corpse— heretofore it has been only a sense of crime committed. This time I saw the body. It was a dead body."

"Let's go," said Susan Perk nervously.

Jane Sprood settled herself more comfortably in her chair.

"Go, nothing!" she said. "Go if you wish, Susan Perk, but I am here and I mean to get to the bottom of this. You may not believe in psychic phenomena except to be scared of them, but as a practicing detective it is my duty to believe more than one thing that I would not believe as a mere human being. Try it again, Mr. Bradley-Orr."

"I don't know that it will happen again," he said. "It does not come when I wish, but when it wishes. But I'll try."

He closed his eyes again. Almost instantly he uttered a cry of horror. He opened his eyes.

"I saw it," whispered Mr. Bradley-Orr in an awed tone. "The corpse! The bleeding corpse. It was—I! I am the corpse!"

"Now," said Jane Sprood in her briskly professional tone, "we are getting somewhere. This is more like it. Susan Perk, did you understand what he said? Far be it from me to say I believe every shilly-shallying tale of ghosts, but such things as premonitions and second-sights do exist. It is well indeed," she said, turning to Mr. Bradley-Orr, "that you sent for us and not for some fool medium. If there is anything in all this, it is a case for a detective. I never expected to detect a murderer for a murder that is not yet committed, but is going to be; but if it can be done, I dare say I can do it. Where were you cut?"

"Cut?" queried Mr. Bradley-Orr.

"You said you were bleeding," said Jane Sprood; "you must have been cut somewhere."

"I did not notice that," said Mr. Bradley-Orr. "If you wish, I will try to find out."

"Do so," said Jane Sprood, and Mr. Bradley-Orr closed his eyes again.

Jane Sprood and Susan Perk watched him eagerly.

"I can see," he said in a dreamy tone. "It is my heart—a knife. It is a knife thrust into my heart."

"Back or front?" asked Jane Sprood.

"Back," said Mr. Bradley-Orr.

"How are you lying?"

"On my side."

"Are you sure you are dead?"

"Yes."

"Where are you? In what place?"

"In my garden."

"What do you see near your dead body?"

"Flowers."

"What kind of flowers?"

"I can't quite see what kind."

"Drat it!" said Jane Sprood with vexation. "Well, what is the knife like?"

"It is a big knife."

"Well, describe it, can't you?"

"It has a wooden handle."

"What sort of a knife is it? Is it a pocketknife? Is it a kitchen knife?"

"I can't quite see."

Jane Sprood was leaning forward eagerly.

"Well, the ground around you—what is that like?"

"Like a flower-bed."

"Is it trampled? Are the flowers trampled down? Are they trampled down as if there had been a struggle there? Are they crushed down as if your body had been dragged down?"

"I wouldn't know how to tell that," said Mr. Bradley-Orr, opening his eyes. "It gets indistinct when I look close. It fades when I look too closely."

"Drat it!" cried Jane Sprood impatiently.

She was now intensely interested in the case. Jane Sprood was no mean believer in the value of advertising, and she saw the fame that would accrue if she were the first to solve an uncommitted murder, using psychic means only. The thing was not impossible. If she could see into the future far enough, as pictured by Mr. Bradley-Orr, to gather a few clues, she and Susan Perk ought to be able to trace back to the murderer. Thus, if the knife-handle bore bloody finger-prints, and she could "see" the finger-prints clearly enough to make out their whorls and lines she might easily trace the would-be murderer. It might be the colored butler, for example. To establish a motive might not be hard.

The great difficulty was, of course, to "see" clearly. The only way in which Jane Sprood could "see" was through the words Mr. Bradley-Orr spoke when in his semi-trance. If these words were gone, all was gone. There was then no murder, no case, nothing.

All that remained was Mr. Bradley-Orr, Jane Sprood and Susan Perk sitting around a small table. It was extremely necessary that Jane Sprood see more clearly into the garden where the corpse of Mr. Bradley-Orr lay. In some way, so to speak, she must put a magnifying glass into the words of Mr. Bradley-Orr so that they might "see" such things as bloody finger-prints, crushed rose-leaves and so on.

"My goodness! Why can't you see more?" she asked.

"I think," said Mr. Bradley-Orr hesitatingly, "it is because the psychic circle is weak. I cannot, alone, supply enough psychic fluid to intensify the psychic optic nerves."

That this was absolute nonsense, Jane Sprood did not know. To those not well acquainted with it, much psychic nomenclature and phrasing sounds like nonsense.

"The psychic fluid created by the psychic circle," said Mr. Bradley-Orr in a suppressed tone, "is like the electric fluid from a storage battery. Perhaps you know something about a storage battery?"

"I have a dry battery in my automobile," said Miss Sprood.

"But, goodness knows, you know little enough about it, to my way of thinking," said Susan Perk.

"An excellent illustration," said Mr. Bradley-Orr, ignoring Miss Perk's remark. "A dry battery is much like the psychic circle. Each unit of a dry battery is like a unit in the psychic circle. If one or two units do not give enough electric fluid to start your car you 'hitch on' a few more. It is the same with the psychic circle. What units are in touch with me in the unseen world, I do not know, but if you would join the circle—"

"How do you mean?" asked Jane Sprood unbendingly.

"I mean that if you, and perhaps Miss Perk, would join hands with me, your psychic values would be added to mine. I might have at my command the psychic strength necessary to sharpen the psychic optic nerves. I might see more clearly, more incisively."

"I am no more psychic than a stone ax is," said Jane Sprood, "and I don't know a thing about such things, but if you have any idea it will help you see better, I will say here and now that I'm here to do detective work and business is business."

With this she put her hands above the table. Miss Perk, more reluctantly, put her hands above the table.

Mr. Bradley-Orr took one of Jane Sprood's hands in his right hand and one of Susan Perk's hands in his left hand.

"If you ladies will join hands under the table, please," he said in his gentle voice, "and try to think of my bleeding body lying in the garden— Do not speak. Now!"

He rapped sharply on the table-top with a heavy ring that decorated his third finger and at the same time tightened his grip on Miss Sprood's hand. He leaned back in his chair and closed his eyes.

"You must be *en rapport*," he warned. "You must not be reluctant. You must wish to help. Your hand seems ever so slightly reluctant, Miss Sprood. You must wish to have me hold it in mine. You do wish to have me hold your hand, do you not?"

"Of course," said Jane Sprood.

"That is good," said Mr. Bradley-Orr.

"I can notice that you are holding my hand more firmly now. In a minute or two I will begin to see. I will see more clearly than I did. Now a silence, please."

There was absolute silence in the darkened room. Now and then one of Miss Perk's shoes creaked a little, for she wore shoes that creaked when their soles flexed. To Jane Sprood it seemed as though the time were lengthening into hours.

"Presently!" said Mr. Bradley-Orr. "Sometimes it takes some time to become quite *en rapport*. It takes some longer than others. I have a friend, Hinckley Martin, who is most difficult."

He paused.

"Perhaps you know Hinckley Martin," he said, in a far-away voice. "He is my best friend. He comes here often. We have great disputes—quarrels almost. To hear us dispute, you might often think we were bitter enemies. We dispute on all varieties of subjects. And sometimes we bet. We bet large sums of money."

Mr. Bradley-Orr was now talking as if in a trance and Jane Sprood pressed Susan Perk's hand meaningly. With her superior intelligence she felt she knew what was happening.

"I am among my sweet peas." Mr. Bradley-Orr continued. "I am down on my knees, a trowel in my hand, loosening the soil. He stands near me. We have been talking. I am speaking to him. I say: 'Given the right to arrange the setting, Hinck. I would exclude no one.' He laughs. 'I know one you would exclude, Brad,' he says. I say to him. 'I don't know who you have in mind, Hinck, but if she is a woman between eighteen and fifty, I'll bet you a thousand dollars she will let me hold her hand for five minutes without trying to draw it away.'"

AT THAT INSTANT the room was flooded with a blinding glare of light, followed by the most intense darkness. Susan Perk screamed. Jane Sprood jerked her hand roughly out of the hand of Mr. Bradley-Orr and jumped to her feet. Then someone turned on the electric lights.

Mr. Bradley-Orr was standing with an apologetic smile on his face, and in the far corner of the room Mr. Hinckley Martin stood, his hand still on the button that had flashed on the electric.

"Of course you will not lay the blame on me, Miss Sprood," he said politely. "All I had to do with it was to tell him you were the one woman he could not possibly get to hold his hand for five minutes. It was, I am sure, a tribute to your stern and unfrivolous character."

Jane Sprood, glaring angrily, looked from one smiling man to the other.

"Well, of all—" Susan Perk began in her high-pitched voice.

"Shut up, Susan!" said Jane Sprood.

"The money, Miss Sprood," said Mr. Bradley-Orr, "I will donate to any charity you may mention. Now, please don't be angry. A bit of harmless fooling—"

He was really very nice about it, but there was no reason why he should not be. That was his cue. Jane Sprood did not feel quite so greatly amused.

"Humph!" she said.

On the mantel close at her hand was a huge Chinese vase, decorated with lilies. With one long stride Jane Sprood reached the mantel. She grasped the vase with the strong right hand Mr. Brad-ley-Orr had held unresistingly for five minutes. With a sweep of vase over her head she gave it impetus, and she brought it down full on the top of a small camera that stood half concealed in the window niche.

"Susan Perk," she said, "come with me."

NOT UNTIL THEY were in the automobile did either speak.

"My goodness!" said Susan Perk. "I left my shooting pistol in the parlor!"

"He held your hand just as long as he held mine," said Jane Sprood, showing that the incident rankled more than she would have admitted. "And as for that fool pistol, it might as well be in his parlor as anywhere else, for all the use you will ever make of it. Why didn't you have sense enough to know there was nothing but nonsense in all that folderol?"

"Why didn't you, Jane?" asked Susan Perk. "Don't you go and blame me!"

The automobile came to an abrupt stop.

"You mean to say I liked it?" demanded Jane Sprood.

Susan Perk said nothing. Jane Sprood got out to crank the car. She climbed into her seat again and sent the car forward.

"Because, if that is what you mean, Susan Perk," she said, "I did!"

"Jane Sprood!" exclaimed Susan.

"And it is nobody's business whether I liked it or not, Susan Perk." Jane Sprood declared, "but if you were half a detective, I wouldn't have to tell you. But, like or dislike, no man is ever going to make a fool of me again!"

The next morning Sam Denning put an additional board on the sign on Jane Sprood's porch. It read: "Jane Sprood & Miss Susan Perk, Detecting Done for Females Only."

VI

WITHOUT A CLUE

FROM HER REAR bedroom window, in her own home in the village of Westcote, Long Island, Jane Sprood, detective, could look out upon a somewhat lovely landscape. By nature Jane Sprood cared nothing for loveliness or beauty, or so she would have declared, but this one charming view had become a part of herself. She had been born in this room; and as soon as she could toddle, she had stood at this window, looking out. Her "own" bedroom, the one she had used until her mother died, looked out through a similar window upon the same scene.

So thoroughly had this bit of landscape become a part of Jane Sprood that it was the first thing at which she looked when she got out of bed in the morning. Being a bachelor woman, Jane Sprood had no husband to distract her morning attention, and being carelessly—even roughly—mannish in her costume and manner, she gave little attention to her morning mirror. Across the window, to the height of her chin, Jane Sprood had placed a sash-curtain. Thus she could dress in safety while looking out, and she invariably did so. She was not aware that this early morning communion with the fields and low hills had become a source of strength and joy to her, but it was so.

Her own back lawn, where stood a great oak tree and the garage that held her noisy old motorcar, was in itself beautiful and restful to the eye. It ended at the tall fence on which climbing roses massed thousands of blossoms in season. Beyond the fence were vacant lots—riotous with wild asters and goldenrod in the fall. Then came a road, and beyond the road lay the great rolling, beautiful field. It was a rather vast field to be found so near the heart of a village. Some day it would be thick-set with houses, but as yet only two had been built on it.

These two houses stood side by side, but they were unlike in size and architecture. One was a small, modern Queen Anne cottage, the home of Colton Butz, who had become the owner of the great, bare field and was holding it until the real-estate market improved. Then he meant to sell it in lots, or possibly build houses on it and sell them.

The other house was a huge old-fashioned, French-roofed house, almost palatial in its size. Here lived Mrs. Anne Jane Perkinson, widow of the late Titherington Overdale Perkinson. All the landscape, as far as Jane Sprood could see from her window, had once been part of the Perkinson estate. Mr. Perkinson had sold it during one of his periods of financial distress, but he had invested the money in Santos coffee-plantations, and dying before he could sell at a loss, had left his widow an estate that had made her many times a millionaire, with a shockingly huge annual income.

Mrs. Perkinson could have bought back the estate ten times over, but she did not want it. She was now a gray-haired woman of seventy, and her mind was taken up with innumerable charities and good works as well as matters financial, and she did not wish to be bothered by a large piece of unproductive real estate. She was deeply interested in the W. C. T. U., the Society for the Prevention of Gambling, the Y. M. C. A., female suffrage, the Armenian Relief, the American Artificial Nitrogen Company, the Boyd-Custer Airship Company and many other concerns.

It was a peculiarity of Mrs. Perkinson that she invested no money in any enterprise that did not promise to better mankind in general. The nitrogen company appealed to her because it promised the world the much-needed cheap nitrogen. She financed the airship concern because it meant to attempt the transatlantic flight and thus increase the friendship of nations. She could never be induced to invest one dollar for the mere purpose of making a profit.

Mrs. Perkinson's neighbor, Colton Butz, was her opposite. Mrs. Perkinson was a tall, gloomy person with a serious bovine face. She wore black continuously, with a hat draped in yards of the deadest, most depressing black crape. Colton Butz, while almost Mrs. Perkinson's age, was a dapper little bachelor. All his life he had been known as Vesty Butz because of his wonderful and unusual waist-coats. It was said he had seven hundred and thirty of these—two for every day in the year—and all brilliant in color and design.

In addition to all these salient characteristics, Vesty Butz was a sporting man. He was a born-and-bred gambler, but he boasted that he had never held a playing-card, a set of dice or a policy-slip in his hand. He never risked money on chance, but he was willing to risk anything he owned on his personal estimate of any living, breathing bird or animal. He would bet on horses, fighting-cocks, dog-fights or anything that breathed and could be watched in any kind of contest. He had, in addition, one great and overwhelming ambition. He wanted to go down in history, not as Vesty Butz, but as Colton Butz, the creator of a new sport on which money could be gambled.

For years Vesty Butz had turned his ambition over and over in his mind, trying to evolve a sporting proposition that would be universally possible. At times he had raced ostriches, promoted flea-battles and staged llama-races, only to learn that these had been attempted far earlier by other men. It was then that he decided he must breed an entirely new variety of competitor, and he thought of the homing chickens.

Mr. Butz' idea was that he could, by selection and inbreeding, produce a strain of chickens that could fly as swiftly as a swallow. Chickens can live in any climate, are domestic to a degree, are pro-lific and cheap, and love to come home to roost. If he could breed a thin, rangy flying chicken that was a speedy racer and at the same time a good layer and a conscientious mother, the homing chicken would soon spread all over the world. "Flying chicken" races would become popular wherever men gambled. The Colton Butz chicken would be as famous as the Plymouth Rock or the White Leghorn, and Colton Butz' name would be immortal.

In the eight or ten years during which Vesty Butz had been at work with the homing chickens he had made wonderful progress. Whenever he heard of a chicken that could not be kept in its coop because it would fly out, he bought it. He had now some fifty homing chickens that could fly a mile or more as straight as a bee and as swift as an arrow. He was well satisfied. In another month he meant to hold the first chicken-race, after which he meant to sell settings of eggs, create a Homing Chicken class at all poultry-shows, and establish the American Homing Chicken Club.

The Colton Butz flying chicken was not a handsome bird as judged by the chunky, squatty standards prevailing for domestic fowl. It had a small, unintelligent head, a long neck, chest-muscles like a buffalo bull, long legs, huge wings and a rudderlike tail. As an article of culinary use it may be said that the Colton Butz chicken would bounce but not break. Vesty had not bred for white meat; he had bred for endurance. In comparison with a Colton Butz homing chicken, an old shoe was as tender as a piece of cheese.

To protect these extremely valuable chickens Mr. Butz had built a coop he felt to be entirely thief-proof. It was of galvanized iron, with shutters of the same material, and each could be firmly locked, as could the door. Even the floor was of galvanized iron. The coop, when closed for the night, was like a money-box.

Across the door were two stout iron rods, each passing through two heavy iron braces. Thus the door had three locks, each of the most improved pattern. To steal chickens out of such a coop seemed an impossibility, but one night in June every flying chicken, with the eggs in the nests, was stolen.

Jane Sprood was awakened by the ringing of her telephone bell and got hastily out of bed, slipping on her robe and slippers. She glanced out of her window, as was her invariable custom. The landscape was as calm and peaceful as ever, and yet it seemed different—she did not know how.

The telephone was close at hand, and Jane Sprood picked it up, still looking through the window.

"Yes," she said, when she had received Colton Butz' agitated message, "I'll take the job. Don't let anyone go near the spot. As soon as I am dressed, I will get Susan Perk, and we will be over. Goodby!"

Hardly removing her eyes from the window, Jane Sprood called Susan Perk's number; for Susan Perk, who lived across the street, was the partner in the famous firm of Jane Sprood & Miss Susan Perk, Detectives.

"Susan," she said, "get right into your clothes and come over here. Mr. Butz's chickens have been stolen, and he has put us on the job."

"Land sakes, Jane!" exclaimed Susan Perk. "Who in the name of goodness stole 'em?"

"That's a bright thing for a detective to ask, ain't it?" said Jane Sprood. "Who stole 'em! Do you suppose Vesty Butz would hire us to find out if he was able to tell us? I don't know who stole them, Susan Perk; so you get on your garments and get over here. Quick!"

"Will a kimono do?" asked Susan Perk.

"Ye gods!" cried Jane Sprood. "Will a kimono do! Susan Perk, did you ever hear of a person going out detecting in a kimono? If you did, wear one. Far be it from me to dictate to you, Susan Perk. If you so desire, you may come with bare legs and a piece of pink cheesecloth, dancing the Spring Song; but come!"

Jane Sprood slammed the receiver on the hook and thumped the telephone-instrument on its table.

"It is a wonder Susan Perk don't drive me crazy," she said, and she hurried into her own clothes. She was standing on the front porch, her wad of hat wrong side before and her hands in her driving-gloves, when Susan Perk came across the street.

Miss Perk was late. She had taken time to dress in the most complete manner, even to a parasol, partly in revenge for Jane Sprood's sarcastic remark, and partly because she expected to see and be seen by Colton Butz. When she saw Jane Sprood's driving gloves, she winced. "You ain't going in the flivver, are you, Jane?" she asked anxiously, dreading the jolting of Jane's remarkable machine. "It's only around the block, ain't it?"

"Nobody ever knows where a detective-chase ends up," said Jane Sprood. "You may be in Alaska before this day's work is over, Susan Perk!"

"Well, if I've got to ride in that car of yours from Long Island to Alaska in one day, Jane Sprood, I resign from this detective firm right now," said Miss Perk.

"You get into that car!" said Jane Sprood. "You can't resign. You're a detective for life."

As soon as the jolting car rounded the corner into full view of the fields, Jane Sprood knew why her favorite landscape had not seemed just as usual that morning. Mr. Butz' chicken-coop was gone. It was not there at all; it was nowhere in the landscape.

Jane Sprood put her foot on the accelerator, and the car jumped a foot into the air. It sped forward like a submarine navigating a stone-pile, and Susan Perk held on with both hands, easing herself a little as the car came down after each jump.

"I want to get there before the ground is all tramped down," said Jane Sprood, for the news of the robbery had already spread, as was evident by the many persons who were hurrying to the scene. In fact, Mr. Colton Butz, in his excitement, had telephoned widely, seeking to learn if anyone in Westcote had seen a bevy of thieves driving off with his chicken-coop.

Jane Sprood, with keen detective instinct, wished to be on the spot before any traces left by the thieves were obliterated. From footprints, buttons caught on bushes, and so on, crimes are often traced. Her car thumped and jangled up to Mr. Butz' door, and she leaped out, landing firmly on the soles of her heavy, mannish shoes. Before Susan Perk had put one old-maidenly foot out of the car—being careful to show no stocking—Jane Sprood was on her way around the house, pulling off her driving-gloves as she went, like a doctor who expects to feel the pulse of his patient the moment he arrives in the sick-room.

Colton Butz, and one other, his aged housekeeper, stood before the scene of the depredation. In spite of the earliness of the hour Mr. Butz had dressed with great care. To Jane Sprood he seemed an example of silly slavery to the extreme of style, but before he spoke of the robbery, he apologized.

"You've got to excuse these duds," he said. "When I expect to receive ladies, I try to look halfway decent, but I'm so excited I have lost my head. That's the truth. If I had thought in time, I would have put on another vest. This vest is one I bought in Paris in 1897, and I never did like it. I wear it now to feed the chickens in. So you can see how excited and worked up I am, when I forget to change my vest for the regular morning vest for this day. I own seven hundred and thirty vests. By that I mean day-vests. I have two hundred evening waistcoats in addition. I could have more, but Prince Albert Edward never had more than that. I make it a rule to have no more than he had. If a man can't be well-dressed with nine hundred and thirty vests and waistcoats, he is not a good dresser. He is a bounder."

Jane Sprood looked at the natty little man with amazement. Miss Perk, who had now arrived, was simply open-mouthed. No other words describe it.

"I thought you wanted me to catch a thief," said Jane Sprood with resentment.

"By all means!" exclaimed Mr. Butz. "But if you think I ought to go in and attire myself properly first—"

"Fiddlesticks!" exclaimed Jane Sprood, and she gave her attention to the scene of the crime. It might have been observed that at that moment Mr. Butz' face, which had worn an anxious look, brightened. The neighbors and others had begun to arrive, and with them came Sam Hornway, the young man who made a good living by reporting interesting local events for the New York and Brooklyn papers at space rates. Mr. Butz shook him warmly by the hand.

"Glad you're here, Hornway," he said excitedly. "This ought to be a big thing for you—a big thing. You ought to get columns out of it—whole columns. I'll go down with you after a while, and have a new photograph made—one of my vests I was never taken in before."

"Odd!" ejaculated Jane Sprood. "Odd, Susan! Not a trace of a wagon-wheel."

"Get that, Hornway?" said Mr. Butz with eagerness that was almost childish. "Big stuff! Chickens gone—all the celebrated Vesty Butz homing chickens—every one. Not an egg or a feather left! Chicken-coop gone—vanished! Middle of the night—not a sound!

Not a thing seen, no trace! Put in it that Vesty Butz was so excited he actually forgot himself and received the lady detectives in a vest he only wears when he feeds his chickens. And the two celebrated female detectives called to the spot the instant the crime was discovered! Regardless of expense!"

He turned to Jane Sprood, who was carefully examining the ground around the spot where the coop had stood, and that spot itself.

"No matter what the expense, I want the chickens recovered," he said to her. "You see!" he added to Hornway. "I don't care what the expense is. Regardless of expense!"

"Just like that!" said Hornway, who was a "kidder."

Mr. Butz looked at him a little anxiously.

"It is not a joke," he said. "You must not make it too frivolous. You know how to write it, Sammy. I've been working for years to breed these racing hens; it is my life-work. Jolly me about the vests—that's what the people like. I'm Vesty to one hundred and ten million readers. But the serious part is that if the chickens are not found, my life-ambition of creating a new sport that men can bet on is ended."

"Don't you fret, Vesty," said Hornway good-naturedly. "You'll get plenty of publicity. Why, if you only buy a new vest, you get a column in every paper in the country. This *is* big, Vesty, and I'm going to keep it going as long as I can. My wife needs new clothes. You can leave it to me."

"Female detectives—chicken-coop and all gone—Vesty in tears," suggested Mr. Butz, and he dropped Mr. Hornway and gave his attention to Jane Sprood.

The center of an admiring and rapidly increasing throng, with Susan Perk hardly less observed, Jane Sprood was standing in deep thought while Susan watched her face. Now and then Miss Sprood walked rapidly around the site of the departed coop with a long, mannish stride. When she returned to the waiting group, she fell into deep thought again.

Jane Sprood found herself baffled.

The chicken-coop, on which her eyes had rested every morning, was gone. Of that there could be no doubt, because it was not there. It was, moreover, gone without leaving the slightest clue. The ground around the late location of the coop was soft, although not spongy, and was free from grass. Its surface was covered with a fine green moss that was hardly more prominent than a thin coat of water-paint would have been. It would have been impossible to trundle an empty wheelbarrow across this surface without leaving a deep wheel-track; yet on no side of the coop was there a wheel-track or a footprint! Even with the most minute observation Miss Sprood could discover no signs that the coop had been removed.

She could, and did, discover abundant proof that the coop had *not* been removed! And yet the coop was not there. It was gone.

A sudden suspicion flashed through her mind, and she turned quickly and saw Vesty Butz once more clinging close to Sam Hornway. With her suspicion in mind, Jane Sprood made another examination of the ground.

There was but one way in which the coop could have been removed. From the bare site of the coop, through the chickenwire inclosure in which the fowls had been allowed to exercise, ran a narrow plank walk. This continued to the kitchen door of Vesty Butz' house. The only possibility was that the chickens had been removed, and that the coop—which might have been built in small detachable sections—had been taken down and carried bit by bit into the house or cellar.

The anxiety of Mr. Butz to get abundant publicity seemed to indicate that he might have staged a fake robbery in order to secure the publicity he always coveted. Jane Sprood looked at the little man sharply and began work on this new field of possibility. Susan Perk "tagged" close to her skirts as she minutely examined the narrow boardwalk.

"Well, I must say, Jane Sprood," Susan said sarcastically, "this is a fine job for two women of our age, to be nosing a plank walk in the sight of half the people of the town! I dare say the next thing will be asking me to get down on my hands and knees and crawl around like a caterpillar. To my mind, detecting ain't no work for elderly females."

"Look close, Susan," said Jane Sprood. "It's little enough help you ever are, land knows! But if you see anything that looks like a nut, bolt or washer, tell me. And as for elderly, if you choose to call anyone that, call yourself and don't call me."

"Elderly we are," said Susan Perk, "and I make no bones of it, Jane. Elderly and far from the material *Sherlock Holmeses* are made from. What may be in your mind, I don't know, but as for me, I have not a thought that would be of any use. I say now, as I have said many times before, I am not a detective either by name or nature."

"My stars!" exclaimed Jane Sprood. "How do you ever expect me to solve anything if you keep up a chatter like that, Susan Perk? Help from you I don't expect. You know as well as I do that you're my partner because it is not proper for an unmarried female to go detecting hither and yon alone, and that is all. But if you can't help, for heaven's sake don't hinder. Don't be a fool!"

Susan Perk was hurt. Never had Jane Sprood spoken to her quite so roughly.

"I am as the Lord made me, Jane," she said, "and not as I made myself, although I am far from saying that if I had myself to make I would make myself to suit you—or could hope to do so. Female I am made by nature, and will no doubt continue so to be."

Jane Sprood said nothing. She had found a rusty screw and was examining it carefully.

"And as the Lord meant me to be," continued Susan Perk, "I am content to be, or would be if you would let me. I dare say the day will come when you will be sending me forth disguised in a false beard or rigged up in coats and vests like that little jackanapes yonder. Such may be your ambition, Jane Sprood, but to me a woman seems far more womanly when trying to be a woman, as Anne Jane Perkinson is, than when seeking to do a man's work in skirts."

"Humph!" said Jane Sprood. "So far as I can learn, Anne Jane Perkinson has a habit of meddling in a great plenty of matters."

"Only such as appertain to females properly, Jane Sprood," said Susan Perk. "Rubbing one's nose along the chicken-walk of a man that wears vests of rainbow hue, and only thinks of turning peaceful hens into race-horses to gamble with, is a different sort of woman's work than that done by Anne Jane Perkinson. You would be far better sitting at home, as Anne Jane Perkinson is, planning to end gambling, than you are when chasing bolts, nuts, et cetera, for a born gambler."

Jane Sprood shrugged her shoulders. From a distance the crowd was watching. She was glad indeed they could not hear Susan Perk's most undetectivelike words.

"Anne Jane Perkinson don't sit at home like a ninny," she said "She finances airships, for one thing, and—"

"And—my lands!" cried Susan Perk suddenly.

An idea had come to her suddenly, and ideas of the sort were so rare a thing with her, that she sat down abruptly on an empty box.

"Jane!" she exclaimed.

"What?"

"What if Anne Jane Perkinson— "

Jane Sprood dropped a bent nail she had picked up and hurried toward her car. Susan Perk, knowing the roughness of the road that led to the airship's resting-place, followed reluctantly, hoping Jane Sprood would forget her; but Vesty Butz touched Sam Hornway on the sleeve.

"Go with her," he said, pointing to Jane Sprood. "She's on the right track. I'll bet a hat this is going to be the story of the year."

"How do you know?" asked Hornway.

"I don't," said Vesty, "but I'll just bet that Jane Sprood knows."

It was a wild ride. Even Sam Hornway, standing on the running-board of the car, admitted that, and Susan Perk uttered but two sentences during the ride.

"What's that you've got your foot on, Jane?" she demanded once.

"Cut-out," said Jane. "Makes us go faster."

"Wish your foot would break off," commented Miss Susan emphatically.

For the most part she could not speak, she was so jolted. She hung on by main strength as the car bounded over ruts and rubble, bumping over a new and half-made road, through wide fields and miniature forests. At a chained gate that bore a signboard with the words "Positively No Admission" Jane stopped the car. She pulled the sign from the post to which it was nailed and used it to pry out the staples that held the chain. Then the car jolted triumphantly into the grounds of the Boyd-Custer Airship Company, and before the great dome of the hangar, came to a stop.

One of half a dozen mechanics who were working on the engines of the monster airship came to the door. He looked at the uninvited trio. It was evident he did not know them. He wasted no time with Jane Sprood. He walked straight to Susan Perk's side of the car.

"You're Mrs. Perkinson, ain't you?" he said. "Well, ma'm, the boss—Mr. Boyd—said to tell you, if you came out here, that he couldn't drown them chickens last night. No ma'm. The coop was a little heavy for the old air-boat, and we sprung a gas-leak, and so we landed the coop over yonder."

They looked where he pointed and saw the metallic coop, well camouflaged with a covering of newly cut brush.

"Well, I declare!" exclaimed Susan Perk.

"Well, ma'm, you mustn't blame the boss. Accidents will happen. We had trouble enough lassoing that confounded coop as it was."

"Is the airship all right now?" inquired Jane Sprood somewhat tartly.

"Yes'm," said the mechanic. "We was just going to run her out and take the chicken-coop out over the bay and sink the thing there."

"Well, don't do it!" said Jane Sprood. "Mrs. Perkinson has changed her mind. She wants the coop put right back where it was. Don't you, Anne Jane?"

Susan Perk gasped.

"Yes," she managed to make answer when Jane Sprood nudged her.

"All right, ma'm," said the mechanic. "And maybe you'd like to ride back in the airship along with us."

"No, thank you," said Jane Sprood. "I shall ride in my own car."

Susan Perk hesitated.

"Well, Jane," she said, "you've done what you came to do. This gentleman is going to fly the chickens back home, although I must say it is the first time I ever heard of chickens flying around the country coop and all. What I want to know is: are you going to put your foot on that cut-out thing on the way back home?"

"If I so desire, yes!" said Jane Sprood.

"Then," said Susan Perk, "I'm going to go home in the airship."

THE DELIBERATE DETECTIVE

BEING A HISTORY OF THE EXTRAORDINARY
ADVENTURES OF MR. STANLEY BROOKE, AND OF
THE STRANGE PARTNERSHIP RESULTING THEREFROM

E. PHILLIPS OPPENHEIM

TALE THE FIRST
THE RESCUE OF WARREN TYRRWELL

Lord Wimbledon was plainly out of sorts with everything and everybody. He looked gloomily across at the young man who shared the compartment with him in the Paris express, an expression of irritation on his severe face. The young man, quite oblivious to the fretful scrutiny, adjusted the golf-bag against the seat and turned to the pages of an illustrated sporting magazine.

"What on earth did you bring those things with you for?" the old gentleman asked, irritably.

The Hon. Stanley Brooke, scientific illuminator of crime, smiled up at him.

"They assist," he replied, "in giving an air of general negligence to our journey. No one would imagine, for instance, that reasonable men would take golf-clubs with them to Paris on an errand like ours."

Lord Wimbledon grunted, fumbled for a moment in his waistcoat-pocket, and finally produced a telegram which he smoothed out and passed across to Brooke.

"If only one could form any idea as to what our errand was!" he remarked irritably. "Read it aloud, please."

Brooke obeyed. The message had been handed in at Paris about midnight on the previous day, and was addressed to Lord Wimbledon:

> Beg you to come over at once,
> Am in great trouble.
> Warren.

"Can you make anything out of it?" Lord Wimbledon asked.

"Nothing," Brooke admitted.

"The most idiotic message I ever received in my life," his lord-ship continued.

"However, I suppose we shall know all about it presently. I hope to goodness he hasn't got himself into any trouble with his chief. Tell me honestly now, Brooke, how does it strike you?"

"To be candid," Brooke replied, "I should say that it does point to some sort of trouble at the embassy. If it had been a private matter, he would surely have written. I must confess, though, that I don't understand it at all. Sidney was always such a careful chap."

"He has never," Lord Wimbledon pronounced, "given me cause for one moment's anxiety."

"That," Brooke sighed, "is what makes it so disquieting. Paris is no place for a young man of that sort."

Lord Wimbledon relapsed into stony silence. It was not until they reached the outskirts of Paris that he spoke again.

"Well, we shall soon know all about it now," he remarked, as they collected their baggage. "Let me come to the window. I shall recognize Warren more easily than you."

The train glided into the Gare du Nord. There was the usual little rush of porters and the bustle of descending passengers. They made their way toward the barrier. The frown on Lord Wimbledon's face grew deeper. There was no sign at all of Warren.

"I can't understand it," he repeated, for the twentieth time. "The boy must know how anxious I feel, and I wired that I was coming on this train. Hello!"

A little dark man had touched Lord Wimbledon upon the arm.

"You are Lord Wimbledon?" he asked.

"I am, sir," was the curt reply. "If you are connected with the press, let me say at once that I am traveling incognito. I do not wish my presence—"

"I have nothing to do with the press," the little man interrupted. "I have come to you from your son, Mr. Warren Tyrrwell."

Lord Wimbledon looked him up and down with disfavor. He was neatly dressed, with pale face a little wizened, but his clothes and manners were of the middle class. He had the appearance of a respectable tradesman—perhaps a detective.

"If you have a message from my son," Lord Wimbledon said, "please let me hear it at once."

"There is a little trouble," the man announced slowly. "It would be best, perhaps, not to speak here on the platform. You have registered luggage?"

"None," Lord Wimbledon replied. "I am proposing to return to-morrow."

"If you will come this way into the buffet," the little man said, "one can speak there with more freedom."

"Lead the way, then," Lord Wimbledon answered sharply. "This is my traveling companion, Mr. Brooke."

They passed hurriedly across the open space and mounted the stairs to the buffet. The little man led the way to a table in the corner.

"Coffee—bring anything," Lord Wimbledon ordered of the expectant waiter—"coffee and brandy will do. Now, sir," he added, "if you will be so good as to get on with your message. You can speak before my friend here; he is in my confidence."

"My name," the little man announced, "is Antin. For the last year your son has made use of me as a guide and interpreter. I am, at the present moment, having been unfortunate with my other work, occupying the position of his valet."

Lord Wimbledon frowned.

"I was not aware that my son had a valet here," he remarked.

"What I have told you is the truth, my lord," the man declared. "It is only during the last two months that I have filled this position, but the season has been a bad one in Paris, and it has provided me at least with a roof and an opportunity to look around me. If you will pardon my saying so, it will be better, for the present at any rate, if you will accept my statement."

Lord Wimbledon nodded.

"Very well, then," he said; "go on."

"Mr. Tyrrwell was, as you are doubtless aware, my lord," the little man continued, "fond of visiting the out-of-the-way corners of Paris and mixing with people of strange nationalities. Considering his official position in this city, it will probably occur to you to wonder whether such a course was altogether wise. In any case, the telegram, is the result of trouble into which Mr. Tyrrwell has fallen during one of these expeditions."

"Tell me at once," Lord Wimbledon begged, "the nature of this trouble—"

"I am coming to it," the man declared. "It is perhaps within your lordship's knowledge that Mr. Tyrrwell's special duties at the embassy lately have been connected with Russian affairs. Mr. Tyrrwell has had lessons in the language and is fairly proficient. He has taken great interest in the Russian colony, and he and I have visited together occasionally some places of which it is well not to speak too openly.

"Yesterday afternoon Mr. Tyrrwell brought back from the embassy a document consisting of about twenty pages of foolscap pinned together. He told me that he should not stir out until he had finished translating them from the Russian tongue. He set to work almost at once with the dictionary, and I made him some tea.

"I understood from him that he had been given special permission to bring the work away from the embassy, as a reception was going on there, and part of the premises being closed for repairs, it was difficult for him to find a quiet corner.

"In the course of his work Mr. Tyrrwell came across several phrases which he was quite unable to translate. He asked for my help, but my knowledge of the Russian tongue is very slight, and I was unable to assist him.

"He did then what at the moment seemed only natural. He sent for a taximeter automobile and drove to the address of the man from whom he received lessons in Russian. That was about eight o'clock last night. Since then I have not seen Mr. Tyrrwell."

"You have not seen him," Lord Wimbledon repeated. "You mean that he has not returned?"

"About half past nine last night," the man went on, "the telephone rang. I answered it, and the voice which spoke to me was the voice of Mr. Tyrrwell. I could tell at once from his tone that something was wrong. He told me that he was down at the café over which the man Grika lives, from whom he has received Russian lessons, and there was something going on which he did not understand.

"He was left alone for a moment, from what I gathered, and had rushed to a telephone in the back room. He seemed to be afraid that they were going to keep him there for some purpose. He begged me to come down at once, but to come quietly. In the middle of the last sentence the telephone was disconnected."

"Disconnected!" Lord Wimbledon exclaimed.

The little man nodded.

"I heard Mr. Tyrrwell's voice suddenly choke," he said. "What happened, without doubt, was that some one had stolen up from behind and dragged him away."

"Good God!" Lord Wimbledon cried. "What did you do?"

"I took an automobile to the place," the man replied. "I saw Professor Grika at once. He was sitting in the café, which occupies the lower part of the premises, with some friends. He seemed surprised, but not in the least discomposed, at my visit. As to your son, he assured me that he had not seen him for ten days.

"I bribed the waiters and a servant. I could learn nothing. I sat for some time in the café, thinking. Then I followed Grika to his room. I spoke to him plainly. I told him that Mr. Warren Tyrrwell was an Englishman of high position; that any attempt to ill-use him or to tamper with any documents he might have had with him could only result in utter disaster.

"I threatened to go to the police. I spoke to him seriously. It was useless. Grika begged me to take any steps I liked, to have the place searched. He treated me as though I were a mild lunatic, and persisted in his statement that he had not seen Mr. Tyrrwell for ten days. Neither could I find any telephone upon the premises. Therefore I came away. I could think of nothing to do. I sent you the telegram in your son's name."

Lord Wimbledon sprang to his feet.

"Why didn't you go to the police at once?" he exclaimed.

"Because if the affair becomes known," Antin replied, "I presume that Mr. Tyrrwell will get into trouble at the embassy. He confided to me that the document which he had brought away from the embassy was one of great importance. It will scarcely be considered discreet that he should have gone to such an unsavory neighborhood with any portion of that document in his possession."

"In a sense that is true," Lord Wimbledon admitted. "On the other hand, my son's personal safety is the chief concern. What do you think, Mr. Brooke?"

"I should suggest," Brooke said, "that you allow me to pay a visit to Professor Grika. It can do no harm and will only delay matters a little."

Lord Wimbledon jumped at the idea.

"I place myself entirely in your hands, Brooke," he declared. "My own impulse, I must admit, is instantly to visit this man myself with a posse of *gendarmes* at my back. Warren's official position, however, must be considered. If that can be saved as well, so much the better. You have gifts in affairs of this sort, Brooke, which have been denied to me. We will await your return."

"Better go to Warren's rooms, I think," Brooke advised. "Get back there as quickly as you can, and wait for me. Now write down this man Grika's address, if you please," he added, turning to Antin. The little man tore off a piece from the menu and obeyed. Brooke turned to Lord Wimbledon, lowering his voice a little.

"If I were you," he said, "I should get back to Warren's rooms as quickly as you can, and take this man with you. I hope I may be able to bring you a report of some sort or another in a very short time." Even the driver of the automobile hesitated when Brooke directed him to drive to 83 Rue de Mont Bleu.

"It is far, monsieur," he objected, "and the roads are very narrow and difficult. One does not often approach the Rue de Mont Bleu in an automobile."

"You will do so," Brooke assured him cheerfully, "and you will receive for *pourboire* another of these when our errand is accomplished."

The man pocketed the five-franc piece and mounted a little reluctantly to his box. He paused for a moment to roll a cigarette, and started off. Even though he drove with the customary recklessness of his class, they reached safely in time the district they sought.

Here their progress became slow. There were stalls out in the street, strange names transcribed in Jewish characters over the shops. The streets were ill-lit, the men and women had little of the air of French people. They were far removed, indeed, from the children of the city of pleasure. There was another turn, a long and silent boulevard filled with decaying houses, a steep climb, and another narrow street. At a café half-way along it the automobile came to a standstill.

"*Voilà, monsieur*," the man announced.

"You can wait," Brooke ordered.

The man looked about him with an air of contempt.

"If one can but obtain a drink in this hole—" he grumbled.

Brooke stepped through the swing-door into the café. The place had none of the characteristics of similar establishments on the other side of the city. It was, in fact, more like an English public house near the wharfs. The illuminations were dim and scanty, the sawdust on the floor was stale, the few customers were gathered together at a table in a remote corner, intent on watching a game of dominoes.

They turned their heads at Brooke's entrance and stared with something in their faces which reminded one of hungry vermin.

Brooke addressed himself to a lady of great size who stood behind the counter. She had very fat cheeks and small black eyes. Her hair was jet-black and showed no signs of any attempt at care or arrangement. Her dress was insufficient.

She looked at Brooke with the palms of her two hands stretched flat upon the counter. She looked at him steadily, and the natural viciousness of her expression was overshadowed for the moment by a certain blank surprise.

Brooke, carefully dressed notwithstanding his journey, his smooth, boyish face unwrinkled, his mouth still a trifle open, his monocle in his left eye, was a type of person of whom madame had had no experience. As she studied him the many wrinkles in her face relaxed. Her lips parted a little and disclosed her yellow teeth. One might imagine that if indeed she were a partner in any nefarious scheme, the advent of the Hon. Stanley Brooke had failed to inspire her with forebodings.

"I understand," Brooke said, "that Professor Grika lives here and that he gives lessons in Russian. I should like to see him."

"Professor Grika has gone into the country for three days," madame declared. "He is not to be found here."

Brooke hesitated for a moment. Without turning his head, he was yet aware that the little group of men in the corner had suspended their game. Their faces were turned toward him. They were all listening.

"It is unfortunate," he continued, "as I have come so far. Madame will be so good as to give me a glass of cognac."

She moved slowly toward a row of bottles and served him. Brooke raised the thick glass to his lips. The liquor which he tasted was like fire. He coughed, and the woman laughed.

"Monsieur is used to milder drinks," she remarked scornfully.

"It is of no consequence," he replied. "I must admit that I find the brandy a little fiery, but it is perhaps suitable for the tastes of your clients. Is it possible, may I ask, that you give me the address of Professor Grika?"

The woman was replacing the cork in the bottle.

"One never knows where he is to be found," she declared. "He comes and goes when he wills. A strange man! He is perhaps visiting the president or the King of England. It is as much as I know."

Brooke turned his head slightly. He could hear the sound of a man's footsteps coming across the sanded floor. A large, loosely built man, collarless and unshaven, wearing only a shirt and trousers, had approached.

"Monsieur was inquiring for Professor Grika?"

Brooke admitted the fact affably. The man pointed to a table.

"We will sit down, you and I," he said, "and for something to drink—"

"Serve monsieur, I pray, with what he desires," Brooke interrupted.

The woman grinned and half filled him a glass out of the bottle from which she had served Brooke. The man led the way to a little wooden table. They sat down before it.

"We speak plainly here," the man growled, folding his arms and looking steadfastly at Brooke. "What is it you want?"

"A few words with Professor Grika," Brooke replied.

His companion looked at him steadfastly. His face was coarse, brutal, vicious, and unwashed. His small eyes had contracted almost into points underneath his lowering brows. He seemed to be subjecting Brooke to a steadfast examination.

Presently he glanced across at the woman. She made a sign to him.

"There are many reasons," he said slowly, "why Professor Grika does not at once receive all those who may choose to visit him."

Brooke's mouth opened a little wider. He kept the monocle firmly in his left eye.

"Political?" he asked.

"Political," his vis-a-vis admitted gravely. "But why not—The professor was exiled from Russia. They called him a nihilist because he was of the people. That is why he came to France—France, which should be a country for the people. Bah!"

The man spat upon the floor. Then he crouched across the table, so close that Brooke leaned back to escape his garlic-laden breath.

"For a *louis*," he said, "you shall see Professor Grika."

"I don't understand," Brooke protested, "why I should pay a *louis* to see a man whom I have come to ask to teach me Russian."

"I tell you," the other replied, "that Grika is a difficult person to see. You might come here a dozen times and be refused. It is worth a *louis*. Come!"

He held out his hand. Brooke affected to hesitate for a moment. Then he placed the piece of gold upon the table. The man pocketed it and rose.

"Come this way," he directed. They left the front room of the café and passed through a door, the two upper panes of which were broken and stuffed with brown paper. They climbed a flight of uneven stairs and arrived on a landing. Brooke's guide, who had been whistling to himself all the way up, whistled a little louder. Then he knocked at the door of a room.

"You can go in," he said. "You'll find Professor Grika there."

Brooke entered the room without hesitation. He heard the footsteps of his guide departing as he closed the door behind him. To his surprise the apartment, though plainly furnished, was clean, the floor carpeted, the walls filled with books and pictures. A man sat writing before a table, with a green-shaded lamp by his side. He looked up at Brooke's entrance. He was a man with a white beard, hollows in his cheeks—a frail man, apparently very old. His voice, when he spoke, shook a little.

"Monsieur desired to see me?"

"If you are Professor Grika, yes," Brooke replied. "I was recommended to you some time ago by an English friend of mine—Mr. Warren Tyrrwell. I wish to take some lessons in Russian."

Professor Grika regarded his visitor thoughtfully. It was curious that, although Brooke's accent as a rule was a matter upon which he prided himself, he was speaking now with a curious, almost a guttural pronunciation.

"Mr. Warren Tyrrwell," Professor Grika repeated. "Yes, yes; I remember the young gentleman perfectly. Why do you wish to learn Russian, monsieur?"

"I am in the German army," Brooke replied. "Staff officers are required to know at least two languages. I have chosen Russian for one, and I wish to make use of my vacation to acquire, at any rate, the rudiments of the language."

The professor nodded gently. He seemed, indeed, a very quiet and harmless old man.

"Sit down, please," he invited.

Brooke took an easy chair close to the table. Professor Grika leaned back in his chair. The light now fell upon Brooke's face and left his in the shadow.

"A German officer, eh—a German officer?" the professor repeated thoughtfully. "To me you speak French more with an English accent."

"I have studied in England," Brooke replied. "In my profession a knowledge of English is a necessity."

"Tell me, in a few words," Grika asked, lowering his tone, "why you chose to come to me for lessons in the Russian language. There are many others more fashionably located."

Brooke sat for a moment immovable. Then he rose from his place and walked carefully all round the room. Professor Grika made no effort to interfere with him. When he resumed his seat he moved a little nearer.

"Because," he said, "not only am I, as I have told you, a German officer, but I am in the Confidential Service. I know very well, among other things, Professor Grika, that you are a secret-service agent of a country which we will not mention.

"You, like all of us, have been working, without a doubt, to get at the truth of the new French mobilization scheme, the caliber of the new gun which has been made so secretly, and the disposition of the new batteries.

"It is possible that you may succeed where we others fail. Very well, I am here to deal with you. If by any chance you should light upon that scheme, or any part of it, it will be to your interest to name the price to me."

The professor remained motionless in his chair. His eyes were fixed upon Brooke as though he would read his soul. Brooke, bland and *insouciant*, had the appearance of a man who had been talking about the latest fashion in cravats.

"What is your name?" he asked at last.

"Captain von Heldermann," Brooke replied promptly.

"I have not heard of you," Professor Grika said slowly. "You put before me a new idea. Such work as I have done I have been promptly paid for from another source. An exile from my country though I may be, I have preferred to use my small gifts in the interests of—?"

"You use them more effectually," Brooke interrupted, "when you study the interests of Germany. This *entente* is an absurdity. No treaties in the world can bridge over the gulf which remains

between Russian and English interests. What is your price for that
scheme?"

"A quarter of a million francs."

Brooke frowned slightly.

"I fear," he said, "that it will require consideration. The funds
at my disposal—"

"One hundred thousand francs," the professor interrupted.

"If the scheme includes for certain the caliber of the gun,"
Brooke continued slowly.

"It does," the professor assured him. "I do not know, Captain
von Heldermann, from whence you derived your information, but
it is most assuredly a fact that a document containing all these
particulars was received at the British embassy yesterday. I cannot say how they procured it, but, unlike all official documents, it
was in Russian, not French. One page of it I have already seen.
The remainder will be in my hands to-night."

"Then at midday to-morrow," Brooke said, "I will be here with
a hundred thousand francs."

The professor sat quite quietly for several moments. His shoulders were hunched. He looked now down at the desk, now into
Brooke's face.

"It is arranged," he declared at last. "Permit me."

He rose from his place and took Brooke by the arm. For a moment he listened. Then he opened the door. Unfamiliar though the
sound seemed from his lips, he whistled softly.

"I shall descend with you," he announced. Brooke was conscious, as they reached the end of the passage, of retreating footsteps. He caught a glimpse of two men stealing away; caught a
glimpse, even, of the knife in the belt of one of them. The door at
the bottom of the stairs was locked. Again the professor whistled.
The woman unlocked it. She stood there with lowering face.

"It is not an affair for our benefit, this, then!" she exclaimed
shrilly. "Jean will be furious indeed—and I! For what are we here?
Why should we let opportunities—?"

The professor held out his hand. "Madame," he said, "all will
be recompensed to you. This gentleman has my safe conduct."

He walked with Brooke through the café to the pavement outside and stood there as his visitor drove away. Brooke drove to the block of flats in which Warren's rooms were situated, changing his automobile twice during the journey. Antin admitted him and he found Lord Wimbledon walking up and down the little sitting-room.

"Well? Well?" the latter exclaimed eagerly. "Have you found him—Is he there?"

"I believe so," Brooke replied, handing his hat to Antin and drawing off his gloves. "To tell you the truth, I never asked."

Lord Wimbledon stared at him.

"Don't you see," Brooke continued, "the great thing is to get Warren out of this without any trouble at the embassy. I have discovered at least this much—that he was not so rash as appeared. He took with him to that Russian one page only of the document in question."

"But where is my boy— What are they doing to him?" Lord Wimbledon demanded.

"One can only hazard surmises," Brooke replied thoughtfully. "I believe that our friend Grika has him safely under lock and key, and the neighborhood is certainly a horrible one. But on the other hand, Grika is much too clever to take unnecessary risks. In any case, we must play the game, for Warren's sake and every one's. You haven't communicated with the embassy at all, sir?"

"Certainly not," Lord Wimbledon replied. "I have done nothing but wait here for you."

Brooke nodded, and for the first time made a careful survey of his surroundings. The small sitting-room in which they were bore every sign of a hurried departure. There were writing materials which had evidently been thrown hastily down upon the table and a small locked safe stood on one side. There were plenty of loose sheets of paper about; no written ones. Brooke nodded approvingly.

"The boy wasn't quite such a mug, then," he murmured. "He locked up the rest when he started out for Grika. Now, sir," he added, turning to Lord Wimbledon, "I want you, if you don't mind, to go into the little dining-room, take Antin with you, and lock yourselves in. Very likely Antin will be able to find you something in the way of dinner. If you hear a ring, don't answer the bell; and if there is a bolt upon the door, don't draw it."

"It would be more satisfactory to me—" Lord Wimbledon began.

Brooke held out his hand. He spoke with unusual abruptness. "I want you to do as I ask this moment," he insisted.

Lord Wimbledon made no further objection. He left the room at once, followed by Antin. As soon as they had departed Brooke lifted the curtains which divided the sitting-room from the bed-room, and drawing an easy chair up behind them, settled down to wait.

He had turned out the lights, both in the sitting-room and the bedroom, but he had pulled a small table up to his side on which was an electric reading-lamp which he could turn on at a moment's notice. For a little more than an hour he sat there waiting. Then the silence of the flat was suddenly broken by the shrill ringing of the electric bell. There was no reply. It rang again, and again there was no response. Then, a few moments later, Brooke beard the click of a key in the outer door, which was at once softly opened and closed. There was the sound of footsteps in the outer hall, the opening of the sitting-room door, and Grika's voice, low, yet commanding.

"Turn on the lights!"

Through the chink in the curtains Brooke saw the little room suddenly illuminated. Warren, white as a sheet, with rings under his eyes, was standing by the side of the switch. A few feet away, still in his hat and overcoat, was Grika. The latter spoke again.

"What are all these papers upon the table?"

"The beginning of my translation," Warren faltered.

"Where is the document itself?"

"In the safe," was the mumbled reply.

"Unlock it at once!" Grika directed. "You have the keys."

The young man hesitated. From where he was Brooke could see that his hands were shaking all the time. About a yard away from him Grika stood, and poised lightly in his fingers was a dull little bar of some springy metal with a leaden top.

"Remember," Grika said softly, "that if you give me the slightest trouble you will go down like a stone once and forever. I shall have the papers anyway—you know that. You know that I shall keep my word, and you know that all my arrangements are made for escaping from here. Unlock that safe."

The young man hesitated no longer.

With shaking fingers he adjusted the combination. The door swung open. Grika drew from it a little roll of papers which he thrust into his pocket.

"It is finished," he said softly. "You have escaped lightly. Others who have visited me in the Rue de Mont Bleu have suffered what you have suffered for a week and more instead of for a few hours only. A month's vacation or a short time in the hospital will put you all right again. See how thoughtful I am. I am going to save even your reputation."

He had drawn a cord from his overcoat pocket. With his hand upon Warren's chest, he was forcing him back into the easy chair.

"I shall tie you hand and foot," he announced. "You will be discovered in a state of collapse. Your reputation will be saved."

Brooke set his teeth. The moment had come. With his left hand he threw aside the curtain and stepped into the room.

"If you make the slightest movement," he said quietly, "I shall fire."

The little man seemed, for a moment, stiffened into some suspended form of life. Then he turned his head very slowly and looked into Brooke's face. There was not the slightest sign of any expression in his features. It was as though he had been turned to stone. Yet Brooke knew all the time that he was thinking, that his brain was working rapidly and fiercely. Warren Tyrrwell, after one little sobbing cry, had fallen forward, stretched upon the floor in a dead faint.

"Take those papers from your overcoat pocket and place them upon the table," Brooke continued. "Don't hesitate. Listen. You are my man if I choose to take you. I don't. You are free. The papers, though—every one of them. You brought the missing sheet with you I notice. Leave it with the others."

Grika drew a little breath. Very slowly he began to empty his pockets. The roll of papers lay upon the table.

"So you mean to save your hundred thousand francs, Captain von Heldermann," he said slowly.

"That is the idea," Brooke admitted coolly. "Be careful there are no odd sheets left in your pockets. Turn the pockets inside out, please—so. Nothing left there, I see. Very well. Now, professor, I have nothing more to do with you."

The man looked at him. His cold blue eyes were filled with reluctant admiration.

"If I might be permitted," he said, "to give you a word of advice, I think, after all, you had better pull that trigger. You have outwitted me to-day and robbed me of a prize which was surely mine. It took only a few hours," he added scornfully, "to make pap of that young man. He was my broken creature."

"To the door, Professor Grika," Brooke ordered. "Leave it wide open and descend the stairs. I shall follow you."

The professor buttoned up his coat.

"I have no wish to stay," he said. "I only hope that we may meet again. Captain von Heldermann."

"Mr. Stanley Brooke," Brooke corrected him. "That young man is a relative," he added, pointing to where Warren lay upon the floor. "A family affair, you see. So you will understand why this little matter has to be kept secret."

The professor removed his hat.

"Sir," he said, "my congratulations are the more heartfelt. I depart. Only," he added, with a little flash of his eyes, "if ever the time should come when it is you whose hands are empty and my right finger where yours is now—"

"Exactly!" Brooke interrupted, as he stood at the top of the steps. "Good night, professor!"

He watched the man disappear and returned to the sitting-room. Lord Wimbledon and Antin answered his summons at once.

"You'll find Warren all right in a few minutes," Brooke assured them quickly. "The papers are all right, too."

The telephone-bell suddenly tinkled. Brooke took up the receiver himself.

"Hello!" he said. "Yes, these are Mr. Warren Tyrrwell's rooms. Yes, Mr. Tyrrwell is in. Who is it? Percival? That you, Percival? I'm Brooke—Stanley Brooke—remember me? Just ran over to look Warren up for a few days. Found him rather seedy, I am sorry to say, struggling with some extra work. Oh, no! He's all right. He's here—hasn't been out all day, he tells me. Right-o! Yes, we shall all be here. Lord Wimbledon is over for a few days, too. So-long!"

Brooke set down the receiver. Then he turned toward Lord Wimbledon. Warren was sitting up in his chair, drinking the brandy which Antin had brought.

"Listen," he said, "the chief has just found out that you were allowed to bring those papers away. They have had a fit of nerves. Percival's coming round at once. Remember, you haven't been out. You've been ill. You've been meaning to get on with the work, but you haven't been well enough because of this attack. That's all. Stick to it and you're safe. If any one thinks that they saw you out, they were mistaken."

Warren Tyrrwell blinked his eyes for a moment and looked around.

"That's all right," he said, a little more cheerfully. "I'm feeling better already. I'm glad it's Percival who's coming."

Lord Wimbledon crossed the room and rested his hand upon Brooke's shoulder. His voice shook a little.

"You have saved Warren's career and the honor of our family," he declared solemnly.

Warren's lips were suddenly quivering. He seemed on the verge of a complete breakdown.

"I should have given up the papers," he sobbed. "I was broken. I can't tell you what they did—"

"Hush!" Brooke interrupted sternly. "All you have to remember is this: You did not give up the papers. You had no real intention of giving them up. Be a man now and see this thing through. Remember that Percival will be here presently."

Brooke sat at supper an hour later with Percival in a fashionable Montmartre restaurant.

"I am afraid, after all, Paris doesn't agree with Warren," the latter remarked, as he sipped his wine. "If he gets the least strain upon him, or a few hours' extra work even, he knocks up."

"He is not strong," Brooke admitted; "but why on earth do you expect a chap to do a schoolboy's task like translating? Why don't you send it out to a teacher or some one?"

Percival smiled in a superior manner.

"My dear fellow," he said, "that document which we entrusted to Warren was a most important political paper. To tell you the truth, it was entirely a mistake that he was allowed to take it away from the embassy, and the chief was in a rare stew when he knew about it."

"Why?" Brooke asked, looking hungrily at the dish which was being prepared for them.

Percival dropped his voice.

"One has to be jolly careful over here, I can tell you," he declared. "There are lots of people in Paris—people whom we know quite well to be agents—secret agents for foreign powers—who would have given a fortune for a sight of those papers."

Brooke smiled at him doubtfully.

"Sort of thing we read about but don't believe," he remarked incredulously.

TALE THE SECOND
THE PRINCESS PAYS

As FULL OF HUMAN weaknesses as his fellows, notwithstanding his gifts of perception, the Hon. Stanley Brooke sat losing his money with cheerful pertinacity at one of the two roulette tables in the Sporting Club at Monte Carlo.

Arrived, after an hour or so of play, at the end of his nightly limit, he watched the disappearance of his last *louis* and, with a sigh, vacated his chair and seated himself on one of the divans which fringed the wall.

Here for some time he indulged in the occupation which, on the whole, he found more attractive even than the gambling. He watched the people as they went by—the women in their brilliant toilets and surfeit of jewels, looking as though the very air of the place had somehow fostered in them an insane rivalry in flamboyance, almost passionate, yet, in this particular corner of the world, not without its picturesque effect. By their side the men seemed more than ordinarily insignificant. There were some whom he recognized, a few with whom he exchanged greetings, many of a class hard to place, difficult even to guess at. On the whole, considering the nature of their surroundings, it appeared to Brooke, as he watched them, that their faces showed very little sign of the emotions.

Large sums were being won or lost, but none of the crowd who passed seemed to carry any indication in their features as to whether they belonged to the fortunate or unfortunate. There were little fragments of character which were, in their way, interesting.

A well-known adventurer passed arm in arm with a rubber magnate of meteoric rise and uncivilized appearance. The heroine of a world-famous murder case, dressed in somber black, pale and emotionless, as she had seemed when she had waited for the news of her life or death, stood with a handful of mille notes in her hand, watching their dispersal without even curiosity.

A German prince passed, in eager attendance upon the lady who was reported to have enslaved his fancy for the moment, and who was walking round from the, baccarat rooms to change her luck. Brooke leaned back among his cushions, mildly amused by it all. . . . And then the first note of real drama!

A woman came slowly down the room, at whom most people turned their heads to glance. She was even more beautiful, more exquisitely dressed, more gorgeously bejeweled than those others. Her carriage was almost imperious. She looked around her with the insolent air of one accustomed to command.

Then, when within a few paces of Brooke, she paused, and he alone, perhaps, in the room, saw the change in her face, which was in itself an epitome of all the passions of life. She seemed suddenly to become rigid, her face chalk-like, her eyes set and staring.

Brooke glanced across the room. Her eyes were fixed upon the face of a middle-aged man who was looking over at the opposite table, craning his neck to watch the result of the turning wheel and quite unconscious of the woman's gaze. She stepped out of the throng and seated herself on the divan.

The little white ball had fallen into its place, the croupier's monotonous voice was heard announcing the number.

"Vingt, noir, pair et passe!"

A little buzz of voices arose from the crowd. The woman turned her head and glanced at Brooke.

"I had the honor of meeting you last night at the Duc de Mendosa's supper," he reminded her with a bow.

She inclined her head.

"I remember you perfectly," she admitted. "You are English, are you not, Mr. Brooke?"

"I am English, princess," he replied.

She looked at him for a moment appraisingly. It was a curious fact; but, in accordance with a recently developed instinct, directly he felt the significance of her look, his features seemed automatically to assume a somewhat fatuous immobility which, to one unacquainted with the quality of his mind, would readily stamp him a vacuous dawdler.

"Listen," she said. "I will tell you something. Come a little nearer to me, please."

He obeyed her at once. Her eyes traveled around the few people in their immediate vicinity. Her fingers played for a moment with the wonderful pearls which shimmered upon her white bosom.

"You know my history?" she continued. "Every one who comes to Monte Carlo knows it. What was it they told me about you—that you were a novelist or an essayist, or that you were interested in people for some reason or other—I forget what. Listen."

Brooke remained silent. He did not specify the particular nature of his interest in his fellow creatures.

"Look across the room," she directed. "There is a man standing there watching the tables—a fairly good-looking, harmless, middle-aged Englishman."

Brooke nodded.

"I see the person you mean," he assented.

"His name is Geoffrey Hardways," she went on. "Well, I will tell you something which may suggest a problem. Everything I possess and am in life I owe to that man."

He looked at her a little puzzled. Once more she played with her pearls.

"I am," she continued, "without a doubt the best-dressed woman in this I room. I have a certain indefinite right to the title which I bear. There are no jewels in Monte Carlo to compare with mine. There are no men who would not come if I beckoned. This I tell you without conceit or false shame, and I repeat that everything I possess and everything I am I owe to that man."

She paused, as though expecting a question, but Brooke remained imperturbably silent. He had, however, the air of one who waits.

"You do not choose to commit yourself," she said quietly. "It is good. Therefore, I must put before you the problem which surely is not without its interest. What do you suppose are my feelings for him? Am I grateful? I have cause, have I not? Or do I wish that he had let me remain the very ill-treated and miserable governess of the lady in whose service I was when he found me?"

"Princess," Brooke replied, "you ask me a very hard question. Supremacy in any walk of life brings with it its own peculiar satisfaction."

"It is the answer," she declared, "of a diplomatist. Now give me the answer of Mr. Stanley Brooke."

"Princess," said he, "I think that if I were Geoffrey Hardways and you looked at me as you looked at him just now, I would leave Monte Carlo."

Very slightly her lips moved. It was scarcely a smile, yet it seemed in some way an indication of her satisfaction with his reply.

"Who knows," she murmured softly, "but that you are right?"

She rose to her feet and left him. Very slowly she continued her perambulation of the tables. Almost every moment some man paused to speak to her. She dismissed every one with a word. She was in one of her moods, a German financier murmured, who had been hoping to introduce a friend. She passed on until she stood at the other side of the tables. She came to a standstill immediately behind Geoffrey Hardways.

Brooke caught a glimpse of her face—white, and with a somber shadow upon it—over his shoulder. Then he saw her fingers touch his arm, saw him turn around to receive a brilliant smile of welcome. They stood talking together. Finally they moved away.

Brooke, upon whom the incident had left a slightly unpleasant sensation, rose and made his way to the bar, where he found an easy chair and made himself comfortable with a whisky-and-soda and a cigarette. He had scarcely been there five minutes when the woman entered, with Hardways by her side. There were several empty places on the other side of the room, but after a moment's hesitation she led the way to where Brooke was sitting.

"Tired of the game already, my friend?" she asked Brooke. "Let me present an old friend of mine whom I have unexpectedly discovered here—Mr. Hardways, Mr. Brooke."

The two men shook hands. Hardways, although passable enough in appearance, was a little nervous and obviously not wholly in touch with his surroundings.

"All new to me, this, you know," he admitted a moment or two later, as they sat together. "Until I met—met the princess just now, I was feeling rather out of it. I've never been on the Riviera before in my life."

"You play, I suppose?"

"Don't understand the game. I play a little bridge at home."

"The Riviera and its life," the princess said calmly, "are all new to Mr. Hardways. He is disposed to be enthusiastic—why not? After all, there is little else like it, especially for those who love gambling. We must teach you to play roulette or *chemin de fer*, Mr. Hardways." He laughed.

"I'd be afraid of losing," he confessed. "I am a poor man."

"So few people lose if they play intelligently," she murmured. "Several of my friends took over a thousand pounds each away last evening. It is so simple. Besides, you can always stop if the luck is against you. Isn't that so, Mr. Brooke?"

"I am not so sure," Brooke replied.

"It rather depends upon one's strength of mind, doesn't it?"

Even as he spoke he found himself noticing the weak droop of the other man's lips, the somewhat covetous gleam in his eyes at the mention of money.

"If I were you," Brooke advised, "I don't think that I should play, unless you first of all put a fixed limit upon what you can afford to lose. It seems to me to be the only way to gamble in comfort."

She laughed at him scornfully.

"You are a timid person, I fear, Mr. Brooke!" she exclaimed.

"If only I could afford it," Hardways muttered, gazing admiringly at his companion, "I'd like to have a plunge."

Brooke made his excuses a few minutes later and left the two together. Somehow the incident of meeting them continued to affect him in a slightly unpleasant manner. He felt a return of the same feeling when, the next evening, he came face to face suddenly with Hardways near one of the roulette tables. The latter greeted him vociferously.

"Hello!" he exclaimed. "Come and have a drink. Look here what I've won! Never saw such luck in my life! The princess stood behind me all the time—must have been my mascot, I think. I had three *en pleins* in six turns of the wheel."

Brooke walked with him to the bar. In a sense, he did so against his own inclinations, for the man failed to attract him in any way. Yet he felt an interest, the nature of which he could scarcely define. Hardways was talking all the time. "By Jove!" he continued. "I really think I am in luck! Never been in the place before, you know. Never understood the game until the princess explained it. I only came to the club by accident. Chap I traveled with in the train advised me to."

"Where are you staying?" Brooke asked for the sake of making conversation.

"Up at one of those little hotels on the hill," Hardways replied, mentioning the name of a second-rate hostelry. "I can't run to the swagger places. I've got a wife and family to look after, and my profession—I'm an architect, you know—doesn't mean big things at any time. By Jove, what a life out here, though! How the people do enjoy themselves! Whisky-and-soda, eh?"

Brooke nodded, and they sat down together. The princess was standing talking to some men on the threshold of the baccarat room. Hardways's expression, as he watched her, was almost fatuous. He stroked his mustache complacently.

"Loveliest woman I ever saw in my life!" he exclaimed. "Do you know," he went on confidentially, "she's an old pal of mine, the princess. I knew her when she was a little governess in Winchester and I was articled to a firm of architects there. She was a pretty little thing then, but I never expected her to blossom out like this. Jove! to think that I nearly married her!"

"In her way," Brooke remarked, "she has made a success of life."

The man laughed good-humoredly. He saw no second meaning in Brooke's words.

"Nothing like being at the top of the tree," he agreed. "She is that, and no mistake. They tell me all the men here are mad after her, but unless she takes a fancy to any one, she won't be seen talking to an ordinary person. Lucky for me I knew her in the old days!"

Brooke remained silent. The man went on talking in his simple, egotistical way of his life in the midland town where they lived, his wife's invitation to stay with an aunt at a hotel in Hyères, and his own visit to Monte Carlo, which he evidently looked upon as something exceedingly dashing.

"I was going back to-morrow," he announced, "but I think I shall hang on for a bit. I can afford it now, anyway. My Heavens, isn't she beautiful!"

The princess came slowly toward them. She was dressed in white chiffon, with less jewelry than usual save for that one rope of magnificent pearls. She smiled at the two men as she approached. Hardways bustled to find a chair for her.

"You must sit down, Violet," he begged. "Do you know how much I've won? Over a thousand francs—forty pounds, mind!"

She looked at him through half-closed eyes; a faint smile of amusement curved her lips. A thousand francs! There was sometimes a hat which she could buy for the sum—not often!

"But you are satisfied with too small things," she laughed. "I have brought thirty mille with me to-night and I am going to risk it presently. Come with me and I will show you how to play."

"Thirty mille!" he gasped.

The whole little world, as he knew it, seemed dwindling away.

"With your luck," she said, "you should be a large winner. You are content with too small things. One must learn to be ambitious—is it not so, Mr. Brooke?"

"That depends," Brooke replied. "My advice to every man who comes to Monte Carlo would be to gamble strictly according to his means. Personally, I think that a mille is a very nice little win for the evening. I think that I should button it up in my pocket and go home."

The contempt in her face was almost withering. She rose to her feet.

"You are both very small men," she declared. "I think that I will play *chemin de fer*. The grand duke is keeping a place for me."

"Come and play roulette," Hardways begged eagerly. "You promised to show me some new *coups*."

"If you have the courage," she replied. "Come, then."

Brooke passed in and out of the rooms once or twice that evening, and on each occasion he saw Hardways and the princess, the former always stooping a little over the table, the other at his elbow, sometimes advising, sometimes encouraging. Hardways's face had lost the sleek, self-satisfied appearance of earlier in the evening. He was alternately pale and flushed. His eyes seemed to have drawn closer together. He appeared to be winning, so far as one could judge from the pile in front of him. The princess and he both held little cards and were evidently playing upon a system.

Brooke left them there to stroll on the Terrace with some friends and did not return. The next morning, however, about twelve o'clock, he met Hardways in the street. The man looked tired but triumphant. He was wearing a new Homburg hat and carrying a great bunch of roses in his hand.

"Just going to leave these at the Paris for the princess," he announced, greeting Brooke. "Let's have a drink first. I want to tell you about last night."

They seated themselves at one of the tables in front of the Café de Paris. The change in Hardways was momentous. His hands twitched nervously, his eyes had grown narrow. He had already lost some portion of his fresh color.

"Last night," he declared, leaning over toward Brooke and speaking in a low, eager tone, "I won eight thousand francs. Just think of it! I'm a poorish man, you know. Think of what it means. Eight thousand francs! It was dead easy, too. The princess has a system. I simply followed. I've got a bit of a head for figures and the money rolled in. I am moving down to the Paris this afternoon."

"Glad you've been lucky," Brooke remarked; "but that sort of thing doesn't always go on, you know."

"Because people don't keep their heads," Hardways explained eagerly. "Now this system of mine, or rather the princess's, if you know when to leave off, is infallible. You win so much a day and you stop. The moment you begin to lose, you chuck it. See what I mean?"

Brooke smiled. "I tell you frankly that I am no believer in systems," he confessed.

Hardways seemed almost angry.

"Anyway," he continued, a little defiantly, "I have won eight thousand francs, and I've made up my mind to win a hundred thousand before I go home. It makes all the difference to me. Just fancy, the whole of my work last year barely brought me in as much as I have in my pocket at the present moment!"

"Supposing you had lost it," Brooke asked, "wouldn't that have been inconvenient?"

Hardways finished his drink. "I didn't lose," he said shortly, "and I'm not going to. No one need if they know how to play. I am just going to drop in at the Casino for half an hour."

He got up and walked away. Brooke strolled up as far as Ciro's to order a table for luncheon and back again toward the Terrace. He passed Hardways coming out of the Casino. The man's air of satisfaction was almost fatuous.

"A thousand francs," he remarked. "Quite easily, too. The system again."

"Wonderful!" Brooke murmured.

The obvious did not at once happen.

Two evenings later Hardways walked into the bar about three o'clock in the morning with his hands in his pockets and a bright spot of color in his cheeks.

"I've done it!" he declared to Brooke. "I've won two hundred thousand francs! I've finished. I'm off back to Hyères tomorrow morning."

Brooke congratulated him, and at that moment the princess came slowly into the room. She was all in black, with a diamond collar around her neck and a diamond star upon her bosom. Hardways watched her come with a peculiar expression in his strained face.

"That's the most maddening woman!" he muttered. "No wonder—"

"Did I hear you say," she asked slowly, "that you were going?"

"I have won two hundred thousand francs," he replied triumphantly. "I'm off back with it."

She smiled, so slowly that the contempt of her lips was scarcely noticeable.

"You have no use for money, then, beyond two hundred thousand francs?" she murmured. "How right I was! Let us talk no more of the matter. Give me some wine, will you? I am tired."

She sank into a chair and Brooke, after a few moments, departed. When he came back Hardways was seated at the table, playing, and behind him stood the princess, her face white and set. An hour later their places were vacant. The princess passed Brooke and paused to whisper in his ear.

"It is the beginning of the end! He has lost half his winnings. He will stay—until he has recovered them."

The next day Brooke played golf above the clouds at La Turbie and dined with some friends at Cap Martin in the evening. He looked in at the Sporting Club only for an hour on the following afternoon, but there were no signs of either the princess or Hardways.

He found a note from her, however, at his hotel, inviting him to a supper-party that night at her rooms. He accepted, owing to some faint curiosity which he could not help feeling as to the fate of the man Hardways.

The company was small but select—a Russian grand duke, a couple of very well-known French actresses, an Englishman with whom Brooke was acquainted, and an American whose yacht was in the harbor. There was no sign of Hardways.

Brooke, who was sitting near his hostess, whispered an inquiry about him toward the close of the meal. Once more that peculiar smile he had never wholly understood played for a moment upon her lips.

"It is finished," she murmured. "It was difficult, for the man's luck at starting was prodigious. It is all over now, though."

Almost as she uttered the words some one pushed on one side the footman who was entering the room. Hardways himself stood there—a broken, dejected, yet threatening figure. He was still in morning dress. He looked as though he had neither washed nor touched his hair for many hours. He glared at them all.

"Princess," he called out, "I want to speak to you at once."

She turned her head and looked at him.

"Gustave," she directed, "you had better remove that person. He has not the *entrée* here."

"*Entrée* be damned!" Hardways shouted. "It's your fault I'm in this mess. The fellow you introduced to cash my checks has stripped me. I'm ruined! I tell you I'm not going back to face it. Lend me a few mille. Let me have one more try. If you don't, I'll shoot myself here."

He actually drew a pistol from his pocket. Not a soul moved.

"Will you lend me five mille?" he cried. "If any one tries to take this away from me I'll shoot him first. Answer!"

The princess's answer was a laugh. She had lowered her lorgnette and sat there, exquisite, maddening, laughing even with her eyes.

"But the man is mad!" she declared. "Mad with presumption, too, to cross my threshold. Shoot yourself by all means, dear M. Hardways. Others have done it before you."

The silence which followed her words seemed to have become possessed of a quality intensely, breathlessly dramatic. One felt that the man's finger had stiffened upon the trigger of his pistol. Suddenly Brooke rose to his feet and walked calmly across the room.

"Give me that," he said quietly. Hardways hesitated, and that moment's hesitation weakened him. He was trembling now like a child. Brooke took the pistol from him and thrust it into his pocket.

"Not even a grain of pluck left!" the princess remarked scathingly. "Throw him into the street, Gustave. See that we are not disturbed again."

The servants, brave enough now, rushed him out. The princess turned round once more to the supper-table.

"A most impossible person," she declared. "I was unfortunate enough to have made his acquaintance when I was a girl, and he has made himself a nuisance to me. That, however, is ended now. Let us go into the salon and play."

Two days later Brooke met the princess in the hall at the Paris. She beckoned him to her.

"I want to speak to you," she said.

"I am at your service, princess," he replied.

She moved toward the lift and they mounted to the fourth floor. She consulted the number of the key which she was carrying and led him to a room at the end of the corridor. It was a small apartment with windows looking out upon the back. There was a heap of masculine clothing upon the bed. The room had apparently been vacated in a hurry. Upon the mantelpiece were some photographs.

"It is Mr. Hardways's room," she remarked. Brooke nodded.

"What has become of him?"

"They do not know," she replied. "He does not appear to have returned here after he left my rooms two nights ago. You see, he has left his belongings. I inquired, and the manager permitted me to inspect his apartment."

Brooke looked grave.

"I suppose, then," he said hesitatingly, "he found the courage. Tell me what really happened to him."

"The tide turned," she answered slowly, "as I meant that it should. I stood over him and I watched him lose—lose all that he had won, all that he had with him. Then I introduced him to Felix, and Felix cashed his checks, one after the other, up to the amount that the man was worth."

"You mean that he is ruined?"

"Absolutely. To the last penny."

Brooke glanced at the photographs upon the mantelpiece. They were commonplace enough, except that the woman had a pleasant face. One was a family group in which Hardways himself was sitting in the garden with three children and his wife grouped around him. It was an undistinguished-looking picture. The princess looked at it through her lorgnette.

"I suppose," she said, "people find happiness in this sort of thing."

"Without a doubt they do, princess," Brooke agreed.

She remained silent. The picture seemed, in a way, to fascinate her.

"Do you know," she said presently, "that I was very nearly in that picture?"

"You were engaged to marry him?" Brooke ventured to ask.

"I was engaged to marry him," she admitted. "He threw me over. I was only a governess. His people were of the small professional class. They considered that a marriage with me would have spoiled his chances. I wonder!"

She moved about restlessly for a minute or two. Brooke looked around the room once more. It was untidy, ordinary. The princess was gazing steadfastly at the photographs. She beckoned at last to Brooke.

"Come with me, please."

She led the way to her own apartments, a magnificent suite upon the first floor. From her desk she handed him a little packet.

"I have discovered," she remarked, "your reputation. You are supposed to be an amateur detective, are you not? You will please find this man Hardways, if he is alive, and give him this."

"If he is alive?" Brooke repeated doubtfully. She shrugged her shoulders.

"It is for you to discover," she said, only her voice trembled a little.

"Give me a letter to the chief of the police here," Brooke suggested. "One can learn nothing without influence. It is no use my searching for Hardways if indeed he has his place already in the little plot."

She wrote a few lines and gave them to him. Brooke took his leave. On the following evening Brooke entered the smoking-room of the Paradise Hotel in Hyères from which Hardways had come. A familiar voice attracted his attention almost at once.

"Time of my life, my boy!" Hardways, who was the center of a little group sitting around the billiard-table, declared.

"Met no end of old pals. Absolutely top-hole, every minute of it."

"Did you make a bit?" some one asked him.

"Came out about level," was the nonchalant reply. "A few mille up one day and down the next. Nothing to speak of. Lost all my luggage on the way back, though."

Brooke strolled a little farther into the room. The man Hardways looked at him, and the hand which held his cigar began to shake. Brooke greeted him with moderate affability.

"How are you? Saw you in the Sporting Club a few evenings ago, didn't I?"

"Yes, I was there," Hardways admitted. "I remember you quite well."

They drifted apart, but when a few moments later Brooke left the room, Hardways followed him.

"Can I have a word with you?" he begged nervously.

"Come outside," Brooke replied. "I have something to say to you, too."

They strolled along the terrace until they came to a seat behind some trees.

"Look here," Hardways said, "I hoped no one would turn up here just yet who was at Monte Carlo when I was. You know what happened to me?"

"I know," Brooke admitted.

"I meant to shoot myself. I wasn't game. It was just the thought of the wife and the kids, if it happened there. I wanted to make it easier for them. I have begun bathing down at the Plage. A chap went with me this morning. I am going alone to-morrow. I sha'n't come back. You see? It won't seem quite so bad." The man was in earnest this time beyond a doubt. He was pale, and his face was twitching.

Brooke produced the packet.

"I have come to Hyères to see you," he said. "The princess sent me. When you first appeared you reawakened in her some impulse of resentment. She did her best to make you lose at roulette. She did her best to break you."

"It is a judgment upon me!" the man muttered, looking steadily before him.

"The princess has changed her mind," Brooke told him, placing the packet in the man's hand. "There are your checks and your losings. You need not mind taking them. Her husband left her three millions."

The man seemed as though turned to stone.

"I can't take her money," he faltered. "I behaved like a cad years ago."

"She has forgiven you," Brooke said calmly. "She can afford, perhaps, to forgive. You must take the money for the sake of your family."

The man's fingers tightened over the packet. His head drooped. Brooke glanced at his watch and rose to his feet.

"Any message?" he asked.

Hardways tried to speak, but he found it difficult. He sat there gripping the packet. Every moment his face began to look more natural.

"Thank her," he said simply. "I'll take the money. After all, she married a prince."

TALE THE THIRD
THE OTHER SIDE OF THE WALL

"Can I speak to you for a moment, sir, if you please?"

The Hon. Stanley Brooke, who had just left the booking-office at Covent Garden Theater and was passing under the portico, turned around at the words, indifferently curious.

A man had touched him upon the arm and stood by his side now, patiently waiting for a reply. At first glance he seemed entirely of the usual type. His clothes were shabby, his expression furtive, his smooth civility of the servile order. He was small, almost undersized; pallid, with narrow lips and protruding chin. The more Brooke looked at him, the less he liked his appearance.

"Do I look the sort of person likely to give money to a man who is out of work, with a wife just recovering from an operation?" he asked patiently.

"It isn't your appearance made me speak to you," the man replied quickly. "It's the fact that you're the Hon. Stanley Brooke, sir."

"You have the advantage of me," Brooke remarked.

"My name wouldn't interest you," the man continued hurriedly. "I'm cadging, right enough, but not in the way you think. I've heard them talking about you—some one pointed you out in Herbert's bar. When I saw you coming out of the booking-office at the theater there I made up my mind to speak to you. You take an interest in queer things and places, don't you?"

"To a certain extent I do—and queer people," Brooke assented.

The man moved a trifle nearer. More than ever, as he stood

there, with his overcoat buttoned up to his chin, looking half fearfully around, he seemed like some hunted animal.

"I could tell you something," he said, "if I had a chance. Will you come to my room to-night, any time after nine? No. 14 Hender Street, off Long Acre—straight up the stairs—There's my name chalked on the door—Robinson."

"What am I to come for?" Brooke asked.

"I'll put you onto something," the man replied, dropping his voice a little—"put you onto a job."

"I think," Brooke remarked thoughtfully, "that if any exchange of hospitalities is to take place between us, I would rather be host. You can come and see me, if you like, at my rooms—No. 10 Peter Street—between seven and eight this evening."

"It wouldn't be any good," the man replied. "What I want to tell you I can only tell you in my room. I dare not come up to the West End, either. I should be followed. You don't run any risk. It's simply a bit of money I want, and you shall have value for it, but I don't want to be seen with you."

Brooke scratched his chin thoughtfully for a moment. It was raining slightly, and he noticed that the man had crept beneath the shelter of his umbrella. His desire to avoid observation was certainly not assumed.

"I know nothing of you," Brooke remarked, "and there are obvious objections to my visiting you in Long Acre. For anything I know, you may be a blackmailer or a thief, or any sort of bad character. Will you come to me if I stand a taxicab?"

"I won't," the man answered. "I tell you it's only from my room you can understand what I want to put before you. You've nothing to be afraid of. I live alone there with my sister. There's no one else on the premises. You could double me up, if I tried to rob you, with one hand. Say you'll come to-night. Don't put it off. It's worth while."

"I'll come," Brooke promised. The man moved away. Brooke turned around and watched him shuffle across the road.

"Let myself in for something!" he sighed.

It happened to be an evening without any engagements for Brooke. He dined in his rooms without changing his clothes, wrote a line or two upon half a sheet of note-paper, with the address to which he was going and the reasons for his visit, and left it upon the table, as was his custom when he was bound upon any unsavory errand.

At nine o'clock he walked eastward, turned into Long Acre, and discovered Hender Street without any particular difficulty. No. 16 consisted of an automobile showroom on the ground floor, which was now closed.

An open door by the side led him to a flight of stairs, at the top of which, as he had been advised, he found the word "Robinson" written in white chalk upon an uninviting-looking panel from which most of the paint seemed to have been scraped off.

He had scarcely knocked before the door was opened from inside. The little man who had accosted him in the street was standing there. He almost dragged Brooke in, stood for a moment listening, then closed the door.

"Did you happen to notice whether any one saw you come in?" he asked quickly.

"So far as I could see, the street was empty," Brooke replied.

He stood looking around him with some curiosity. The room was barely furnished, lit by one common lamp, close to which, upon an uncovered deal table, was a worn and battered typewriter. Seated before it was a girl.

She turned her head at his approach and looked at him. She was very pale, but there were about her appearance contradictions which puzzled Brooke. She wore a crimson serge dress, which gave her a general impression of tawdriness. Her hands were well-shaped and white, however; her hair neatly arranged.

The hat which hung on a peg by her side—a most dejected-looking piece of millinery—was trimmed with flowers of faded brilliance. Still when she looked at him, curiously, yet with a certain indifference, he was surprised at the quality of her eyes.

"It's my sister," the man explained. "She gets a little typing sometimes, as you see. One of the offices sends her some work."

"And what do you do for a living?" Brooke inquired.

The man hesitated.

"Anything," he replied, a little defiantly. "I've been in prison three times. I expect I shall be in again before long. Sit down, sir, if you will."

Brooke looked at the one wooden chair and shook his head.

"Thanks," he said, "I'd rather stand. Please be as brief as possible."

"You've nothing to be afraid of," the man declared, with the first note of resentment in his tone.

"Possibly not," Brooke agreed, watching the girl. "You brought me here, though, and I want to know what for."

The little man cleared his throat.

"It's the house next door," he said. "It's locked up in front—bolts and bars across the window. The back entrance is locked, too. It's been empty for months. The Miller Automobile Company had it and failed."

"Well?" Brooke remarked. "I saw that it was empty—dust all over the windows. What about it?"

"Step this way a moment, sir." Brooke obeyed the summons. The man was standing close to the wall by the side of the fireplace.

"This house and the next one were connected a few years ago," he said. "This wall has only been built up lately. It's nothing but lath and plaster. Look here." He removed a picture, cut out from some illustrated paper, which had been pinned upon the wall. From the spot which it had covered he took out a brick, thrust his arm in, and pulled out two more. He laid them softly upon the floor. All the time he was almost holding his breath.

"Stoop down and look!"

Brooke obeyed him. There was one more brick apparently still remaining, but the mortar had slipped away, and from all around it came a little gleam of dull light.

"Get your head as near as you can," Robinson whispered. "Listen!"

Brooke obeyed. At first he heard nothing, however. There was some sort of light in the room, but no sound. He was on the point of withdrawing his head when the silence was suddenly broken. A man's voice was heard—a man's voice which seemed to come with queer, rolling regularity. Brooke listened hard, but was unable to make out any word. Then there was silence, broken almost immediately by the sound of several voices speaking in unison. This time there seemed to be no doubt about it. The reply was a sort of monotonous chant. One man had spoken and others had replied. Brooke listened with more interest. The same thing happened several times. Then again there was silence. Brooke stepped away from the wall.

"What on earth is it all about?" he asked.

The man Robinson shook his head.

"I know nothing," he said, and his voice sounded weak and faint. "Only, if you go downstairs, you will find that the entrance to the house is locked and barred, and the back entrance is locked, too. Neither I nor any one else sees people enter. And yet there is that!"

Brooke brushed the dust from his clothes.

"It is certainly curious," he admitted. "What do you think about it, young lady?"

She raised her eyes and looked at him.

"All that I think of it is," she said, "that it is safer in this world, and in this little corner of London, to mind one's own business. That is what I tell my brother."

"Can one live by minding one's own business?" Robinson exclaimed excitedly. "Don't laugh—I was a gentleman once. I'm anything you like now, down to a gutter thief, but I have something of the tastes left. I want money—God knows how I want it!"

"What is your proposition?" Brooke inquired.

"Not much of a one, anyway. There's a mystery there, and you're a lover of mysteries. I've disclosed it to you, as much as I know of or dare know. Help yourself and pay me. It ought to be worth a ten-pound note to you. You're rich, they say, and just go round looking for adventures. You can have all the adventure you like if you can get into that room. I know nothing about it, but I'll guarantee that. Give me a tenner."

"Do you propose to assist me in any further steps I might take toward the elucidation of this affair?" Brooke asked curiously.

The man began to shake as though he had an ague.

"Not for my life!" he declared. "I've seen too many queer things in this city. If you're curious, I'm not."

"What about your room here?"

"Your last visit," Robinson insisted feverishly. "I'm not going to be connected with anything that happens. Do you hear? I tell you I won't be! I just want a ten-pound note from you, and out you go and forget you've ever seen me. And if you want excitement—my God! you'll have value for your money!"

Brooke shook his head. "You are a little mistaken as to my vocation and tastes," he explained. "I am not a curious person. If any one consults me, and I can help him, I do so. On the other hand, I should say that an affair like this, with which I am not connected in any way, is a matter either for the police or for the tenants of the flat."

"You mean you won't do anything?"

"Nothing at all, thank you," Brooke replied, taking up his hat. "If you will accept a sovereign as a loan or gift or whatever you like to call it, it is yours, with pleasure. So far as I am concerned, that is the end of the matter."

The man was obviously disappointed. He accepted the sovereign, however, with eagerness.

"My advice to you would be," Brooke concluded, as he prepared to depart, "to give information to the police as to anything that may be going on in the next house. They will probably reward you, if your information turns out to be worth anything."

Robinson said nothing, but his face seemed to grow tense.

"I may have to," he muttered. "I'm up against it. I want money. After all, one's life isn't worth much if one starves. Go down quietly, please."

Brooke turned toward the girl, but she was already bending over her work. He lingered upon the threshold. There was a queer sort of tired grace in the stiff, unbending lines of her figure.

"Good night, young lady," he said pleasantly.

"Good night!" she replied, without raising her head.

Brooke strolled back down Hender Street into Long Acre and returned to his rooms. Once or twice he paused as though to look into a shop-window, but he was not able on that night to verify absolutely his suspicions.

Yet from the moment he left the little house in Hender Street he had the impression that he was being followed. The same idea came to him once or twice during the next few days. He had always the uncomfortable sense that he was under surveillance.

He thought little more of his visit. There were possibly lawbreakers of some sort in the place—very likely by arrangement with the landlord. In any case, the affair did not greatly interest him. It was not until the third day, when he picked up the morning paper and read that a man named Robinson had been found dead on the Embankment, within a dozen paces of Scotland Yard, that he felt any real interest in the matter.

Late that afternoon Brooke found his way once more to the house in Hender Street. He passed along the passage, climbed the stairs, and knocked at the door. The girl's tired voice bade him enter. She did not rise from her seat. She simply glanced around as he entered. He noticed with a little thrill of horror that she was still wearing the crimson-colored gown.

"What do you want?" she demanded.

He closed the door behind him. She awaited an answer to her question with her fingers still resting upon the keys.

"Is this true that I have read in the papers about your brother?" he inquired gravely.

"It is true," she answered. "What of it?"

Brooke was a little staggered. Her utter lifelessness of tone and manner was incredible. It was as though she were without feelings or any sort of emotion.

"It is a very terrible thing," he said. "I am very sorry for you."

"Why are you sorry?" she asked. "And why is it a very terrible thing? Death may seem terrible enough to you people who lead happy lives. To us, who are facing broken hour after hour upon the wheel, death is the night which is all we have to look forward to."

He sensed a chill in his blood. Somehow he felt that ordinary forms of speech were wholly out of place with this remarkable young woman. She had leaned a little back in her chair, however, as though willing to desist, for a moment, from her labors.

"Are you going to remain here?" he asked, a little diffidently.

She looked at him with cold scrutiny.

"Whether I live here or elsewhere, whether I choose to live at all or to die," she remarked, "is no concern of a stranger."

"I am sorry if I have offended you," he began.

"Will you kindly tell me why you have come?" she interrupted. "You will be able to go the sooner."

"I have come," he explained, "because I want to know what you think about your brother's death. The papers are divided in their opinion. Some say that he fell down and got concussion of the brain; others seem to think that he was murdered."

"If it interests you to know the truth," she said, "he was murdered on his way to give information at Scotland Yard about the next house."

Her matter-of-fact words, delivered in her quiet, tired tone, seemed to Brooke the most thrilling he had ever heard. He had never realized more completely the presence of tragedy. He moved a little nearer to her.

"Look here!" he exclaimed; "doesn't this thing move you? Doesn't it seem terrible to you? Can you sit there and tell me, without the slightest emotion, that your brother was murdered?"

"He knew very well what would happen," she replied. "He has known for weeks what would happen if he approached the police. That is why he chose rather to come to you; only, you see, you very wisely declined to meddle in an affair which has nothing to do with you."

"Then what, in God's name, is this affair?" he demanded. "Who are these people who murder rather than have information as to their doings given to the police? And how did your brother become connected with them?"

"Because," she replied, "my brother was employed by one of them until he was thrown out for unworthiness."

"For unworthiness?" Brooke muttered. She nodded.

"There is honor, you know, among thieves and criminals and sinners of every description," she said. "My brother had sunk so low that, although he was willing to pilfer himself, to rob in any way, to rob with violence if he had the strength or the courage, he was yet equally willing to make money by giving away those whose sins were of a different order to his. He had sunk so low that a man can sink no lower."

"He is dead!" Brooke whispered, shivering.

"Don't you think you should remember that?"

"I have no sentiment," she answered scornfully. "For this last year I have known him to be one of the lowest things that crawls. You are surprised, perhaps, that I am not in black, weeping over his memory. The earth is a cleaner place for his absence. That is all that I feel about his death."

"Nothing else?"

"Perhaps one little spark of admiration," she replied defiantly, "for the men who have the courage to remove such as he from their path."

Brooke had lost his imperturbability. He was horrified, and showed it. He tried one counter stroke, however.

"If," he asked, "your point of view is as you suggest, why do you sit here grinding out a miserable living from that battered old typewriter? Why don't you join the great crowd of those who fatten upon the fools of the earth?"

She turned and faced him. Something very grim, but which might almost have developed into a smile, trembled at the corners of her lips.

"Because," she told him, "I do not happen to have come into contact with any illegal means of earning my livelihood. The ordinary methods of my sex, unfortunately, do not appeal to me. I have no ideals, I do not value character a straw, but I have certain tastes and preferences, the gratification of which keeps me from—any word you choose to give it," she added, looking him full in the eyes.

"I speak, perhaps, rather of the past than of the present," she continued. "I am older now and a little tired. There were times when I was considered good-looking. May I ask whether you intend to keep me much longer answering your questions?"

"I will pay you for your time," Brooke declared bruskly.

"Thank you," she replied, "I accept payment for the work I do. This isn't work."

"So you are proud," he remarked. "You would like to be a criminal, but you won't take money, you tell me."

She shrugged her shoulders scornfully.

"You belong to those who don't understand," she said shortly. "Any one can see that you are half a fool."

"I am going to prove," Brooke retorted, "that I am a whole one. I am going to solve the mystery of the next house."

For a single second a shadow of something new appeared in her face.

"If I were you," she advised, "I wouldn't."

"You wouldn't care to help, then?"

"I should not!"

"Do you mind if I listen once more at the wall?"

"You can do as you like," she answered indifferently.

Brooke made his way to the spot which Robinson had showed him, carefully removed the bricks, and listened. There was, without doubt, some one in the adjoining room. One voice only was audible—the voice of one man apparently speaking in a monotonous singsong, as though he were delivering some sort of an address.

Punctuated by those level sentences, every now and then came a fainter sound, to which Brooke listened with something like dismay. It was like the moan of an animal—or was it a child in pain— He replaced the bricks.

"I wonder," he said to the girl, "whether the police have ever searched that house?"

"Why not save your own skin and go and ask them to?" she suggested.

Brooke came and stood by the side of her typewriter.

"Listen," he continued; "I am going through with this little adventure myself. Isn't there anything you can tell me?"

"Why should I?" she asked defiantly. "If they are criminals who meet there, why should I be on your side more than theirs? I am a fragment of the debris of the world myself."

"You are not," he answered steadily. "You have courage. I believe that you have other gifts."

She set her teeth.

"In any case," she declared bruskly, "I have nothing to tell you. If you want my advice, you've had it, but I'll give it you again. Don't meddle in things that don't concern you."

"Will you do some typewriting for me?" Brooke asked.

"At nine-pence a thousand words and three-pence extra for carbon copies," she assented. "I'd rather do it for any one else. That doesn't matter."

"I will take the liberty, then," Brooke replied, moving toward the door, "of coming to see you later on."

Again, as he left the house, Brooke was conscious that he was being shadowed. He stopped once or twice and retraced his steps, but he was never able definitely to decide whence came the subtle, ever present feeling.

Finally, with a shrug of the shoulders, he abandoned his half-formed intention of examining the premises from the outside and, turning into Long Acre, took a taxicab back to his rooms.

On the hall table was a letter addressed to him in a bold masculine handwriting and with a London postmark. He opened it at once. A single line written in thick, black ink, with several notes of exclamation, seemed to stare up at him from the half-sheet of paper:

Keep away from Hender Street, Mr. Brooke!!!!

Brooke thrust the letter into his pocket. At last he had some definite proof that he was not wasting his time. In the morning he paid a visit to the house-agents and learned that the empty house in question had been leased to the manager of the defunct automobile company, who was now abroad. The agreement had one year to run, and the agents had had no notice of any sub-letting.

Brooke walked from their offices to Hender Street. Without any attempt at concealment, he examined the front of the house. It was not only locked and barricaded, but there was dust upon the fastenings. He made his way to the back entrance. The gate leading into the little strip of asphalt was fastened with a chain. There was no sign that it had been disturbed for a long time.

He made his way to the front again. Suddenly the door of the adjoining house was opened and a man was literally thrown into the street. Brooke caught a glimpse of a negro in the background—a stern and ferocious-looking figure. Then the door was closed.

A thin, weedy-looking young man picked himself up from the ground, took off his spectacles to be sure that they were not broken, and began to knock the dust off his clothes. He saw Brooke regarding him with astonishment, and smiled faintly.

"Just my luck to run up against this sort of thing!" he exclaimed. "All in the day's work, though."

"Did you annoy any one?" Brooke inquired.

"It seems so," the young man answered. "I am a reporter on the *Weekly Post*, and I went to interview Kinsey Brand."

"The African traveler?" Brooke asked quickly.

The young man nodded. They had fallen into step together and set their faces southward.

"Yes," he replied. "That was his servant who just hurried me out. He's got two of them. He need never be afraid of burglars with two beauties like that on the premises!"

"Better have a drink," Brooke suggested—"pull you together."

The young man assented readily. They entered a bar and sat on high stools.

"What did you want to interview Kinsey Brand about?" Brooke asked.

"Oh, they say he's brought home a new religion—discovered it among the natives, where they have been practising it for two thousand years," the young man continued. "All the magazines have tried to get him to write about it, but he won't, and every reporter in London has tried to get at him, unsuccessfully. They generally end where I did!"

"This," Brooke murmured, "is very interesting."

The young man felt his back.

"What I should like to do," he declared, "would be to get Jack Johnson to stroll in there with a note-book and ask him a few questions. As a matter of fact, I never saw Kinsey Brand at all. I was just giving the negro half a sovereign when I heard a voice that sounded like a bellow, and out I went."

"Queer place for the man to live," Brooke remarked.

"He's got a bit of money, too, I should think," the reporter continued. "Lots of skins and things about the place. Smelled like a corner of the zoological gardens."

"What is this religion—do you know?" Brooke asked.

"No idea," the young man answered. "Seems to make 'em tolerably muscular! The only reporter who got Brand to say a word was Ted Foales, of the *Express*. He told him that all he wanted to do was to be left alone; that he wanted neither converts nor critics."

"It's not a money-making job, then," Brooke remarked thoughtfully.

"About the only religion that ain't," the young man murmured, looking into the bottom of his empty glass. "I don't know that I blame 'em, either. If I'd got a brand-new religion to foist on the world, I'd run it for all it was worth. One would be able to stand a gentleman a drink then, in return for any little civility one might receive."

Brooke took the hint and the young man's glass was replenished.

"Between you and me," the latter said, moving his stool a little closer to Brooke's, "if I had the time and the money and the physique and the courage I should like to stick to this Kinsey Brand. There are some queer stories going about.

"They say he went mad on the voyage home from West Africa, and that he brought home a negro and a native priest. If so, he's got 'em in that house. While I was there I heard a man making noises in a tongue which made you feel as though you were in a monkey forest. The only visitors he ever has are three or four old cronies, all West Africans, and they almost live in the place."

"It all sounds very mysterious."

"I was too scared to look about me much," the young man continued; "but just inside that passage what do you think there was, hanging down from the ceiling? A long, double-edged knife, hung by a piece of gold thread! The knife was stained all over, and I'll swear it was blood. Nice, cheerful sight to greet you when you step in!"

"I should imagine," Brooke remarked, "that Mr. Kinsey Brand's instincts are not hospitable."

The young man grunted.

"Anyway, I've done with him," he declared. "Any one else can take up the job!"

At ten o'clock that night Brooke sat in his rooms with an open letter and a pile of newspapers by his side. The former he had just received from the librarian of a large book-shop from whom he made occasional purchases. It was not very long, but its contents were interesting:

> Dear Sir:
> I am sending you the file of papers, procured with great difficulty, and I beg that you will take every care of them. It is a very remarkable circumstance that the letters from Mr. Kinsey Brand, for which the *Times* was paying a large sum, ceased abruptly on the eve of his projected visit to one of the most interesting spots in Africa. Since then, notwithstanding the large offers which have been made to him, Mr. Kinsey Brand has not, so far as we know, set his hand to paper at all, either in the form of articles or volume. It is understood that his health was affected by privations, and that he had no further inclination to write of his travels. The affair, however, is in some respects mysterious, and I may say that many efforts

have been made, even up to the last few weeks, to obtain some explanation.

> Faithfully yours,
> S. Clowes.

The interest of the newspapers culminated in the issue of latest date. For the second or third time Brooke was reading some extracts of a letter written about two years ago and signed "Kinsey Brand":

> To-morrow I expect to reach the holy village of Nah-u-weh. If reports are true, I shall have an opportunity there of studying the primeval religion of these Western tribes, founded, they say, upon a contemplation of the extinction of life. They make a cult of watching the death struggles of animals and, on certain days of the year, human beings. The soul, as it escapes, is declared to be visible to the priest, who is able to transmit by it messages to the Supreme Being. This, however, is all hearsay. I shall know more about it in my next letter.

There was a knock at the door. Brooke's servant entered, bearing a note. Brooke took it and glanced at it, carelessly at first and then with a sudden interest. It was addressed to him in typewritten characters, and in the corner it was marked "Urgent." He tore it open and read the following:

> Mr. Brooke:
> If you are still interested in the house next door, you had better come here at once. Some thing is going on at the other side of the wall. It seems to me that they have discovered the opening and are enlarging it from their side.
>
> Constance Robinson

Brooke sprang to his feet, made a few hasty preparations, took a taxicab to the corner of Hender Street, passed up the passage and the stairs, and knocked at the door above. There was no reply. He turned the handle and entered. The room was empty.

On the floor was the typewriter, lying on its side, broken. By the side of the wall were half a dozen loose bricks and a quantity of plaster. There was a hole in the wall, stuffed up with paper, large enough for a man to pass through. Brooke stood for a moment, rooted to the spot. Caught on a corner of the fender was a torn fragment of something red. He recognized it at once—it was a portion of the girl's dress.

Then, as he stood there slowly collecting his senses, he distinctly heard a low, half-stifled moan from the interior of the room beyond. The sound suddenly awakened his energies. He scarcely paused for thought.

He tore off his overcoat and coat, threw himself on all fours, and made one plunge at the mass of paper which alone blocked the opening. He was through in a moment and on his feet in the room on the other side of the wall before any one could seize him.

For a few seconds there was a grim and ghastly silence. Brooke looked around him wildly. The apartment was unfurnished, save that the floor was covered with thick rugs, and three benches were placed near the farther wall. There were six men present altogether, three of whom were sitting with folded arms upon the farthest bench. They had the air and attitude of spectators.

Directly facing them was a man as black as ink, dressed in a yellow robe, and holding a long knife of thin blue steel in his hand; not far off stood a gaunt, strange-looking person, with parchment-white skin and burning eyes, whom Brooke recognized in an instant, from his pictures, as Kinsey Brand, the explorer. Behind the two men a gigantic negro was standing with lamps in his hands, and in front of them the girl, bound with cords which cut deeply into her dress, was lying stretched upon a block of wood.

Her face was absolutely colorless, her eyes black and staring.

There was a curious, sickly odor which seemed to come from the lamps which the negro was swinging. All these things were before Brooke like a flash. For some reason or other, probably owing to the fact that the ceremony at which they were assisting had reached what to them was its most impressive stage, no one stirred from his place during those few seconds. Brooke had time to withdraw his hand from his hip pocket. He stood there with his feet firmly planted upon the ground and his back to the wall. In his hand the revolver glittered like silver in the light of the red flame. Then, without removing his eyes from the priest, he shouted as though to unseen followers:

"Come on, you men! I've got them! They are all here! See that the house is surrounded!"

The priest, for such he seemed to be, suddenly raised the knife which he was holding and crouched as though for a spring at the intruder. Brooke, who had never shot at a human being in his life, felt scarcely a tremor as he pulled the trigger of his revolver and saw the man go swaying over with a hideous cry and his hands above his head.

His downfall, the flash and report of the revolver, seemed to spread confusion among the remaining occupants of the room. The three spectators, followed by the negro, rushed for the door. Brand remained for a single moment glaring at Brooke.

Then he muttered something, something which sounded to Brooke at first like gibberish, and afterward like music, something which ended in a little impressive cry—a denunciation, perhaps, for one hand was lifted to the ceiling. Then he, too, turned and left, walking with a strange dignity.

Brooke, for the first few seconds, was dazed. Then he seized the knife and commenced to cut the cords which bound the girl. Once he paused. The atmosphere had become unbearable.

The sound below was unmistakable—the crackling and roaring of flames. He glanced at the window. A long tongue of red fire had shot up. He hacked furiously at the rope. The girl was almost fainting.

"Get through the hole," he begged, "if you can. Can you crawl?"

She nodded. He dragged her toward the opening. As he pushed her through he glanced back. A great zigzag crack had spread itself out across the opposite wall and a hissing puff of smoke rushed in. Outside he could hear the calls in the streets and the throb of the fire-engine. The girl seemed suddenly inert. She was only half-way through.

"Make an effort!" he shouted.

She disappeared. He flung himself into the opening. He, too, reached the other side. The girl was half on her feet, swaying.

"Don't faint," he implored. "Cling to me. We must make a rush for the stairs."

"Who said anything about fainting?" she replied.

"Come on!"

They rushed for the stairs, his arm around her. Below they could hear the crashing of hatchets as the firemen forced their way into the next house. A volume of smoke met them, but they reached the street in safety. The crowds of people closing in on either side cheered as they emerged from the house and made way. Some one helped her into a taxi. They drove off. She was only half conscious.

"My typewriter!" she murmured.

"We'll get a new one from the insurance company," Brooke whispered comfortingly, "Keep your courage up for a minute or two."

Her lips moved, but she had no strength to speak. Brooke drove to a nursing home, where the matron was a friend of his, and where they willingly took her in.

At eleven o'clock the next morning Brooke called at the nursing-home. The girl was lying on the sofa in her room. She looked at him steadily as he came and sat by her side.

"Well?" she asked.

"The two Africans were burned," he told her quietly. "They had planned to destroy the place by fire if anything happened, but the flames spread too quickly and their own escape was cut off."

"What about the man Brand?"

"He was found dead in his room."

"And the three spectators?"

"They must have got away," he replied. "There were no other casualties. Tell me what happened."

"I was sitting at work," she said, "when I heard them boring at the wall. I wrote a note and went down into the street to find a boy to take it to you. When I got back the African was in the room. He seized me, put something over my mouth and dragged me through to the other side of the wall.

"They tied me to that block and chanted all sorts of strange things I couldn't understand. Just as you appeared the priest had lifted that knife as though he were going to stab me, and I heard Kinsey Brand cry out in English: 'Watch for her soul!'"

Brooke shuddered.

"They were all as mad as men could be," he declared.

"Will it be in the papers?"

He shook his head.

"No one would believe it! We'd better keep it to ourselves. Both houses were burned to the ground—completely destroyed."

She breathed a sigh of relief.

"What about my typewriter? asked weakly.

"Burned to ashes, and about time too," he replied briskly. "The 'g' crooked and the 'w' had a twist in the middle. You shall have a brand-new one and plenty of work as soon as you are able to start."

She fidgeted for a moment and frowned. Then she sighed. There was something a little pathetic in the abnegation of her ill manners.

"You are very kind," she said, her voice shaking a little, "you have been very kind indeed. You saved my life, too. I wanted to die, but not—like that!"

"You've got to make up your mind that it was all just a dream— a nightmare, if you like," Brooke declared cheerfully. "The program is three days here, three weeks at a branch of this place at Bournemouth. After that as much typewriting as you like. I can get you bushels of work."

She covered her eyes with her handkerchief as though weary. Her lips trembled.

Brooke stole away.

TALE THE FOURTH
THE MURDER OF WILLIAM BLESSING

I

THE HON. STANLEY BROOKE leaned back in his steamer-chair and yawned. A pleasant and bracing west wind blew in his face the white-topped waves were all aglint with sunshine. His surroundings were altogether delightful. There was, in fact, only one circumstance which made him inclined to regret this suddenly arranged trip across the Atlantic. This was his third day out, and he was bored.

The usual distractions were offered him.

"Care to make a fourth at shuffleboard, sir?" a bare-headed young man asked, pausing tentatively before his chair and brandishing a fearful looking implement with a scooped-out end.

Brooke shook his head.

"I'm not very keen on deck games," he confessed; "thanks all the same."

A head was thrust out from the smoking-room window. Its owner caught Brooke's eye.

"Will you come and make us up at bridge?" one of his table companions asked.

Brooke refused even more decidedly.

"I never play cards until after dinner," he declared.

He was left alone presently and fell to studying the people as they passed. He was beginning to realize that lately all other interests in life had become with him subordinate to this.

He appreciated the elasticity of one's powers of observation when properly ministered to, the possibility of tragedy and crime beneath the smoothest and most commonplace exterior. He had developed a habit of watchfulness. The lines about his mouth had tightened.

It was more of an effort with him now to assume that bland aspect of juvenile imbecility which had stood him more than once in such good stead. Yet it certainly seemed that upon this voyage there was little enough to engage his interest. The boat was a medium-sized one and not one of the fastest. The people were mostly Americans of the tourist type, a handful of business men—and Gordon Black. Brooke, whenever he tried to think of any one of them, found himself always thinking of Black.

The man passed as he sat there—tall, hard-featured, his hands clasped behind him, his eyes bent upon the deck. The invalid who lay flat in a chair by Brooke's side stretched out a hand and touched his neighbor on the coat-sleeve.

"Tell me," he asked in a quavering voice, "is that really Mr. Gordon Black?"

"That is his name," Brooke replied. "He looks rather an interesting character. Do you know anything about him?"

The little man looked at his questioner wonderingly. He was a small, frail person, with white hair and wasted face, and there were rumors that he was dying. He had been carried on board at Southampton, and he only appeared on deck for an hour at a time.

"Know anything about Gordon Black!" he repeated. "Why, a year or two ago he was the most talked-of man in the States!"

"Why?" Brooke asked. "Is he a celebrity, then?"

The little man—he called himself Dr. Browning, but admitted that he was only a dentist—sighed.

"Of course, you're English," he remarked, "and you wouldn't read our papers. Gordon Black was the head of a great railroad trust. He ran up against another trust, controlled by Seth Pryor, and they had the greatest financial struggle that the history of American finance has ever known.

"In the end. Black was maneuvered into a false position. He broke the law and had to leave the country. It has always been understood that there was some sort of an agreement between him and his enemies that, if he left, his followers should be spared. That's the idea, at any rate.

"Anyway, during the last two months Seth Pryor has suddenly begun to squeeze Black's followers. Black is on his way back to fight him, and Seth Pryor has sworn that as soon as he sets foot in New York he'll have him arrested."

"It sounds interesting," Brooke confessed.

"It is interesting," the other declared. "It's a romance, sir—a wonderful romance. I have never spoken to Mr. Gordon Black myself, but he is going back to face the music because he thinks it his duty, and for my part I hope he pulls through."

He leaned back in his chair and closed his eyes with the air of one fatigued by conversation. Brooke took up his book and set it down again. Afterward he decided that it must have been some mesmeric instinct which prompted him at that precise moment to struggle up from his comfortable seat, throw aside his rug, and stroll along the deck.

On his second time around he came to an abrupt standstill at the aft extremity of the promenade-deck. A few yards away from him, but in the second-class portion of the ship, a girl, whose profile was turned toward him, was leaning over the rail, bending far forward with folded arms, in an attitude which seemed to him somehow familiar.

He stood perfectly still, watching her, and then a curious thing happened. The thrill was doubtless caused by the recollection of those few breathless moments of life and death through which they two had lived together, but it is certain that Brooke felt suddenly the rush of warm blood through his veins and the singing of strange things around his heart. Without a moment's hesitation he crossed the narrow plankway and stepped to her side.

"Miss Robinson!" he exclaimed eagerly. "It really is you, then!"

She turned and looked at him. She was a little startled. Taken so completely by surprise, she seemed to forget for the moment her somewhat uncompromising attitude. Her beautiful eyes were lit with something very like pleasure, her lips parted into almost tender hues. The moment was a revelation. For the first time Brooke realized that she was beautiful.

"It really is you, then," she murmured.

"But what on earth?" he began. "I thought you were going to a post in the country."

Already her manner was stiffening. A touch of the old sullenness was in her tone. She had been taken by surprise.

"A new country," she corrected him. "I am tired of England."

"You are going to America for good?"

"Precisely," she replied. "I am an emigrant."

"I think that you might have told me," he protested.

She was already in revolt.

"And why?" she demanded. "I have already accepted charity from you. I have lived for twenty-four years in England, twelve of which have been blankly miserable. I am going to start again."

"Are you going to New York?"

"To New York," she assented.

"You have a position?"

She hesitated. She answered him grudgingly.

"I have a place," she admitted. "Forgive me, but you must go now. First-class passengers are not allowed here."

"I wonder," he said deliberately, "why you treat me as though I wanted to pick your pocket. I want to be your friend."

She turned away, her manner reluctantly ungracious.

"It is not possible," she said. "My friendship, anyhow, isn't worth having. Good-by!"

She disappeared through the companionway. Brooke retraced his steps slowly to his own deck. As he crossed the bridge he was conscious of being watched. He raised his eyes. Mr. Gordon Black was leaning over the rail, deeply interested now in the uncoiling of a rope below.

II

THAT NIGHT, or rather in the small hours of the morning, the silence of the great ship was broken by the sound of hurrying footsteps along the passage outside Brooke's stateroom, a hoarse murmuring of voices, the flying feet of an urgent messenger. Brooke put his head out of the alleyway leading to his cabin.

"Anything the matter?" he asked.

The steward whom he addressed seemed scarcely to hear him. Brooke made his way to the spot where the little group was congregated. Something dark was stretched across the passageway. Brooke looked down upon it with a shudder.

It was the body of a man—a crumpled-up heap, with the head half covered by one distorted arm. His white lips, from which the last groan had issued, were still parted. He could have been dead only a few seconds.

"Did any one see it happen?" Brooke demanded.

No one answered. No one even seemed capable of speech. Brooke turned on another of the electric lights and looked up and down the dimly lit gangway. There was not a soul in sight. The doors of every one of the adjacent staterooms were closed. The place seemed wrapped in gloomy silence; there was nothing to be heard but the thud and roar of the engines below. The only people in sight were the three who stooped over the body—Brooke's own bedroom steward, a bathroom steward, and a boy from the engine room still carrying a handful of waste.

"Didn't any one see it happen?" Brooke repeated.

The bedroom steward staggered to his feet and shook his head.

"I passed along here not three minutes ago, sir," he declared, "and there wasn't a sign of any one. I just put away some hot-water tins in the closet there. While I was doing it I thought I heard a funny noise. I came back again—and he was lying here. I couldn't have been away altogether more than sixty seconds."

"Do you know who he is?" Brooke inquired.

"He's got the end stateroom a little further along," the bathroom steward declared. "I dunno his name."

Brooke looked steadily down, trying to fix the little scene in his memory. The man was lying on the right-hand side of the gangway and had, therefore, probably been attacked from the left. The blow on his head, too, was on that side. His coat was open and a letter was protruding from it. His right hand lay across his chest, as though he had striven to clutch at something there. There were few other details worth noticing.

Then the captain arrived, followed by the doctor, and presently Brooke retreated to his cabin.

III

A BRUTAL MURDER committed upon an ocean steamer on the high seas, where the passengers rely for their casual conversation upon an occasional marconigram or fragments of gossip concerning one another, is naturally an absorbing subject of discussion.

From early morning until the bugle sounded for luncheon all games were suspended and all conversation rang the different changes around this most extraordinary and dramatic happening. Brooke threw himself thoroughly into the role of careful and attentive listener. Apart from all manner of vague rumors, however, all that was definitely known was trivial. The man's name was Blessing. He was of cheerful and sociable disposition, and appeared to have talked to every one on board.

He had never mentioned his profession, but a card in his pocketbook bore the inscription of "Agent," with an address at an office on Broadway.

He had never been seen to quarrel with any one.

The half-torn letter in his pocket was domestic and unimportant.

The staterooms opposite the spot where he had been found were empty with the exception of two, one of which was occupied by a Mr. Baines, who was with the doctor in his room at the time the affair occurred; and the other by Dr. Browning. Robbery was an impossible motive, as the murdered man had frankly confessed himself short of money, had made application to the purser for a loan, and had despatched a marconigram for a clerk to meet him on the quay with funds.

The cause of death was a blow dealt with some blunt instrument which was not forthcoming.

Brooke listened to the gossip, listened to what every one had to say, and made a few inquiries on his own account. They led him, however, to nothing in the shape of a definite conclusion. Then, a little later, while talking with the captain in his room, the latter handed him a marconigram.

"What do you make of this?" he asked. "It was addressed to Blessing. Under the circumstances, I felt justified in opening it."

Brooke glanced at the flimsy sheet. It consisted only of a few words:

LOOK OUT: T IS ON BOARD.

"Unsigned," he murmured.

"Unfortunately," the captain replied. "If we only knew who sent it, we might know who 'T' was."

"And 'T,'" Brooke added, "might be sitting in irons at this present moment."

"Precisely," the captain agreed dryly. "I don't like these things on my boat. I'm not a detective. I can't detain my passengers. The murderer will probably walk off the gangway at New York and no one will be able to stop him. I may even shake hands with him without knowing it."

"Hard luck!" Brooke declared. "Try one of these."

The captain accepted one of his visitor's cigarettes and parted from him, a few minutes later, without any very exalted opinion of his young friend's intelligence. Brooke paced slowly down the deck with his hands behind him. As he neared the spot where, on the preceding day, he had seen Constance Robinson, he glanced up. She was leaning against the rail in almost the same position, only this time she had turned a little sidewise. She was facing him, and, as he raised his cap in salutation, she beckoned him to her. He crossed the dividing bridge at once and stood by her side.

"You've heard about the murder, of course?" she asked bruskly.

"Naturally," Brooke admitted.

She looked at him for a moment, a grim smile upon her lips.

"I forgot," she went on. "The solution of crime is rather in your line, isn't it? Solve this one."

"I can't," Brooke confessed.

"Who murdered Mr. Blessing?"

"No idea!"

"And you on the spot!" she exclaimed derisively. "Fancy calling yourself a man of observation!"

Brooke looked at her steadfastly. Without a doubt she was a different person. Her hair, a little disordered in the wind, was unexpectedly luxuriant; her dark, splendid eyes were lit with gentle laughter; the glow of a new health was already stealing into her cheeks. In her plain, tight-fitting, blue serge costume, her entire absence of ornaments, she appealed to him in a subtle and entirely novel way.

"In this instance," he said simply, "I am afraid that I must confess myself a failure. I have made a great many inquiries, but they have led nowhere. Perhaps you can help me?"

She suddenly became grave.

"As it happens," she replied, "I can. Come nearer."

He stood close to her side. A few yards away an Italian squatted, playing a concertina; four men were throwing quoits; a mother was sitting with her three children. Constance glanced around and drew him to the side of the boat.

"Mr. Blessing was murdered by a man named Gordon Black," she told him. "Perhaps, as I can tell you the name of the guilty person, you can do the rest."

"How do you know?" Brooke asked.

She frowned.

"Mr. Blessing was my new employer," she told him. "He was a private detective in New York. I did some typing for him, and he formed the idea that I was intelligent enough to be of use to him permanently."

"What do you know about Gordon Black?"

"I know that Mr. Blessing had been to England to collect evidence against him for complicity in the Jersey River Railway scandal, whatever that may be, and I know that he had succeeded. That evidence was in Mr. Blessing's possession when he boarded the steamer. I expect it is in Gordon Black's now!"

"I think," Brooke suggested, "that you had better come with me to the captain."

"What is the use?" she replied impatiently. "There is work to be done yet—your share of the work. I have pointed out the man. It is for you to forge the links. You start knowing who he is. You have only to work a little way backward."

"All the same," Brooke persisted, "I think that you ought to come with me to the captain."

"I'll come when I think best," she answered tersely. "Gordon Black has seen me with Mr. Blessing. If he sees me with you on the way to the captain he'll suspect something. See what you can do on your own. I'll come in afterward.

"I'll tell you this much more, if you like. Less than forty-eight hours ago Gordon Black offered Mr. Blessing twenty-five thousand pounds for a document in his possession—an illegal transfer, or something of the sort. Mr. Blessing refused. He was acting for a client—Gordon Black's great enemy."

Brooke made his way back to his own part of the ship. He spent nearly an hour in putting a few cautious inquiries. Then he rejoined Constance, who was still sitting in her corner reading, and who watched his approach with evident displeasure.

"You are very foolish," she said, as she put her book down, "to come over here so often. I have told you that Gordon Black has seen Mr. Blessing talking to me. He will be on his guard."

"It does not appear to be of much consequence," Brooke remarked. "Listen. There is no doubt whatever as to the time when the murder took place. It was between half past eleven and five and twenty to twelve."

"Well?"

"From ten o'clock until the news of the affair was brought there Black was playing bridge in the smoking-room."

The girl frowned.

"Is that certain?"

"Absolutely," he assured her. "I have it from the smoking-room steward, and Major Bryce—who was one of the four. Without a doubt he was in the smoking-room when the affair took place."

She seemed a little staggered. For a few moments she said nothing.

"Failing Mr. Gordon Black," Brooke continued, "I presume you have no other suggestions? I'm getting rather keen."

She shook her head. "It must have been Gordon Black," she declared.

"But the man has a perfect, a truthful alibi," Brooke ventured to point out.

"I can't help it," she persisted obstinately. "Mr. Blessing told me himself that he was afraid of him. Those papers included a forged transfer. He meant having them. He had offered Mr. Blessing twenty-five thousand pounds for them and was refused."

Brooke pointed to a school of porpoises.

"Let us talk about something else," he suggested. "What are you going to do when you get to New York?"

"Give evidence against Gordon Black at his trial for murder, I hope," she replied doggedly. "Afterward—well, I shall find something."

IV

WHEN BROOKE RETURNED to his chair he found that his invalid neighbor had been brought on deck and was lying in the next one, smothered over with rugs. Brooke spoke to him pleasantly, and would have passed on but for the other's obvious disappointment.

"You're going to sit down for a few minutes, aren't you?" the fellow piped out, his thin voice shriller and weaker than ever. "I've had a bad night, and I'm nervous this morning. Say, what day do you reckon we shall fetch New York?"

Brooke seated himself. The cheering up of the man seemed to be a charge upon the whole ship's company.

"About Friday morning," he replied cheerfully. "Nothing to make us late that I can see."

The little man began to count upon his fingers.

"Let me see—to-day is Tuesday. Then there's Wednesday and Thursday—two whole days! I reckon I'll last that long—somehow," he added wistfully.

Brooke laughed at him. "Of course you will," he declared encouragingly. "Why, I heard you walked across the deck alone yesterday morning!"

Dr. Browning smiled—a little vaingloriously.

"Not all the way—very nearly as far as the rail," he admitted. "My book blew away."

He was silent for a few minutes, looking out across the sea.

"You know," he continued, "when I started on this voyage I wasn't afraid, because I felt that I'd just as soon die at sea as anywhere else. I took kind of a fancy to end it all out here. Directly I got on board and looked through a port-hole I changed my mind, though. Queer thing, eh? I was afraid!"

"I wouldn't think about it at all, if I were you," Brooke advised. "Make up your mind that you're going to get better. That's the way."

A queer little smile flickered for a moment upon the gray lips. The man's face was almost ghastly.

"There isn't any chance of that," he said simply. "I'd like to live out the voyage—that's all."

"Have you friends who are meeting you in New York?" Brooke asked.

"Perhaps," the other answered. "I cannot say for certain. My people live out in the West."

The purser came along and paused to talk cheerfully for a few minutes to the ship's invalid. Afterward a benevolent old lady brought up her camp-stool to his side. Brooke lay with half-closed eyes, looking out upon the sea.

His thoughts wandered from the pathetic little figure by his side to Mr. Gordon Black, who was strolling up and down the deck smoking a cigar. Brooke felt a peculiar interest in studying the dark, handsome face.

That the man had been a bold adventurer, a buccaneer of finance, was true without a doubt. Was there really the shadow of that ghastly crime concealed behind the mask of those set features and level brows?

He stood smoking his cigar stolidly, one hand grasping the rail of the steamer, his eyes fixed upon the silver streak which fringed the horizon. Brooke felt that this quiet sea voyage had been touched unexpectedly with the hand of tragedy, and try how he would to put him in the background of his thoughts, this man stood out the central figure in it. There was a shrill blast from the foghorn; they had passed into a little bank of white mist. Immediately afterward a cabin steward came up, looked around the deck for a moment, and, finally advancing to Gordon Black, touched him on the shoulder and presented him with a note.

"For me?" Brooke heard him ask.

"Left in your cabin, sir," the man replied, as he turned away.

Brooke watched his neighbor break the seal of the letter and read its contents. They seemed to consist of a few lines only, yet the seconds passed into minutes and the eyes of the reader were still riveted upon the half-sheet of paper.

He seemed at first a little dazed; he had the appearance of a man who struggles with a message sent him in some foreign language. Then Brooke saw the blanching of the man's cheeks, the sudden shiver, the quick, stern effort to recover his self-control. There was no longer any doubt. Tragedy and Mr. Gordon Black walked hand in hand!

V

BROOKE WENT BACK again to Constance Robinson that evening. He found her promenading alone on the lower deck, her hands clasped behind her back. She welcomed him with a smile which, dubious though it was, gave him an unreasonable amount of pleasure. He fell into step by her side. It was a dark, windy night and the sea sang to them.

"Any progress?" she asked.

"None to speak of," he admitted frankly. "I fancy I'm not lucky this time."

She turned upon him almost fiercely.

"I wonder how you dare mention the word to me!" she exclaimed. "You have just the glimmering of an idea as to what my life has been up to now. Well, I get another chance—a good salary—a new profession in a new country—and this is what happens. My employer is murdered on the way out. I haven't even drawn my first week's pay!"

"No good brooding over it," Brooke remarked briskly. "You've health and strength, and you're bound for a country where those things count. Do you mind going a little slower? It's a treat to see you walk, but I'm out of breath."

She slackened her pace at once. She had been walking with the long, free paces and swift-footed grace of some forest animal. She glanced doubtfully at her companion. His tone seemed to indicate a certain change in his attitude toward her.

"Oh! I'm not afraid," she declared. "I'll find work—only—I wish to God, when I start out to look for it, that I were a man!"

He understood, and this time was silent. The mood passed, and he was careful to take no advantage of it. Presently she stopped at the end of the deck nearest to the first-class quarters.

"Good night!" she said. "I'm sorry you're not succeeding."

"By the bye," he asked, "you didn't, by any chance, send a note to Mr. Gordon Black, did you?"

"I—Of course not! Why?"

"He had one from some one which upset him pretty badly."

"Find out who sent it," she insisted eagerly.

"My idea," he replied. "I was just waiting till I'd spoken to you."

"It's very likely the beginning of negotiations," she declared. "Remember that whoever killed poor Mr. Blessing, even if it wasn't Gordon Black, has those papers and the forged transfers."

Brooke sighed. "I'm afraid," he said, "they'll begin to tumble to me soon, but I'll do my best."

VI

THE NEXT DAY they ran into a storm. The skies were leaden, the ship developed a very ugly pitch, the decks were deserted, swept with rain and spray. The steamer-chairs, even on the covered deck, were lashed to a rail. The whole outlook was unspeakably dreary. About eleven o'clock a cabin steward came to Brooke in the smoking-room.

"I beg your pardon, sir," he said. "Dr. Browning, the old gentle-man who is ill, would take it as a great favor if you would step down to his stateroom for a moment. The poor gentleman's very bad indeed, sir," he added confidentially. "Don't look as though he'd last the day."

"Sure he meant me?" Brooke asked, a little puzzled. "I've only spoken to him once or twice on deck."

"Certain, sir," the man replied. "He wanted to speak to you most particular."

Brooke made his way down below at once. The little man was lying half-dressed upon the sofa berth and his appearance was ghastly. He motioned Brooke to close the door.

"Sorry to find you queer," the latter remarked cheerfully. "This weather's enough to knock any one over."

"I'm nearly done." was the reply. "I didn't reckon upon this. Please listen."

"Anything I can do for you—" Brooke began.

"Two nights ago," Dr. Browning interrupted, "the man Blessing was murdered just outside my stateroom there—only a few feet away, mind. I was lying where I am now. I heard the scuffle, the blow, the groan."

"Great Heavens!" Brooke exclaimed. "You didn't see the fellow, did you?"

The doctor shook his head. He was speaking with the utmost difficulty.

"I saw nothing, but I heard the fall of something just outside my door, which was about a foot open. I dragged myself there. I picked up this."

He opened his coat; a long envelope, apparently stuffed with papers, was lying there. Brooke gazed at it with fascinated eyes.

"Why haven't you mentioned it before—told the captain or some one?" he asked.

The little doctor paused for several moments to recover his breath.

"I made up my mind that this packet should go straight from my hands to the chief of police in New York," he said. "Everything is talked about on board ship. I decided to keep silent. Since then I have been terrified—almost to death. Last night and the night before a man has been in my room. My trunk, the cushions here, have been searched. I lay shivering in my bunk. The packet was between my two mattresses."

"Who was the man?" Brooke asked.

"I couldn't reach the light—I dared not have turned it on if I could have done so," was the almost plaintive reply. "It might have been a steward. I had courage once—but now—you see what I am. I can't bear another night. I want you to take this packet."

Once more he produced the envelope. Brooke took it.

"What am I to do with it?"

"Keep it until we are safely off the steamer," Dr. Browning begged. "Bring it to me the moment after we land. I shall be at No. 387, the Waldorf-Astoria. My room is already engaged. I shall lie there and wait for you."

Brooke fingered the packet irresolutely.

"May I ask you this?" he said. "Why do you select me as your confidant? We are complete strangers, and many of the other passengers upon the ship have talked with you more."

"I choose you," Browning replied, "because you are an Englishman, and a person whose appearance, forgive me, renders you free from any suspicion of being mixed up in this affair. You are so obviously a young Englishman of good family, with no particular occupation and no particular interests in the world. There is a widespread plot which turns upon these papers, and if, before I die, I can help toward an act of justice, it will make me happy. You are just the person whom no one would suspect of complicity in it."

Brooke thrust the packet into the breast pocket of his tweed coat, which he buttoned up closely.

"Very well," he promised, "I'll do as you say."

The little man leaned back upon his sofa.

"I shall sleep now," he declared, with a sigh of content. "I never closed my eyes all last night."

Brooke tiptoed his way out of the stateroom and sat in his steamer-chair upon the deck for an hour without moving. Then he rose and made his way to the second-class portion of the ship, where he found Constance in a sheltered corner.

"Supposing," he said, "I was able to help toward the clearing up of this little affair, I take it that it would be a sort of satisfaction to you?"

"It would be more than that," she answered firmly.

"Very well, then," he continued. "I am by way of making a bargain. Supposing I succeed, will you lunch with me at the Waldorf-Astoria at one o'clock on the day after we arrive, and will you promise to let me know your whereabouts for the first month of your stay in New York?"

She looked at him, a little softened—and yet suspicious.

"I can't see what satisfaction that would be to you," she remarked.

"My lookout, that, isn't it?" he reminded her gently.

"I haven't any clothes to come out to luncheon in," she told him.

"If you will wear the clothes," he replied, "which you wore when you came on the steamer?"

"Well, I had to have a new frock," she interrupted, a little defiantly, "and I couldn't come abroad without a new hat, could I?"

He laughed.

"It's a bargain, then."

"Aren't you going to tell me anything?" she asked.

"Not at present," he replied. "To tell you the truth, there's so much that I don't understand myself."

VII

THE END OF THE VOYAGE, so eagerly looked forward to by many of the passengers, was certainly not disappointing in the matter of sensation.

The steamer was boarded in the harbor by two detectives, whose every movement was watched with intense interest. They made their way at once to the captain's cabin, where they remained for at least a quarter of an hour.

When they returned to the deck they came face to face with Mr. Gordon Black. He was smoking a large cigar and, so far from showing any signs of discomfiture, accosted the two men and shook hands with them. A slight sense of disappointment began to manifest itself among the passengers. They were now almost up to the landing-stage and nothing had happened. Mr. Gordon Black, whose arrest by the New York police had been looked upon as a certainty, remained very much at liberty. The two detectives were talking to no one nor showing any signs of imminent action. It seemed, too, as though the murderer of Mr. Blessing were to walk off the ship unmolested. Then there was a little commotion at the companionway. Two of the stewards emerged, carrying a steamer-chair upon which Dr. Browning was stretched out. He was wearing a shore-going hat, and, though his appearance was ghastly, he was doing his best to exchange farewells with those of the passengers whom he passed. His chair was set down close to the gangway and within a few feet of the detectives. At that moment Brooke strolled up. He pointed to the chair.

"I give that man in charge, officer," he said to the nearer detective, "for the murder of William Blessing on this boat."

Brooke had spoken without raising his voice in the least, but his words had been perfectly distinct. What followed seemed nothing short of miraculous.

With a single bound Browning was at the side of the ship. He sent sprawling a passenger who inadvertently barred his path, and a seaman who made an instinctive movement toward him he tripped up with a dexterity which was simply amazing.

They saw him for a moment and heard a splash. Then every one rushed to the side of the ship.

"Your man, right enough," Brooke remarked to the detective.

"That's Tim, sure," was the prompt reply. "I wish to God I'd believed it, and we wouldn't have bungled the job!"

The steamer was within forty yards of the dock, and the only open space around was the space which had been left for her to clear. Two sailors dived, and a dozen boats were in the water within five minutes. Nevertheless, the passengers were obliged to disembark without learning what had become of their late steamer companion.

VIII

CONSTANCE ARRIVED punctually at the Waldorf on the following morning. Brooke led her to the table which he had reserved and watched the color stream into her cheeks as she bent over the roses which were lying by her plate.

"Well," he announced cheerfully, "I've ordered luncheon—all manner of weird dishes, with just one or two we are sure of. I didn't order champagne because I thought you'd prefer that for dinner."

"What do you mean?" she asked, half indignantly.

"Never mind," he replied. "I can see you are bubbling over with questions. Read the papers this morning?"

She shook her head.

"I've been too busy."

"Then I'll have to tell you a few facts first," he said. "The whole affair hinges around the great struggle between Gordon Black and Seth Pryor. Black stepped over the line a bit and had to leave the country. The documents which would have incriminated him were in England.

"Blessing went over, as Pryor's agent, to buy them. Our little friend. Dr. Browning, who has a dozen aliases, and who is more wanted by the New York police than any other man on earth, was also on to the game, only what he wanted was to steal the papers. Very well. Blessing gets them. Gordon Black, acting on a hint he received from New York, sails for home.

"Dr. Browning—Tim, the New York police call him—books on the same steamer. Tim murders Blessing and gets hold of the documents. Having got them, he tries to think out the safest way to make use of them. Blessing was murdered outside his door. On the whole, it is safer for him to land in New York without those documents in his possession.

"He pitches on the most ingenuous-looking of his fellow passengers and hands them over to me to take care of. One or two little things about the man, however, during the last few days, gave me to think, as one says. I watched him like a lynx for the last twenty-four hours and was convinced that he was shamming. The rest is obvious."

"And what about Mr. Gordon Black?" she asked.

"Therein," Brooke replied, "lies the humor of the situation, if one can use such a word at all in connection with the affair. The two great factions headed by Black and Seth Pryor made peace one day last week. The documents for which our little friend hoped to get a million dollars, and for which Mr. Black had actually bid twenty-five thousand pounds, are valueless. Quite a dramatic little business, wasn't it?"

"What about the note which you saw Mr. Gordon Black receive on deck?"

"That was from Browning, although he didn't sign it," Brooke explained. "It was just a little reminder that those documents were still in existence."

"There isn't anything in life," she said softly, "so wonderful as to realize these things going on around you; to watch other people and wonder what secrets they are carrying about with them."

"I'm glad you feel like that," Brooke answered, "because that sort of thing is a bit of a hobby of mine, too. Found another post yet?"

"Not yet."

"I offer you one," he declared, filling her glass with hock. "Secretary, companion, and—"

She put out her hand, checking him, as if his words had smitten her with poignant edge,

"No, no," she pleaded, her soft eyes appealing to him sorrowfully; "wait, please wait!"

He lapsed into thoughtful silence. Perhaps he was pushing the matter rather indelicately, somewhat hastily. So he reasoned, after a minute's cogitation. Better wait, indeed, than ruin it all.

"You had joined Blessing," said he slowly, looking at her with frank directness, "and meant to help him in his detective work."

She nodded, the flush of excitement, due to the crisis which she had staved off, brightening her cheeks and lips. Brooke wanted to kiss her. He wanted to tell her so. But it might be wiser—of course it would be wiser—to wait.

He leaned his elbows on the table, talking across to her confidentially. "What do you say to a partnership—business—with me

as the other member of the firm?" he suggested. "Let's open a detective bureau in London—there's a world of work waiting—on
equal terms."

She shook her head. "I have no capital for such a venture," said
she. "I must stay here and fight."

"You have your brains and your typewriter," said he, his face
glowing with the heat of his new idea. "You can't remain here
friendless, with no business connection, you know. Say that you'll
put your typewriter and business experience against my capital and
join the venture."

"There's a great field—with your well-known talent as a business asset," she admitted, catching some of his fire.

"Then let's call it done!" he exclaimed "We'll return by the next
steamer, and I'll have you near me, at least, while I—" he caught
himself, his face paling, as if afraid.

"While you?" she smiled.

"Wait," said he.

She offered her hand. "A strictly business partnership, Mr.
Brooke," she blushed. "And you must promise me not to mention—
not to—to—" There was a supplication almost painful in her sol-
emn eyes.

"I'll wait," said he.

TALE THE FIFTH
THE DISAPPEARANCE OF MONSIEUR DUPOY

SIX MONTHS HAD PASSED since the day that unique partnership was entered into across the breakfast table in the Waldorf-Astoria, New York. To all appearances Constance Robinson had resumed her vocation as public typist, except that the contrast between her comfortable office of the present, and the bare room in Render Street in which Brooke first met her, was pleasantly sharp. Brooke sat by, watching her fingers dance through the transcription of a page.

"What we want," he declared, from the depths of her easy-chair, "is a holiday—a proper summer holiday."

"What you may want," Constance asserted, with emphasis, "has nothing to do with me. What I want is to finish this typing."

He glanced at the machine contemptuously.

"I cannot understand," he exclaimed, "why you go on grinding away at that wretched copying! You get ninepence a thousand words for it. It isn't in the least worth your while."

"Perhaps not," she admitted, "and yet I fancy that I know my own business best. I have explained to you before that it is not the money it brings me in so much as the fact that it gives me a definite station in life. If any inquiries are made about me, I can easily prove that I am a professional typist, with work coming in all the time. It would be very much better for you if you had some corresponding occupation."

Brooke evaded the point. "Will you come out somewhere for a drive this afternoon?" he asked.

"I will not," she replied calmly. "You ought to have gone down and played golf. As you did not, I wish you would go round to your club or somewhere. You distract me."

He shrugged his shoulders and left her. He found Constance sometimes almost unendurable. Her resolution, her indomitable front towards all his attempts to alter in any way their relations, was beginning to tell upon him.

It was impossible, however, to believe that she was not like other girls. There had even been moments when he had fancied that she had looked at him more kindly, moments when he had certainly permitted himself to hope. Only it was a long time! Personally he felt as far away from her now as on that first day.

She had begun by piquing his curiosity. His vanity had been a little ruffled by her calm resistance of his advances. Then the other things had come—not all at once, but gradually. To-day he knew that there could never be any other woman in the world for him.

At the club he was distrait. He wandered from the card-room, which bored him, abandoned the billiard-room without an effort to play, and finally found himself in the library, the most deserted spot in the club. Its only other occupant laid down his paper at his approach and welcomed him.

"Mr. Brooke," he said, "your coming is rather a coincidence. I was on the point of ringing the bell to ask whether you were in the club."

Brooke looked at the speaker in surprise.

"I didn't even know that you remembered me, Sir William," he remarked, a little dryly.

Sir William Dennison smiled as he drew up his chair. He was a tall, gray-bearded man, well groomed, his beard trimmed Vandyke fashion, a single eyeglass in his left eye. He held an official position under the government, and was quite the most distinguished member of the club.

"On the contrary, I remember you very well," he declared. "It was in Vienna that I last met you."

"I am flattered," said Brooke, easily, "to have remained in your memory so long."

Sir William glanced around the room as though to make sure that they were alone.

"I have heard of you once or twice lately," he announced, "through a friend of mine whom I need not name—you and a young lady—Miss Constance Robinson, I think."

Brooke sat quite still.

"I am told that in one or two cases," Sir William continued, "you have shown, between you, an unusual amount of determination and ingenuity. I have a commission to offer you. Are you prepared to take it?"

"Without a doubt," Brooke answered.

"It doesn't seem, on the face of it, a very interesting affair," Sir William went on. "One can't tell, however, what it might lead to. These are the facts.

"About a fortnight ago a Monsieur Dupoy came over to this country, indirectly on behalf of the French government. I may say that we have received from them, within the course of the last few months, a strong protest against our neglect in the matter of war balloons and aeroplanes generally.

"Dupoy was sent here to attend some experiments at Aldershot, and to be entrusted by us with a complete scheme of our proposed reorganization. He was to have received these at the War Office at twelve o'clock last Friday week. He presented himself at the appointed place at that time but we were not quite ready, and we asked him to call again the next day.

"Dupoy was perfectly willing. I happened to be there myself, and I invited him to dine with me that night, an invitation which he accepted at once. Since then nothing whatever has been seen of Monsieur Dupoy."

"He disappeared?"

"Absolutely!"

"Are you sure that he did not return home?"

"Quite," Sir William replied. "We have communicated with the French government, and through them with his relations. No one has seen or heard anything of him since he left here last Friday week."

"I haven't noticed anything about it in the papers," Brooke re-marked.

Sir William smiled.

"The disappearance of Monsieur Dupoy," he said softly, "is not one of those cases which are advertised in the press. It may, of course, have been due to an accident in the ordinary way. The hos-pitals, however, have been thoroughly searched, and no trace dis-covered of him. It is a significant fact that, so far as anybody knew, he left the War Office a week ago last Friday with our proposals and our complete scheme in his pocket."

"Where was he staying?" Brooke asked.

"At Delacher's Hotel, on the Embankment."

"Some inquiries have been made there, of course?"

"Naturally. Dupoy was reported to have paid his bill on the Friday morning, to have ordered his bag brought down, and to have gone out for half an hour to buy, he told the hotel clerk, a present for his wife. Since then he has not been heard of."

"Do you suspect any one?" Brooke asked next.

Sir William shrugged his shoulders. He had risen to his feet and was lighting a cigarette from a case which he passed over to Brooke.

"Not with any reason," he answered.

"Curiously enough, however, this is the third disappearance from Delacher's Hotel within the last six weeks. It is possible that something may have happened to Dupoy quite apart from the fact that he was supposed to be carrying with him very important po-litical documents.

"I don't know whether the affair appeals to you. If it does, my department will pay exceedingly well for any satisfactory elucida-tion of the mystery, and will, in any case, be responsible for your expenses if you care to have a look round."

"I am awfully obliged to you, sir," Brooke replied. "Perhaps in a day or two I may have something to report."

Brooke sought no longer to distract himself at bridge or bil-liards. He took a taxicab and drove back to his rooms, calling, on his way, to see Constance. She looked up at him ominously as he entered, but he only smiled.

"This," he declared, "is no idle visit. Work! Do you know anything about Delacher's Hotel?"

She nodded. "I know that a few weeks ago there was a diamond merchant from Hamburg who disappeared from there; and a little time before that, a mysterious young woman from St. Petersburg, who had come over to look for a situation as a teacher of languages, went out one morning and never returned."

"Good!" Brooke exclaimed. "There has been a third disappearance—a Frenchman this time."

"How did you hear of it?" she asked quickly.

"A friend of mine," he explained, "a member of the government now, has placed the affair in my hands."

"He has probably heard of you," she remarked quietly, "as my assistant."

"He will hear of me some day as your—" Brooke began.

"Don't be rash," she interrupted. "What are you going to do?"

"I am going to stay at Delacher's Hotel," he replied. "And you?"

"I am going to finish this typing. Tell me, before you go, about this man who has disappeared?"

Brooke imparted to her in a few words all the information he had gained from Sir William. She listened thoughtfully. When he had finished, she turned back to her work.

"I wish you luck. Don't get into trouble," she advised him.

Brooke opened his lips, but the click of the typewriter drowned his words. He moved slowly away. At the door he looked back. Constance was absorbed in her work. He could see only the top of her light brown hair and the flashing of her fingers. With a muttered word he went up to his room.

An hour later he made his way to Charing Cross and, waiting until the arrival of the Continental train, mingled with the little stream of alighting passengers and took a taxicab to Delacher's Hotel. A hall porter received his bag and ushered him in. Brooke, whose French was perfect, asked for a room in the name of Monsieur

Dupoy. The clerk stared at him for a moment. The head porter, who was a tall, olive-skinned person, with a black mustache, also leaned forward with interest.

"Monsieur Dupoy!" the clerk repeated, with the pen in his hand.

Brooke nodded, and glanced around as though to make sure that no one else was within hearing.

"To tell you the truth," he announced, "I come here on behalf of the family. Only the week before last, a cousin of mine was staying in this same hotel. He was to have returned to Paris last Friday week. He did not arrive. We have sent him many messages and letters. There has been no reply. It was arranged that I should come over to make inquiries."

"We have already written," the clerk remarked, "informing Madame Dupoy that her husband left here on the Friday morning, for the purpose, he said, of buying her a present. He did not return. He had so little luggage that we imagined he had been kept until the last moment and then had taken the train without it, sooner than be delayed."

Brooke nodded. "Up till last night," he declared, with a little gesture, "my cousin had not returned. Therefore, I am here. Give me a room. I do not know what I can do, but we shall see. One must try the police."

The clerk handed him a round ticket.

"You can have the room which your cousin occupied. Monsieur Dupoy," he said—"No. 387, on the third floor. As to the police, it is, of course, your affair, but I trust you are satisfied that nothing happened to Monsieur Dupoy under this roof?"

"Entirely," Brooke replied. "All the evidence goes to show that he left here, as you have told me, to buy this present."

Brooke was ushered to the lift. Until he disappeared, he noticed that the head porter was watching him with ill-concealed curiosity. He was shown into an ordinary hotel bedroom on the third floor, with an outlook on the Thames.

The furniture was of the plainest, and there was no communicating door into another room. Brooke opened his bag, took out his clothes, and glanced at his watch. It was a quarter to eight. He decided to dine in the restaurant downstairs without changing, and accordingly rang the bell and ordered some hot water. The chambermaid wished him good evening pleasantly. He slipped a half-crown into her hand.

"I may leave at any moment," he explained. "I give you this now."

She grabbed the money and beamed at him.

"The gentleman is very gracious," she declared, with a strong German accent.

Brooke broke into fluent German.

"You knew the occupant of this room," he inquired, "who was here the week before last—Monsieur Dupoy?"

She nodded.

"He left his bag behind him," she said. "He departed in a great hurry."

"You didn't happen to see him before he started, I suppose?" Brooke asked.

"Yes!" she answered. "Yes! He came in and washed his hands. It was the middle of the morning. He went out to eat. I know because he said to me: 'The food downstairs,' he said, 'it is good, but the room is dull. I will go somewhere more lively.' He said that to me while I poured out his hot water."

"Nothing about buying a present for his wife?" Brooke inquired.

The girl shook her head. "Not to me did he speak of such a person."

Brooke whistled softly as he went downstairs. As he crossed the hall he heard the sound of voices raised in altercation. The head porter was speaking angrily to a subordinate, who had apparently come late to relieve him. Brooke bought a paper and went into the restaurant.

He dined fairly well, but his surroundings were certainly depressing. A band, not of the first order, was playing. There were only a few diners, and these were obviously foreigners of the commercial type. One or two of the men seemed to be talking business. There were barely half a dozen women in the room. As soon as he had finished his meal, he strolled out into the hall. The man who had relieved the head porter was standing on the door-step. Brooke strolled up to him and lit a cigarette.

"Disagreeable looking fellow, your head porter," he observed.

"It is a wonder," the man grumbled, "that any of us stay here with him. If the management only knew—"

He hurried off to procure a taxi for a departing guest. Brooke awaited his return.

"Queer-appearing fellow altogether," he said softly. "He looks more like a head-waiter than anything."

"He was a waiter before he took on this job," the porter remarked. "He has got a restaurant of his own now, they say. Shouldn't care to go to it myself."

"Why not?" Brooke inquired.

The man hesitated. He looked more closely at his questioner.

"No particular reason, sir. I don't like Paul, that's all. You'll excuse me, sir."

He walked off to attend to some alighting passengers. Brooke noticed that he seemed rather to avoid returning. When he was disengaged, however, Brooke called softly to him.

"Tell me, what is your name?" he asked.

"My name is Fritz, sir," the man replied.

"Do you happen to know mine?" Brooke continued.

"No, sir!"

"My name is Dupoy."

"Indeed, sir—We had a Monsieur Dupoy here quite lately."

"My cousin," Brooke declared. "He was to have returned to Paris last Friday week. He never came, and we have been very anxious. That is why I am here."

The porter edged a little away.

"I should go to the police, sir, and make inquiries," he suggested.

"There are certain reasons," Brooke said slowly, "why I would rather not do that. I thought I might be able to pick up some information here. I am willing to pay for it."

The man smiled in somewhat mysterious fashion.

"If I were you, sir," he whispered, confidentially, "I should ask—"

"Whom?" Brooke demanded.

"Paul!"

Again he went about his business, and again Brooke waited. When he came back, however, he was uncommunicative. He kept looking behind toward the office.

"You will forgive me if I speak plainly, sir," he said. "My first instructions when I got the job here were to keep my mouth shut. I've got a wife and children and I can't afford to run any risks. If they see you here with me and know you're making inquiries, they'll think I'm gassing."

Brooke slipped a sovereign into his hand. "What time does Paul come on duty?"

"Not for another hour, sir," the man replied. "He is having his dinner."

Brooke strolled back into the hotel and asked for the manager, Mr. Delacher, who turned out to be a very polite but somewhat somber-looking personage. Brooke introduced himself as a cousin of Monsieur Dupoy.

"I don't know," he said, "whether you remember my cousin? He stayed here for a day or two, and then, on the day when he should have returned home, he absolutely disappeared."

"I remember Monsieur Dupoy perfectly," the manager admitted. "It is true that he did not return, but as he had paid his bill and said that he was going by the two-twenty, we concluded that he would send for his luggage afterwards."

"You cannot help me in any way, then?" Brooke asked. "He has a wife who is altogether in despair at his absence."

Mr. Delacher was only mildly sympathetic.

"My guests," he explained, "come and go. Of their doings I keep no count. How Monsieur Dupoy spent his time I cannot tell. All that I know is that he paid his bill, which seems to prove that he meant to depart. You will probably find, sir, that he will return presently. He is perhaps at home by now."

"I thank you very much," Brooke said. "By the bye, the face of your head porter seemed to me so familiar. Have I seen him at any of the hotels on the Continent, I wonder?"

Mr. Delacher shook his head.

"Paul has been with me for twelve years. Before that, he was at the Savoy in Berlin. He is a very valuable servant."

"Without a doubt," Brooke assented. "I suppose, then, if I want to find my cousin you would advise me to apply to the police?"

Mr. Delacher shrugged his shoulders.

"I can see no other course, monsieur."

Brooke strolled out along the Embankment for half an hour. When he returned, Paul was on duty—tall, austere, magnificent. He saluted Brooke in a dignified manner, but he watched him all the time as one who was scarcely satisfied. Brooke came to a standstill.

"Paul," he said, "it is a saying in Paris that the chief porter at a London hotel can tell you anything in the world you may want to know."

"It is an exaggeration, monsieur," the man replied.

"It may be," Brooke admitted. "Who can say? I search everywhere for my cousin, Eugene Dupoy. It is you who saw him last. You cannot even tell me where it was that he intended to lunch before he returned for his bag?"

Paul regarded his questioner in melancholy fashion.

"I cannot tell monsieur that," he admitted.

"You did not know, even, how he spent his time here?"

Paul shook his head.

"He seemed to be occupied with affairs," he announced. "On the morning of his unexpected departure, he left in a state of some excitement. He had an important engagement, he said, at twelve o'clock."

Brooke nodded.

"That is so," he said, confidentially. "The appointment, however, was postponed."

Paul turned slowly round. His manner, in a sense, was changing.

"Some papers which my cousin was expecting were not completed," Brooke continued. "A little affair of business. I myself am to fetch them to-morrow from the same place. That, however, is beside the point."

There was no doubt but that Paul was an altered man. His frigidity of demeanor had departed. He apparently took the liveliest interest in his questioner.

"I am very sorry indeed, sir," he said, "that I cannot help you. Monsieur Dupoy was a charming guest. He will, I am sure, return home safely. Monsieur remains with us long?"

Brooke shrugged his shoulders.

"What is the good?" he demanded. "Where am I to look for my dear cousin? I cannot tell. I shall finish the little matter of business which he was obliged to leave undone, and return to Paris."

"You are not anxious, then, about your relation, sir?" Paul asked.

Brooke shook his head.

"This," he declared, "is London. Things do not happen here. It may well be an affair of a letter, ill-directed or missing. Eugene may have gone on the Continent. Who can tell?"

Paul was standing with his hands behind him. It was between nine and ten o'clock and there was nothing whatever doing.

"It seems strange, monsieur," he remarked, "that your cousin did not finish his business here, after all."

"It is nothing," Brooke answered. "Certain papers were not ready. I myself take possession of them at eleven o'clock to-morrow. I think that I shall do exactly what Eugene would have done—pay my bill when I leave here in the morning, return for my bag, and catch the two twenty."

"I will give orders, sir," Paul said. "You will lunch here, sir?"

"Probably," Brooke replied. "It is not amusing but, although I speak English so well, I am almost a stranger in London."

"If I might venture," Paul suggested slowly, "there is a little restaurant in a street leading off Shaftesbury Avenue—I could give monsieur the address—where the cooking is altogether French. A most interesting place! Monsieur might see there a great singer, a dancer, an artist. The French ladies who have succeeded in London, they go there at midday. It is worth a visit."

"The place for me, Paul!" Brooke exclaimed. "Write it down on a piece of paper."

Paul obeyed promptly.

"It is called the Café Hollande, monsieur," he said, handing over the card. "There are two floors. You go downstairs and ask for Jean Marchand. You will, I think, be exceedingly well served."

"I'll try, at all events," Brooke decided. "I suppose I shall have plenty of time to return here and catch the two-twenty?"

"It would be advisable, monsieur," Paul proposed, "if your bag were sent to the station to meet you. The account could be paid before you leave in the morning."

"It is excellent," Brooke declared. "Good night, Paul!"

The man saluted.

"Good night, monsieur!"

Brooke slept well, was called at a reasonable hour in the morning, visited the hairdresser after his breakfast, and at eleven o'clock strolled out to the front and instructed Paul to procure him a taxi-cab.

"I shall do as you suggested, Paul," he remarked. "I have paid my bill. After I have finished my business, I shall call at Scotland Yard and inquire about my cousin."

The man assented gravely.

"I trust, monsieur," he said, "that you will receive good news. Also that you will like my little restaurant. *Bonjour et bon voyage, monsieur!*"

Brooke was driven in a taxi to the War Office. Sir William, who happened to be in the building and disengaged, received him at once.

"Any news?" he asked, laconically.

"Not yet," Brooke replied. "So far, it has been an affair of routine. I am supposed to be here to receive a document from you—drawings, and all that sort of thing. Can I have a bundle made up?"

Sir William nodded and gave a few instructions.

"When one comes to think of it," he said thoughtfully, "it is rather a serious thing that this fellow Dupoy should have disappeared in the heart of London. Where are you going when you leave here?"

"I am going exactly where Dupoy went. I am going to lunch in a little restaurant off Shaftesbury Avenue, strongly recommended

to me by a person whom I suspect was interested in Dupoy's disappearance. I expect there to obtain at any rate a hint."

Sir William nodded in an interested manner. "You fellows do
get some fun out of life," he remarked, a little enviously. "I should
rather like to lunch with you."

Brooke shook his head.

"I wouldn't, Sir William," he advised. "If I am on a clue at all, it
is a very thin one, and this sort of people are easily put off. I think
I had better go alone."

"Anyhow," Sir William suggested, "you'd better let me know
the name of the restaurant, in case you do the disappearance trick,
or anything of that sort."

Brooke scribbled it down upon a piece of paper. Then, with a
sealed packet in his hand which he had the air of endeavoring to
conceal as much as possible, he left the building and reentered his
taxicab.

He drove first to Scotland Yard where, for the sake of appearances, he made a few aimless inquiries about Inspector Simmons,
who was out of town. At a quarter to one he was set down outside
the Café Hollande. He entered the place and looked around him
for a minute. Although it was early, a great many of the tables were
occupied, nearly all apparently by foreigners. There was a small
orchestra playing from somewhere below, a large desk at which an
elderly woman was busy making out accounts, mirrored walls,
muslin curtains not absolutely clean, the usual appurtenances of a
restaurant on the borders of Soho. A little dark man came hurrying towards him, his face wreathed in smiles.

"Jean Marchand?" Brooke asked.

"But certainly, monsieur," the little man replied. "It is Monsieur Paul who has sent you here?"

"Paul of Delacher's Hotel," Brooke admitted.

Jean glanced around the room. "Up here, monsieur," he confided, "it is at all times a little noisy—not entirely *comme il faut*. I
recommend to monsieur my favorite table below. This way."

Brooke followed his guide down the stairs into a large and
somewhat empty apartment, in which were set a few tables only.
At the bottom of the stairs an orchestra of three musicians was

playing. At the farther end of the room was a long table covered with bottles, watched over by a *maître d'hôtel*. There were only one or two people lunching.

"It is not yet one," Jean explained. "Between one and half past this room will be crowded. There are celebrities who come here. I myself will point them out to monsieur. I recommend this table—the one in the corner."

"But it is already occupied," Brooke remarked, glancing with a slightly puzzled air at the girl in the corner, who seemed on the point of raising her veil.

"The adjoining table, then, monsieur," Jean begged. "Monsieur may make himself comfortable. I myself will return to take his order for luncheon."

Jean retreated with smooth haste. Brooke advanced slowly towards the corner of the room indicated. Then he stopped short. The girl had raised her veil.

"Constance!" he exclaimed.

"You!" she echoed.

Brooke took a seat opposite to her.

"What on earth does it mean?" he cried.

She tore open a letter which lay on the table by her side. She glanced through the few lines and passed it across to him.

"A man called upon me this morning," she explained. "He asked for my aid in a certain private matter. The first step was that I should lunch here at a table which should be pointed out by a *maître d'hôtel* named Jean Marchand, and that I should open this letter if a neighbor should take the adjoining place. Read."

Brooke snatched at the half sheet of note paper. Across it was written in a bold, sprawling hand—

> Good fortune and good appetite to Monsieur Dupoy
> from Paris, and mademoiselle, his charming part-
> ner!

Brooke looked up at Constance and met her eyes steadily fixed upon his.

"This means?" he said slowly.

The wrinkles began to form around her eyes. She was beginning to laugh.

"It means that you have run up against some one even cleverer than we are," she declared.

He looked at her with a little of that old-time cast of imbecility on his face.

"A philosophical attitude," Brooke insisted at length, "is our best role. We came here to lunch—we will lunch. We will lunch well."

Certainly there was nothing to be complained of in the cooking at the Café Hollande. The service was a little slow and there was a queer sense of emptiness in the room. All the time there was a great tumult of voices and footsteps upstairs, but Jean's prophecy as to the filling up of this particular room was in no way carried out. As though by mutual consent, neither Constance nor Brooke talked of the disappearance of Dupoy. It was only over their coffee, during the last few moments, that the subject was mentioned.

"I made a mistake, of course," Brooke confessed. "It was foolish of me even to show myself at Delacher's Hotel."

She nodded. Soon afterwards they rose and, Brooke having paid the bill, they ascended the stairs and walked out into the street, without having seen anything further of Jean Marchand. As they passed along Shaftesbury Avenue, Constance, who had been looking into a shop-window, touched Brooke on the arm.

"We are being followed," she whispered.

"A man who stood on the other side of the street as we came out, is trailing us now."

"What is he like?" Brooke asked, with a sudden hope.

"He looks like a porter of some sort at an hotel or club," she answered. "He has on dark blue trousers, an ordinary coat, and a cap. He is rather florid—"

Brooke gently guided her down a narrow street which they were passing.

"It is the man I wanted to see," he declared softly. "Is he still following us?"

She nodded. Almost directly he stepped up.

"You want to speak to me, Fritz?" Brooke inquired.

"Yes, sir," the man replied, "but not here. If you please—"

He plunged through the door of a public-house. Brooke and Constance, without hesitation, followed him. It was an ordinary little place, half café, half public house, almost empty. They sat at a small table away from the window. Brooke ordered something to drink. Fritz leaned forward.

"This morning," he announced, "after you left, I was dismissed. That man Paul, he thinks that all are fools. He thinks that one sees nothing. He is wrong. Monsieur Dupoy, I am here to speak of your cousin."

"It is good," Brooke said, nodding. "Go on."

Fritz looked around him.

"I am a poor man," he continued. "I had a good place until one day Paul he took a dislike to me. Now I am turned away. Places are hard to get. I have a wife and children. I must do the best I can. It is for that reason that I said to myself—'Why should I not profit by the things which I have observed?'"

Brooke brought out his pocketbook.

"You are an exceedingly sensible fellow, Fritz," he declared. "Now tell me what information you have to offer, and we will talk business."

Fritz nodded.

"Directly," he said, "but first, monsieur, what were you doing so long in the Café Hollande?"

"I had lunch there," Brooke told him, dryly.

The face of Fritz seemed suddenly blanched. He stared at them both.

"*Monsieur* lunched there!" he repeated.

"Downstairs?"

"Downstairs," Brooke admitted.

Fritz took the glass of brandy which had been offered, and drank it off.

"You have the good fortune, monsieur," he muttered. "It was not so with your cousin when he lunched there downstairs."

"What happened to him?" Brooke asked quickly.

Fritz shook his head.

"There are things," he declared, "which, if I knew, I would not dare to speak of. Indeed, I do not know. This is my offer to monsieur. For twenty pounds I will take him to his cousin."

Brooke placed the money without hesitation upon the counter. Fritz buttoned it up in his pocket and rose.

"Understand, monsieur" he said in the doorway, "that when I point to the house where you will find Monsieur Dupoy, I have finished. If you seek for me, it will be useless. I know nothing. I keep my bargain when I show you the house which shelters Monsieur Dupoy."

"It is agreed," Brooke assured him. They walked out into the street. Fritz kept about a dozen yards ahead. They crossed Shaftesbury Avenue, traversed another narrow street for a short distance, and then turned abruptly to the right. There was a news agent's shop, with a notice in the window—"Rooms to let for single gentlemen." Fritz pointed to it.

"There, monsieur!"

Almost as he uttered the words he stepped aside to avoid a passing dray. When it had gone, Fritz, too, had disappeared. He had plunged once more into the throng of people.

Brooke and Constance entered the shop. A Frenchwoman was behind the counter, stout, untidy, with black hair all over her face. Brooke took off his hat.

"Have you, madame," he asked, "a lodger here of the name of Dupoy?"

She stretched out her hands.

"But, monsieur," she said, "I have a lodger here whom I do not know. His name is as likely to be Dupoy as anything else. Monsieur would like to see him?"

Brooke followed her up the crazy stairs. Constance came behind. They were ushered into a tiny bedchamber. A man, partly dressed, lay upon a sofa, his head propped up by two or three pillows. He stared at them eagerly as they came in, and his lips moved, but he said nothing. His clothes hung about him shapelessly. He had a beard of a week or so's growth upon his chin. His head was tied up with a bandage.

"Dupoy?" Brooke exclaimed.

The man stared at him but remained speechless. Madame shook her head.

"He talks only nonsense," she declared. "All the time he asks who he is. But listen, it is the doctor who comes. You shall speak with him yourself."

The doctor knocked at the door and entered. He bowed with a little flourish to Constance.

"Ah!" he exclaimed, "it is perhaps the friends of the unfortunate monsieur?"

"Tell me what has happened to him?" Brooke asked.

The Frenchman stretched out his hands.

"Madame can tell you as much as I," he said. "Last Friday week he tottered into the shop, very much as he is now, his head bound up, desperately ill. She fancies that an unseen hand propelled him. That may or may not be so. His pockets were cut open as though he had been searched. She brought him upstairs and sent for me. Since then I have attended him every day. He was suffering from a terrible blow on the head, which has unfortunately produced, as you see, a complete loss of memory."

"If his head was bound up, he had already been treated for the blow when he came in?" Brooke remarked. "It was not an accident, then, which had happened in the street?"

The doctor shook his head in most mysterious fashion.

"Monsieur," he said, "almost I felt it my duty to communicate with the police. The wound when I examined it—it is beginning to heal now—gave me the impression of having been made by a surgeon's knife. It takes a certain course. Its effect has been this loss of memory and apprehension. The poor fellow knows nothing. The wound is healing, but for the rest, who can tell?"

There was a brief silence in the room.

"He had money?" Brooke asked slowly.

The woman's eyes were suddenly covetous. She exchanged a rapid glance with the doctor, who coughed and looked away.

"He had money," she admitted slowly. "There is little left now, though. We have taken for his board and the doctor has taken for his bills. There is little remaining."

Again there was silence. The doctor was affecting to examine his patient. Brooke walked to the window—dusty, and smothered with a filthy muslin blind. He looked across the housetops for a moment. The instinct of the detective was suddenly crushed by a stronger feeling—a passionate sympathy with this poor stricken creature, an angry craving for revenge.

The woman had sidled out of the room. They could hear her heavy footsteps upon the stairs. The doctor was bending over his patient. Brooke turned back to Constance.

"We have found Dupoy," he said, "after all, but there are other things to be done."

WITHIN A WEEK, several things happened. Dupoy was formally identified, and died without having recovered his memory. The Café Hollande was searched quietly but closely from floor to ceiling, without the slightest result. The body of Fritz was discovered floating in the Thames.

Paul was so much upset by these and other happenings that he was confined to his room for a fortnight with a severe nervous breakdown. Ultimately, however, to the great satisfaction of a large number of travelers, he was able to take up once more his duties as head porter at Delacher's Hotel.

TALE THE SIXTH
THE SPIDER'S PARLOR

BROOKE MISSED the sound of the typewriter as he entered her room, but, to his immense relief, Constance was there. She was sitting back in her easy-chair, her eyes were half closed, she seemed pale and tired. The windows were wide open but the air of the little room was stifling.

"Constance!" he exclaimed, "I beg your pardon, Miss Robinson—you see I am back again."

She seemed suddenly to pull herself together. The lines were still under her weary eyes, but she held herself upright and she spoke briskly.

"So I observe," she remarked. "I am sorry—"

She hesitated, looking at his dark clothes and black tie. He came over to her, dragging a chair with him.

"I am not going to try and be a hypocrite," he said. "It was an uncle whom I have seen only half a dozen times in my life, and he has left me a little money. He was eighty-one years old. Why on earth should I be sorry?"

"No reason at all that I can see," she admitted, smiling. "I suppose you have come to tell me, then, that our partnership is at an end?"

"On the contrary," he answered swiftly, "I have come to beg for a new one."

She was conscious, almost as soon as she had spoken, of the opportunity which her words had given him. She shrank a little away but he caught at her hands and held them boldly.

"Constance," he said, "you've known all the time, of course. You're horrid to me, and I haven't cared to say much before because, after all, I had only what I could earn with you and through you. I've a reserve fund to fall back upon now. Will you marry me, please, dear?"

She drew her hands firmly away.

"Most certainly and decidedly not," she declared.

Brooke sighed.

"It sounds a little uncompromising," he remarked.

"It is exactly how I feel," she assured him. "I have not the slightest desire to marry you or any one. What I've seen of married life," she went on, a little sadly, "has been quite enough to prevent my ever thinking about it for myself as long as I live."

"But surely," he pleaded, "you do not allow yourself to be influenced by one, or even two, unfortunate marriages?"

She shook her head.

"I cannot discuss it," she said. "Fortunately for me, I am one of those people who are able to take care of themselves, who can live alone and not feel the want of any one's society. You see, I am not at all the sort of girl men like. I am a little hard, a little bitter. There have been things in my life which have made me so. The world is full of girls, Mr. Brooke, who would make you excellent wives, and who are only waiting for the opportunity. Please put away all such thoughts in connection with me."

He sat in silence for a few moments.

"I wonder," he remarked, "is there anything in your life which accounts for your unnatural attitude towards matrimony?"

She sighed.

"Some day," she answered, "I may tell you—certainly not at present. Now, please, get all these foolish ideas out of your head. There is some business to talk about."

"I will talk business in five minutes," Brooke said. "Before I do so, I insist upon knowing what has happened to this room."

He looked around him wonderingly.

Constance sat quite still, but her lips were quivering.

"I have got rid of a few articles of furniture which I did not require," she declared. "Nothing else has happened to it that I know of."

"Your little water-colors have gone," he pointed out, "your two bronzes, all the china from your cabinet, all the silver from that little what-not. Were you thinking of moving, or—"

"Or what?"

"Have you sold them?"

"I do not consider, Mr. Brooke," she said, "that this matter concerns you at all."

"We are partners," he objected.

"We are partners inasmuch as we divide the profits of certain of our undertakings," she replied. "We have done that, and there is an end of it."

"If we are partners in good fortune," he insisted doggedly, "we are also partners in ill fortune."

"I am not prepared to grant anything of the sort," she rejoined. "Since you are so ill-bred as to be inquisitive, I will admit that I have sold some of my things. I had a pressing claim and I had to satisfy it."

"But why on earth couldn't you telegraph me?" he exclaimed. "You knew where I was."

"Why on earth should I?" she replied.

"You know very well that what I have—"

"What you have has nothing to do with me," she declared firmly. "I have a burden to carry through life and I mean to carry it myself. What it is I have no idea of telling you—at any rate for the present. If you find out, it will be against my will. Sometimes it keeps me poor. At other times it is no trouble at all. Whatever it is, it is my affair and mine alone. Now, will you please sit quite still? I want to talk to you about something else."

Brooke kept silent with an effort.

"Very well," he muttered. "For the present, then—only for the present. You can go on."

"I suppose," she began, "I have been wasting my time the whole of the fortnight you have been away. I couldn't help it. I am going to make a confession. That downstairs room in the Café Hollande has fascinated me. I haven't been able to keep away from it. I think what makes it the more attractive really is that they hate the sight of me there."

"The place has been thoroughly searched, hasn't it?" he interposed.

"From cellar to attic. Directly the manager was spoken to and it was hinted to him that suspicions had been aroused concerning the restaurant, he placed all his keys at the disposal of Mr. Simmons, and he insisted upon their searching every room and cross-questioning whomever they chose.

"Not a single suspicious circumstance came to light, not a single thing to connect the place with Paul of Delacher's Hotel, or with any other person. Mr. Simmons himself told me that he was sure there had been some mistake. I told him about Fritz, the man whose dead body was found in the Thames. I told him how genuinely terrified he was when he heard that we had lunched there. Mr. Simmons only shook his head. You know how obstinate he is. He had made up his mind.

"Very well, I said no more. But since then the Café Lugano has seen little of me. I have lunched in that gloomy room downstairs at the Hollande nearly every day. Sometimes I have dined there as well. They keep on charging me more and more. They bring me indifferent things to eat. They keep me waiting an unconscionable time. I say to myself 'Never again will I set foot inside this place!' and in a few hours I am back again."

"This isn't like you," he remarked, wonderingly.

"Not a bit," she admitted. "I have never believed in presentiments. I haven't cared about anything but direct methods. Yet I am going to tell you something. I know perfectly well that there are things connected with the Café Hollande which have never been discovered. Do you know what I call it to myself—the Spider's Parlor! Things go on there which no one has any idea of."

"But in what part of the place?" Brooke asked.

"I do not know," she answered, "only I feel quite sure that there is something mysterious about that half-underground room, with just those few tables and the three musicians. They are turning people away all the time upstairs. It would be perfectly easy to add fifty more tables downstairs, instead of which they keep it empty. The few people who are there seem either to have drifted in by accident, or to have some special interest in the place. However, there is something more to tell you."

She glanced at the clock, which was just striking four.

"To-day," she went on, "as I came out, I stopped to give something to the musicians. The man who plays the piano was the only one there. The other two had turned away for a minute. I wonder whether you remember him? He was a strange, dark-looking creature, with queer eyes."

Brooke nodded.

"I remember him perfectly."

"He seemed to have a sudden idea when I spoke to him," she went on. "There was no one within hearing. He asked me in an undertone for my address."

"The infernal cheek—" Brooke began.

Constance shook her head.

"Don't be absurd," she said quietly.

"He did not ask in that sort of way. The only other two words he said were 'Four o'clock.' Now suppose you go to the door and open it."

There was a sound of knocking outside. Brooke obeyed. It was indeed the musician who stood there. He wore a long black overcoat, notwithstanding the heat of the day, and he carried a soft black hat in his hand. He stared hard at Brooke with one eye, and blinked rapidly with the other.

"Miss Robinson?" he asked.

"She is here," Brooke replied. "Come in."

The man came into the room. Constance rose to her feet.

"This gentleman," she said, indicating Brooke, "is a friend of mine. You need not hesitate to speak before him. What is it you wish to say?"

The man laid his hat upon the table.

"Young lady," he began, "I do not quite know why I spoke to you. I was beside myself this morning. They have dismissed me, those people at that rathole. I sat there thinking when you passed. You, too, have been in that place often, and I wondered, as the others wonder, for what purpose. I said to myself that we would speak with one another. Who can tell what may come of it?"

"I have nothing whatever to conceal," she told him. "I have been so often into that wretched little room at the Café Hollande because the place seems to me so mysterious, and because I am interested in unraveling queer things and visiting strange places. I have always a fancy that there are secrets almost within the reach of one's hands there."

The man leaned forward. He was English enough, and yet there was a strain of some foreign blood in him. His gestures were theatrical but natural.

"It is the truth!" he exclaimed. "There are things going on there which no one knows of. There are certain visitors who are brought with much ceremony to the little room downstairs, and on those nights we are sent away early. What happens? Who knows? But that visitor never comes another time. He is never seen again.

"You," he went on, pointing to Brooke, "were brought down there one day, and the young lady. Nothing happened. The young lady has been often since. Yet believe me or not, as you choose, never do I remember any one else escorted down those stairs by Jean whose face I have ever seen again!"

"But there are always a few customers there," Constance objected.

"Dummies!" the musician declared. "They are creatures of the restaurant. There is barely a single genuine customer. Why should they come? The place is nearly empty. Only one or two tables are set there; it is cold and drafty, the service is slow. Mademoiselle is the only one from the outside world who has been there often, and I have seen them watch her—watch her from upstairs, watch her from the other places. Sometimes I have had it in my mind to speak to her."

"Tell me," Brooke asked, "you seem to have been suspicious of this place for some time. Have you discovered anything?"

"A trifle which may not be a trifle," the musician answered. "It was only yesterday. There was a wine merchant who called. Jean complained bitterly of some wine. We could hear them upon the stairs.

"It was arranged that Jean should go into the cellars and bring up several bottles at hazard. Jean passed us, went behind the bar, opened the trap-door and stepped down. I saw him disappear with my own eyes. In a moment or two the wine merchant came down the stairs. He inquired for Monsieur Jean. I pointed to the open trap-door.

"'Ah!' he exclaimed, 'he has gone to fetch the wine. I will help him.' He hurried across the room and began to descend the steps. Presently he returned. 'There is no one there,' he declared.

"It was in the intervals of playing. I myself descended with him. The cellar was empty. We searched it everywhere. Then we both ascended. While we spoke of this thing we heard footsteps. Jean appeared with the bottles. I turned away. I heard Jean explain that he had been behind a bin in the corner, but I know better. Jean was not in the cellar at all."

"But surely it is not impossible," Brooke interposed, "that there should be another way out of the cellar?"

"There is a way for letting cases down from the street," the man replied, "but that is almost perpendicular, and Jean could not have been hidden there or gone out that way. I know a short time ago there came men who searched those cellars, searched them carefully, yard by yard. They found no other exit. It was for that they were looking. To-day I know that they were wrong. There is another exit. That is all I have to say."

"I do not quite understand, after all," Constance remarked, "why you have come to me. You have realized that I was interested in the restaurant, but is that all?"

The man took up his hat slowly.

"I know," he declared, "that you are an enemy of the place. I have seen Jean's face grow black when you have entered. I have heard orders given that you were to be served slowly and badly. I know that for some reason they are afraid of you there. Therefore, it seemed to me that, hating the place as I do, you were the person to whom I might bring the little information I have."

Brooke put his hand in his pocket.

"If a trifling loan," he suggested, "while you are out of work—"

"I shall accept it with pleasure, sir," the man replied. "And if anything should come of this?"

He wrote down his address upon a piece of paper.

"There may be other questions," he continued, "matters which have seemed to me unimportant."

"There is just one thing I should like to ask you," Constance said, as he turned to go. "Besides myself there seems to be one *habitué* of the place from the general public—a little man with gold glasses, who is always reading a paper. They treat him almost as rudely as they do me."

The musician nodded.

"He is a doctor, miss," he told her, "who has a surgery near. That is all I know. I have seen them look at him, also, as though they wished him somewhere else. He comes in, I think, because it is near his place. They serve him, too, badly, but he takes no notice. He reads always more than he eats. Good day, miss! Good day, sir!"

"Entirely as a matter of business," Brooke proposed, as the door closed behind their visitor, "I suggest that we dine to-night at the Café Hollande."

"It would perhaps be advisable," Constance assented.

They were met at the head of the stairs by Jean, who hurried along the crowded room towards them.

"If I could only persuade mademoiselle," he begged, "to dine here! I will arrange a round table for two. Downstairs it is so *triste* and damp."

"Another time, Jean," Brooke declared. "I have been away, and we have a little matter to talk over, mademoiselle and I. We like the quiet down there."

Jean shrugged his shoulders. It was unaccountable. However, it must be as mademoiselle preferred. He escorted them down the stairs himself.

"We are having plans made," he confided to them, "for turning this into a large grill-room. It is only the kitchen accommodation which is difficult. Mademoiselle will like her accustomed seat?"

They decided to move farther into the corner, however, and found themselves at the next table to the little gentleman with the gold spectacles, who favored them with a bland but benevolent stare. He called Jean to him.

"Waiter," he said, in a smooth, cultivated voice, "I have dined here for two months and I have never made a complaint."

"I am glad that monsieur has been so well served," Jean remarked.

"I have been abominably served," was the indignant reply. "I care little for my food. I come here only because it is quiet and because I may read and because it is near my work. But even a worm will turn. I desire to inform you that your food is the worst I have ever tasted, that it reaches me half cold, that your service is abominable and your charges exorbitant. After to-night I shall look for another restaurant. It is all."

The natural instinct of the *maître d'hôtel* seemed for the moment to triumph in Jean. He started to make apologies, but the little man waved him away.

"It is my first complaint," he declared. "It is my last."

Jean departed. The little man was settling down again to his papers. He glanced for a moment, however, at Constance.

"I trust," he said, "that I have not made myself objectionable? You, madam, also have been, I believe, an *habitué* here. I must confess that I wonder at it."

Constance smiled.

"I certainly have not come here to dine—well or cheaply," she admitted. "I think really I have come because I am fond of the unusual and because there is something about the place which rather mystifies me."

"In what way?" the little gentleman asked.

She shook her head.

"Just an idea."

The little gentleman drew his newspaper closer to him.

"Madam," he said, "I have no faith in ideas. I am a physician. Science is at once my mistress and my hobby. It provides me with all the mysteries I require. As for this place, it is nothing but a drafty, ill-managed hole. I have finished with it. Pardon me."

He plunged into his paper with the air of one who has concluded a conversation. There were only two other customers in the room— one a powerful, sunburnt man in tweed clothes, who sat with a bottle of wine in front of him and a newspaper propped up against it, dining, apparently, entirely to his satisfaction. The other had the appearance of being one of the staff. The dinner was a little better than usual, and curiously enough it was served almost precipitately.

"One would imagine," Brooke remarked, "that they wanted to get rid of us."

Constance looked around the room. The tablecloths had been removed from the other tables and there were no signs of any other diners being expected.

"What about our friend there?" she inquired, moving her head slightly towards the sunburnt man.

"A countryman or colonial," Brooke decided, "wandered in here by accident. Probably didn't care for it upstairs because of his clothes and thick boots."

"He looks like that," she admitted. They finished their dinner presently. There seemed to be nothing to wait for. The little doctor had lit a pipe and was reading over his coffee. The sunburnt man was leaning back in his chair, apparently thoroughly satisfied with his dinner. As they passed out, Brooke obeyed a sudden impulse and spoke to him.

"Do you mind if I take one of your matches?" he asked.

The man pushed them to him without a word. Brooke made some difficulty about striking one.

"Everything down here seems damp," he remarked. "Gives one the feeling of being half underground, doesn't it?"

The sunburnt man looked up at Brooke and frowned. Then he turned a little away, crossing his legs, and took up his paper again.

"Hadn't noticed it," he declared, shortly.

Brooke caught Constance up, smiling.

"Your friend with the red cheeks," he told her, "has about the worst manners of any man I ever knew. He seemed afraid of being spoken to." She laughed.

"I noticed that he didn't seem to take to you," she remarked. "At any rate, he seems very well able to take care of himself." They passed Jean, descending the stairs with a bottle of old brandy in his hand. Brooke left the place almost reluctantly.

"Well?" Constance asked.

"I suppose that fellow's all right," Brooke said thoughtfully. "The little doctor was just getting up to go as we came away. He will be the last one in the room."

"I never saw any one who looked better able to take care of himself," Constance murmured.

The night was hot, the streets were light as day. As though by common consent, they walked. At the corner of Piccadilly Circus, Brooke halted.

"What do you say to a ride on the top of a motor omnibus?" he suggested.

"It would perhaps be pleasant," she assented.

"There's one at the corner there, for Hampstead," he said. "Come."

They were crossing the road when Constance felt a light touch on her arm. She turned quickly around. Inspector Simmons of Scotland Yard was walking by her side.

"Stroke of luck, seeing you, Miss Robinson," he remarked.

"I am glad you think so," she answered. "You know Mr. Brooke, don't you?"

Mr. Simmons bit his lip.

"Of course I do. Sorry! I only caught sight of you that moment. Are you in a hurry, Miss Robinson?"

"I am never in a hurry," she replied, "if there is anything to be done."

"Will you please both step into the Monico with me, then?" he begged. "We will have some coffee. I want to show you a letter."

"Certainly," Constance agreed.

Mr. Simmons escorted her politely to the door of the restaurant. Brooke looked a little regretfully at the top of the motor omnibus, and followed. They found a small table against the wall and Mr. Simmons ordered coffee. Then he drew from his pocket a letter, which he did not, however, at once open.

"I wonder," he said, "if you have either of you heard of the Eburian Copper Mine?"

"Of course," Brooke replied. "The annual meeting is to-morrow, isn't it? They say there's going to be an awful row."

"There probably will be," Mr. Simmons assented. "I know we've orders to draft a hundred police down to the Cannon Street Hotel. Let me remind you of the facts. Miss Robinson may not know them.

"There have been six hundred thousand pounds' worth of shares issued and paid for on the strength of certain reports. A month ago there was a sensational article in the *Financial Times*, absolutely discrediting the mine. There was a fearful panic, of course, and the company sent out the greatest known mining expert—a man named Haslem—to make an independent report. He has not been allowed to send a telegram or a letter. He arrived in London secretly to-night. The meeting is to-morrow."

Brooke and Constance were both interested now. Their coffee stood before them, neglected.

"To-night," the detective continued, slowly unfolding the letter, "I was in my office when this was brought in—this with an enclosure. I will read the letter first. It seems to be from Haslem and it is written from Delacher's Hotel:

"Dear Sir,
"I received the enclosed letter on my arrival in London this evening. I am sending it on to you as a matter of form, for I think I can take care of myself. You may know me by name. I have to give evidence at the Cannon Street Hotel tomorrow with regard to the Eburian Mine.
                    "Faithfully,
                    "John Haslem."

Brooke and Constance had exchanged swift glances.

"Delacher's Hotel!" she murmured.

"Now for the enclosure," Mr. Simmons continued. "Here it is—the usual sort of thing—plain paper, typewritten, and all the rest of it. Let me read it:

> "Mr. Haslem.
>
> "Sir,
> "To-morrow you are going to give evidence which will practically ruin half-a-dozen of the most unscrupulous company promoters in London. Read the advice of a friend. Take care of yourself to-night. London is not altogether the city of safety one is apt to believe.
>
> "From One Who Knows."

"What have you done about this?" Brooke asked quickly.

"I sent a new man whom no one would recognize, to Delacher's Hotel," Mr. Simmons announced. "He did his work quite satisfactorily. Haslem arrived at about five o'clock and must have sent that note off to me very soon afterwards. He took a bedroom and asked Paul, the head porter, for some quiet place where he could dine without being noticed, as he didn't wish to be seen in London at all till next day. Paul directed him to—where do you think?"

Constance was sitting quite still. Her eyes seemed to have grown larger.

"To the Café Hollande!" she cried.

The inspector smiled a little indulgently.

"I know you have that place on the brain, Miss Robinson," he said. "Personally, as I've searched it plank by plank, I don't exactly—why, what's the matter?"

Constance was already half-way towards the door. Brooke dragged the inspector to his feet.

"Haslem was at the Café Hollande when we left," he exclaimed, "and, by Heaven, he wasn't there for nothing! Quick! We'll explain on the way." They hurried into a taxicab.

"Look here," Brooke said, "notwithstanding your search Mr. Simmons, there's something wrong about that place. Paul sent Dupoy there, and you know what happened to him. Haslem is another man with enemies. I tell you he was sitting down there twenty minutes ago. They'd got him."

Mr. Simmons was an unprejudiced person. To a certain extent he believed in Constance, and he believed in Brooke.

"We'll fetch him out, then, at any rate," he declared. "Is there likely to be any trouble, I wonder?"

"If so, we can deal with it," Brooke replied. "Miss Robinson can stay outside and bring in a policeman or two after us, if we don't reappear."

"Miss Robinson will do nothing of the sort," she retorted. "If this is any one's affair, it's mine."

The taxicab pulled up at the corner. They all three hurried across the pavement. The upper room was still filled with a cheerful crowd. They hastened towards the staircase. A waiter intercepted them.

"It is closed downstairs, monsieur," he announced.

Brooke flung him out of the way. They descended quickly. The band had ceased to play, half the lights were out, the doctor had left.

Only Jean was there, standing by the table at which Haslem had been sitting. There was a broken glass upon the floor, the tablecloth seemed to have been dragged sideways. Jean himself was swiftly setting things to rights.

He started and turned round as he heard footsteps. His face was suddenly almost ghastly. He clutched at the table and stared at them.

"Where is the man who was sitting at that table?" Brooke demanded.

"He has left, monsieur," Jean faltered, "five minutes ago. He had had too much to drink."

Brooke glanced towards the other vacant table.

"And the doctor?" he asked.

"He left at nine o'clock, as usual, sir," Jean answered. "He never varies his time. He has patients to receive." For one second Brooke hesitated. His first impulse was to plunge down into the cellar. Then Constance seized him by the arm.

"Quick!" she almost sobbed into his ear. "Quick!"

She tore up the stairs and they followed her. She flashed through the restaurant, through the swing doors, out into the street and turned sharply down the narrow thoroughfare past the left hand side of the building.

Brooke and Simmons were only a few yards behind. At the end of the restaurant premises stood a narrow house, on the door of which was a brass plate. Outside in the street an ambulance wagon was standing.

Constance leaned with her finger upon the bell. The man looked over from the box seat of the ambulance. He was half frightened, half angry.

"Don't do that!" he cried. "There's some one ill inside."

They took no notice of him. They heard footsteps in the hall. The door was cautiously opened by a woman dressed like a hospital nurse. They broke past her and Brooke threw open the door of the room on the left.

Haslem was there, unconscious, breathing heavily, stretched out on what seemed to be an operating table. The little doctor with the gold spectacles, dressed now in a long linen smock, turned and faced them. Outside, they could hear the ambulance galloping away.

"Drop that knife," Brooke shouted, "or, by Heaven, I'll wring your neck!"

The knife slipped from the man's fingers. For a moment there was silence. A draft was blowing through the room. Brooke glanced away for a single second; a door in the wall stood a little ajar.

"Take that fellow, Simmons," Brooke ordered. "We must get a doctor at once."

The little man with the gold glasses beamed upon them.

"My friends from the Café Hollande!" he remarked. "After all, then, the young lady has wits. Pardon!"

His fingers flashed from his waistcoat pocket to his mouth. He waved Brooke away as he sank into an easy-chair.

"Quite unnecessary," he murmured. "I shall be dead within five minutes. Another martyr to the cause of science! I never could resist these little affairs. One learned so much."

MR. HASLEM WAS ABLE, after all, to give his evidence at the Cannon Street Hotel on the following day, but would-be lunchers at the Café Hollande were disappointed. The doors of the restaurant were closed, without any reason with which the public was ever made aware other than the painfully sudden death of the proprietor, and Jean—his chief *maître d'hôtel*.

The disappearance of Paul was wrapped in mystery. He received a telephone message late in the evening and strolled away from the hotel in his full uniform a few minutes later. When the police arrived, he was not to be found. His escape was one of those episodes not mentioned by persons of tact before Inspector Simmons. Brooke and Constance stood outside the restaurant the next morning and watched the locked doors with complete satisfaction.

"At last," she sighed, "I can go back to my dear little café. Already I am longing for one of Charles's omelettes."

"On this occasion only," Brooke started to plead.

"Very well," she acceded, "you may come."

TALE THE SEVENTH
THE SILENT PEOPLE

ON THE FIRST SUNDAY in May there occurred in the heart of London a tragedy simple enough in itself, yet with a strange and sinister meaning for those who cared to study life a little way beneath its exterior crust. Among the well-dressed crowd of London's fashionable people swarming in Hyde Park between midday and one o'clock on Sunday a woman, whose rags were only partially concealed by a rusty black shawl, was seen suddenly to reel and fall. She was picked up dead. Upon the bosom of her threadbare gown were pinned a few words of writing, which afforded to the smug press of the country an opportunity for many rhetorical flourishes. They led, too, to other and more serious things, for there were those who accepted them as a message.

These were the words, written very correctly in faint but straggling characters upon a half sheet of coarse white paper:

> I am thirty years old. I am going to die. I am tired out. There is no hope in this world for the poor. I have done my best. I have a husband and four children. My husband earns twenty-one shillings a week. I cannot feed him, myself, and four children on twenty-one shillings a week. I have tried.
>
> My children are thin and hungry. My husband never smiles. He, too, is losing his strength. I myself am the withered remnant of a woman. I have no hope. I know that there is a life, but, for some reason, I

am not asked to share in it. This morning, for once,
I go to see the sunshine. I go to see the other women.
Perhaps I shall understand what it is they have done
to deserve life and I have not done. And then I shall
rest.

When the newspapers had finished with their stories, and a
satisfactory fund had been raised for the children of the dead
woman, things began to happen.

A millionaire employer of labor, who had closed his yards and
turned seventeen hundred people into the streets because one of
the commodities used by him had reached a price which he declared made his business unprofitable, was shot dead as he crossed
the pavement from his house in Park Lane to step into his motorcar. His murderer turned out to be one of his unemployed work
people whose wife had gone on the streets to find bread for her
starving children. The man defended himself from the dock with a
rough eloquence which paralyzed even the law.

Within a few days other events happened which pointed to some
systematic effort. Four factories in different parts of the country,
whose owners were deservedly unpopular, were destroyed either
by dynamite or fire. A trades-union official, who was reported to
have accepted a bribe from a federation of employers to prohibit a
strike, even though he was in possession of large funds subscribed
by the work people, was missed for several days and discovered
with a cord around his neck in the Thames.

Then a leading daily paper published a mysterious document
which had been dropped into its letter-box by an unknown hand.
It was headed:

> To the People of England!
> There are millions who have been waiting for a sign.
> Eleven days ago a woman died in Hyde Park, and
> the message found pinned to the rags which covered
> her withered body has been accepted as that sign.
> England is governed by laws—laws ill-made by man

for his kind. The old laws are hard to break; the new laws are difficult to frame. From our place in the wilderness we who send this message have spent many weary hours pondering over the great subject—how and in what fashion shall we make heard the voice of the sufferers?

A short time ago hundreds of women, nourished in comfortable homes, educated, civilized, apparently respectable, called attention to a grievance from which they imagined themselves to be suffering by great and wanton destruction of property. Their grievance is to ours as the light of a candle to the burning of the sun. There are those who have approved their methods. They have taught us a lesson. Cause and effect shall be dissociated in our minds. Until you listen to us we will kill, burn, and destroy. When the moment has come we will point to you the way to freedom.

To-morrow the king drives through the city to the Mansion House. The king to-morrow will be safe. But between Ludgate Bridge and St. Paul's Cathedral one of the horses drawing his coach will be destroyed.

The Silent People.

This document was scoffed at by nearly every one who read it. Even the editor of the paper was derided for publishing an anonymous hoax. That morning, however, half-way up Ludgate Hill, a spectator was seen to break through the little line and, taking a deliberate aim, to shoot one of the horses of the king's coach through the head.

He was at once arrested—in fact, he made no effort to escape. He made no reply to the charge and remained absolutely dumb, both at the time and subsequently. He was committed to prison during the king's pleasure, a fate to which he submitted with the utmost indifference. On the following day the letter-box of the

Daily Observer was watched by the cleverest detectives in London. The sub-editor, however, discovered in the morning another communication among the rest of his correspondence. This document was headed in the same way:

> To the People of England!
> We have a thousand men like William Clarke ready to do our bidding; ready to kill, burn, or destroy, as we choose. We are tired of our labor members and our magazine-writing socialists. The people speak now for themselves. We adopt the tactics of a more educated class. On Thursday one of the masterpieces in The National Gallery will be destroyed.
> > The Silent People.

This time, short of closing the National Gallery, every possible precaution was taken, but about three o'clock in the afternoon the Madonna of Giotto was discovered cut into strips.

The perpetrator of the deed was easily arrested. His name was Johnson. He was a weaver by trade, out of work, and poorly dressed.

He made no reply to the charge, no reply in the police court, and, refusing to answer the simplest questions, he was committed to prison indefinitely.

On the third day another communication was received and published in *The Observer*:

> We of the people have been accused always of ranting, of shouting our wrongs from the house-tops. Let us hope that our new tactics will be approved. We have left off words. We have come to deeds, and those who do our bidding have learned silence. To-morrow there will be wrecked the house of one whose name is held by us as the name of an enemy.
> > The Silent People.

Throughout London a certain thrill of anticipation seemed to quiver in the air from hour to hour. Who was there who could be called an enemy of the people? In great black head-lines the evening papers told the story.

In a suburb of London the house of a member of the government who had risen from the ranks, and to whom such measures for the relief of the poor which a temporizing government had devised had lately been entrusted, was completely wrecked.

The man himself had escaped, but his house was in ruins. He stood branded as an enemy of the people. On this occasion the thrower of the bomb remained undiscovered. The house was one of those which had been left unwatched.

II

IT WAS ABOUT this time that Stanley Brooke made a thrilling and amazing discovery, which at first threatened seriously to alter his relations with his partner. He arrived home unexpectedly early one night to find a note asking him to call in and report. He discovered the door of her flat unfastened and the door of the inner room wide open. Hearing his footsteps, she called out:

"Please come here at once."

After a moment's hesitation he obeyed. He advanced even to the threshold of the inner room and, for the first time, saw inside. He stood quite still, transfixed with surprise.

Every detail of her sitting-room was always rigidly reminiscent of Constance herself. Even the easy chairs were a little severe, and the furniture which she had added from time to time was of a somber and decorous type. Her color-scheme was gray; the pictures which hung upon the walls were nearly all landscapes; her whole environment always seemed so thoroughly in keeping with her clothes, her manner of speech itself of prim, almost Quakerish simplicity.

He had pictured her own room as something like this: a simple bedstead, a few prints, an apartment clean and bare and chaste. He looked instead into a chamber utterly unlike anything he could have imagined.

The walls were colored a faint rose-pink, and there was a carpet on the floor of almost the same hue. The bedstead was of white, with a top of hooded muslin tied up with ribbons. There was an easy chair and a large divan, chintz-covered, luxurious; a dressing-table covered with dainty trifles; and on the bed, by the side of an empty basket, a little heap of garments which seemed to him like a sea of lace and muslin, with blue ribbons stealing from unexpected places.

Everything was spotless, exquisitely dainty. It might well have been the sleeping apartment of a princess.

Brooke stood rooted to the spot. His final shock of amazement came when he realized that Constance herself was wearing a dressing-gown of white muslin, that she seemed like a bewildering vision of fluffiness and laces and ribbons. He was absolutely incapable of any form of speech. He simply stood and stared while her face grew darker.

"How dare you?" she exclaimed, advancing rapidly toward the door.

"You called me," he declared. "I got your note and hurried down. When I came inside you called me."

"I thought it was Susan, you idiot!" she retorted, slamming the door in his face.

He walked slowly away. The maid whom Constance had recently engaged for several hours a day entered hurriedly, almost at the same moment, from the outside door. She smiled at Brooke as she passed.

"I am afraid that Miss Robinson will think I have been gone a long time, sir," she remarked. "I could not find the shop."

She disappeared, closing the door behind her. Brooke threw himself into an easy chair. So there was another Constance, after all, a Constance who loved the things a woman should love, a Constance who was as dainty and sweet as anything he could have conceived in his most sentimental moments.

He felt his heart beating with the pleasure of it. Her life, then, was to some extent a pose. At heart she was like other girls. He sat with half-closed eyes, dwelling upon those few seconds—seconds full of exquisite imaginings.

It seemed to him that he had never in his life looked upon anything more beautiful than that little chamber and its contents. Even Constance, when she at last appeared, could not dispel his dreams. She was dressed in severe and homely black, unrelieved even at the neck. A vision he seemed to have had of silk stockings was dissipated by the sight of her square-toed shoes. She came toward him in an absolutely matter-of-fact way. He rose, a little embarrassed.

"If I was rude just now," she said calmly, "I am sorry. The fault, I suppose, was mine."

"I certainly," he explained, "would not have dreamed of—"

"That will do," she interrupted. "We will not discuss the subject again, ever. I hope you will humor me so far as to forget the occurrence. I sent for you because I wanted to talk."

He nodded. "It is three weeks since we did anything."

"I have nothing definite to propose now," she went on. "I wanted to speak about the Silent People."

"There is a reward of a thousand pounds offered this morning," he remarked.

"They are doing all they can to break the thing up," she said. "People are growing uneasy. The question is whether, supposing we were successful where others have failed, we could take that thousand pounds' reward with a clear conscience."

"What do you mean?" he asked.

"I mean that I am not at all sure," she continued, "that my sympathies are not with the Silent People."

Brooke, whose habits of mind were conventional, even though his views were broad enough, shook his head.

"One may see weak points in our laws, in our whole social system," he observed, "but the attacks made upon it must be legitimate. I say that it is the duty of every one to uphold the law."

"Yours," she replied, "is the point of view of the man in the street. I will not tell you exactly what I think. Only this—if you join with me in a certain scheme which I am about to propose, it must be on this one condition only: that in the event of success, the claiming of that reward—that is to say, the denouncing of these people—must rest with me."

"I do not mind that," he assented.

"You understand," she repeated. "Even if we are successful—supposing we find out who it is that writes those notices and who has planned these outrages—if I decide that the knowledge is to be forgotten, it must be so."

"I agree," he said. "I think that your instinct will be too strong for your humanitarianism."

"We shall see," she rejoined. "There are a good many threads hanging loose, a good many which have been tried already and thrown on one side. Now tell me, you have done what I asked you this afternoon?"

He nodded. "I was at the House of Commons at four o'clock. I heard Cammerley bring in his bill."

"What did you think of him?"

Brooke hesitated. "At first," he said thoughtfully, "I was disappointed. Then he began to impress me. His is rather a curious personality. Nothing about him suggests in any way a leader of the people. He has a thin frame, he stoops, and he wears gold-rimmed spectacles. He spoke almost without gestures and his voice at times was quite low. It was not until he had been speaking for some time that one realized that he was, after all, in his way an orator.

"He had no notes, he spoke with perfect assurance, and he said some startling things. But he didn't attempt to make the points that these labor men nearly always do. There wasn't a touch of rhetoric in anything he said. He simply spoke of the coming of the people as though it were written."

"He believes that," she murmured.

"On the whole," Brooke concluded, "I should put him down as a dangerous man."

"Why dangerous?"

"He is a revolutionary. One could almost imagine him a Robespierre."

"Even that," she remarked, "may come."

"And now," he asked, "tell me exactly why you wanted me to hear him. You had some reason."

"I had," she admitted. "I think that if you could see inside his brain you wouldn't have much trouble in earning that thousand pounds."

"He is one of the Silent People!" Brooke exclaimed.

Constance waited for a moment.

"You know," she said then, "that I am a member of the Forward Club?"

"You told me so the other night," he replied. "I remember how surprised I was."

"There is nothing for you to be surprised at," she continued calmly. "Anyhow, I was there the other afternoon. Cammerley was having tea with a woman at the next table. They were talking together earnestly. You know how acute my hearing is. I caught a single sentence. It was enough."

Brooke was obviously interested.

"If Cammerley is really mixed up with those people," he said, "it would cause a sensation if it were known. He has been getting quite a little following of his own lately. The other side have rather taken him up. The *Daily Mail* had a leading article on him one day last week."

"Why not? He is a strong man. In a few years' time, unless accidents happen, the country will have to reckon with him."

"Accidents?"

"I mean if he does not come to grief," she explained. "It is his pose at present to be a moderate man. They say that at heart he is a red-hot anarchist, ready to sacrifice the country, the lives of millions, if necessary, to his principles. That is why I wonder whether we should not be doing good rather than harm if we were to take that thousand pounds' reward."

"You would have to get your proofs first," he reminded her.

"We might fail," she admitted. "On the other hand, we might succeed. What I cannot make up my mind about is whether we might not do more harm by succeeding."

"But you are not a socialist yourself!"

"I am not so sure about that," she answered.

He shrugged his shoulders. It was certainly not the place or the time for arguments.

"In any case," he begged, "tell me just what you have in your mind."

"You are still in touch with the *Daily Observer* people," she said. "Well, go and interview Mr. Cammerley on their behalf. Talk to him in his own house. See if anything occurs to you."

"No hints?"

"None. I am not keeping anything from you. I simply heard a sentence pass between him and a woman whom I know very well by repute. Go and see what you think of him."

Brooke glanced at the clock.

"I'll go to-morrow," he promised; "—but in the mean time?"

"I am going to dine at my club tonight," she interrupted, a little ruthlessly. "I shall be leaving in a few minutes."

"You wouldn't like to take me with you, I suppose?" he suggested.

"I should dislike it very much indeed," she replied. "I don't see the slightest reason why I should pay for your dinner."

"It's only eighteen pence," he ventured hopefully.

"The amount is not so serious, perhaps," she admitted. "It is the principle. Besides, I want to make a few inquiries there about Mr. Cammerley's friends. I shall be better alone."

"Constance," he began, suddenly inspired by a recollection of that little room. Her eyes flashed a warning.

"I consider the use of my Christian name a liberty, Mr. Brooke!" He turned on his heel and went out. It was not until he had left the room that her lips relaxed in the least. Then she smiled.

III

BROOKE PRESENTED HIMSELF at two o'clock the next day at a large and gloomy-looking house in Bermondsey, a house which had once belonged to a manufacturer of leather who had chosen to live near his works, but which stood now in almost pitiful isolation, with a tan-yard at the back of it and a row of small shops on either side.

A woman admitted him, a woman who was neatly dressed but who wore no cap and had not the manners of a servant. He passed along a bare hall and was shown into a large, untidy-looking study. Mr. Cammerley looked up from his desk as Brooke approached, but did not offer his hand or attempt any form of conventional greeting. He pointed, however, to a plain deal chair close at hand.

"I do not understand," he said, "why you have come to see me. Your card says that you are a journalist. One paper has already turned me inside out and indulged in a photographic representation of the person I am not, and given a faithful description of the things I did not say and the views which I do not hold. Surely one is enough?"

"These are curious days," Brooke remarked, setting his hat upon the table. "The whole reading public is crazy for personalities."

The man behind the desk looked at him steadfastly. It seemed to Brooke that those light-colored eyes were growing larger behind his spectacles.

"What is the name of your paper?" he asked.

"I am a reporter on the *Daily Observer*," Brooke told him.

"You are also a liar," Mr. Cammerley said calmly. "Your name is Brooke, and, with a certain young lady as your partner, you have been teaching Scotland Yard its business for the last few months. Now, sir, what the devil do you mean by coming to see me under false pretenses? Is there any mystery connected with me or my life? Is there anything you wish to discover?"

Brooke shut up his note-book. He had the curious sense of being in the presence of a man who could read his innermost thoughts.

"To tell you the truth," he confessed, "I was wondering whether you could not give me some information with regard to the Silent People?"

Mr. Cammerley continued to look steadily at him.

"Supposing I could," he asked, "why should I? You are a stranger to me. There is a thousand pounds' reward, I believe, offered for information about these people. Why should you associate me with them in any way?"

"You are a socialist," Brooke reminded him. "You speak with wonderful restraint, but that very restraint is impressive. I heard you yesterday afternoon in the House of Commons. I may be wrong, but to me you seemed to represent the type of man who would go to any lengths if he considered himself justified by his principles."

"For an inquiry agent," Mr. Cammerley declared, "you certainly do seem to be possessed of a certain amount of perception as regards elementary facts. How much of this interview is going in your paper, Mr. Brooke?"

"Not a word," Brooke replied.

"So I imagined," Mr. Cammerley remarked dryly. "Then listen. You are right. I am an anarchist, if you like to use the word. That is to say, I would, if I had the power, rend this country from north to south that the better days might dawn. I would do evil that good may come."

"It is a dangerous doctrine."

Mr. Cammerley raised his eyebrows. "A surgeon cuts off your leg that he may save your life."

"He obeys fixed laws," Brooke retorted, "and disease is a matter of fact, not principle."

Mr. Cammerley smiled indulgently. He glanced at the papers before him.

"Mr. Brooke," he said, "you are wasting my time. I have no desire to make a convert of you."

"Tell me something about the Silent People," Brooke persisted, "and I will go."

Cammerley rose slowly from his place and moved to the door. He held it open and turned his face toward the stairs.

"Lucy!" he called.

An answer came from above. Cammerley remained with the door open. In a few moments a woman appeared, a woman broadly built, with a dark, square face, a slight down upon the upper lip, and beautiful eyes—the eyes of an enthusiast. Her hair was parted simply in the middle. It was black and shiny, and there were large quantities of it. Her dress was plain in the extreme. She looked from Cammerley to Brooke.

"It is a young man," Cammerley explained softly, "who has come here in the guise of a reporter to know if I can tell him anything about the Silent People." Not a muscle of her face changed, only a sudden light shone in her eyes. Brooke, who was glancing at her, shivered. For some mysterious reason he felt that he was in danger.

"This visitor of ours," Cammerley continued, looking at Brooke dispassionately, "has been associated with a young lady in various investigations during the last few months. He would call himself, I suppose, a private-inquiry agent, or something of the sort. He has become interested in the craze of the moment. He is exceedingly curious about the Silent People."

The woman sighed. When she spoke it was with a slight foreign accent.

"What is it that one hears about them?" she murmured. "There have been others who have sought to discover their identity—others who are themselves silent now forever."

"The young man," Cammerley said thoughtfully, "is of a harmless type."

Brooke, as he stood there, was conscious of soft footsteps in the hall—footsteps which seemed to gather volume all the time, not the footsteps of one or two people, but the footsteps of dozens.

"You were looking for adventures, perhaps, my young friend," Cammerley continued. "You have been successful. Some one who visited me once remarked that this might well be a house of mysteries, so strangely situated in such a neighborhood. Perhaps it is. Look!"

He pushed the door a little further open. The hall seemed filled with men—men who were waiting patiently, men who exchanged not a syllable, pale-faced most of them, dressed in the garb of operatives, with something curious about them which, although he did not understand it, made Brooke shiver. Cammerley closed the door again.

"As I think you already knew before you came," he said quietly, "you are in the presence of the Silent People—Lucy Fragade and I myself. Those outside have also learned the gift of silence. They are some of those who do our bidding."

Brooke stared at the woman. The name was well enough known to him—Lucy Fragade, who had been expelled from Russia, imprisoned in America, imprisoned again in Germany, and forced to escape from France; the daughter of an anarchist, a woman who preached force and bloodshed with an eloquence which no man of her cause had ever approached. He recognized her from her portraits. She was gazing at him fixedly. She was more like them now than ever.

"There is a room at the back of this house," Cammerley continued, "into which others have been invited who have come as you have come, and the world has seen no more of them. The river flows within forty yards of my back door, and the tanyard is empty at night. I am afraid, Mr. Brooke, that the public will have to wait a little time for that interview with me which you proposed writing."

Brooke looked from one to the other. Up to the present moment, at any rate, he had felt no fear. Yet there was something a little disquieting in the expression with which they regarded him; something ominous, too, in that sense of men waiting without. He remembered several disappearances lately. He knew suddenly that murder had been done in this place. Yet he was still without fear. Perhaps he was, to some extent, a fatalist. Death seemed to him always a thing so unlikely.

"I shall be missed," he remarked affably. "Miss Robinson knows that I have come to see you."

Cammerley nodded.

"The young lady who overheard our conversation at the Forward Club," he explained to Lucy. "It is a pity that she did not accompany you, sir."

"Perhaps," Brooke replied, "she is better where she is!"

The telephone-bell rang. Cammerley held the receiver to his ear.

"This is Mr. Cammerley speaking," he declared. "What can I do for you? Yes, Mr. Brooke is here. You are Miss Constance Robinson."

Brooke made a movement toward the telephone, but stopped.

"No, I am afraid that I cannot say," Cammerley continued, "what time Mr. Brooke will return. He will leave this room in a few

minutes. As for the rest, it is difficult. Yes, I understand." He listened for some time. His face showed no change of expression. He
glanced toward the clock.

"Very well," he said, "the course you suggest will be quite agree-
able to me. It would give me great pleasure to meet you personally. Yes, pray, come. As you say, it is only an affair of ten minutes
in a taxicab."

Brooke sprang toward the telephone.

"She shall not come here!" he shouted.

Mr. Cammerley handed him the receiver.

"Really," he said, "you people are wasting a lot of our time this
afternoon. Tell her yourself to keep away, then."

Brooke snatched the receiver.

"Miss Robinson!" he called out. "Constance, are you there?
Constance!"

"Miss Robinson is here," was the calm reply.

"You are not to come to this man's house!" Brooke exclaimed.
"If you do, don't come alone! You understand?"

"Quite well. There is probably a slight misunderstanding. *Au
revoir*!"

"Listen!" Brooke begged.

The connection was gone. Cammerley removed the instrument
out of reach with a little sigh.

"My dear Mr. Brooke," he said, "the young lady is evidently
accustomed to having her own way. Who can blame her? Miss
Fragade is a little like that, too. Now how shall we spend the time
until Miss Robinson arrives? Would you like to see around the
place? Would you care to stroll through the tan-yard down to the
river? There is a room here which Lucy calls our chamber of horrors. Perhaps you would like to see that? Or would you like to make
the acquaintance of our bodyguard—fifty strange-looking men?
Most of them now, I suppose, have gone back to their posts, but
there will be a few remaining."

He swung open the door. There were a dozen men still in the
hall, standing against the wall almost like statues. Their eyes were

fixed upon Cammerley. They seemed ready to obey his slightest gesture. Brooke glanced at the door; Cammerley smiled.

"The only modern thing about the place," he remarked. "A double lock of really wonderful pattern. Would you like to see some of my books? Or would it amuse you to hear Lucy talk of her Continental experiences?"

The telephone-bell rang again. Cammerley spoke, apparently, to a whip in the House of Commons.

"I shall be in my place at four o'clock," Brooke heard him say. "The division, I suppose, is not likely to come on before dinner-time? Thank you!"

"An interesting thing, the telephone," he continued, replacing the receiver and turning to Brooke. "It seems to bring one so into touch with the outside world from the most impossible places, doesn't it? Ah, the taxicab! Stay here, please, Mr. Brooke. Miss Robinson will be properly received, without a doubt."

Constance was ushered into the room, a moment later, by the gray-haired woman who had admitted Brooke. She was, as usual, exceedingly quiet in her manner and very self-composed.

"It is Mr. Cammerley, is it not?" she inquired, holding out her hand. "And I am sure that this is Lucy Fragade? It is very interesting to meet you both." Cammerley smiled.

"Without flattery," he remarked, "I may say that there have been many who have found it interesting."

Constance was standing between Lucy Fragade and Cammerley. She seemed very small.

"I have come," she announced, "to take Mr. Brooke back with me."

Lucy Fragade looked at her curiously. Cammerley smiled.

"Mr. Brooke was a little lonely," he said. "I have no doubt that he will find your coming of benefit to him."

"Ours must be only a flying visit," Constance continued quietly. "Before I go, there is a question I have wanted to ask Mr. Cammerley ever since I knew of his existence. This will probably be my only chance. Should I be too exacting if I begged for—say, thirty seconds in which to ask it?"

"I have no secrets," Cammerley replied. "Pray ask your question."

Constance looked at him intently.

"It was a question," she murmured, "which occurred to me first when I heard that Blanche Fragade was indeed—"

"Lucy Fragade," the woman interrupted. Constance accepted the correction, but she did not at once continue. She was looking steadfastly at Cammerley. There was perhaps no one else in the room who noticed any change in him. Yet Brooke, who was nearest, and who found the temperature of the apartment on the cold side, was suddenly surprised to see two little drops of perspiration standing out on the man's forehead.

Cammerley looked toward the woman and said something to her in a tongue which neither Brooke nor Constance understood. She nodded and left the room.

Cammerley leaned, a little toward Constance as she passed out.

"Go on," he said.

"Is there any need?" she asked calmly. "I have a friend in Cyril Mansions. The letter is ready for the post—if we do not return."

Cammerley's face was, for a moment, like the face of a skeleton. His eyes shone large behind his spectacles. His lips had parted, showing his strong, yellow teeth.

"Your terms?" he whispered.

"This is not our affair," Constance said softly. "I was wrong to send him here," she added, motioning toward Brooke. "I, too, am of the people. So long as it is not life you take, he and I are silent."

Cammerley asked for no pledge. He understood. For a moment he listened.

Then he led the way toward the door. In the hall several shadowy figures came stealing toward them. He waved them back and opened the front door.

"You will find a taxicab at the corner," he said.

At the corner of the street they stopped to look around them. Brooke glanced back at the house they had left. Behind it was the tanyard, and a little farther away they could see the masts in the river.

"A queer place," Constance observed composedly. "They say that he is a real philanthropist. His house is filled with all sorts of outcasts from the streets, to whom he gives temporary shelter. That is the reason he lives there."

"Is it?" Brooke replied dryly. "There is nothing would please me better than to go over it with half a dozen policemen at my back."

She shook her head.

"It is forbidden. I think those two people, mistaken though they may be, represent things with which we do better not to interfere."

"At least," Brooke asked, "I may inquire who Blanche is?"

"But for Blanche," Constance told him, "I should never have suffered you to go to that man's house, because I know that they are suspicious of you and of me. Blanche is Lucy Fragade's sister. She left her home mysteriously some years ago. Lucy does not know where she is. Philip Cammerley does. There are only two things in life greater than that woman's devotion to her cause. One was her love for her sister; the other her passion for Cammerley. I should say that he was a man who feared but one thing in the world. When I spoke he saw the possibility of it."

Brooke handed her into a taxicab.

"There seems to be a weak spot in the life of every strong man," he remarked, "and that weak spot is always a woman. Even with myself—"

"Don't talk nonsense!" she interrupted

TALE THE EIGHTH
THE GLEN TERRACE TRAGEDY

BROOKE WAS CONSCIOUS of a variety of most disquieting sensations. In the first place, he had completely lost his appetite. Furthermore, he was furiously and unreasonably angry. Charles hung around him continually, aware that all was not well with his favorite patron.

"It is not one of monsieur's regular days for luncheon here," he ventured. Brooke was scowling across the room toward the small table against the wall, at which Constance and a companion were seated.

"It isn't," he admitted. "That accounts for it."

"Accounts for it, *monsieur*? But for what?"

Charles glanced wonderingly across the room—and understood. The perplexity upon his face disappeared.

"Monsieur perceives that the young lady in whom he was interested has found a companion," he remarked confidentially. "They sit together to-day for the third time. On Tuesday evening he dined with mademoiselle!"

"The devil he did!" Brooke muttered.

"One notices these things," the waiter continued, glancing around to be sure that his services were not required elsewhere.

"For so many months the young lady has been so retired, so lonely. It was monsieur who first spoke of her. Always she sits alone, she is reserved, she avoids notice. It is not until one looks carefully that one realizes that *mademoiselle* has an appearance. The gentleman who is with her now," Charles went on, leaning a

288

little closer toward Brooke and dropping his voice, "he asked about her one day last week very much as monsieur did."

Brooke muttered something between his teeth and poured himself out a glass of wine. "The young lady would probably object to our discussing her," he remarked grimly. "You can fetch me my coffee. And this afternoon I will take a liqueur—the old brandy."

"Monsieur shall be served," Charles murmured, and hastened away. It was not until he had served the coffee and generously filled the liqueur-glass above the line with the deep-brown brandy that he spoke again. He leaned forward confidentially.

"It is for monsieur's private ear, this," he whispered. "We do not, as a rule, speak of such things. The gentleman who is with her now—he wrote a little note to mademoiselle here in the restaurant at luncheon one day. Mademoiselle replied, and he took his coffee at her table."

Brooke waved the man away impatiently. "That will do, Charles," he said. "There is probably some explanation. It certainly is not our business."

Brooke lit his cigarette, and while he smoked he looked across the room. The man was apparently a little less than middle-aged, dark, with small, black mustache, well-groomed, well-dressed. He would, without doubt, rank as good-looking. His manner indicated an interest in his companion which to some extent, at any rate, she seemed inclined to return. Constance was certainly more animated than usual. The pallor of her cheeks was undisturbed, but her eyes were exceptionally bright, and she was listening with obvious interest to all that her companion had to say. Beyond the faint uplifting of her eyebrows and the grave nod with which she had acknowledged his greeting upon his entrance, she had taken no further notice of Brooke.

That no more familiar intercourse should take place between them in public beyond that form of recognition was a condition to which she had rigidly adhered ever since their strange partnership began. Brooke hated it and obeyed. To-day he was more than ever a rebel.

Presently he paid his bill and went. Constance, although without doubt she saw his preparations for departure, took not the slightest further notice of him. She was talking all the time, and her manner, for her, toward this new acquaintance, was positively friendly. Brooke jammed his hat upon his head and walked round to the club.

"Bridge!" he muttered to himself. "A debauch at bridge, and the Lord help my partner!"

The morning had been hopelessly wet, which was the reason Brooke was not playing golf. There was plenty of bridge; there were also billiards and other sane amusements to be found at the club. Brooke passed the time away as well as he could, but he found it a task of some difficulty. His usual cheerfulness seemed to have deserted him. He revoked at bridge, lost two games of billiards, and contradicted a member of the committee; altogether a disastrous afternoon. About five o'clock, just after he had sent his tea away for the second time, a page came in search of him.

"Wanted on the telephone, sir," he announced.

Brooke rose promptly. "Any name?" he asked.

"There was no name, sir," the boy replied. "The gentleman is waiting on the line now."

Brooke hurried downstairs, passed into the telephone-box, and took up the receiver.

"This is Brooke," he said. "Who are you?"

"I am Inspector Simmons," the voice answered. "I am speaking from Miss Robinson's rooms."

"Is Miss Robinson there?" Brooke asked.

"She is not here at present," the man replied. "I rang up to ask whether it would be quite convenient for you to step round here."

"Of course I'll come," Brooke assented. "There's nothing wrong, is there?"

The voice hesitated a moment.

"Not that I know of. Perhaps it would be as well if you came round."

Brooke rang off, put on his hat and coat, caught a taxicab, and in a few minutes' time presented himself at Constance's rooms. To his surprise the inspector, who admitted him, was still alone there.

"Where is Miss Robinson?" Brooke demanded.

"That's exactly what I'm not sure about," the inspector explained. "I had an appointment with her here this afternoon at three o'clock. I arrived quite punctually, rang the bell, and as there was no answer, I went away. I came again half an hour ago, and as there was still no one here, I took the liberty of entering. Miss Robinson, as a rule, is very particular about her appointments."

"She was lunching with a friend today," Brooke remarked gloomily.

"Where? What sort of a friend?" the inspector asked.

Brooke hesitated. The inspector's tone was eager, almost impatient.

"It was a man I think she met at the Café Lugano, just a restaurant acquaintance."

"Was he dark, with a small, black mustache, brown, freckled complexion, well-dressed, looked like a military man?" the inspector asked quickly.

"That is an exact description of him," Brooke admitted. "Who is he? What do you know about him?"

The inspector glanced at the clock.

"What time did you say they were lunching?" he asked.

"Between half past one and two," Brooke replied. "I left them there."

"That confirms my information," the inspector said, half to himself, "It is now past five o'clock. You'll excuse me for a minute, if you please."

He went to the telephone and gave a few rapid orders. Then he turned round to Brooke.

"You've heard of the Glen Terrace tragedy, Mr. Brooke?" he asked.

"Of course! What about it?"

"The man whom you saw lunching with Miss Robinson is the man we are shadowing for it," the inspector declared. "We can't arrest him at the moment because there isn't sufficient evidence. All that we can do is to watch and see that he doesn't get away. I'm as confident that he did it as that I'm standing here at this moment, but if we try to put our hands on him too quickly, and he once gets away, he is safe for life.

"Miss Robinson took the matter up entirely on her own account. She had an idea that she could get the evidence we are lacking. I told her it wasn't a proper case for her to mix herself up in. She only smiled at me. She is a determined young lady, as I dare say you know. Anyway, she has been meeting this man for the last few days, and she told me to be here at three o'clock. She expected, I believe, to have something definite to say. I don't mind confessing that I am a little worried about it. It seems—"

"You say your men are shadowing him?" Brooke interrupted quickly. "Can't we find out exactly where he is?"

"They lost him after leaving the restaurant," the inspector replied. "It seems he went in by the hotel and must have come out by the restaurant entrance. We could have had our hand upon his shoulder any time during the last three months, and there isn't the least chance of his being able to escape out of the country. But where he is at this precise moment I must admit I don't know."

"Shall I go to the restaurant," Brooke asked, "and find out if any one remembers their leaving?"

"I have gone as far as that myself," the inspector remarked. "What I was told bears out what you say. Miss Robinson and Delamoir left the Café Lugano together in a taxicab at five minutes to two."

Brooke glanced at the clock. "My God!" he muttered. "That was more than three hours ago!"

II

THE SUN WAS SHINING between the showers and the sky was unexpectedly blue when Constance and the man with whom she had been lunching left the little restaurant in Old Compton Street. They stood for a moment upon the pavement, and Constance, with a farewell nod, prepared to turn away.

"Good morning, Mr. Harold," she said. "We must have another talk some day about these fancies of yours."

"Why not this afternoon?" he asked. "Don't you see how beautiful it is just now? Couldn't you spare—say, one hour? Do you know what I was going to do? I was going to take a taxicab and drive about alone. Come with me."

She looked at him thoughtfully for a moment. Her hesitation made him the more insistent.

"Do come," he begged. "You know how nervous and broken-down I am. To have any one near as calm and self-centered as you are is like a sedative. Please come, just for one hour."

"I will come," she agreed.

He called a taxi and handed her in.

"Is there anywhere you wish to go particularly?" he inquired eagerly.

She shook her head.

"I have no choice," she replied, "only we must not be longer than an hour."

"To Putney," he told the driver. "I will direct you again."

He took his place by her side. In this clear sunlight there were things to be noticed about him not easily apparent in the dimmer light of the restaurant. He was dressed in mourning, with a black tie, and a black band around his hat. There were lines upon his face and a strange restlessness in his deep-set eyes. Every now and then his lips twitched. He looked about him all the time with little abrupt movements of the head.

"If I were you," she suggested, "I should see a doctor. Over-work should never make any one quite as nervous as you seem to be. It is so easy to cure oneself if one has the will."

"It is not only overwork," he muttered. "Let us forget it for a few minutes. How wonderful to be so calm and collected as you are always! Do you never feel emotions, little lady?"

She turned her head and looked at him.

"My name," she said, "is Miss Robinson."

"I beg your pardon!" he exclaimed quickly. "It shall be just as you say. Only, somehow or other, I have been feeling so lonely, and you are such a strange, quiet little person. You have such a gift of making one talk and of listening."

She smiled.

"If you will keep your part of the bargain," she promised, "I will stay with you; not otherwise."

"I will keep it," he agreed.

They were passing through St. James's Park, toward Buckingham Palace. Now that they had left the more crowded streets behind, he seemed a little more at his ease.

"Let me advise you seriously," she begged, "to go and see a nerve specialist. There is a man in Harley Street—I could give you his address—to whom ever so many barristers go, and members of Parliament."

He laughed curiously.

"You think it is overwork only," he groaned. "I wish—oh, I only wish I dared tell you!"

She looked steadily ahead. There was so little about him that she did not know—one thing only. "Why don't you?" she murmured."

"You are so sensible," he muttered. "You would not go into hysterics."

"I am certainly not given to that sort of thing," she assured him.

"You are a woman, too," he went on—"very different from her, but still a woman. In a way you would understand. Promise not to jump out of the taxicab?"

"I promise you that under no circumstances will I attempt anything of the sort," she replied.

"My name is not Harold," he confessed, gripping the strap by his side and shaking as he spoke. "My name is Richard Harold Delamoir—Delamoir, you know!"

She turned her head.

"I seem to have heard the name lately," she murmured.

"Heard it!" he exclaimed. "Haven't you heard it at every street corner, seen it on every newspaper placard?"

"Of course," she assented. "You are the Richard Delamoir whose wife was found poisoned in your house at Putney."

He looked at her, his lips parted, his eyes blinking rapidly.

"You don't mind?" he cried. "You are not terrified?"

"Not in the least," she assured him calmly. "Why should I be?"

"You don't know the worst," he told her. "The police are watching me all the time. They think I did it. They think I murdered her. Everybody thinks so. The bus drivers, the tradespeople, the children in the street—they all stare at me curiously as I go by—the man who poisoned his wife! The women look at me from behind the curtains. The men hurry when they pass. It's worse than overwork, this, Miss Robinson."

"Yes," she admitted, "it is worse than overwork."

"There isn't a soul," he continued, "except the doctor, whom I've dared to speak with about it. I haven't been near my club, I've had to leave my favorite restaurants alone—that's why I turned up at the Lugano, where I first saw you. I thought the doctor might have talked to me now and then. We used to be quite friendly once. I went to see him the other night—just dropped in to have a pipe, as I used to. He only said a few words, but it was the way he looked at me. I understood. I remembered his evidence at the inquest. Did you read about the inquest, Miss Robinson?"

"I did," she confessed. "It rather interested me."

"Ah!" he groaned. "They say that after the doctor's evidence it was a toss up whether I was arrested or not. Do you know why I wasn't? Do you know why I am free now? They are waiting to get a little more evidence. They are afraid they might try me and I might get off, and then they'd find out too late. Evidence! I could give them all the evidence they wanted."

"Then why don't you?" she asked.

He laughed harshly.

"Why should I? Is it my business? Let us talk about something else. Miss Robinson. I want to get away from it for a little time. You know the worst now. I've nothing to hide from you. You know that I am Richard Delamoir."

She watched him from her corner without flinching.

"Is it true," she asked, "that you have inherited a large sum of money by your wife's death?"

"Quite true," he answered; "quite true. Oh, I am rich! I hadn't much before I married her, but she left me everything. I thought of stealing out of the country, but they are so clever, these detectives. They'd think I was running away. I should feel a hand on my shoulder just as I was getting into the train. Ugh! If only there was some one to go with me! If only I could get away from this infernal solitude!"

He looked at her eagerly. There was very little encouragement in her emotionless face.

"Have you no friends or relatives at all?" she asked.

"No relatives—not one," he replied. "I was born in Australia. Most of my friends over here were my wife's friends, and—"

His voice seemed to leave him for a moment. He tried to speak and failed.

"They keep out of my way," he went on, after a moment's pause. "I don't know why. Can you think? They can't believe—not all of them. Let us talk about something else. Have you ever been a nurse, Miss Robinson?"

"Certainly not," she answered. "Why do you ask that?"

"I don't know, except that you are so restful and so strong," he declared. "You make me feel almost like a child. That's because my nerve is gone, of course. Are you very well off, I wonder?"

"I am not at all well off," she told him. "I am a typist."

"If I were to give you a large sum of money," he went on eagerly, "would you go abroad with me—just as my nurse," he explained hurriedly, "just to be with me and to keep me from being frightened always? You could have plenty of money, beautiful dresses. Dresses would make such a difference to you—dresses and hats. You are queer-looking, you know. You look old-fashioned and dowdy, and your face is so still and quiet that one forgets that you have really beautiful eyes. It would change you tremendously to be well-dressed."

Her eyes were half closed with silent laughter. There was something about the laugh a little cruel.

"You are afraid of me!"

"Who—I?" she asked. "I afraid?"

"I didn't mean that!" he exclaimed. "I mean that you are afraid I should want to make love to you. Do you know, sometimes I think that I shall never want to make love to another woman."

"How old are you?" she inquired.

"Thirty-nine," he replied. "I was twenty-six years old when I married Maggie. She hadn't her money then. She was just a chorus-girl."

"Is it true that you used always to quarrel?"

"We used to quarrel a good deal," he admitted. "I am afraid I was impatient and a little jealous. Maggie was always having flirtations. She was crazy for admiration."

Constance sighed as she looked away. After all, there were all the commonplace elements of tragedy here.

"You really wish to talk about something else?" she asked. "Come, I will try. You shall tell me about your life in Australia. I think you said that you were born there."

"It isn't any use," he answered. "I want to talk about something else and I can't. It always comes back."

"Then if you won't talk about anything else," she said, "tell me what you meant when you said that you could give the police the evidence they needed."

He shook his head. "No," he muttered, "I couldn't trust anybody with that, not even you!"

She was silent. He sat by her side, and his manner gradually became calmer.

"It is odd," he went on, half to himself, "how much I have told you, really; you—just a little stranger whom I spoke to in a restaurant. Why did you let me speak to you?"

"You looked lonely," she answered. "I am never afraid to speak to any one. I can take care of myself."

"Yes," he admitted, "I should say that that was true. You can very well take care of yourself. Would nothing terrify you, Miss Robinson? Would nothing shake your nerves?"

She smiled. "I have no opportunity of judging. My life is a very uneventful one."

"Try them this afternoon," he begged eagerly. "You see where we are? We are close to Putney. The third turn to the left, then another turn, and the fourth house is where I live. Not a soul has crossed the threshold since that day. Come in with me. Sit with me for a little time. Perhaps it will help. Perhaps after that I shall not be so terrified. If only I can feel another human being breathing the same air in that sitting-room where we used to be! Will you come?"

She did not hesitate. She had no fear. She felt easily his master.

"If it is any satisfaction to you," she assented, "I will come."

His eyes flashed. He gave a direction to the driver, who looked at him curiously. In a few moments they turned off the main street. In less than five minutes the taxicab was pulled up outside one of a little row of villas. As they stepped out Constance was half conscious of people peering from behind the windows. Some women opposite, who had been pointing out the place to a stranger, stared open-mouthed. Constance followed her companion composedly into the house, the door of which he opened with a latch-key. He closed it behind them.

"Why have you sent away the taxicab?" she asked.

"You won't hurry?" he pleaded. "Why should I keep it there? People always gather round if they think I am here. They stare so. Come!"

He opened the door of a little drawing room, a queer apartment, half Oriental, with a tented divan in one corner and a curious smell of incense. The wall-paper was of bright yellow and the curtains black. There were withered flowers in the vases and cigarette-ash upon the carpet. The atmosphere was almost unbearable.

"Do you mind opening a window?" Constance begged. "I couldn't possibly sit here like this."

He nodded and threw up one of the side windows.

"I have only just put my head in here since," he explained hoarsely. "I couldn't bear it. This is where we used to sit. Maggie had such queer taste. I don't think," he went on, "that she had really a healthy nature. She liked everything exotic and unnatural. Poor woman! You see the black curtains and the black carpet. She thought they went with the bright yellow walls and that they helped her complexion.

"She was older than I am, you know, and she used to fancy sometimes that she was losing her looks. Yes, I can breathe now there is some one in the room with me! Sit just where you are, please. Miss Robinson. She used to sit over in that corner, and often she would lie down on the divan there.

"I couldn't bear all the stuffy hangings, but she loved them. Now shall we talk about something? Shall I show you some views? There's an album there of my wife's notices. Or shall we talk about—Australia?"

She shook her head. "You know very well, Mr. Delamoir," she said, "that, however hard you were to try, you couldn't talk—about anything except—"

"Of course you are right," he interrupted. "It isn't any use. I can no more talk about anything else than I can think about anything else. If you want to see her picture, there it is on the corner of the mantelpiece. I can't look—I don't know why—I can't!"

He had turned his back upon her. Constance moved to the mantelpiece and took up the picture. It gave her at first almost a shock. It was the picture of a woman, haggard, painted, with darkened eyebrows, false hair, in a ball dress cut absurdly low, and a satin skirt absurdly tight. She remembered the words Inspector Simmons had used in speaking to her of the case:

"A woman any man would be glad to be rid of!"

Her companion drew the curtain a little.

"There are some boys outside!" he exclaimed irritably. "And those women? their eyes seem never off the place. Do you mind the blind being down?"

She shook her head. There was still a long shaft of sunlight piercing the gloom of the room. Presently he came and sat opposite to her.

"If there were any way," he said, "of ending this?"

"What way could there be?" she interrupted. "You must travel soon and try to forget."

"Forget!" he repeated. "Would you forget, I wonder? Could you carry about with you the horrible knowledge I have locked in my heart, and forget? No one could."

"Well, then, why not tell the truth and have it over?" she asked calmly.

He sprang from his seat. She sat quite still, unflinching. His passion, however, was not one of anger.

"If only I could!" he moaned. "If only—"

He stopped short.

"Stay where you are, Miss Robinson," he implored. "Stay just where you are. Don't move. I shall be back in a moment."

He left the room. She heard him climb the stairs and remained where she was, looking about her. It seemed to her that in all the adventures of her life she had never found herself in such an atmosphere. She looked at the picture of the woman, worthy presiding genius of such an apartment. And yet there was something in the eyes—was it terror or despair—something piteous shining out from the midst of the wreck; just in the same way that, on a table only a few feet away, a little marble statuette of exquisite design struck a strange note in the midst of the flamboyant furniture and vulgar gewgaws with which the place was littered.

She heard his footsteps descending the stairs. He entered the room. There was a new look in his face, white and strained. He carried in his hand a little volume, bound in violent purple arid tied up with ribbon. He held it out to her.

"The evidence," he muttered—"I spoke of the evidence! Only a page or two, mind. You can read; then you will understand. You will be the only person in the world except myself who understands. Don't begin at the beginning—that's all rubbish. Begin there—there!"

His forefinger showed her the place. She began to read. The entries were sprawled all about the book in a loose, untidy handwriting, and without regard to keeping within the limits of the dates.

> Began to-day worse than ever. I got up at twelve and passed the looking-glass on my way to the bath. I almost shrieked. I can't be like it! I had forgotten my hair! I dressed very quickly. Such beautiful things I put on. Then for a long time I could not make up my mind. I put on my lilac dress and my ermine, with a new hat that came last night, and a thick veil. I spent quite an hour with madame in her parlor. Then

I walked slowly away down Bond Street. At first no one looked at me at all. Then a man and a woman passed and I heard the man laugh!

I looked in at a shop-window—perhaps my front was a little crooked. I went down to the theater. I thought to-day, perhaps, there might be a chance. Madame had taken a lot of pains. The stage-door-keeper smiled when he told me that Bunsome was out. Liar! Bunsome came down the passage just a minute later. I told him what I wanted. He looked at me in a queer sort of way.

"Can't see whom I'm talking to," he muttered. "Take off your veil." I took it off. Perhaps my fingers trembled, perhaps I took it off clumsily. He turned away. I could have sworn that he was laughing!

"My good woman," he said, "we want girls!" . . . . I got out somehow, crossed the road. I went into a public house. I had two glasses of port—filthy stuff, but they won't sell me drugs in quantities big enough. Never mind, when I got home I forgot!

Constance looked up. He was still standing over her. "Go on," he ordered. "Turn to the next page. Turn quickly." She obeyed him.

Last night I cried myself to sleep. It doesn't matter crying in the night-time. I was in the West End all day, and I wore my new tailor made gown, the patent shoes with the gray suede tops, and gray stockings. I met Peter face to face. It doesn't seem long ago since he used to beg me to go out to luncheon with him. He hurried on. I tried to stop him, but he muttered something about an appointment, looked at me as though there were something wrong about my appearance, and kept glancing around nervously, as though he were afraid that some one would see us.

I went in to madame's and looked at myself in a glass. Glasses are such liars. I know I don't look like that. Every woman has to use a little rouge and a little false hair nowadays to keep in the fashion. I hate looking-glasses! . . . I lunched at Prince's; got rid of Dick. No one ever takes any notice of a woman if she's with a man younger than herself. I am going to write the truth. I can't bear it! I don't think I will ever lunch there alone again. The men glanced at me as they came in, and then looked away. There wasn't one who had that expression in his face I used to see always when I lunched alone and men passed. It frightened me.

I couldn't eat anything. I went into the ladies' room afterward and I ventured to look in the glass. It was madame's fault. She had put too much rouge on my left cheek. Yes, it must have been madame's fault! I shall try again.

Constance put the book away from her. Her voice was not altogether steady.

"I don't want to read any more," she said.

"One more page," he insisted. "One more, please. You are beginning to understand. One human person in this world understands besides myself! I think that I shall go about with a lighter heart."

She turned the page.

To-day I feel will be different. Laroche has sent me home the most wonderful white velveteen gown. I have rested until twelve o'clock. Now I have just put it on. It fits me divinely. One would say that I had the figure of a girl. It is marvelous. I have put on my big black hat with the feathers and a thinner veil. Yes, I am going to risk a thinner veil!

I shall go to madame for an hour, and then I will take all my courage in my hands. I will go once more to Prince's. I know that Stephen will be there. I will stop him as he passes my table, and I will watch him. I shall see. He used to love me in white. Somehow or other I feel younger myself to-day. As to being old, it is absurd. I am not old.

I have sent Susan for a taxi, and I have made Richard go away for the day. He bothers me so, wanting to go about with me. What admiration can a woman have who has a young husband with her! He doesn't seem to understand. . . . I don't know why I feel so excited to-day. I think it is the white velveteen gown. I shall put on my white silk stockings. It is a little daring, perhaps, but Stephen loves white. . . . Now I am going. I don't think, after all, I shall ever need to use that little packet.

The writing sprawled down to the end of the page. Constance looked up. Delamoir's eyes were upon her.

"Turn over," he ordered.

She obeyed.

I can scarcely hold my pen. My God! I have seen the truth! It is the end! Madame called in little Emilie to look at me before I left. "Madame," she declared, "is *ravissante*!" I paid her and went out. Just as I reached the door I fancied I heard a laugh. At the time I thought that it must be fancy. Now I am not so sure! I went to Prince's, I got my table just inside. I waited. Every one who passed seemed to be in such a hurry.

Bunsome came in, and Elliman, and Captain Jenks, but they none of them appeared to see me. And then Stephen! He saw me, and he was alone, but he was going to pass. I held out my hand and I smiled at him.

"Stephen," I said, "won't you stop and speak to me?" He seemed quite awkward about it, but he stopped. I looked at the place by my side.

"Are you alone?" I asked very softly. He muttered something about having to join a party. I looked at him intently; he used to say that he liked me to look at him like that.

"Why are you in such a hurry?" I asked him. "Can't you stay for a little time and talk?" He shook his head. Then I felt suddenly queer and giddy. Something came into my heart and I held him when he wanted to get away. I said, "Stephen, tell me the truth. Why do you avoid me? Why do those others hurry by? You men used to crowd around me, not so very many years ago. Why is it?"

He hesitated for a moment. Then he looked me straight in the face.

"Since you've asked me that question, Maggie," he said, "I'll tell you, as much for your husband's sake as your own. It's because you are close upon sixty years of age and you dress up to make yourself look like a girl and sit about and expect men to be-have as though you were still attractive. And you're not. You're an old woman, and you know you are. Leave off painting yourself and wearing clothes thirty years too young for you and we'd all be glad to see you now and then and talk to you. But no man likes to be seen talking to a guy. . . . I don't mean to be unkind," he went on, for I suppose I was looking at him in a queer sort of way. "I've just told you this from myself and the others, for Richard's sake as well as your own. Now be a sensible woman and give it up."

I think that he went away then. I am not quite sure what happened to me. I found myself in a taxi-

cab, and here I am—here I am! Fortunately, I didn't
have to buy anything. I've had the stuff with me for
years. I am leaving this in case there should be any
trouble. Whoever reads this, if it shouldn't be Richard, please tell him there's a letter for the coroner
on the next page. . . . I don't know what it's going to
be like on my next page, but it won't be worse than
to-day. I'm going to—turn over!

He took the book from her fingers.

Constance suddenly felt cold.

"I loved her!" he muttered hoarsely. "Don't you understand that
I shall have to hang before I could show that book?"

She gave him both her hands. "Yes," she said, "I think I understand."

III

CONSTANCE WALKED into her rooms at a few minutes after six. Brooke
and Inspector Simmons were on the point of leaving. She looked
at them in some surprise.

"May I ask what you are doing in my apartments?" she inquired,
beginning to take off her gloves.

"You forget that you had an appointment with me here at three
o'clock," Simmons remarked.

"Quite right," Constance admitted. "I had forgotten it."

"And as we had information," Brooke continued, "that at five
minutes to two this afternoon you left the Café Lugano with a certain notorious person called Delamoir, you may understand that
we were becoming a little uneasy."

She sank into her easy chair. The two men looked at her. Every
muscle in Brooke's body seemed to stiffen. "Something has happened!" he exclaimed. She drew a little brown-paper parcel from
her pocket.

"Mr. Simmons," she said, "I started out this afternoon to try to
trap a man into a confession of his guilt. I have instead succeeded
in becoming acquainted with his innocence. The proofs are here."

Simmons moved swiftly forward, but Constance retained possession of the parcel.

"This," she went on quietly, "is his wife's diary. It is my belief that Delamoir would have gone to the gallows sooner than have given it up. I have talked to him for some time, and he has let me have it for two hours, on one condition.

"You are to read it, and the superintendent. Beyond that, no other person. Not a word of it is to be breathed to the press. Sooner than have had a single line appear in any newspaper, Delamoir would have hung.

"There is no doubt," she continued, "about its being his wife's diary. You will find inside some of her letters, in her own handwriting, and there is also one addressed to the coroner, which is in itself conclusive.

"If, however, you have any remaining doubts as to the genuineness of this diary, you have only to go down to the Hilarity Theater and interview some of the young women who are mentioned in the earlier pages. Remember, however, that I part with the book only on the terms I have mentioned."

Simmons accepted the parcel and his charge.

"Queer," he remarked. "I know quite a lot of people who never believed in Delamoir's guilt; who even declared that he had an odd sort of affection for his wife, weird creature though she was."

Constance's eyes suddenly shone. For a single moment she was beautiful.

"There are many strange ways," she said, "in which a man may love a woman."

The inspector took his leave.

Brooke turned to her earnestly, her last words sounding in his ears. "But his task is," said he, "to make the woman believe and understand."

Constance felt her cheeks burn. Her eyes would no longer stand to their posts, arrogant sentinels, cool defenders against love's assaults. They turned, cowardly, in that moment, and took refuge behind their fringed curtains, while she answered, softly, very, very softly indeed:

"But I have known, Stanley, dear boy, all along. I have known—and understood."

"And the other partnership that I have proposed before to-day," said he, eagerly as a thirsty man, "the closer partnership, Constance?"

"I think," she answered slyly, "that we may have the papers drawn."

COACHWHIP PUBLICATIONS

COACHWHIPBOOKS.COM

DETECTIVES

2

MISS CAYLEY'S ADVENTURES
GRANT ALLEN

HILDA WADE
GRANT ALLEN

ISBN 978-1-61646-125-6

DETECTIVES 2

LOVEDAY BROOKE
CATHERINE LOUISA PIRKIN

LADY MOLLY OF SCOTLAND YARD
BARONESS EMMA ORCZY

ISBN 978-1-61646-112-6

COACHWHIP PUBLICATIONS

COACHWHIPBOOKS.COM

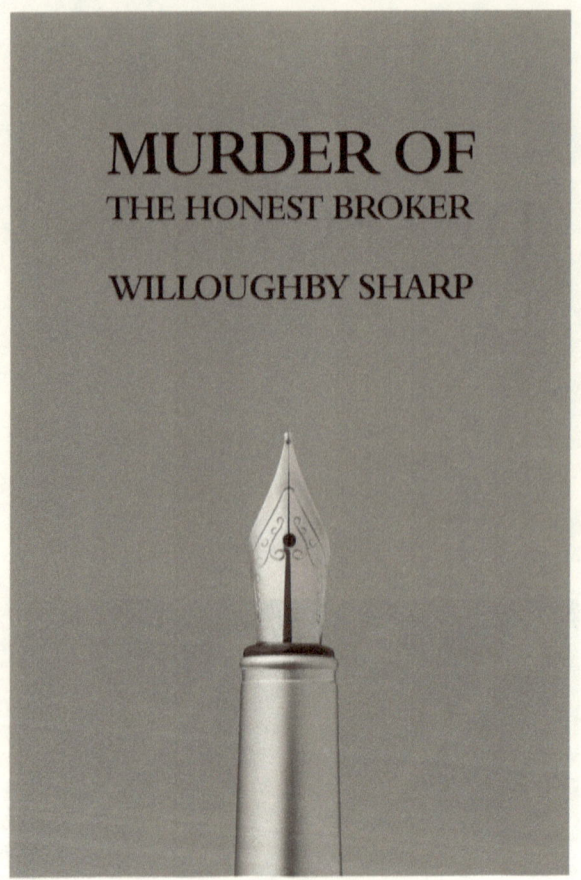

MURDER OF
THE HONEST BROKER

WILLOUGHBY SHARP

ISBN 978-1-61646-211-6

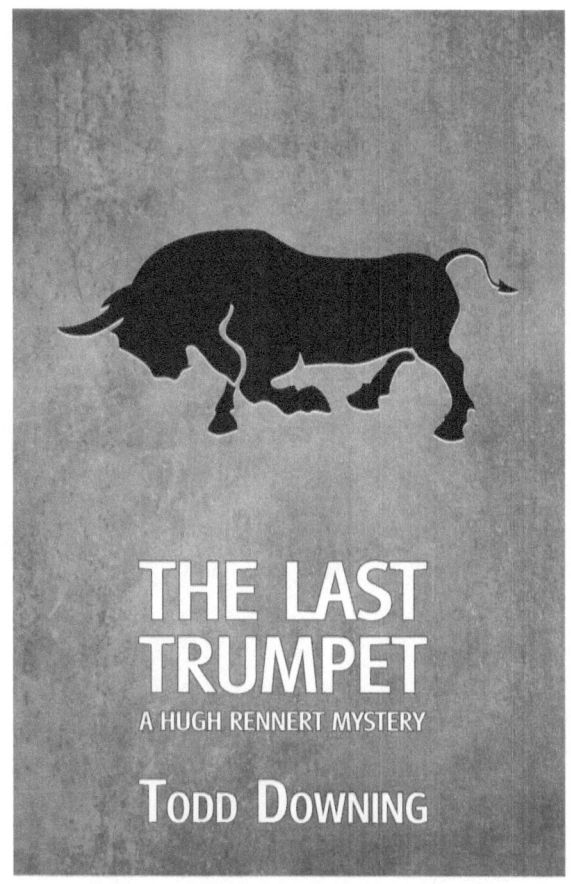

THE LAST
TRUMPET
A HUGH RENNERT MYSTERY

TODD DOWNING

ISBN 978-1-61646-152-2

COACHWHIP PUBLICATIONS

COACHWHIPBOOKS.COM

MURDER

À LA RICHELIEU

THE ADELAIDE ADAMS MYSTERIES

ANITA BLACKMON

ISBN 978-1-61646-222-2

THE
WINE ROOM
MURDER

STANLEY VESTAL

ISBN 978-1-61646-225-3

www.ingramcontent.com/pod-product-compliance
Lightning Source LLC
Chambersburg PA
CBHW020538020726
47494CB00006B/1822